**NO MATTER WHAT,
I HAD TO PROTECT THE CHILDREN
FROM THE EVIL THAT HAUNTED
THE RUINS OF THE CLOISTER.**

I guided the horse along the narrow path through the high walls of cane, then up the hill to the cloister door. I jerked the weary beast to a stop, then froze as I realized that the door was standing open!

Trembling, I lifted the gun and stepped through the door. It was dim inside, but nothing moved, so I set the gun down long enough to light a lamp, then moved cautiously through the rooms.

Though each door I opened brought a fresh wave of hope and fear, I found nothing. The rooms appeared much as I had left them, except that all were now empty of life. No babies slept in the tiny beds, no children dreamed on their cots. Every bed was rumpled, as though its occupant had been roused from sleep and taken . . .

SHARON WAGNER
DARK
CLOISTER

ZEBRA BOOKS
KENSINGTON PUBLISHING CORP.

Chapter 1

"If the weather holds, we shall reach St. Devina tomorrow, Miss Ames," Captain Hawkes stated, looking pleased—no doubt because he would no longer have to answer my questions. I had a strong suspicion that he would be delighted to see me down the gangplank and safely off the *Sea Hawk.*

"I shall make sure my belongings are ready, Captain," I assured him. Not that I would have to do much packing, since I had taken out only the most essential of my belongings during the voyage from Philadelphia, Pennsylvania. The first few days I had been too ill, and after that, there had seemed little point.

A nod was his only answer as he left me at the rail with only the creaking of the mast and the rustle of the sails for company. Since the *Sea Hawk* was actually a trading vessel and carried only two other passengers, I swallowed a sigh. Had I known how lonely my journey would be, I might have packed more books in my small trunk and consigned a larger portion of my clothing to my luggage in the hold.

But now it was ending. Tomorrow I should be landing on the Caribbean island of St. Devina, where the Reverend Paul Michaels would be waiting to escort me to the island of Bell Harbour and my new life. A shiver traced along my spine in spite of the heat of the summer afternoon.

A new life, indeed. After spending the past three years as a student at the Middle Brook Christian School for Young Ladies, I was on my way to my first teaching position, an assignment that would take me into a world totally different from anything I had ever known. I closed my eyes, trying to remember how thrilling it had seemed when Reverend Bennett had given me the news a bit over six weeks ago.

"As our most promising student, Rachel, you have been chosen for a very special assignment. Not only will you be teaching those less fortunate, but you will also be assisting our own Paul Michaels in the worthy task of organizing an orphanage to care for those who have no one else. A demanding duty, but one I am sure you will find joyous, as you will be using all your gifts in doing the Lord's work." His praise and confidence had made me blush. That, and the mention of Reverend Paul Michaels.

The other girls at Middle Brook Christian had been wildly envious of my assignment, since most new teachers were sent either to posts nearby or to schools close to their homes. But of course, most of them had families to live with; I had no one, beyond some distant cousins and an uncle who had gone west seeking his fortune several years before I'd lost my parents in a terrible fire. That had been nearly seven years ago, when I was but fifteen.

I sighed, not wanting to remember the loneliness of living with my grandmother. Life had been more cheerful after I was accepted at Middle Brook Christian. The Bennetts had been kind, and the other girls were almost like the sisters I never had. Almost—but not quite. Sisters were forever; schoolmates finished their training and left to begin their new lives.

6

I forced the sad thoughts away. It was time to look ahead, not back. Still, I could not help wondering if my assignment would have been different if my grandmother had lived to see me complete my studies. Would I have gone back to Greensville to live with her and teach in the small school there? Or would the Reverend Bennett still have given me the opportunity that he claimed I had earned by my diligence?

Knowing that I should never get the answer to that question, I left the rail and found a shady spot near a well-secured stack of deck cargo. During the endless days of the voyage, I had spent many hours seated on a canvas-covered bundle, sometimes rereading the papers that the Reverend Bennett had given me, but more often watching the ever-changing panorama of sky and sea and wondering what lay ahead. And thinking about Paul Michaels.

Reverend Michaels had come to Middle Brook Christian twice, both times during the hot summer months, when only two other students remained at the school with me. Since classes were not in session, we shared meals with Reverend and Mrs. Bennett, and as Paul was their guest, we had the chance to get to know him. I remembered every minute of those meals in vivid detail.

At thirty, Paul was at least twenty years younger than Reverend Bennett, but they had become friends while Paul was studying to become a minister. That friendship had continued after Paul's graduation, and from things Reverend Bennett said when Paul was not about, I suspected that he had helped secure Paul's assignment to establish a mission school on an island called Bell Harbour.

Not that a dynamic man like Paul needed any assistance. He fairly glowed with enthusiasm for his work on the island, and when he spoke of his mission and all that he hoped to accomplish there, I found him the most fascinating and exciting man in the world. And now I was to be a part of it. The very thought knotted my stomach and made my heart beat faster, though I could not be sure whether it was the prospect of seeing Paul again or the thrill of the assignment that caused my disquiet.

To remind myself of why I had been sent, I took the small packet of papers from the pocket in my skirt and unfolded it once again. Reverend Bennett's neat handwriting was slightly blurred now—the result of too many readings, no doubt. Not that it mattered; I knew the words by heart.

Because Paul had written to Reverend Bennett several months earlier about the heavy burdens of his work, I was being sent to assist with the small school Paul had opened in the village on Bell Harbour. According to Reverend Bennett, I would be expected to teach the younger island children, especially those who might need extra supervision. And though eventually Paul hoped to open and staff a proper orphanage in which I would be working, I carried with me a letter from Reverend Bennett asking Paul to make arrangements for me to be housed on the Harrison estate, under the protection of Jarvis Harrison.

Sighing, I pondered again the remarks Reverend Bennett had made when he'd escorted me aboard the *Sea Hawk*. "I mislike sending you out alone like this, Rachel. I would have preferred waiting until I could arrange for you to have a proper chaperone; but from Paul's last report, I suspect he needs help now, and I have no one else to send him. Still, I know you are a mature and resourceful young woman, and I have met Mr. and Mrs. Graves, who will be sailing on the ship, too. They have given me their solemn promise to see that you have a safe voyage."

Safe, but deadly dull. I squirmed on the hard bundle. For the first week, Mrs. Graves had done nothing but weep for her home in Pennsylvania; and Mr. Graves had said no more than a dozen words to me during the entire trip. My only diversions had come when the ship had stopped at the various islands to unload cargo and take on more. Even then, however, Mrs. Graves had refused to leave the dock area, fearing that the ship might leave us behind, so I had seen precious little of this strange new world.

I reread the few facts contained in the papers, wondering, not for the first time, why there were no more, since Paul had been on the island for nearly a year. And why the urgency about my leaving? Why had I not been allowed to wait for someone more pleasant to travel with?

Tomorrow I would finally have the opportunity to find out the answers to many of my questions. That is, if Paul had received the notification of my arrival that Reverend Bennett had sent as soon as I accepted the assignment. If all went according to Reverend Bennett's plan, Paul would meet me in St. Devina, and then we would sail to Bell Harbour on a smaller ship.

I swallowed hard, reminding myself once again that I must start thinking of Paul as Reverend Michaels. It would never do for me to appear too familiar toward the man I had come to assist. Even though he had asked me to call him by his given name when he'd last visited Middle Brook Christian, that did not mean he would feel the same now. There was no way he could know how much his missionary fervor had inspired me—or how often he had slipped into my dreams.

"Oh, dear, I shall miss you, Rachel." Mrs. Graves gripped my hand as we stood near the rail, watching as the captain eased the *Sea Hawk* up to the long dock that extended out into the brightly colored water of St.

Devina's harbor. "I don't know what I should have done on this voyage had I not had you to keep me company."

"It would have been most lonely for me, also, Mrs. Graves." I did my best to be polite, but I was hard put to keep my gaze on her instead of searching the crowd on the dock for a familiar figure, one with Paul Michael's golden hair and stocky form.

She seemed to sense my feelings, for she turned to look at the harbor area, her thin lips twisting with disapproval. "I still cannot believe that you have been sent alone to this heathen place. You are but a young girl, Rachel."

"I am two and twenty, and a trained teacher," I reminded her, having heard her words numerous times before. "And I am to assist in the missionary work already begun by Reverend Michaels." I turned to search the crowd, hoping to locate him in the colorful throng that had come to greet the ship. Many faces, some black and some white, turned my way, but all of them belonged to strangers.

I swallowed hard, fighting a lump that threatened to close my throat completely. Could Reverend Bennett's message have gone astray? What if Paul did not meet me? I clutched my small purse, well aware that it contained far too small an amount to purchase my fare back to Philadelphia.

The sale of the house that was my legacy from my grandmother had scarcely brought enough to cover my tuition and expenses at Middle Brook Christian. What was left had gone for the personal supplies I expected to need during my first year on Bell Harbour. Beyond that, I would need every penny of the respectable salary that was being offered by the Harrison, Travis, Ferguson, and Chalmers families of Bell Harbour.

"If you will come with me, Miss Ames." Captain Hawkes broke into my worried speculation. "Once you

10

have made sure that all your luggage is here, I will escort you to the Harbour Inn." He signaled several of the crew, who came forward with my trunks as well as the large containers that the Reverend Bennett had shipped for delivery to Paul.

"I was hoping to be met," I murmured, as I caught up with the captain, who was already on the dock. "I am to go on to Bell Harbour Island, and . . ." I let it trail off, sensing that Captain Hawkes had no interest in my plans.

"Perhaps someone at the Harbour Inn will know where your escort is. I have very little cargo to unload here, so I cannot remain long in port." His words and expression made it clear that I could expect no sympathy or assistance from him.

I lifted my chin and managed a polite smile. "I am sure you are correct, Captain, and I thank you for your consideration during the voyage."

His surprised look was my reward. He had undoubtedly expected me to weep and wail at the prospect of being left here. Well, he was wrong. I much preferred being here—or I would once Paul came to meet me.

He looked slightly chastened as he continued, "It was the Reverend's suggestion that I see you safely to the nearest inn, so that you might wait in comfort."

His reference to Reverend Bennett made me feel much better. Undoubtedly, delays were to be expected when one journeyed to distant places or even between islands. Perhaps Paul had arrived earlier and no one had told him that the *Sea Hawk* was due in today. He might have left the area to take care of some business. My spirits lifted as we neared the open door of the Harbour Inn, then plummeted as we entered.

The place was dark as a cave after the brightness of the tropical sun, and the air felt heavy and damp, thick with the scents of cooking fish and another odor that I suspected was from some sort of spirits. Loud voices filled the air, and I could see that most of the tables in the room were occupied by men.

"Surely there is some mistake, Captain," I began, my hard-won assurance fading at the prospect of being abandoned here. "I cannot wait here for Pa ... Reverend Michaels. 'Twould not be seemly."

The captain's scowl told me that he had come to the same conclusion. Still, he refused to retreat, taking my arm and guiding me across the room to where a burly older man leaned on a counter, watching the crowd. "Harry?" he called. "Harry Ryder?"

The man turned hooded dark eyes our direction and nodded. "You be Capt'n Hawkes?"

The captain nodded. "And this is Miss Rachel Ames."

"Been 'spectin' you." The man straightened. "This be left for the lady, and he said for her to store her goods with me." He handed me a folded piece of paper. "Ole Charlie's awaitin' out back to take you to him, Miss."

"Charlie?" I murmured, wanting to open the note, but aware that I would likely be unable to read it, thanks to the gloom of the room. "Who is ..."

"This way." The man headed for a door that opened from behind the counter.

The captain released his hold on my arm and gave me a little shove. "You had best go with him, Miss Ames. I shall see that your goods are properly stored. Farewell." Naturally, the captain was in a hurry to be rid of me.

Since I apparently had no choice, I followed Mr. Ryder and was relieved when the door opened onto a dusty street where an old cart and driver waited in the shade beneath a flowering tree. "This be her, Charlie," Mr. Ryder said, handing me up to the hard wooden seat without a by-your-leave. "Your goods'll be awaitin',

Miss, when you be ready." He disappeared back through the door before I could say a word.

"Afternoon, Missy." The black face beneath the thick silvery curls seemed friendly enough and his smile was gentle as he slapped the reins on the back of the fat bay, startling him into a slow walk.

Not sure what to do, I unfolded the note, hoping that it would tell me where I was to go. It did, though the message was discouragingly brief.

Miss Ames,
    Forgive me for not waiting. I will explain everything when you get to the cathedral.

It was signed with a single initial, an "N." My heart dropped to the dusty toes of my shoes. Paul had not come; I was being met by a stranger—and one who had thoughtlessly gone off and left me to fend for myself. I swallowed hard. This was not exactly the auspicious beginning that I had envisioned for my new life.

Not sure what else to do, I turned to the driver. "Do you know where the cathedral is?" I asked, with a calmness I was far from feeling.

"Yes'm. I's takin' you ta Mista Nick."

Nick. So that was what the "N" stood for. But who was he, and why had Paul sent a stranger to meet me, instead of coming himself? And why in the world would this Nick want me to meet him at a cathedral? Though Reverend Bennett practiced Christian charity when it came to people of other religions, I could imagine no circumstance that would necessitate his going to a cathedral.

To quell the hordes of butterflies that seemed to be rising within me, I turned my attention to the area around me. Now that we had left the shabbiness of the harbor, the vista was breathtaking. Handsome, colorfully painted houses sat behind the low fences that lined the dusty street, and each was surrounded by a spectacular garden. Huge trees shaded the street, and busy birds fluttered among the bright red blossoms that occasionally drifted on the light breeze.

A number of children ran shouting and laughing through the gardens, but only a few adults were about in the sticky heat of late afternoon. I felt their curious gaze as the cart moved along the street and tried to smile at them in a friendly fashion. To my surprise, several nodded, and one woman even waved. At least the people here seemed welcoming; I could only hope that would also be true on Bell Harbour Island.

The road curved inland, away from the harbor, and smaller houses crowded closer to the road, their paint less bright. Porches sagged, fences were tumbling down, and many roofs bore patches of rusted metal. Here, the gardens more often contained vegetables than flowers. We had entered a poorer neighborhood, I realized.

The houses quickly gave way to a number of shops and stalls and the streets grew crowded with people, many of whom came rushing toward the cart with baskets of fruits and vegetables or other items that they held out to me, calling loudly to get my attention. I cringed, half-frightened by their urgency.

Charlie tightened his grip on the reins, shouting at them angrily, ordering them back. Much to my relief, they obeyed, though they muttered sullenly as they withdrew. What sort of place was this, where people were hawking their wares on the streets? Had we come to some kind of native marketplace?

"How much further?" I asked, suddenly wishing myself back on the *Sea Hawk*.

"Just 'round the hill." Charlie slapped the reins, hurrying the bay a little in spite of the throng of children that continued to race back and forth nearly under the poor beast's hooves.

The congestion eased once we'd left the area of shops and the street suddenly widened into a pleasant, tree-shaded square. A fountain splashed tranquilly in the middle, and people either strolled quietly in the shade or sat on the benches that surrounded the fountain. It was a charming scene, reminding me of a painting I had once seen.

Charlie guided the horse around the fountain, then stopped at the base of a flight of worn stone stairs. I gasped as I looked up at the imposingly handsome building. I had not expected so grand an edifice on an island. This was, indeed, a cathedral, not simply a church.

"We's here." Charlie offered me a hand, helping me from the cart to the shell-paved ground in front of the cathedral. "Mista Nick awaitin'."

"Where?" I looked around, wondering if one of the men seated near the fountain could be Paul's representative. From the curious stares I was receiving, it seemed doubtful.

Charlie just shrugged, then climbed nimbly back up to the seat, obviously sure that he had completed his task. He was going to leave me! The thought nearly paralyzed me. "Wait!" I gasped.

"Missy?" His worried look made it clear that he had heard the panic in my voice.

"I should pay you," I murmured, embarrassed by my own fear. Everyone had told me how mature and capable I was, and now I was behaving like a frightened child. If Paul saw me, he would probably agree with Mrs. Graves's opinion of my aptitude for service; he might even send me back to Philadelphia on the next ship.

"Mista Nick took care 'o me, Missy." Charlie's wide grin returned as he slapped the reins on the bay's back. Before I could think of anything to delay him further, he

15

was moving on around the square, leaving me very much alone at the foot of the stairs.

Feeling out of place in my wrinkled and too-heavy brown traveling suit, I looked around. The elderly men on the bench were still watching me, but no one else seemed to have noticed that I had simply been abandoned in a strange village. Swallowing the lump that was forming in my throat, I turned my back on the men and looked up at the imposing double doors of the cathedral.

What was I supposed to do—go up and knock? Or maybe walk in and shout the name Nick? The image was so foolish, I should have laughed, had I not been so frightened. I took a deep breath and forced my shaking legs to carry me to the bottom step. If my escort to Bell Harbour was inside, I had to find him.

Before I could begin my climb, I heard a door slam somewhere off to my left. Not minding a distraction, I looked past the vine-covered wall of the cathedral to what appeared to be a narrow opening. Perhaps this Nick was not inside after all. Maybe he was waiting for me in . . .

A shriek interrupted my speculation. "No! No, I won't let you!" The child's voice was high and thin, but it was filled with agony. "You cannot take her, she's all I have!"

My fears vanished as I lifted my long skirt and raced toward the opening. If a child was in trouble, I had to help. My shoes slipped on the broken shells as I entered what appeared to be an alleyway. I was forced to slow my pace, for the late afternoon sun scarce penetrated the narrow space between the walls. Part way along, a break in the wall admitted a bar of light, and as I looked ahead for the source of the scream, I caught my first glimpse of the child I had heard.

"She's mine!" The little girl crossing the patch of

sunlight was small and thin, her deeply tanned arms and legs flailing like wind-tossed sticks as she leaped toward the shadowy figure of a man. "Give her back to me!"

The violence of the child's attack stopped me. Never had I seen such desperate fury in one so young. Not that I counted myself an expert, though I had spent much of the past year teaching the younger children and caring for the orphans whom the Reverend Bennett took in from time to time.

"Stop that, Elena." The man's voice was surprisingly gentle as he easily fended off the girl's attack. He was, I could see, holding something just out of the child's reach. A bundle, or perhaps a doll of some sort.

A new wailing echoed off the enclosing walls and I gasped, realizing that what the man held was another child, one not much more than a babe. As my eyes adjusted to the dimness, I saw the girl grab the bare foot of the babe, and its screams grew louder as its small arms reached down toward the older child. Fury banished my shock and I raced down the alleyway to stop their tormentor.

"What in the world do you think you are doing to these children?" I demanded, skidding to a stop in front of the man. "Give me that babe before you hurt it." I held out my arms.

Silence settled over the dim passageway like a pall as three pairs of eyes turned my way. The children's faces were full of fear and wet with tears. I did my best to smile at them reassuringly before I turned my gaze back to the man. For a moment he just stared. Then, to my surprise, his look of confusion faded. He did not, however, hand me the smaller child.

"Miss Ames, I presume." His coldly assessing gaze made me want to retreat. "If you will go back out front and wait for me, I shall join you shortly."

"Leave?" I nearly choked on the word, but before I could go on, the babe began to cry again. Not loudly this time, just the heartbreaking whimpering of a child that has no expectation of getting what it cries for. It was a sound I had heard often enough among the children brought to the orphanage. Sensing its need, I tossed back my escaping curls and glared at him. "I know not who you may be, but I will not leave you with these two children, not until you tell me what is going on."

"He be takin' my sister away," the older girl sobbed. "She be all I have left and he be givin' her away. I kin take care of her, I swear it. Please make 'um give her back to me." Tears spilled from her dark eyes and flooded down her cheeks.

Touched by the agony in her voice, I reached out and pulled her into my arms. "It will be all right," I whispered, hoping that I was right. "We can find a way, I am sure." I hugged her trembling body close and sent a pleading glance toward the man. "Surely there must be something . . . ?"

He looked down at me, still frowning. "Miss Ames, this is nothing that should concern you. I had hoped to have it all resolved before you arrived, but now . . ."

Anger stiffened my spine. How dared he act as though I was somehow interfering in his personal business? "If you know who I am, you must also realize that children are very much my concern. I have no idea what is going on here, but I cannot believe that anyone would wish to make two children so miserable."

"What is going on out here, Nick? I thought you said that everything was under control." A black-robed, middle-aged priest stepped through a door beside me, startling me so I stumbled back a step, releasing my hold on the child.

Nick? My heart dropped. This was the man sent to

meet me. I swallowed hard, aware that had I not been so distracted by the children's plight, I would have suspected his identity the moment he'd called me by name.

"Father Sebastian, thank heavens you have returned." The man turned to the priest with obvious relief. "Will you please explain to Miss Ames that I am no blackguard out to do harm to innocent children?"

"I shall happily clear your name, but first I shall need to know the source of all the shrieking and wailing." The priest's tone held amusement, and that rankled, even though I realized that both children had now stopped crying. "I thought you had reached a satisfactory agreement with the good sisters."

The man's hard features softened with a wry grin. "With the sisters, yes; but not with Elena." He shifted the babe to hold her gently against his broad chest, and she seemed quite content there. Her thumb slipped into her mouth and her eyes seemed about to drift shut. "If we could go inside . . ."

The priest nodded, then offered me a smile. "If you would join us, Miss Ames, I am sure that we can sort all this out." He held his hand out to Elena, and to my surprise, she took it without hesitation. Feeling relieved and confused, I followed them along the dim alleyway to where a gate opened into a small private garden behind the cathedral.

We entered the rear of the cathedral, and before I could protest, both children were sent off with Mrs. Mendez, the priest's housekeeper. I was then escorted into what appeared to be a handsome parlor. Feeling a bit disoriented by the heat and all the strange things that had happened since I'd left the ship, I turned to face the man Paul had sent to meet me.

"Mr. . . . a . . ." I was embarrassed to realize that I did not even know his last name. In all the confusion with the children, there had been no time for introductions.

19

"Harrison, Nick Harrison." He took my hand and bowed slightly over it. "I am delighted to make your acquaintance, Miss Ames, and I do apologize for the unfortunate circumstances of our meeting. I had hoped to have all this in order before your arrival."

The words of proper greeting formed in my mind, but when I looked up at him, I found myself unable to speak. In the shadowy alley, I had not truly seen his face, nor had I realized how large he was, how strong and obviously male. When I looked into the green- and gold-flecked depths of his eyes, I felt a little dizzy, which was why I did not immediately think to free my fingers from his grasp.

"Are you all right, Miss Ames?" His frown penetrated the fog that seemed to have settled over my mind.

"Of course, I . . ." I paused, took a deep breath, then forced my gaze away from his mesmerizing hazel eyes. This would never do; I must gather my wits and behave as a proper lady. "I am pleased to meet you, Mr. Harrison."

"I suggest that we sit down, Nick, Miss Ames." Father Sebastian came to take my hand once Nick released it. "I suspect Miss Ames is rather overcome by her tumultuous arrival here. I have asked Mrs. Mendez to bring lemonade and some spice cookies. I hope that will be acceptable, Miss Ames?"

The priest's touch was gentle, his hand soft, quite unlike Mr. Harrison's hard fingers; still, his interruption helped me overcome my odd weakness. I settled myself carefully on the edge of the sofa. "That would be most kind, Rev . . . er . . . Father Sebastian. I fear I am a bit confused. You see, I was told that Reverend Michaels would meet the ship, so . . ."

"Do you know Paul?" The sharp note in Mr. Harrison's voice drew my attention back to him. He frowned as he raked a hand through his thick russet hair. One springy lock fell across his deeply tanned forehead, slightly softening the impact of his frown. He was, I had to admit, a most attractive man, though a thoroughly confusing one.

"We have met." I had no intention of telling him more, though I could see the bright gleam of curiosity in his eyes.

To my surprise, he turned away, shaking his head and muttering, "And he still allowed them to send you here. I cannot believe even Paul would be so foolish."

Chapter 2

For a moment I was too shocked to react, then the full impact of his words struck me and a blaze of anger released my tongue. "How dare you?" I demanded, leaping to my feet.

"Miss Ames, I am sure that Nick . . ." The priest rose, his frown showing his concern. He seemed ready to step between us, as though he feared we would come to blows; but Mr. Harrison was too quick for him. Before I could say another word, he was nearly toe-to-toe with me, and his eyes were blazing.

"I dare say what I believe, Miss Ames, and that is that you should be on the next ship back to that safe world you left behind. Bell Harbour is no place for an innocent young girl like yourself."

Gritting my teeth in frustration, I took a deep breath, trying hard to keep my temper in check. Why did everyone always assume I was too young to accomplish what I set out to do? "I can assure you, Mr. Harrison, that I am a fully trained teacher, and quite capable of assisting Reverend Michaels in the handling of the mission school on Bell Harbour Island. I would not have been sent here, if that were not the case."

"If it were just the school . . ." he began, then seemed to catch himself. "How old are you, Miss Ames?"

For a moment, I considered simply refusing to answer such an impertinent question, but there was something about Nick Harrison's expression that warned me to tread lightly with him. He was, after all, the one on whom I must rely until I reached Bell Harbour and the welcome I hoped Paul would offer. "I am two and twenty."

"And fresh from the protection of a church school, I wager. Have you had any experience teaching or caring for children like Elena and Inez?" His tone challenged me.

"I taught the younger children all during my last year, and I worked with the orphans through most summers, having full charge of them the past few months. I assure you, Reverend Bennett made certain that I would be worthy of this assignment."

Mr. Harrison looked as though he would like to dispute that fact further; but before he could say anything, Mrs. Mendez arrived with sweat-beaded glasses of lemonade and a large platter of cookies. I sank down, grateful for the reprieve, though I was sure that I had not heard the last of Nick Harrison's complaints.

After Mrs. Mendez left, Father Sebastian smiled benignly at me, then turned to Nick. "Before you and Miss Ames get back to your discussion of the conditions on Bell Harbour, I fear we must talk further about the future of Elena and Inez. What happened out there? Why were they so upset?"

Mr. Harrison took a large swallow of his lemonade, then sighed. "I was just taking Inez across to the orphanage. The sisters agreed to keep her for me until such time as she can be taken back to Bell Harbour. Unfortunately, Elena refuses to understand why her sister has to stay. She followed me out and started screaming." He turned toward me. "That was when Miss Ames came to the rescue."

His mocking tone brought a blaze of heat to my cheeks. "I had no way of knowing what you meant to do to that poor babe or her sister," I snapped, furious with him. Then my temper cooled slightly as I realized what he had said. "Why must the little one be left behind? Is she ill?"

"Inez? No, she is healthy enough, but we have no place for her on the island." Mr. Harrison's mouth twisted in a wry smile. "No matter what Paul has reported back to your Reverend Bennett and his other backers, there is no orphanage being organized on Bell Harbour. Elena is old enough to begin training as a servant, but Inez will be better off with the sisters for now."

"That could be a problem, Nick." The priest's round face was creased with worry.

"But I talked with Sister Maria just this morning and she said she would be pleased to keep even both children, if I wished." Nick set his glass down and got to his feet, his restless pacing shrinking the room around us until I felt nearly overwhelmed by his sheer size and energetic movements.

"I, too, have been discussing the future of the children, and I find that there are many on this island who resent their being placed in our orphanage since they are not of our faith. Right after the accident, it was necessary to take them in; but since you have come over from Bell Harbour . . ." The priest let it trail off, shrugging. "I did try, Nick, but we have many mouths of our own to feed, and the Verdugos had been on St. Devina only a short time before it happened."

"Before what happened? Where are their parents?" I was too caught up with curiosity to observe proper decorum.

Father Sebastian turned my way at once. "The girls' mother, father, and two older brothers were all killed when the family's fishing boat went down in a squall about two weeks ago. Since the family had been on St. Devina only about four months, they had no close friends here, so the girls were brought to us."

"Have the girls no family on Bell Harbour?" I asked, looking to Mr. Harrison for answers.

He shook his head, sorrow shadowing his lean features. "That was part of the reason they decided to leave. They hoped to give their children a better life away from Bell Harbour." He sighed. "If Inez had not been ill that day, they'd all have perished together. Elena was left home to care for Inez while the others went out on their boat."

I shuddered, remembering only too well how my own life had been forever changed. I had injured my ankle in the morning, so had been forced to stay home from the party at the Holmbees'. That event seven years ago had ended in a devastating fire that had taken both my parents from me forever. At fifteen, I had been totally destroyed by my loss; I could scarcely imagine how much worse it would be for two children as young as Inez and Elena.

"If you have no orphanage, what do you plan to do with Elena?" I asked, blinking back my sympathetic tears as I did my best to be practical.

"She can enter service with one of the families. At eight, she is old enough to work." Though he spoke firmly, I sensed that Mr. Harrison lacked confidence in his plan.

"With no time to mourn her family? Without the comfort of her only remaining relative? I cannot imagine even you finding that an acceptable answer to their plight." Anger at his lack of understanding brought out the full force of my temper, and I was in no mood to control it. I pushed back the tendrils of my pale brown hair and plunged on. "If Bell Harbour Island has no orphanage, perhaps it is time it started one. I shall be happy to run it and to care for Inez and Elena."

"I have told you . . ." Mr. Harrison's furious tone made it clear that I had struck a painful spot with my words.

"Wait a bit, Nick." Father Sebastian interrupted the tirade I was expecting from Mr. Harrison. "Miss Ames may not be what you expected, but she does have spirit and the will to help. I think perhaps you should give her an opportunity to try. She's not the troublemaker you are battling and she has the necessary training. Surely there is a place on one of the plantations where she might set up a small orphanage."

Nick Harrison's gaze was mutinous, and I could see the fire of temper burning in his face, but after another turn about the room, he returned to his chair. The silence grew heavy as he finished his lemonade and methodically munched his way through a cookie. I tried to do the same, but my hands shook when I lifted my glass, and I scarcely tasted the sweets.

Finally, Father Sebastian cleared his throat. "What is it to be, Nick? Are you prepared to abandon Inez here, or will you give Miss Ames the opportunity she has come so far to accept?"

Mr. Harrison sighed, then slowly turned to me. "I hope you will accept my apology, Miss Ames. It has been a most trying day, and I fear I have directed my frustration toward you, when you deserve only a proper welcome to our islands. If you are truly determined to continue on to Bell Harbour, I shall do my best to help you in your endeavor."

My heartbeat quickened as I met his gaze. The challenge was still there, but it had somehow softened. Once again, I was struck by the sheer magnetism of the man. I had never felt that way about anyone before, not even Paul, and it frightened me. "And the children?" I asked, trying to concentrate on what must be most important to me. "May I take charge of both of them?"

"We shall take them back to the island, but beyond that, their fate will be in Paul's hands." His lips, which had seemed almost tender, now thinned, and the warmth was gone from his face. "And yours, of course."

Relief flooded through me, and I would have assured them both of Paul's delight, had I not been forestalled by Mr. Harrison's abrupt turning to Father Sebastian. "May I beg another night's lodging for the children, Father? I have no desire to annoy your parishioners, but I cannot start for Bell Harbour this late in the day—not with two children and a young lady." His tone became mocking. "I should not want to risk Miss Ames's reputation by bringing her ashore in the middle of the night."

Father Sebastian's smile deepened. "There is no cause to trouble the sisters for one night. I am sure Mrs. Mendez will be quite happy to keep the children with her. She has become rather attached to the little one. Says she is about the age of her smallest grandchild."

Mr. Harrison rose and offered his hand to the priest. "I am in your debt, Father. If I can ever be of service . . ."

"We shall all need each other in the days ahead, I fear." The priest smiled as he spoke, but I could see the sadness in his dark eyes, and it chilled me. What could he possibly mean? As far as I could remember, there had been nothing in Paul's reports about trouble on Bell Harbour. They had, in fact, been filled with hope and plans for the future of the islanders he had come so far to serve and care for.

Before I could frame a question that would not be too impertinent, Mr. Harrison turned to me. "Well, Miss Ames, if you are sufficiently rested, we should go to the Harbour Inn and reclaim your belongings. I should like

27

to stow them safely aboard the boat, for I doubt that Harry Ryder will keep them for us past nightfall. He could turn a pretty profit selling them, and all he would need to do is claim they were washed ashore on the tide."

My gasp was covered by the priest's chuckle. "You hold wicked thoughts, Nick," he said, patting my shoulder as I got to my feet. "You will be frightening this young lady, if she believes your tall tales."

I stiffened at once, determined not to let either man see just how anxious Mr. Harrison's teasing had made me. It had been far too many years since my father had teased me thus. "I am sure Mr. Ryder must be trustworthy or Mr. Harrison would never have asked him to direct me here." I favored them both with my sweetest smile.

Father Sebastian's appreciative laughter filled the corridor as he led us through several halls to a door, which opened in what I judged to be the rear of the cathedral building. He turned to me as we stepped out into the steamy heat. "You may yet surprise us all, Miss Ames." He then directed his attention to Mr. Harrison. "And, Nick, you would do well to remember that even the softest kitten has claws and the courage to use them to protect itself."

"If you will excuse me, I shall fetch the cart." Nick moved away without acknowledging the priest's warning.

Father Sebastian sighed, his expression becoming solemn. "You will need to be patient with Nick, Miss Ames. Things are not simple for him these days."

His words gave me the opening I needed. "I do not understand, Father Sebastian. What is wrong on Bell Harbour? Has something happened since Reverend Michaels requested an assistant?"

I felt the priest's too-knowing gaze on my face,

though I was too embarrassed to meet it. I should not be requesting information from a stranger, I reminded myself. Reverend Bennett would truly have been scandalized to know that I had been entertained in a cathedral, and now to . . . "Forgive me," I murmured, aware that the silence had grown long between us. "I should not have asked."

"You must ask questions, Miss Ames. How else will you learn the truth? Just be aware that not everyone will answer you honestly. As I counseled Nick, you, too, must follow your heart and do your best; beyond that, whatever happens is God's will." His tone was soothing, yet after he helped me into the small cart beside Nick, I realized that he had not answered any of my questions.

That realization set my head to spinning so that we were leaving the square before it occurred to me that I had no idea where we were going. "Mr. Harrison," I began, trying to find just the right words to inquire about our final destination, since I hoped he would not expect me to spend the night in a place like the Harbour Inn.

"I think it might be best if you called me Nick, since we shall be spending quite a bit of time together." His smile was charming, distracting me momentarily.

"Then you must call me Rachel," I agreed, though I was far from comfortable with such familiarity. Reverend Bennett would not have considered it seemly, but perhaps such formalities were handled differently in the Caribbean. I was, after all, a long way from Philadelphia.

"A lovely name for a lovely young lady." He sighed. "I really am sorry for my behavior earlier, Rachel. You just took me by surprise. When my father asked me to meet the *Sea Hawk* and escort Paul's assistant to the island, I expected an older woman, someone more suitable . . ."

I stiffened, regretting my momentary weakening. I

29

had had more than enough of being treated like an incompetent child.

"Suitable for what?"

"For life on Bell Harbour Island, blast it!" Nick turned to face me. "I have no idea what Paul has been telling his superiors in his reports, but it cannot be the truth, or you would never have been sent here."

"What do you mean by that?" I had reached the end of my patience—unfortunately, never a long journey in the best of times. "There is obviously a need for my help, yet you behave as though I have come to make trouble for you."

For a heartbeat, I could see the flash of temper in his eyes, then it was gone and he merely looked weary. "It is none of your doing, Rachel, I know that. In fact, under ordinary circumstances, you would be a most welcome addition to our island; unfortunately, things have not been normal on Bell Harbour for over a year."

"And why is that?" I was beyond caring about proper decorum. "Can you not tell me what is wrong?"

Nick opened his mouth, and for a moment I thought he was going to give me the answers I sought. Then he closed his lips again and shook his head. "I think it would be best for you to hear the answer to that from Paul. It is mostly his doing, anyway, and I am sure he will expect you to be a part of his grand plan for our people."

I wanted to ask him what he meant, but we had entered the market street and the vendors were again crowding in, shouting and offering their wares. Nick had his hands full keeping the spirited horse under control as several of the baskets and trays bumped his sleek sides.

By the time we left the crowd, my thoughts turned back to my earlier question. "Where are we going, Nick?" I asked.

He appeared surprised. "To the Harbour Inn."

"No, I mean, after that." I swallowed hard. In all my life, I had never stayed at an inn; but I was sure that Mr. Ryder's establishment was not suitable. "You left the children with Father Sebastian, but you never said where I . . ."

His stern features softened immediately, and I was fascinated to discover that when he grinned, a dimple appeared in his left cheek. "Are you saying you do not wish to enjoy the comforts of the Harbour Inn?"

"I . . ." Was he teasing me again? I wished mightily that I had been allowed to spend more time in the company of young men, for I felt woefully inadequate to judge Nick's mood. "I saw little of the establishment, but it seemed . . ." Words failed me.

"Unsuitable? Rough? Disgusting?" Nick's eyes were bright with laughter. "You have excellent taste, Rachel. It is all of those things and more. We are simply going there to reclaim your trunks and whatever supplies you brought so I can stow them on the *Island Belle*."

I was relieved by his words, but that still left unanswered the question of where we were to spend the night. "Is there another inn on St. Devina?"

"I fear the Harbour Inn is all the island has to offer." Nick seemed to be concentrating on guiding the horse, though we were simply following the same road I had traveled earlier with Charlie. "Of course, the *Island Belle* can sleep four comfortably enough, so . . ."

His casual words struck me like icy water on a winter morn. "Mr. Harrison!"

His bellow of laughter told me that he had been teasing again, but I was in no mood to be amused. In fact, I was hard put not to dissolve in frustrated tears. I had not traveled so far just to provide sport for some . . . My limited life experiences at Middle Brook Christian left me without a suitable description of Nick Harrison.

31

The creaking of the cart and the muffled sounds of the horse's hooves were all that broke the silence between us after Nick stopped laughing. I could feel the red shame burning in my cheeks, yet I knew that he was in the wrong, not I. He was not the first person to laugh at me, but I had never hated it so much before.

"Rachel." His voice was soft.

I ignored him, keeping my gaze on the distant blue of the water in the harbor. If he found me so amusing, perhaps he could talk to himself for a time.

"I was but teasing you, Rachel. I had no thought to hurt or anger you." He did sound sincere. "I have two sisters, and they are forever telling me that I go too far with my joking; but I never meant to . . ." He stopped.

I stole a peek at him, keeping my eyes downcast so my lashes hid my eyes from him. He no longer appeared so pleased with himself. In fact, he looked decidedly uncomfortable.

"We will be staying the night with George and Sarah Kasper. This is their cart. When your ship had not arrived by noon, I knew that we should have to remain until morning, so I took the liberty . . . They are old friends from Bell Harbour and will be happy to welcome you."

Since he did sound contrite, I turned toward him. "Could you not have simply told me that?" I asked, unwilling to let him escape responsibility. "I know that I am somewhat naive, Mr. Harrison, but I do not enjoy being made sport of. I am not familiar with your ways here, and since I have no brothers . . ."

Before I could stop him, he took my hand. "I was not laughing at you, Rachel, only at your expression of outrage. You were truly like a cornered kitten, so sweet and soft, yet spitting with outrage and baring your claws. If I swear to behave myself, will you agree to call me Nick again?"

His fingers were warm, and I felt the hardness of a callus as he lightly caressed the back of my hand with his thumb. It was impossible to cling to my righteous anger; it vanished like mist under the heat of the sun.

"All right, Nick." I had to yield; he was irresistible. "It is only that all this is very strange for me, and I am most anxious to reach Bell Harbour, so I may take up my duties there."

"And you were expecting Paul to meet you." He released my hand, though the horse seemed to have no need for his guidance.

"That was what Reverend Bennett told me."

"How well do you know Paul, Rachel?"

For a moment I thought that he might be about to tease me again, but his expression was solemn. "I had an opportunity to get to know him during the past two summers. He was close to Reverend and Mrs. Bennett, so he came to stay with them when he was free. Since I had no family to spend time with, I remained at Middle Brook and helped in the orphanage."

"You have no family?" The compassion in his eyes seemed quite genuine.

"An uncle and a few distant cousins, but no one close. My parents were killed in a fire when I was fifteen. I lived with my grandmother after that, but she died while I was at Middle Brook Christian." I spoke quickly, not wanting to be pitied. "The Bennetts were wonderful to me, treating me almost like a daughter. I think they had expected to keep me on at Middle Brook to help in their expansion plans; but when Paul wrote of his need for an assistant . . ." I gladly let my recital trail off when Nick stopped the cart at the front of the Harbour Inn.

I was delighted when he insisted that I remain in the cart instead of entering the establishment. My comfort lasted only a short time, however, for I soon found myself the center of attention from those who worked along the waterfront. Also, food smells wafted out the open door along with the raucous laughter and shouts of the men within. My stomach rumbled, reminding me that I had not eaten since morning. I was relieved when Nick and several burly young men emerged with my belongings and the containers of supplies.

I was more than happy to leave the waterfront behind once everything but my small trunk was stowed aboard the *Island Belle;* still, I could not help being concerned about the supplies entrusted to my care. "Are you sure everything will be safe?" I asked, as Nick started the horse along a road I had not noticed earlier.

"There is little danger of theft on an island this size, Rachel. Everyone knows everyone else, so the guilty person would easily be caught. Besides, Samuel will sleep on board."

Remembering the silent blond giant who had shifted my heaviest trunk as though it weighed nothing, I was reassured. "Is he a friend of yours?"

"An employee. He works for Harrison Enterprises, but he has a sister on St. Devina, so I asked him to come along as crew so he would have a chance to visit her and her family."

"Harrison Enterprises?" I scarcely contained a gulp of shock. How could I have overlooked the fact that Nick Harrison bore the name of one of the powerful families that, according to Paul, controlled everything on Bell Harbour?

There was a flash of amusement in Nick's eyes as he grinned at me. "My father is Jarvis Harrison."

"Your father is the one who brought Paul to Bell Harbour?" I was too shocked even to notice that I had called Paul by his first name.

Nick nodded. "At the time, it seemed a good idea. The islanders wanted their children to learn to read and

34

write, and old Reverend Hale was too ill to conduct services for his flock. My father wrote to several men in Boston and Philadelphia that he'd known from his days as a ship's captain. One of them suggested that Father write Reverend Bennett, and he, in turn, recommended Paul Michaels."

There was a note of disapproval in Nick's tone that rankled for a moment, but I held my tongue. Much as I wanted to jump to Paul's defense, I could not without knowing for what he was being blamed. I sat up straighter, determined that once I was on Bell Harbour, I would find a way to make Nick appreciate how wonderful Paul truly was.

Since hearing Nick talk about Paul bothered me, I decided to change the subject. "Could you perhaps tell me a little bit about the Kaspers, Nick? I feel most uncomfortable imposing upon them this way."

"Entertaining you will be their pleasure. They travel extensively in the Caribbean for their business, but because of the War Between the States, they have never visited your country. Of course, Sarah's grandfather came from South Carolina, as did mine and most of the other families on Bell Harbour, so she has reason to be curious about America."

"Your family is from America?" I was astonished. It seemed there was a great deal about the people on Bell Harbour that I had not been told.

Nick nodded. "According to my father, when the first rift between the northern and southern states began to spread, six families who held no belief in slavery decided to leave South Carolina and Georgia. My father was a young man then, but he had his own ship, and he had sailed over much of the Caribbean. It was he who found Bell Harbour and saw its potential."

"Then your family was one of the first on the island?" His words conjured up intriguing images in my mind.

"The first in many years. The islanders welcomed them eagerly. They were a motley lot, dirt poor, living mostly in hovels and feeding themselves from the sea and their gardens. They were more than happy to hire out to the families as they arrived. Outside of the cloister, most every building on Bell Harbour dates from those days."

"Built by the islanders for your family and the others who came down." I suddenly remembered something I had heard Paul say last year. I had been outside, sitting in the garden with the children; but the windows had been open, and because of my feelings about Paul, I had listened shamelessly.

"Four families hold all the good land, and they employ the poor souls from whom they stole that land. True, they claim to have no belief in slavery; but the people must work for them or starve. I am expected to teach these poor children to read and write, yet what will that do for them except make them more valuable employees? They will still have nothing, while their masters reap all the profits from their toil." Paul's voice had rung with righteous passion, thrilling me even though I had scarce understood the meaning of his anger.

"It is truly a beautiful place, and for the most part, a happy one—or it was." Nick sighed, then seemed to shake off his melancholy. "But enough of the past. Look up ahead, that is where we are going."

I gasped as I followed the direction of his pointing finger and saw the handsome white house that seemed to cling to the curve of the hill we were climbing. Though only one story, it was on several levels, following the contours of the land. It was painted white, yet so large that one of the wings reflected the pink and orange

36

of the setting sun, while another was already tinged with the blue of twilight.

"Sarah will be pleased to know that you are taking both Inez and Elena back to Bell Harbour. She is the one who sent word to us of the loss of the Verdugos. She was very worried about the children."

So worried that she had left the children with the sisters in an orphanage, instead of taking them into her home? Since I had been taught it was wrong to judge others, I did not speak my thoughts; but I no longer looked forward to meeting Mr. and Mrs. Kasper. Not that I had a choice, I reminded myself, as the horse trotted between the ornate stone columns and followed the narrow pathway that wove through the handsome gardens to the magnificent veranda.

"You look so troubled, Rachel," Nick said, as a boy came to take the horse's head and Nick helped me from the cart. "You must not be anxious, you will love the Kaspers, everyone does. They will give you a proper island welcome, I promise."

I tried to smile, since his wide grin was once again revealing the intriguing dimple in his cheek; but my heart felt heavy and I was almost too weary to stand. I swayed slightly. It seemed I had been on St. Devina forever and nothing had gone as I had expected.

"Are you all right?" Nick had been about to lift my trunk from the cart, but he turned instead to slip a steadying arm about my waist.

I opened my mouth to protest this familiarity, but before I could speak, the door opened and light spilled out to banish the shadows that had settled over the veranda. A small woman came sweeping down the broad steps, trailing laughter and the scent of flowers.

"Nick, thank goodness you have finally come. We saw the ship set sail so long ago, we were beginning to worry that something might have happened to the teacher." She stopped before me, holding out her arms. "Welcome to our islands."

Chapter 3

Before I could respond, I found myself clasped in Sarah Kasper's warm embrace. Though she was a bit shorter than my five-foot-one, she fairly bounced with enthusiasm, and I was immediately caught up by her friendliness. Still, my weakness returned the moment she let me go and I had to lean against the cart to stay on my feet.

Concern brought a frown to her round face. "Are you ill? When was the last time you ate?" She stepped back to study me. "Did you have an evening meal?"

I shook my head. "There was no time . . ."

Her unladylike snort told me she did not believe that for a moment. "You mean this great lummox never bothered to ask you if you would like to take the time for a decent meal?"

Embarrassed, I glanced in Nick's direction and was surprised to see that he had not taken offense at her words. "We were pretty busy with Elena and Inez," he explained. "And at the cathedral, Father Sebastian offered lemonade and Mrs. Mendez's cookies."

"Which I expect you devoured." Sarah—though I tried, I could not think of her as Mrs. Kasper—shook her head. "I have no doubt it was much more important to make sure the *Belle* was properly loaded and to make any of a dozen other stops rather than have a care for our guest. Come along, my dear, I will have a meal set out by the time you have refreshed yourself." She twined her arm through mine and led me up the stairs and into the house.

For the next few moments I felt I had entered a dream world; everything was so lovely, it seemed impossible that it was real. Not that I had any chance to fully appreciate the rooms we passed through. In the short distance between the entrance of the house and the room I was to occupy, Sarah told me that she and her husband had just recently returned from a trading trip to the Bahamas. She inquired about the girls, saying she had not been to visit them today. She commented on my youth, then assured me that I was needed on Bell Harbour, before telling me not to think too harshly of Nick, since he was unused to seeing to the needs of proper young ladies.

When we reached the handsome guest bedchamber, she gestured me inside, then told me to ask the maid if I needed anything else and invited me to join them on the rear terrace whenever I was ready. I gratefully returned her quick hug before she left, then sank down on the bench at the foot of the bed to catch my breath. Being around Sarah Kasper was exciting, but exhausting.

A tap on the door roused me, and I welcomed the arrival of my trunk and a shy young maid. A glimpse of my disheveled self in the framed mirror that stood near the heavy darkwood chest had been enough to convince me that I needed help. The damp air had my light brown hair curling wildly about my face, and my once-neat brown traveling suit was now crushed with wrinkles and marked by the dust from the streets.

While the maid unpacked my few dresses, I stepped behind an ornate screen to strip off my heavy suit so I could make good use of the soap and water that had

40

been set out for me. Much refreshed, I slipped on the least wrinkled of my gowns, a deep pink cotton with a round neck edged with white lace and short puffed sleeves. Since my hair refused to be subdued into a proper knot on the back of my neck, I finally allowed the maid to tie it back with a bit of pink ribbon.

"Would you like me to show you to the terrace now, Miss?" she asked, picking up my traveling suit, which she had offered to launder and have ready for me in the morning.

A last look in the mirror told me that there was little more I could do to improve my appearance, so I nodded. A flutter of anxiety had me wondering if I should plead fatigue and ask for a tray in my room; but I could not, for then I would have missed my chance to get acquainted with Sarah—and to spend more time getting to know Nick, something I very much wanted to do before we set sail together tomorrow.

I heard Nick's deep rumble of laughter even before we reached the terrace and felt an odd shivering deep inside me, rather like the sensations I had felt once or twice when I listened to beautiful organ music. That thought made me smile. Nick Harrison and organ music? It seemed a strange combination, yet I could think of nothing else that had affected me thus.

"Ah, there you are, Rachel." Sarah came to greet me, her smile as bright as her wide green eyes. "Come along and meet my husband George, then I promise you peace to enjoy your meal. From all that Nick has been telling us about conditions on Bell Harbour, you will need your strength tomorrow."

That ominous statement might have sobered me a little; but Sarah seemed unworried by it, so I decided to concentrate on enjoying the present and forget about tomorrow. Thanks to a teasing conversation mostly composed of amusing tales told by Nick, Sarah, and George, I found that surprisingly easy to do.

Since the night was balmy and bright with starlight, Sarah had ordered our meal served at a table on the terrace. The food was as exquisite as the house, each dish perfectly prepared and served with a flourish. Had I been at the Bennetts' table, I should have been shamed by my appetite, but here everyone seemed eager to offer me more of each course. By the time the last dishes were cleared, I felt that I had more than made up for the privations of the day.

"That was a wonderful meal, Sarah," I moaned, "but I fear I have eaten more than I should."

"A stroll through the gardens will help that," Nick said. "I always need a walk after I dine with Sarah and George."

"I think we could all do with a bit of exercise," Sarah agreed, getting to her feet and taking my arm again. "When we were talking before you came out, Nick told us that it is your intention to care for Elena and Inez yourself. I think that is very commendable of you."

"Setting up an orphanage is a part of my assignment. Reverend Michaels had written of the need for one, so I assume there are other children on the island in the same circumstances as Elena and Inez. Is that not true?" I looked to Nick for information.

"In these times, of course there are. Most, however, do well enough with relatives or go into service with one of the plantation families. We take care of our own, Rachel." Nick's tone was sharp, almost defensive.

"Is that why you intended to leave Inez here?" I countered just as sharply.

"Surely you were not planning to split up those two children, Nick?" Sarah gasped before he could answer me.

"Only until I could find someone to take care of Inez.

42

She is barely two, much too young to be entrusted to Elena's care. Besides, I had thought to see Elena safely in service with one of the families." Nick sighed. "As it is, I have no idea where Rachel will be setting up her orphanage. So far as I know, Paul has done nothing about finding a suitable building. He may even have forgotten now that his school is gone."

"Gone?" I stopped abruptly, freeing my arm from Sarah's so that I could face Nick. "What are you talking about? In his reports Paul wrote of the school he helped build in the village, and I am sure it was his intention to add rooms to it for the orphanage."

Nick's expression hardened as he met my gaze. "The school was burned to the ground three weeks ago, and so far as I know, there has been little talk of rebuilding it. What few classes are being held are conducted in the church."

"The school has burned?" I found it hard to take in. "But how . . . what happened? Was anyone injured?"

"I would venture a guess that someone on the island felt that Paul was teaching far more than the reading, writing, and ciphering he was hired to teach." Again Nick's gaze challenged me, and I had the impression that he expected a certain response, though I had no idea what it might be.

"You mean someone actually burned down the school?" I gasped, hoping that I had misunderstood.

Nick nodded. "I am afraid so. That is why I wanted you to return to Philadelphia, Rachel. Luckily, no one was hurt this time, but the unrest continues. There is no way you are going to be living in the village, of that I am sure."

"But where . . . ?"

"You will stay at Sunrise, of course." His gaze met mine and I felt the strange quickening inside me again.

"Sunrise?"

43

"My family's home. You said yourself, you are to be under my father's protection, so where better?" Nick took my hand and tucked it beneath his arm. "Surely you cannot expect to stay in the village unchaperoned."

The tingling excitement I felt at his touch made me wonder if I would be safe living in the same house with him, but I could not speak of such a shocking thought. Instead, I forced myself to think of more practical matters. "What of Elena and Inez? And if there are other children in need of my care and protection, I must make provisions for them, too. Would that not be a terrible burden to place upon your family?"

"That is a matter to be taken up with Paul and my father when we get home." Nick's tone was adamant as he led me around a fragrant planting of pale flowers.

"Is there no building on your estate that could be used for a temporary orphanage?" I asked. "Surely once people see that I am there only to help the children, I would be safe enough."

"Elena and Inez will be welcome at Sunrise." Nick's confident smile was evident even in the dim light.

"What of the cloister, Nick?" Sarah asked, reminding me that Nick and I were not alone out here. "Why could that not be made into an orphanage?"

"That would be impossible." Nick's tone was even, but I felt the sudden tension in his arm muscles through the sleeve of his shirt.

Sarah seemed unaware of his feelings as she continued, "Why? I cannot believe no one has thought of it before. The building is large, and there are many rooms that could be converted to Rachel's special needs. Everything is there, even a kitchen and dining room. It would be perfect."

"It is out of the question." There was anger in Nick's tone as he turned to face Sarah. "The building has been deserted for years. I fear it would be unsafe now. Remember how often we were warned to stay away from there when we were children."

I looked at Sarah, sensing strange undercurrents beneath the words that were being said. Her expression showed both confusion and anger, but she bit her lower lip instead of arguing with him further. The silence seemed to swell, draining the pleasure from the evening.

"What is this cloister?" I asked, hoping to somehow ease what was rapidly becoming a very awkward moment.

Nick gave Sarah one last warning look, then turned to me with a smile that did nothing to thaw the coldness in his eyes. "It is an old stone building. According to local legend, it was built by the Spanish about the same time the cathedral was begun on St. Devina. It was to be home for a small group of monks, who planned to put the island under cultivation while they went about saving the souls of the islanders."

"If it is as well constructed as the cathedral . . ." I began, then let the sentence trail off as I encountered the anger in Nick's eyes.

"It is," Sarah said, seemingly deciding to ignore Nick's displeasure. "I always adored it. In fact, I used to tell my father that I wanted to live there when I grew up."

"You never told me that," George said, smiling down at his wife.

"She outgrew that foolish idea by the time she was eight or nine," Nick supplied, sounding like a man trying to control his temper.

"Actually, it was about the time my father informed me that I should have to marry a Harrison if I wished to live in it." Sarah's tone was bright with laughter. "Since you were but a child of six or seven . . ."

Nick chuckled, and I sensed the easing of his tension. "That was near twenty years ago, Sarah. Times have

45

changed, and so has the cloister. 'Twould not be a suitable place for Rachel or the children, believe me." He took my arm and started along the path again. "Now, let us talk of happier things. Tell me what you found in Nassau, George. Was the trading good, now that the war in America is over?"

George answered enthusiastically, and within moments he and Nick were busy discussing various products and the deals that he had made. I tried to follow the conversation at first, but the names meant little to me, and my thoughts returned to the subject Nick had sought to dismiss.

Why was he so adamant about my not opening an orphanage on Bell Harbour? Was it because he feared I would stay? That thought hurt, since it would mean he did not like me. And why should he resent the idea of my using an empty building? If it was as perfect as Sarah had said, what harm would I be doing if I used it to care for innocent children?

Thinking of children reminded me of the way Nick had cuddled Inez after my first encounter with him, and I also remembered his gentleness with Elena. He was obviously not a cruel or unfeeling man, yet he seemed unwilling even to discuss an orphanage. Why? Was it because he did not approve of me, or did it have more to do with the resentment he seemed to feel toward Paul?

That thought brought with it a sweeping sense of despair. If Nick disliked Paul and resented what he was trying to do on Bell Harbour, there was truly little hope for our success. My enjoyment of the garden and the company faded as my exhaustion returned, making me stumble and cling tightly to the support of Nick's arm. I ached to escape into sleep.

"Are you all right, Rachel?" Nick's question broke through the swirling fog of my fears.

"Only a little tired. It has been a trying day, and now I feel so unsure of what lies ahead." I was ashamed of the way my voice shook, but I was too disturbed to hide my feelings.

"I have upset you." Nick looked guilty. "Please, forgive me. I should never have told you about the school being burned. I really meant to wait and let Paul explain."

"It will be all right, Rachel." Sarah came to add her reassurances. "The islanders will adore you. Whatever trouble is brewing on Bell Harbour has nothing to do with you."

I wanted to believe her, but somehow I could not. My need to escape grew stronger. "Perhaps it is just that I am so weary," I murmured, wanting only to return to the pretty bedchamber Sarah had given me and hide beneath the bedcovers.

"And we have thoughtlessly kept you up." Now Sarah looked guilty, too.

"You have been wonderful to a stranger, Sarah," I assured her, summoning up my strength. "This has been a lovely evening, and I only wish that it could go on forever." A heartfelt truth, since I felt safe here with Sarah.

"We shall spend more time together, I promise. I visit Bell Harbour quite often, and you shall have to return to St. Devina, too. You will bring her back, will you not, Nick?"

"As often as possible." The warmth in his eyes as he smiled down at me made me forget my weariness. Though I still did not understand Nick's objections to my starting an orphanage on Bell Harbour, I was suddenly sure that he liked me. That made my step much lighter as we returned to the house and added a touch of reluctance to my "Goodnight" as I left him on the terrace.

Having become quite independent during my sea

47

voyage, I declined Sarah's offer to summon the maid to help me prepare for bed. I needed to be alone so I could ponder all that had happened to me since I'd left the *Sea Hawk*. Tomorrow I would have to take charge of Elena and Inez, the first of my orphans. And later I would see Paul Michaels and take my place as his assistant.

That thought sent a shiver down my spine, though I could not be sure whether it was of anxiety or anticipation. I had set sail with such high expectations, been filled with grand plans for dedicating myself to helping Paul; but now . . . I tried to picture Paul as I had seen him last, but it was Nick's face that filled my mind, sending another shiver through me.

What was happening to me? I wondered, as I slipped between the sweet-scented bed linens. Why should I be thinking of Nick instead of Paul? I was far too mature to be fluttering on about a man like some ninny. I had come to teach, and to help Paul by caring for the children; I would have no time for foolish romantic feelings.

I closed my eyes and composed myself for sleep, but the images of Nick refused to vanish. As I drifted into dreams, I was still remembering the way his hair seemed touched with fire when the sun caressed it; the arrogant tilt of his brow when he questioned something; the fascinating dimple that appeared in his left cheek when he laughed.

The room was filled with sunlight when I woke. For a moment, I just stretched and sighed, reluctant to abandon my dreams; then reality intruded. Where was I? I sat up, looking around as memories of last night filled my mind. This was the day I was to go to Bell Harbour.

Sounds of childish laughter came drifting through the open window on a flower-scented breeze. I frowned, remembering that Sarah had told me that she and George had not yet been blessed with any children. Curious when the sounds grew louder, I slipped from the high bed and padded barefoot to the window.

I had no difficulty recognizing Elena as she skipped across the thick grass in pursuit of a large brown dog. A moment later, Inez came toddling after her, crowing with excitement. They were so happy, it was several moments before I remembered that Nick and I were to have collected them from the cathedral on our way to the *Island Belle*.

Guilt swept over me as I saw Nick sitting in the shade of a flowering tree, watching over them. Obviously, I had overslept by a number of hours. Heat rose in my cheeks as I remembered the romantic dreams that had filled my night and much of the morning—dreams of Nick Harrison. What had come over me?

I still had no answer to that question by the time I was dressed in my freshly pressed brown suit. Leaving the maid to pack my belongings in my trunk, I followed Sarah to the terrace.

"Please stop apologizing, Rachel," she chided me. "We had no wish to wake you this morning. The voyage to Bell Harbour will take only a few hours if the winds are favorable, so there was no need to leave early. You must have some bread and fruit before you go. The girls are having fun and so is Nick, I suspect." Sounds of masculine laughter from the other side of the house seemed to confirm her words.

"I just hate to cause any delay. Nick may have business to attend to once he returns home. The late arrival of the *Sea Hawk* has already delayed him overnight."

"I doubt you will hear Nick complain. He used to take any excuse to leave the island for a while. Of course, things have been different since his father's illness." Sarah poured each of us a cup of tea and settled

49

down at the table as one of the maids brought me a plate of food.

"Mr. Harrison has been ill?" My anxiety returned. How could I take the children into the Harrisons' house if there was an invalid to be cared for? "Nick said nothing about it."

Sarah's eyes were sad. "I suspect he dislikes speaking of it. Jarvis Harrison never was one to take kindly to weakness, and I am sure he has been a trial to live with since his heart has been troubling him."

"I do hope my arrival with the children will not make things worse for the poor man." I closed my eyes, not liking the images her words conveyed.

"If anything, I suspect you will be a welcome distraction. Mr. Harrison will be delighted to have someone else to order about." Sarah's smile seemed unperturbed, which I found reassuring.

Though I would have liked to have asked more questions, I was given no opportunity, for at that moment George came out to join us. A short while later, Nick and the children came around the corner of the house. Long before I was ready, I found myself seated on the deck of the *Island Belle* with Inez on my lap and Elena beside me.

I found the thought of leaving the dock on such a small ship frightening; but I took great pains to hide my fears from Elena and Inez, aware that they had already lost everything but each other to the sea. Fortunately, because of my pretense, I quickly forgot my fears and began to enjoy the sheer excitement of the voyage.

At first, Nick and Samuel were very busy, as they had to slowly maneuver our ship through the crowded harbor. Once we left the other boats behind, however, things were different. The *Island Belle* fairly leaped through the waves, leaving St. Devina behind.

"Are you all right, Rachel?" Nearly an hour after we

came on board, Nick startled me by placing a hand on my shoulder. "The motion of the ship does not bother you?"

I shook my head, delighted to discover that it was true. "I suffered on the first few days of my voyage down here, but not even in the storms after that."

"So you are a natural sailor." He seemed pleased. "Would you like me to take Inez below? I suspect she will sleep most of the way."

I looked down at the child in my lap and was surprised to discover that she was, indeed, sound asleep. "Will she be safe?" I asked, as Nick gently lifted her in his arms.

"I'll stay with her," Elena offered, her dark eyes shadowed as she looked out at the sea. My heart ached for her as I followed them inside, yet when I offered to stay in the small cabin with her, she shook her head. "I can care for my sister, Miss Ames. She'll always be safe with me."

I wanted to protest, to hold Elena in my arms as I had held Inez earlier, but Nick drew me away. "You cannot take their sorrow, Rachel," he counseled gently, as we returned to the deck. "This first voyage will be difficult for Elena since she made the journey many times with her family, but she will get through it. She has Inez to care for; that will give her strength."

"But perhaps I could comfort her, help her bear the pain." I stood beside him at the rail, staring out at the passing waves, yet not really seeing them.

"Even the good sisters found that impossible. She refused to lean on any of them. I suspect she needs time."

Memories swept over me. How many people had held out their arms to me in the days after my parents' deaths? And how often had I turned away, refusing their comfort? I sighed. "I know you are right, for I remember how it was. When my parents were taken from me,

51

I felt that I could trust no one to comfort me because those I trusted most had left me. And I was fifteen, much older than Elena."

"Caring for orphans must stir up a lot of painful memories." Nick's eyes were soft with sympathetic understanding, and when I gazed into them, something inside me seemed to melt, spreading warmth through me.

"At first it was difficult, but when I discovered that I could help the children, it made my own grief easier. Reverend Bennett said that I had a special gift for the work. I truly believe that is why he chose me to be Reverend Michaels's assistant."

Nick nodded. "I expect you are right. I only hope that you have the opportunity to use your skills properly. I can call to mind at least a half-dozen children on Bell Harbour who could use your love and understanding."

"All I need is a place, and perhaps someone to help me. In one of his reports, Reverend Michaels mentioned a woman who might be interested, but . . ." I hesitated, suddenly aware that I had once again ventured into the forbidden subject. I swallowed a sigh, hoping that I had not destroyed the magical feeling of closeness that seemed to be spreading between Nick and me. If only I knew what had caused him to resent the idea of the orphanage, I should know better what not to say to him.

"Before you seek help, you will need a place." Nick stepped back from the rail. "But enough of that, you should enjoy this voyage. Look off there to the left and you can see Palm Isle."

Though he was only a few inches further away and the air was balmy, I felt the chill of his withdrawal, even as he continued, "We shall soon be nearing another small island. In fact, we will rarely be out of sight of land the entire way."

I tried to sound enthusiastic as I replied, looking obediently in the direction indicated and admiring the smudge of green that floated indistinctly between the blue of the sky and the indigo of the sea. Meantime, I ached to demand that he tell me why he was so adamantly against my having an orphanage, but I dared not. I had no right—and I had no desire to anger him. Oh, no, I definitely did not want Nick angry at me.

It was a relief when the wind began to rise and Nick had to leave me to help Samuel with the sail. I withdrew to a sheltered corner of the deck, wondering if there would always be this strain between us.

And why should I care? It was Paul I had come to help, not Nick. If he continued to refuse to secure a place for my orphanage, perhaps Paul would know of a building. I sighed, remembering that Paul was undoubtedly very busy finding a building for his school. But if they could be combined . . .

I closed my eyes, remembering life in Philadelphia. There I should have known exactly what was expected of me. To my surprise, the possibility of returning held little attraction. There was no Nick Harrison at Middle Brook Christian.

"Rachel, Rachel, come and see. We're almost home!" Elena's voice roused me from my dozing.

I leaped to my feet, embarrassed to be caught napping in the late afternoon sun. My heartbeat quickened as I got a good look at the rocky cliffs that rose above the hungry, seeking waves. As we drew nearer to the island, I could see lots of trees and flowering bushes, but I caught only quick glimpses of the large houses they shielded.

"Where do we land?" I asked, seeing no break in the rocks that extended out beyond the shore.

"The harbor is just ahead, around the point." Elena's eyes never left the island. " 'Tis the only place where a boat this size can land. The rocks are too near the sand everywhere else."

The moment we rounded the rocky headland formed by one of the arms that protected the cove, everything changed. The water calmed, and for the first time I could see the glorious colors of Bell Harbour. We skimmed lightly over shimmering patches of green, blue, azure, aqua, and turquoise water as we eased toward the shore.

It was several minutes before I lifted my attention from the water to the small cluster of houses that rose above the long dock that extended out into the cove. Though they were painted in colorful pastels, and flowers seemed to bloom everywhere, I could see at once that the area was very poor and neglected.

A soft wail from below deck claimed my attention and I left Elena at the rail while I went down to comfort Inez. I was still trying to explain where we were when I felt the ship bumping against the dock. Heart pounding, I carried her out into the sunlight.

"It is about time you returned, Nick." Paul's impatient voice carried easily to me. "Where is the . . ."

The sun was behind Paul, shining in his fair hair and shadowing his eyes, but not so much that I missed the look of utter shock and disbelief that passed over his familiar features.

"Greetings, Reverend Michaels." I tried to smile at him, but my face seemed frozen.

"Rachel Ames! By all that is holy, what are you doing here?" Paul's gray eyes reflected nothing but dismay.

"She is to be your new assistant." Nick's tone was no happier than Paul's, but there was a biting touch of mockery beneath his words as he continued, "She has even brought the first two orphans for your orphanage."

"We have no orphanage as yet." Paul's frown deepened.

"So I informed her." Nick sounded almost amused.

Anger flooded through me as I looked at the two men, then down at Elena and Inez. "We are here whether or not there is an orphanage," I snapped. "And the children are tired and hungry, so I would appreciate being allowed to leave the boat with them."

Paul appeared shocked at my vehemence, and the amusement vanished from Nick's eyes. "I see the wagon coming," he said. "We can leave for Sunrise as soon as your belongings are loaded."

I looked to Paul, expecting him to offer some protest or comment, but he only shook his head and turned away. My heart sank. I had arrived ready to accept my assignment, but it appeared that it was not going to be easy.

Chapter 4

Though Paul's name rose to my lips, I kept them firmly closed, refusing to plead for his approval. I turned my gaze back to Nick, surprised by the ease with which he had accepted my demands. He seemed about to speak, then turned away instead, following Paul off the boat.

For a moment I was tempted to do the same, but Paul's displeasure had been too obvious. If he had no wish to have me here, I knew there was nothing I could say or do to change his mind. When Nick stopped Paul, I feared a confrontation; but the two men just talked. I watched them closely, wishing that I could hear their words.

After what seemed an eternity, Paul nodded and left without a glance in my direction. Nick stayed where he was until the large farm cart reached him. He spoke to the darkly tanned driver, then came back to the *Island Belle* looking much happier.

"Paul will see to the transport of the supplies that you brought for him, so we can go as soon as your belongings and those of the girls can be put on the cart." Nick brushed past me to show Samuel and the cart driver which bales and boxes went where.

"Please, Miss Ames, be we stayin' with you?" The

painful urgency in Elena's soft whisper forced me to forget Paul's uncaring treatment and turn my attention to her. The dark fear in her eyes made my heart ache.

"Of course, Elena. Nick has promised that I can care for both you and Inez. We are to go to his home for now, and later, when we have a place for the orphanage ..." I let it trail off, wondering now if I would be given the opportunity to stay. What if Paul's rejection meant that I would be sent back to Philadelphia? What would become of Elena and Inez? I hugged Inez tighter, hoping that neither child would sense my fears. They obviously had enough of their own.

Before I could think of anything more to say, several people came hurrying out of the buildings across the dusty street from the dock and one of the women called out to Elena. Within moments, both my charges were being welcomed by the islanders and I was free to turn my attention to Nick.

Not sure exactly how to approach the subject uppermost in my mind, I moved to the rail, where he now stood. He glanced at me, but said nothing, his expression speculative. I swallowed hard, then began, "Reverend Michaels seemed surprised to see me."

Nick's chuckle revived my anger. "It seems your Reverend Bennett never saw fit to inform him about the assistant he was sending. Perhaps because he feared Paul would question his choice."

That hurt, but I blinked back my quick tears, hiding my feelings under a shroud of anger. "Why do you think so little of me? Does no one trust Reverend Bennett's judgment? Am I to have no chance to prove myself?" The hot words fairly exploded from my mouth.

Nick lifted a hand, stopping me before I said more. "No one is questioning your ability, Rachel. The problem is that everyone, myself included, expected him to send an older woman, perhaps a widow, someone experienced in the ways of the world. A very pretty young miss arriving here alone is bound to cause some upset, which is the last thing we need on Bell Harbour."

Though his gaze had softened as he'd spoken the last words, I was in no mood to be distracted by compliments, no matter how welcome. "Am I to be sent back?"

"Sent back?" Nick's shock was obvious. "Of course not. At the moment, you are expected at Sunrise. Even Paul had to admit that is the best place for you now."

And what else had Paul said? I wondered, but dared not ask. I could only hope that once he recovered from his surprise, Paul would come to talk to me. Surely when I explained my dedication to caring for the children, he would welcome me and we could begin making plans for a real orphanage.

I thought no more about Nick's words until we were all settled in the cart on our way out of the village, then the implications struck me. Could it be true? Had Reverend Bennett purposely not told Paul that I was coming? But why? If he was sure that I would not be welcomed, why send me at all? It made no sense, and in all the time I had known Reverend Bennett, he had never seemed a man to be capricious in his decisions. Which had to mean that he believed I could serve a purpose here.

Drawing strength from the belief, I straightened my shoulders and turned my attention to the lovely land through which we were passing. The earth must be wonderfully rich, for crops grew vigorously on both sides of the road. I recognized sugar cane in several large fields and healthy rows of vegetables in another. Neat stone walls separated the fields, and beyond the vegetables stretched a vast meadow broken only by thick groves of trees and bushes.

"Is this your land?" I asked Nick.

"No, this part of the island belongs to the Chalmerses. The plantation is called Emerald Acres, for obvious reasons." His lazy grin warmed me more than the lowering rays of the sun.

"It is truly lovely here." My response to him confused me. Now that I was here, I must forget how pleasant he could be. I had to be ready to take my place at Paul's side, if he wanted me. And if he did not? I refused to even consider the possibility.

"This part of the island was settled first, but I prefer the land around Sunrise. It may be wilder, but there is a special beauty . . ."

I could hear the love in his voice and felt a sharp pang of homesickness for the house I had shared with my parents, a feeling I had thought was long behind me. The beauty of this land lost its allure as I remembered home.

"I had not thought to make you sad, Rachel." Nick's voice broke into my thoughts, shaming me.

"I was only thinking that it has been years since I felt thus about some land and a house. Not that my parents owned a plantation, but our house was special to me, and . . ." I stopped, afraid that the lump in my throat would become a sob if I continued.

"You must let my family make you feel at home here. They will welcome you, I promise."

When I looked into the intriguing depths of his hazel eyes, I had to believe him. There was a warm promise there that made the dark sorrow inside me melt away like the snow in spring. Though outwardly nothing had changed, my heart lifted and the lump vanished.

Disturbed by the way he made me feel, I again turned my attention to the passing scene, but I continued to be aware of the warmth of his arm when it brushed mine as the cart bumped along. A disturbing feeling, yet not unpleasant, I decided. Rather the way I felt about Mr. Nick Harrison himself, truth be told. That thought made me smile, for I was sure it would amuse him, too.

After what seemed an endless stretch of silence, Nick leaned forward, searching the land ahead. Curious, I sought for some clue to what he might be seeking, and my breath caught in my throat as the road curved around a thick growth of flowering bushes. The stone building rose magnificently from the crest of a small rise, so draped in clinging vines, it was almost a part of the rich foliage that surrounded it.

"What is that?" I gasped, though a part of me already knew.

" 'Tis the old cloister. We are on Sunrise land now." Nick's tone held a mixture of pride and resignation.

"Oh, 'tis lovely. Could we not stop for just a moment . . ." I began, then gasped at my own forwardness, mortified. "Forgive me, I have no right to ask such a favor. It is just so . . ." Words failed me.

"Mysterious and intriguing?" Nick's sigh held a note of amusement. "That was what Sarah always said, and she was right; but I think we should wait a few days before you explore the place. Right now, I suspect my father is pacing about the house, impatient for our arrival."

"But how would he know . . ." I let it trail off, suddenly realizing that the arrival of the cart had been a bit too fortuitous, a fact I would have noted sooner had I been less upset.

"Papa undoubtedly sent someone to watch for us from the headland. We sailed past Sunrise on our way to the harbor."

I swallowed hard, thinking of the handsome mansions I had glimpsed from the ship. Not that I was surprised, for Paul's stories had made it clear that the landowners of Bell Harbour Island lived well; but Nick seemed so

. . . not ordinary, certainly, but still practical, and very real to me.

"Are you disappointed, Rachel?" His gentle question brought a blush to my cheeks.

I tore my gaze from the vine-covered stone edifice we were passing and managed a smile. "Because I shall have to wait to see the cloister? Of course not. It is just so much larger than I had expected."

"It was built at least partially as a fortress to protect the first Spaniards who landed on the island. Once they had determined that the natives were peaceful, the settlers began to arrive and the monks were given the building as their own. It has a long and varied history."

Something about his tone told me that not all that history had been happy, but I had no opportunity to ask for further details, for Elena was now tugging at my sleeve. "We be arrivin' soon, Miss Ames? Inez be frettin'."

I looked to Nick for an answer. He nodded, then reached down into the bed of the cart to lift the whimpering girl into his lap. "We shall be there soon, and if I know Cook, she will have a grand tea prepared to welcome us. Would you like that, Inez? Sweet honey cakes and coconut pudding, perhaps, or ripe fruit and molasses drops."

Inez stopped whimpering immediately, her dark eyes growing round at the prospect. Elena sighed softly. "For us, too?"

"Of course. You will be staying at Sunrise, Elena, I told you that." Nick's expression was sad.

"I be workin' at Sunrise." Elena's frown made it clear that she was unsure of what Nick's words meant. "And Inez be with Miss Ames."

Nick reached back to pat her narrow shoulders. "I think perhaps you should be allowed some schooling before we talk about your entering service with any family, Elena. You will assist Miss Ames for the time being. I am sure that, should she start an orphanage, she will have need of help."

I started to protest that I was perfectly capable of handling children, but when I saw the glow of hope in Elena's eyes, I held my tongue. "I am sure Elena will be a great help," I agreed. I would never have expected a man like Nick to be so sensitive to a lonely child's need for a place to belong.

I gazed into his eyes for a moment, then I had to look away quickly for fear that he would see how deeply his words had touched me. Since I knew little about men, the strange new feeling disturbed me. Mrs. Bennett had been most clear about not trusting the sweet talk of strange men, and for all that we had spent more than a day together, Nick Harrison was still very much a stranger to me.

To distract myself from thoughts of Nick, I concentrated my attention on what he had said Elena should help me with—the orphanage. Did his words mean that he thought I might actually be given a chance to stay and create a haven for the orphaned children of this island? Or was he only offering hope to a weary child who needed to be coddled?

And what of Paul Michaels? His disappointment at seeing me still rankled. I had thought him a kind and compassionate man, but now ... Though Nick's description of the tea that awaited us at Sunrise had set my stomach to grumbling, my confusion about my future as Paul's assistant killed my appetite. Nothing was turning out as I'd imagined it would.

"That is Sunrise just ahead." Nick broke into my dark thoughts and I gladly set them aside as I looked in the direction he indicated.

The huge white house lounged like a dowager queen in the midst of the most lush gardens I had ever seen. There were flowers everywhere and the grass grew thick as emerald velvet. Three floors the building rose, the second-story balcony shadowing an inviting veranda that wrapped around the two visible sides of the house.

When I tore my eyes from the building, I became aware of Nick's gaze. I took a deep breath, not sure what he expected of me. "It is magnificent."

His grin made my heartbeat quicken. " 'Tis the grandest house my grandfather could remember from his visits to Charleston and Savannah. He always dreamed of inviting some of his old friends down for a visit, but it took so long to build the place, and then the war came . . ." His grin faded. "Anyway, it is home."

Home, indeed. It would have held everyone from Middle Brook Christian, with plenty of room left over. My family's comfortable house outside Philadelphia seemed shabby and small compared to the mansion we were approaching. "Why is it called Sunrise?" I asked, uncomfortable with the comparison. Reverend Bennett had told me often enough that envy was sinful.

"You will see tomorrow. This end of the island catches the first rays of the rising sun for most of the year and dawn turns the house pink and gold each morning." His eyes sparkled with mischief and his grin brought the intriguing dimple back to his left cheek. "At least, that is what the early risers tell me."

"I shall look forward to seeing it," I murmured, feeling heat in my cheeks, though I was not sure why his words made me blush. Perhaps it was the intimacy of speaking about dawn with him, or it might be the caressing way his gaze moved over my face. For whatever reason, I was glad that we had reached the plantation house, for I desperately needed some time away from the distracting Mr. Nick Harrison.

As the cart came to a halt at the foot of the wide stairway, the handsome mahogany double doors swung open and a portly gentleman came striding out. "About time

63

you arrived, Nick," he thundered, though his wide grin belied his gruff words. "I was beginning to think you had run the *Island Belle* aground somewhere."

Nick's laughter boomed out and he jumped to the ground, then turned to offer me a hand. Though the man's hair was gray instead of deep russet, their grins were so much alike, I had no need to wait for introductions to know that this man must be Nick's father—and Paul's benefactor, Jarvis Harrison.

"What have we here?" Mr. Harrison demanded, as Nick set me on the bottom step and turned back to lift Elena and Inez out of the cart. "I thought you went to fetch the assistant Reverend Michaels requested."

"Papa, I would like you to meet Miss Rachel Ames, recent graduate of Middle Brook Christian School for Young Ladies, and Paul's new assistant."

I could hear the touch of amusement in Nick's voice and it rankled almost as much as the instant dismay I read in his father's face. I lifted my chin and smoothed back the curls that had escaped from my pins. I was getting used to being unwanted, but that made it no more palatable. In fact, I ached for someone to welcome me to my new life with hope. "I am pleased to meet you, Mr. Harrison," I murmured, wishing it were true.

He studied me for what seemed an eternity, his hazel eyes unreadable, then his lips turned up in a smile and the same gleam of mischief came into his eyes that I had seen so often in Nick's. "Well, this should be interesting. How did the Reverend react?"

"He was surprised." Nick moved closer to me, his tone surprisingly serious. "It was clear he had no more idea who was being sent than we did."

"Where is he?" Mr. Harrison was frowning.

"He said that he had several matters to take care of before he could begin to make suitable arrangements for Miss Ames. I suggested that she come out here for the time being. These days the village is no place for an unchaperoned young lady."

"And these children?" His father's gaze had now moved to Elena and Inez, who were cowering behind my skirts, looking as miserable as I felt.

"Miss Ames has made it clear that she wishes to open an orphanage on Bell Harbour Island and these two will be her first charges."

Anger stiffened my spine. They spoke of me as though I were unable to speak for myself. I took a deep breath and forced myself to meet Mr. Harrison's gaze. "I was given to believe that my mission here was to assist Reverend Michaels with his teaching duties and to care for the children who had no one to watch over them. Elena and Inez Verdugo needed someone, so . . ." My courage drained away as Mr. Harrison turned to his son. "I am sorry if my arrival is an imposition, but I . . ."

"You are quite welcome here, Miss Ames, though these two would keep you out here in the hot sun until you melt." The woman's voice interrupted me and brought our eyes to the middle-aged woman who came across the veranda to join us. "Please come in. I am Eudora Harrison." Though tiny and plump, she appeared very much in command of the situation as she offered me a cool, pale hand and led me up the stairs and into the most magnificent entry hall I had ever seen.

I had no chance to catch my breath or speak as she began issuing orders to a bewildering collection of servants. A sweet-faced young maid was entrusted with Elena and Inez, while the driver of the cart was ordered to take my belongings to my room. A second maid was instructed to take me to my room and to aid me in any way I needed.

"We shall be serving tea shortly, and you will have a chance to meet the rest of the family then, Miss Ames,"

Mrs. Harrison informed me, as I followed the maid to the handsome staircase that rose from the far end of the hall.

Feeling very much at sea, I glanced over my shoulder, hoping for a sign from Nick; but he was already deep in conversation with his father. Obviously, I was once again on my own in a strange new place. I took a deep breath and hurried after the sturdy young woman, who at least seemed to know where we were going.

Though I certainly had not been expected, Mrs. Harrison's arrangements made me feel most welcome. I even felt a tingle of anticipation as I smoothed down the least wrinkled of my gowns and carefully retraced the route the maid had used to take me to my elegant room. Though my stay at Sunrise would likely be brief, I meant to enjoy it to the fullest.

"Ah, there you are." Nick separated himself from a shadowy corner of the wide entry hall and came to take my arm. "Mother has everyone waiting in the library."

"She has been most kind." I murmured the proper words, though my attention was on the strange warmth that seemed to spread through me from where my hand rested on Nick's arm. Why should I feel thus whenever we touched? What did it mean?

"Your accommodations are comfortable?" Nick kept his gaze away from me as though he, too, felt something odd.

"Very." As I spoke, I remembered a play that I had seen as a child; in it, the people spoke as we did, as though their thoughts were occupied elsewhere.

Before I could puzzle it further, we entered a charmingly cluttered room that opened off the entry and what had seemed a pleasant buzz of conversation halted as everyone turned to stare at me. The faces of my host and hostess offered smiles; but for some reason, the others seemed less pleased to see me.

Nick introduced me to the three young women who sat with his parents. His sisters, Pamela and Olivia, murmured words of welcome, but I sensed a reserve behind their polite smiles. The third woman, Geraldine Chalmers, seemed older than his sisters, perhaps closer to Nick's age, and was by far the most beautiful woman in the room. Her shining black hair framed an aristocratic face dominated by huge blue eyes, which I noted were directed most often toward Nick.

Once the introductions were finished, I took the seat to which Nick directed me and did my best to enjoy the lavish tea that was served. I was, I realized, developing a talent for swallowing around the lump of anxiety that I feared had taking up permanent residence in my throat. Still, eating gave me something to do besides admire the books that lined the walls of the room while I listened to the conversation that ebbed and flowed around me.

Miss Chalmers, I learned, was the daughter of another of the powerful planter families, and an old friend of the Harrisons. She had ridden over earlier in the day to visit Pamela and Olivia—or so she said. I, however, had ample time to notice that her attention was more often directed toward Nick than toward either of his sisters.

Was she his intended? I wondered, hating the way that thought made me feel. He appeared quite fond of her, yet he also seemed to enjoy being near me. Or was he simply being kind to me because he sensed my discomfort and shyness? I told myself sternly that I should not be entertaining such thoughts, but it was hard to make them go away when Nick was so close and so dreadfully handsome. I tried to concentrate on the books.

Miss Chalmers came to sit beside me as the servants were clearing away the tea things. "So you are here to assist Reverend Michaels, Miss Ames. Are you a teacher?" Though her smile was polite, her tone held a touch of derision that grated on my already strained emotions.

Having had enough of being looked upon as a useless child by everyone I met, I gazed at her with the firmness I had seen Mrs. Bennett use to quell even the most rebellious children. "Yes, I have been trained as a teacher, but I was chosen because I also have spent a great deal of time working with orphans. It was hoped that I could help Reverend Michaels create a proper orphanage here on Bell Harbour Island. Something he had said was badly needed."

"An orphanage?" Miss Chalmers seemed surprised.

"Rachel and I brought back the Verdugo children, Elena and Inez, so I suspect we shall have to do something about housing them even while Paul is still trying to find a new location for his school." Nick spoke from behind me, his tone stern.

His words seemed to have quite an impact on Miss Chalmers. For a moment, I could see flashes of fire in her eyes, then she lowered her thick, dark lashes, and when she looked up again, her smile seemed to reach out to me. "What a brave undertaking for one so young. I do admire you, Miss Ames, and I should like to help if I can."

Her tone was so friendly, I responded without thinking. "Please call me Rachel, and I do thank you for your offer. I shall surely need all the help I can find, if what Nick has told me about Reverend Michaels's school is true."

"And I shall be Geraldine. We will be great friends, I am sure. Please, have no worry about what happened in the village. You cannot let what a few angry islanders did deter you from your work here. I assure you, I shall be happy to help you find just the right place for your orphanage." She directed her smile over my shoulder to where Nick still stood. "Even Nick will have to admit that I know the island as well as anyone."

"Every nook and cranny." His tone held a mocking note that made me wonder just what their relationship might be, but he continued in more kindly tone. "If Geraldine helps you, I am certain you will find just what you need."

"That is most generous," I began, but before I could go on, Mr. Harrison joined us with some questions about the supplies I had brought with me and I was soon caught up in a discussion about my life in Philadelphia. When I looked around again, both Nick and Geraldine had vanished.

Feeling deserted, I turned to Mrs. Harrison. "Perhaps I should attend to Elena and Inez," I murmured, remembering belatedly that I had promised to see to their care. "I should not like them to feel neglected."

"I doubt that they will, with all the servants fussing over them, but if you wish . . ." Mrs. Harrison waved the hovering maid forward and instructed her to take me to the girls.

Sensing that I was being dismissed, I thanked her for her generous welcome, then followed the girl from the room. Had I annoyed Nick's mother by asking to see the girls? I wondered, as I followed the maid to the rear of the huge house. But surely she must understand that I felt responsible for bringing the girls here and meant to assume my duties toward them immediately.

"Where are the children?" I asked, a bit confused when the maid opened the door to what appeared to be the back staircase of the house.

"They be on the third floor, Miss. Cook fed 'um, then I was told to take 'um to the old children's wing." The girl kept her gaze on her toes. "They be safe there."

Sensing her discomfort, I changed my tone at once.

69

"I had no doubt that they were well cared for, I only wondered where they had been taken. The house is so large."

"I kin show you." The girl led the way up the steep stairs and I hurried after her, finding this area of the house more familiar than the grandeur of the front entry. Though life at Middle Brook Christian had been comfortable, there had been nothing lavish about our living arrangements and there had always been work that needed to be done.

Work that would soon be commanding all my time and effort, I reminded myself, as I climbed the second set of stairs and followed the maid along a hall far plainer than the one outside the door of the room I had been given. I swallowed a sigh, aware that I probably should request a room up here, near the children. It would never do for me to become too used to the luxury of living at Sunrise, since I would soon be moving to wherever the orphanage was to be housed.

"They be in here, Miss." The maid opened a door and stood back.

The huge room was dim, and it was several seconds before I could take in the entire scene. This had obviously been the children's playroom, for child-sized furniture still stood about the vast expanse and the shelves that lined the walls seemed to contain more toys than I had ever seen before. There were rocking horses and small carts, dolls and all manner of stuffed and carved toys, plus a number of large boxes and trunks. In fact, there was so much to see, it took me quite a while to realize that the room appeared empty of life.

"Where are they?" I asked, but there was no answer. When I looked around, I realized that I was alone. The maid, evidently feeling that she had fulfilled her mission, had gone back downstairs.

Heart pounding, I stepped into the room. "Elena? Inez?"

My voice echoed back at me and the dust rose as my skirt swept the wooden floor when I hurried across the room to open the curtains that covered the windows. Light spilled in, dispelling the worst of the shadows, but giving me no clue as to where the children could have gone.

Guild flooded over me. Where could they be? I closed my eyes, imagining how they must have felt when they were abandoned here by the same maid who had brought me to this room. Had they believed that I no longer cared about them? Or might they have gone in search of me?

And where had I been? Bitter pain knifed through me. I had been sipping tea and eating cakes with one of the planter families. I remembered clearly all that I had overheard Paul telling the Bennetts about how little these people cared about the islanders.

But Nick was not like that! The thought filled my mind so forcefully that I nearly looked around to see who had spoken. Then, realizing that I was still alone, I forced the images of his face from my mind and focused on what was truly important. I had to find Elena and Inez—now!

With the addition of light, I could see clearly that a door opened off each end of the immense room, and I headed for the nearest one. A soft sound came to me even before I had the door open. Candlelight flickered in the draft from the door and two tearstained faces turned my way.

"Elena, Inez, thank the good Lord that I found you. I was most distressed." I dropped to my knees and held out my arms as they both ran to me.

"We be most skeered, Miss Ames," Elena gasped, obviously fighting a sob. "We dint know where you be, and . . ."

"I am so sorry." I hugged her tight, feeling the trembling of her slender body. How could I have neglected them? What sort of woman was I, that I could not be trusted to watch over two helpless children? Had Nick bewitched me?

"Wanna play." Inez pulled away from me. "Kin I?"

"Them things not be ours, Inez." Elena's gaze followed her sister's, and I could read the matching longing in her eyes. Suddenly I understood that much more than my seeming neglect was involved here. "You kin look, but not touch."

I opened my mouth to tell them to go ahead and enjoy the treasures that were spread about the room, but I stopped myself. Such permission was not mine to give, though I could not believe anyone would be cruel enough to put the children here and not allow them to play with the toys.

"I shall go down and ask if you may play with the toys." I got to my feet and carefully dusted off my skirt. "Will you be all right here, while I am gone?"

"We be fine, Miss Ames." Elena slipped a protective arm around her baby sister. "Just please hurry. Inez ain't never seen such wonderful things."

Nor had she, I suspected; but I said nothing more as I used the hem of my skirt to wipe her tanned cheeks. Elena would need all her dignity and courage in the days ahead, so I would have to help her by allowing her to be responsible for Inez.

I was halfway across the playroom when the door to the hall opened and Nick entered. When our eyes met, his smile stole my breath away, and for just a heartbeat I forgot everything except the strange feelings that quivered through me. Then a sound from the small bedroom where Elena and Inez waited broke the spell.

"Mother just told me that she had the children brought up here." He looked around. "Where are they?"

I pointed to the closed door as I recovered enough of my composure to remember where I had been going. "I was just on my way to ask your mother's permission for the children to play with the toys here."

"There's no need to ask. They are quite welcome to enjoy everything. I do, however, think that someone should stay up here with them at all times. One of the maids . . ."

"I should be the one to stay with them," I broke in. "They are my responsibility."

"But you . . ." he began, then seemed to reconsider. After a moment, he nodded. "Whatever you choose, Rachel. There is a suite of rooms at the other end that was used by our governesses, so I can have your belongings moved up here, if you wish."

I could read disapproval in his gaze, but I forced myself to ignore it. It would be best if we both realized that I was not a real guest in his house. If I was to be of use to Paul in his mission on this island, I must put distance between myself and the allure of Nick's friendliness. Moving up here would be a good first step. "I would be most grateful," I murmured, wishing that I spoke the truth.

Chapter 5

Within an hour I was again unpacking my belongings; but this time my surroundings seemed much more familiar, though I still had more space to myself here than I'd ever had at the school. Thanks to the efficiency of the maids, my two rooms now sparkled, and the breeze from the window carried with it the scent of the oil used to polish the furniture that filled both my bedroom and the tiny sitting room.

I stood in the doorway that opened into the playroom and watched as Elena and Inez continued their explorations. My heart ached for their silence in the face of such wonders, yet I understood that their grief and loss had robbed them of the natural exuberance of children. Still, it was good to see their smiles, and I hoped that their laughter would soon follow.

My gaze strayed to the door that led to the hall, and I found myself wishing that it would open again and that Nick would return. I shook my head at the foolishness of such a thought. I would do better to wish that Paul would appear there, for he was the one to whom I needed to speak.

Sighing, I returned to my unpacking, wondering as I did so where I should next be hanging my dresses and tucking away my underthings. Both Mr. Harrison and

Nick had been adamant about my not living in the village, but if not there—where?

The image of a huge stone building filled my mind. What was the cloister like inside? Was it an impossible ruin, or could I make enough of the vast area livable for Elena, Inez, and me? It had looked so peaceful, and yet so . . . enduring. Surely we could be safe there.

Safe. I shook my head, not wanting to believe that anyone could harbor ill feelings toward a good man like Paul Michaels. What had happened here? Why would the very people to whom Paul had promised his help burn down the school he was using to teach their children? There was so much that made no sense to me.

A tap on the door that led from my sitting room to the hall broke into my thoughts and I hurried to answer it, my heart pounding at the thought that it might be Nick. My joy faded as I faced a stout woman in a black dress. Mrs. Harrison had introduced me to so many of the household staff, it took me several minutes to remember the housekeeper.

"Yes, Mrs. McGinty, what is it?"

"Miz Harrison asked me to inquire if you wished to join the family for the evening meal. She thought that since you were so concerned about your charges, you might prefer to eat with the children." The words were delivered without inflection, and there was no warmth in the cold gray eyes that appraised my dusty gown and untidy hair. Clearly, Mrs. McGinty felt I had no business dining with the family.

For just a moment, I had pictured the pleasure that would come from sharing another meal with Nick. But Nick and I would share the table with his parents and his sisters, and possibly Geraldine Chalmers. My pretty daydream faded quickly under the bright light of the real world.

"Miz Harrison said I was to tell you that one of the

maids would be available to help you dress, should you wish to join them." Mrs. McGinty shifted her feet, obviously eager for my answer.

I had no need to glance at my small wardrobe to know that I should need more than help with dressing. Even my finest gowns were far out of fashion and hopelessly plain. I had no desire to have Nick see how poorly they compared to what his sisters would be wearing.

"I think it would be best if I shared my meals with the children." I spoke quickly, shamed by my own thoughts. First envy, now vanity. I was beginning to understand why Reverend Bennett so often lectured about the temptations that existed outside the walls of Middle Brook Christian. Thanks to the strange effect Nick had upon me, it seemed I was not handling them too well.

"I will instruct Harriet to bring up a tray for you." Mrs. McGinty turned and was halfway down the hall before I could even thank her. I closed my eyes, fighting a strong desire to call her back, to tell her that I had changed my mind.

The happy sound of giggles from the playroom broke through the longing and recalled me to my duty. I was here to care for the children, not to moon after Nick Harrison like some foolish young girl. Besides, I told myself grimly, it was very likely that he was already promised to Geraldine Chalmers, so there was really no reason for me to think about him.

Though I was resolute about following my own advice, it proved more difficult than I had anticipated. Images of Nick kept straying into my thoughts, distracting me from the games I devised for Elena and Inez. When I looked at the toy soldiers on the shelf, I could imagine a little boy with russet hair playing with them. Had he whipped the battered rocking horse to race across imaginary fields? Was one of the tattered books his favorite? Had he sat there and . . .

A tap on the door broke into my thoughts. I turned, expecting it to be Harriet with the tray from the kitchen. My heart turned over as Nick stepped into the room. A smile came unbidden to my lips, then froze there as he frowned at me.

"Is there something amiss?" I asked, glancing nervously at the mess the children had created. "Should I have waited to give them permission . . ."

"I have come to speak with you." His frown disappeared as he smiled at the laughing children, then he took my elbow and steered me across the room, away from Elena and Inez.

"What is it? Have you thought of a place where I . . ." His stern expression stopped me.

"Why have you refused to dine with my family?"

"Refused?" I was perplexed that he should be so angry. "I thought only that it would be better for the girls not to eat alone, since this is still a strange place for them."

"Then you have no objection to taking the meal with us?"

"Of course not, you family is charming." I spoke quickly, caught between anticipation and anxiety.

"Then you shall. Harriet can bring up the girls' tray in a bit and stay with them. She can even see them into bed, if you wish. That will give you plenty of time to yourself before you join us." His pleased grin made me feel warm all over. "I know it takes my sisters an eternity to prepare for a simple dinner."

His words destroyed the sweet images forming in my head, reminding me of my meager wardrobe and my original doubts about sitting at table with the elegant Harrisons. Dreading his laughter and fearing to meet his gaze, lest he read too much in my eyes, I studied my dusty gown as I tried to formulate a proper excuse for staying away from this meal. "I fear I have had no time to prepare my clothing since the voyage ..."

A strong hand caught mine, startling me so that I was forced to look into his eyes. "'Tis not a formal meal, Rachel. Just a family that would like to know you better and to have you get to know us."

My heart seemed to stop for a moment, then raced wildly as I felt the compelling warmth of his gaze flooding over me. I would never have expected the gentle understanding I could read in his expression. "Father would like to hear more of your plans for the orphanage, and I am sure my sisters would love to hear about the fashions in Philadelphia."

As I looked into his eyes, I knew I could never refuse such a special invitation. "Then I shall be delighted to join you."

His smile left a glow surrounding me that lasted until Harriet arrived with the tray for herself and the children. "Miz McGinty says I should eat up here," she explained, as I ordered the children to wash their hands and faces before they sat down at the small table.

"I think that is a fine idea," I assured her, sensing that she was a bit uncomfortable. "I disliked the idea of having them to eat alone."

"I'd be right happy to see to them as much as you wish." Harriet's gaze was directed at the girls, and I could see that it was full of longing. "I be missin' my little brothers and sisters something fierce since I come into service here."

"How long have you been here?" I asked, surprised at her confession.

"Two years, Miss."

"And do you not have time at home?"

She looked away, fussing with the dishes. "My folk be gone. Went to Pine Isle long time ago. I stayed 'cause . . ." She sighed. "No matter, Miss. Excuse me for speaking out. Cook say I be forever talking too much."

Sympathy swept over me as I recognized her loneliness. I remembered well how it felt to live among strangers and long for those I loved. "I like to have you talk to me, and I should be grateful for any time you can spend with the girls. I have no idea what demands will be made on my time while I am staying here, and they have been alone too much."

Harriet nodded. "Cook told me about them losin' their folks, poor little tykes."

I watched over the three of them for a few moments after Elena and Inez returned from their ablutions, then I left them to see to my own preparations. Not that there was a great deal I could do. My choices were limited by wrinkles and the fact that I had brought mostly dresses more suited for the classroom than the sure-to-be-elegant dining room at Sunrise.

Still, as I worked to subdue my riot of tawny curls, I was pleased to note that the sun had brought a glow to my skin and my brown eyes fairly danced in the candle's glow. Or perhaps it was my growing anticipation that I saw reflected in the mirror. At least living at the school had forced me to learn to manage my own hair, I thought wryly, as I used my combs to hold the neatly brushed waves back, then stepped away from the looking glass.

It was too small for me to see much, but I already knew that my green cotton grown fit well, for I had made it myself during the last weeks at Middle Brook. Only the pale expanse of my throat troubled me, for it seemed to cry out for an adornment. Not sure what I wanted, I opened the small box of ribbons that I had unpacked and smiled as I found a bit of the same green ribbon that trimmed my gown.

79

Armed with the ribbon, I turned my attention to my small carved box of treasures, seeking through my tiny collection of jewelry until I found my mother's creamy cameo. I felt closer to her when I threaded the ribbon through the cameo, then tied it about my neck. Still, I had to wonder what she would have thought of her daughter, had she seen me here, so far from home and facing so many problems as I accepted my first assignment as a teacher.

Luckily, I had little time to wonder, for Harriet tapped on my door. "If you be needin' someone to show you the way back down, Annie be here for the tray, and she could help you." Harriet's expression told me that she recognized the anxiety I was feeling, and I should have been ashamed of being so transparent, but instead I was grateful.

"Thank you, that would be kind. I fear I paid little attention earlier, as I was most concerned about the girls." I smiled at her, hoping that she would think my fear was only of getting lost, for now that the time had come, I was beginning to wonder if I had made a mistake. Was I really ready to spend several hours with the Harrisons?

I was given little time for worry, for Nick was waiting on the narrow second-floor landing. "Thank you, Annie, I shall see to Miss Ames from here." He took my arm, leading me out of the back stairway and along the second floor hall to the wide front staircase.

As I looked down the grand length of it, I could hear the sound of voices from below. I swallowed hard, my fear growing. Nick's warm fingers closed over my hand as it rested on his arm. "Everyone is most eager to spend more time with you, Rachel."

"And I am eager to know them better." I did my best to make it sound like the truth, though I was far from ready for whatever lay ahead.

To my surprise, the evening proved a genuine pleasure, mostly thanks to Nick and his father. Jarvis Harrison was a man of many interests, and he quickly made it clear that he expected me to tell him all I could of life in Philadelphia now that the terrible war against the South had ended. Though it made me a little homesick, I was happy to oblige.

Pamela and Olivia were less friendly until after the meal, when the men left us and Mrs. Harrison inquired as to what the latest fashion was among society ladies. Once I began describing some of the gowns I had seen during a visit to a friend who was a dressmaker, they seemed to forget that we were strangers. By the time we rejoined the gentlemen on the veranda, we were chatting like old friends. At least we were until Nick came to sit beside me on one of the benches that sat along the side of the house.

"How are the children, Rachel?" Mrs. Harrison asked. "Have they been made comfortable?"

"They were most appreciative of the opportunity to play with the toys, ma'am," I answered, surprised by the question, since no one had asked about the children during the evening, even though Mr. Harrison had talked a little about the need for a place where the orphans of the island could be cared for. "It gave them a chance to forget how much they have lost."

"I am sure they are most grateful for your care." Pamela's friendly smile had vanished. "They must miss you whenever you are out of their sight."

"Do you think they will be frightened, being alone for so long?" Mrs. Hamilton added her voice to Pamela's.

"Harriet offered to stay with them," I began, sensing the censure in their tones, but unsure why it was being directed my way.

"Harriet?" Olivia's frown was visible even in the weak starlight that penetrated the shadowy veranda. "I thought she was attending to the pressing of some of my gowns this evening."

"Your dresses can wait," Nick snapped. "I instructed her to care for Elena and Inez. They have need of a friendly face here."

Sensing the swirling anger that was building among the family members on my account, I got to my feet. "That face should be mine. I do thank you for your kind invitation to dine with you and I did enjoy the evening, but I should be with the girls. They are my responsibility now and I must see to them. Goodnight." I slipped into the house before anyone could speak.

Tears burned in my eyes as I ran up the wide staircase and down the hall to the door that led to the backstairs. What had I done to make them change? Why had they been so friendly as we sat at table, then become so angry with me when we moved to the veranda? Had I somehow overstepped? Were there customs here of which I was not aware?

No answers had come to me by the time I reached the third floor and made my way carefully to the door I now knew led to the rooms I had been given. Like much of my life in recent days, the animosity of the Harrison women made no sense to me. As I hurried across the playroom to the bedchamber that Elena and Inez occupied, I vowed to find a place for my orphanage as soon as possible. I had no desire to stay where I was not wanted.

Harriet smothered a yawn as she got to her feet to greet me. From her sleepy gaze, I suspected she had been dozing in the chair while she awaited my return, and from Olivia's remarks, I could understand why. Undoubtedly, she would still have to do whatever chores had been assigned her, though the hour was late. I thanked her, wishing that I could offer more.

I needed to speak with Paul—no, I must now think of

him as Reverend Michaels, I realized as I readied myself for bed. Whether or not I was the person he wanted here, here I was, and there were plans we must make. I should never have allowed him just to walk away from me as he had at the dock.

I smiled at my own thoughts as I blew out the candle and settled myself beneath the light quilt. And how should I have stopped him? By stamping my foot and demanding his attention? Had I been less weary, I might have laughed at the images that filled my mind. The Reverend Michaels I had encountered today was a far cry from the Paul of my girlish daydreams, a fact that would have kept me long awake had I not been so exhausted.

So began my stay at Sunrise. After what had happened on the veranda, I was determined to stay out of the family's way. It proved to be more difficult than I had expected, however, for Nick seemed equally determined to draw me into his family circle by inviting me to every meal. I refused as often as I could, but he was not a man easily dissuaded.

I tried to keep away from Nick, not because he was unkind, but because being near him was so pleasurable that I knew I would hate the day when I should have to leave Sunrise. But Nick would have none of my evasions. He insisted on taking the girls and me for daily walks and rides about the plantation. And he paid at least one visit each day to the playroom. By the third day, my heart leaped at the sound of his steps in the hall, and when he grinned at me, I forgot my vow to keep my distance.

Realizing how much I had come to look forward to his visits, I decided I must take some action. "Have you heard anything from Reverend Michaels, Nick?" I asked that third afternoon.

He shook his head.

"Would it be possible for me to send him a message?" I looked out the window at the rolling green lawns, not wanting him to see the worry I felt. "I really cannot stay on here. There are plans that should be made, and I can do nothing without his permission."

"You may stay here as long as you like, Rachel. Father is delighted with your company, as am I." His tone drew my gaze to his face and I could feel the heat rising in my cheeks at his open admiration. Never had a man paid me so many compliments. I knew not what to say to him.

Forcing myself to look away again, I tried to concentrate on the reasons for my being here. "But what of the other children who have need of my protection and care? Your lovely home was never meant to be a shelter for orphans, Nick, and if we stay much longer, it will be harder for Elena and Inez to adjust to whatever home we are to share."

His eyes darkened and a frown marred his tanned forehead. "If I had my way . . ."

"But I am here to serve God's way," I reminded him quickly. "And to help Reverend Michaels."

Nick sighed. "I have twice invited him to Sunrise, but he has refused both invitations. I suspect he is avoiding a meeting with my father."

"But why? Did your father not bring him here in the first place?"

"A decision he has sometimes had cause to regret." Nick's tone was cold. "Perhaps in a few days I shall be able to arrange a meeting for you in the village. The girls would doubtless enjoy seeing some of their old friends, and you could discuss all your plans with Paul at that time. If he has any plans."

"What do you mean, if?" His tone had nettled me.

"He has certainly kept his own counsel since your arrival." I glanced his way to see if he might be mocking me, but his expression was grim.

"Perhaps he has been busy with other, more pressing matters." It was the reason I had given myself every time I wondered about Paul's neglect.

"Of that I am sure; I only wish I knew what those matters were." Nick moved restlessly to finger one of many toy soldiers that lined a nearby shelf. "And I don't see how anything could be more urgent than seeing you safely settled."

"If he is doing God's work . . ." I let it trail off, suddenly sure that Nick wouldn't understand. My needs and those of the girls would simply have to wait.

Another idea occurred to me. "What about the cloister?" I asked. "Could we perhaps visit there on one of our rides? I should truly love to see what it is like."

"I told you, 'tis not a proper place for you." Nick looked beyond me to where the girls were playing. "Come along, Elena, Inez, I have the pony cart waiting. We shall go down to the beach and build sandcastles. Would you like that?"

Since the girls would gladly do anything Nick suggested, we were soon on our way; but Nick's refusal to take me to the cloister bothered me. The lovely stone structure seemed perfect, so old and peaceful beneath its green mantle of vines; it had haunted my dreams ever since I'd first seen it.

"Is something troubling you, Rachel?" Nick's question forced my attention back to the present and I realized that we were already nearing the steep path that led from the top of the bluff to the pocket of sand that served as a beach for Sunrise.

I looked into his eyes and wished that I could confide my thoughts to him, even though they were chaotic at the moment. When he gazed at me with such warmth, I truly forgot everything but the wonder of being a woman. Never had I felt so odd, so at the mercy of forces I had never known before. Luckily, the excited children claimed his attention, giving me time to bring my wayward thoughts back under control while he cautioned them about the path to the shore.

"I hope 'twas not my words about Paul Michaels that made you so pensive." Nick lifted me from the cart, then took my hand before he reached back into the cart for the basket Cook had sent along. "I meant no disrespect for your calling; I am only concerned for your safety and comfort."

My heart fluttered so at his touch that I spoke quickly, hoping to distract myself in order that I not play the fool. "Perhaps I should send word to Miss Chalmers. She did offer to help me find a place for my orphanage."

"If you wish to write her a note, one of the servants can take it to Emerald Acres." His tone lacked enthusiasm, which made me curious, especially when I realized that he had not mentioned her name since the day we arrived.

"She seemed most kind, but I should not want to take advantage of her offer, if you think it was made merely for politeness."

"Geraldine never does favors without a reason and she can be very helpful when she wishes." He grinned. "I believe you should allow her the opportunity to do something good for the island."

"I shall write her a note tonight."

"Why are you so anxious to escape Sunrise, Rachel?" He tightened his hold on my fingers as he slowed at a narrow point on the trail, forcing me to face him. "Are you so unhappy in my home?"

"Of course not. As I told you before, it is only that

86

I wish to begin the work I came here to do, and I cannot so long as I am a guest in your home. Several of the servants have mentioned other young children who should be in my care, and I was sent to help Reverend Michaels teach the children to read and write and do numbers."

"You would willingly trade Sunrise for an orphanage?" His gaze seemed almost angry, though I had no clue why.

"The orphanage is my mission here, Nick. I have trained for such a post much of my adult life. I accepted responsibility for Elena and Inez on St. Devina and I cannot properly discharge that responsibility until I have made a place for them here." I looked deep in his eyes and swallowed hard as I felt my firm resolve melting under the warmth of my longing to please him. Fearfully, I conjured up an image to strengthen my defenses against his charm. "Reverend Bennett expects nothing less than my best efforts."

"Of course." Nick let go of my hand and moved down the rocky path ahead of me. "I should have realized that."

When we reached the beach, he set the basket on the sand, then hurried after the children, leaving me to wonder at his change of mood. Had I offended him in some way? I took a few steps after him, seeking through my mind for words of explanation; but how could I tell him that he was the reason I must leave Sunrise? I hardly dared admit it to myself. I sank down beside the basket, wishing mightily that I had some older woman to confide in, for I was sorely in need of advice.

The rest of the afternoon passed without incident, and Nick was pleasant but distant on the short journey back to the plantation house. There was no invitation to take the evening meal with the family, so after I shared a tray with the children, I settled myself at my desk and composed a short note to be dispatched to Miss Chalmers. I finished it just as Harriet came to fetch the tray.

"That be for Miss Chalmers?" Harriet asked, eyeing the paper curiously.

I nodded. "How did you know?"

"Mister Nick say you be needin' someone to carry it to Emerald Acres." Her shy grin lit her dark eyes. "My Digger say he do it."

"Your Digger?" I lifted an eyebrow, remembering the strong young islander who had driven the cart that had met us when we'd arrived on Bell Harbour Island. "Are you two promised?"

Her giggle made me long for the companionship of the girls I had left behind in Philadelphia. "Not yet, but one day soon."

"He seems a fine young man." Just saying the words made me feel as old as Mrs. Bennett, and I wondered suddenly if I should ever feel as Harriet did about a young man. Nick Harrison's image filled my mind and brought heat to my cheeks. How could I be thinking of him in such a romantic way?

"He say someday soon we be havin' a place of our own, and ..." She stopped, her grin fading. "We be dreamin' like. I be takin' your note to him."

She left so quickly, I scarce had time to thank her, which surprised me. I had grown used to Harriet spending as much time as she could with us. But then, I reminded myself, Digger would be waiting for her, so perhaps she would return later to talk and to play with the girls before they went to bed.

The evening dragged by, however, without any visitors. I did my best to keep my spirits up by reading to Inez and Elena; but after they were tucked into bed, the loneliness seemed to settle around me like a dark fog. Was this to be my future? Would I become a respected spinster lady, given to good works, caring for other women's children in an orphanage here or on some other island?

That had been my dream as I neared the end of my training, but now ... What was different? Was that not God's plan for me? I remembered Reverend Bennett's thrilling words as he spoke of feeling called to serve those who needed our care and protection. I had been so sure ...

And I still was, I told myself firmly. It was only that I had been too long at Sunrise. Already the elegant way of life and the pleasure of being near Nick was making me forget what was important. I closed my eyes, wanting to deny that thought, but unable to. I must leave Sunrise soon, before the temptation to stay became too strong.

Harriet brought a note with my breakfast tray. "It be too late when Digger come ridin' back last night," she explained.

"Thank him for me, please." I unfolded the note with shaking fingers, suddenly not sure that I had done the right thing in contacting Miss Chalmers. She had seemed friendly, but if she truly disapproved of what I had come to do ...

The note was short.

> Rachel,
> I shall come for you about ten. We can seek a proper site for your orphanage together.
> Geraldine.

"Would you be free to care for the children today, Harriet?" I asked, suddenly realizing that I could never take Elena and Inez along on a ride with Miss Chalmers.

"I'd be pleased, Miss Rachel."

"I should never want to take you from your duties."

"Mr. Nick, he say you might be needin' me."

Nick again. I suddenly wondered if he had read my note or Geraldine's. He would certainly have every right to know what I wrote and to be interested in my comings and goings, yet I resented the idea. I had come here to work with Paul, not to spend my time with Nick Harrison.

It took only a moment to make the necessary arrangements with Harriet, then I was free to think about the day ahead and what I had set in motion with my note to Geraldine Chalmers. If she was truly helpful, I could, I realized, be leaving Sunrise as soon as tomorrow. The idea of seeing no more of Nick brought a dreadful sense of loss.

What did that mean? I closed my eyes, trying hard to conjure up the dreams that had filled my mind as I'd sailed from Philadelphia, but they eluded me. Even my cherished memories of meetings with Paul at the school were tarnished by the way he had reacted when he'd seen me on the deck of the *Island Belle*. And by the fact that he had made no attempt to contact me since.

Was Paul planning to send me back? Had he perhaps written to Reverend Bennett for instructions, or to ask that someone older and wiser be sent to assist him? The possibility horrified me. I had no desire to return to Philadelphia. Paul might not have welcomed me, but others had, and I loved the island. And I was needed here; even Nick admitted that.

Nick! Why did my thoughts always circle back to him? What was the strange hold that he seemed to have over me? It had to be more than just my innocence and lack of experience in dealing with men that had me so confused. I had always prized my strong and logical mind, yet in the past few days I hardly recognized myself.

But that would all change soon, I told myself firmly. With luck, after today I would be too busy to entertain such frivolous thoughts. Once I spoke with Paul, surely he would see that I was as devoted to the islanders as he, and then we could begin making plans for the orphanage. Nick would have no place in my life once I was occupied with the care and teaching of the islanders' children. Then I would be safe.

That thought stunned me. Safe from what? Nick had always been the perfect gentleman; he had taken no liberties with me. I swallowed hard as the realization swept over me. I wanted to leave Sunrise not because I was afraid of what Nick might do, but because of what I was feeling. I was running from temptation!

Chapter 6

Since I knew Nick was aware of Geraldine Chalmers's visit, I half-expected him to be waiting in the entry hall or on the veranda when I came down at nine-thirty. But he was nowhere about as I settled myself on one of the beautifully carved hardwood benches to await her arrival. Was he staying away because he disapproved? But that would make no sense, for he had encouraged me to contact Geraldine and ask for her help.

I frowned out at the sunlit gardens, cursing the fact that I understood these people so poorly. Life had been simpler at school, for we had all come there as strangers and were learning together, but here . . . here I was an outsider, sensing, but never understanding, the undercurrents that flowed between family members and servants alike.

"Are you so troubled, Rachel?" Geraldine Chalmers's voice made me start and I looked up, shocked to find her standing at the corner of the veranda.

Her smile was warm, but when I gazed into her eyes, I found them unreadable. "I did not hear you."

"I left my horse with the stableboy. He needed a drink after the drive over here." She looked around with studied casualness. "Are you all alone?"

I had no need to ask for whom she was looking, for neither Pamela nor Olivia had paid a call on her since my arrival. I found myself wondering again if there was an understanding between her and Nick. "No one was about when I came down."

"Well, then, how may I help you, Rachel? Have you decided upon a place for your orphanage, or are you simply tired of being so far from the man you came here to assist?" She settled herself in á rocker, appearing quite at home here.

The note of reproof in her tone stiffened my spine. "I have had no word from Reverend Michaels as yet."

"And 'tis not likely that you shall, so long as you remain at Sunrise. Dear Paul spends little time at this end of the island. Perhaps we could offer you room at Emerald Acres for a time. That way you could take a pony cart into the village each day and help him with his work."

"Are you near the village?" I was too stunned by her offer to reply to it, so I asked the question merely to fill the silence between us.

"Nick has certainly kept you tucked away out here. One would think that he . . ." Geraldine's gaze moved from my face to the doorway behind me and her expression warmed at once. "Good morning, Mr. Harrison."

I turned to greet my host, oddly relieved to have him join us. I had forgotten how unnerving Geraldine Chalmers could be. While I was trying to unscramble my thoughts, Geraldine repeated to Nick's father her suggestion that I move to Emerald Acres, giving me no chance to respond myself.

Jarvis Harrison listened attentively as she listed the reasons, emphasizing the fact that I should be able to go daily to the village, perhaps even help Paul find a suitable building there for the orphanage. As she spoke, I found myself nodding, aware that she was right; yet my heart ached at the idea of leaving Sunrise . . . and Nick.

I was so sure that Mr. Harrison was going to agree with her that I was shocked when he shook his head. "I think not, Geraldine. After what happened to the school, I would prefer to have Rachel remain at Sunrise for the time being. There is no reason why the orphanage must be in the village, and as for the teaching, I doubt that the Reverend has more students than he can handle at the moment."

"If what I hear is true, he has fewer than before," Geraldine reported. "It appears that the islanders are beginning to mistrust the good Reverend."

"How can that be?" I asked, not caring that I was interrupting their conversation. This was very much my business, since I had come here to help Paul. "I thought that he was much loved by those he came here to help."

Jarvis Harrison sighed. "Change is never easy, Rachel, and there are those on the island who fear it. I still believe that teaching the island children to read and write and do sums will eventually benefit us all; but there are some who disagree."

I sensed the undercurrents again as Mr. Harrison and Geraldine exchanged meaningful glances. Refusing to be left out, I asked, "Is that why I cannot stay in the village?"

Mr. Harrison looked uncomfortable, and good manners dictated that I should take back my question, but I could not. I met his gaze firmly, doing my best not to let him see how his words had disturbed me.

"I feel it would be better for all if the orphanage and the school were kept separate, at least for now. Tempers need time to cool, and the children must be protected. Once we find a location on this end of the island and move you and a proper staff into it, we can build something positive and the islanders will come around. Even the Reverend must understand that when I explain it to him."

"You and Reverend Michaels have not yet spoken about the orphanage?" I tried to hide my disappointment, but I failed miserably. Despite Nick's words, I had been hoping that he was wrong about Paul's lack of interest in my future work.

Jarvis Harrison patted my shoulder in a fatherly manner. "Now, you must not trouble yourself about it, my dear. Just enjoy your drive with Geraldine. I shall speak with the Reverend and we will make the necessary arrangements."

For a moment I was reassured, then something strange happened. For the first time in my life, I found myself resenting his fatherly attitude. It made me feel like a child, and that was wrong. I was here to care for children, to be responsible for their physical and spiritual needs. It was my future he was deciding, and it seemed as though I was to have no part in the decision.

"Perhaps we should be on our way, Rachel," Geraldine said, getting to her feet. "We must not take more of Mr. Harrison's valuable time with our chatter."

I wanted to argue, but as I followed Geraldine along the veranda, I realized that I should be grateful to her. Never had I come so close to behaving badly. Had I truly been considering arguing with my host, the man who sheltered and fed not only me, but Elena and Inez as well? What was happening to me?

Once we were settled in the handsome trap, Geraldine slapped the reins on the bay's back and gave me a wicked smile. "Now you can see why so little has been done. Jarvis Harrison is a kindly, well-intentioned man, but if you leave it to him, you will still be living at Sunrise when the new year comes."

I had a horrible feeling that she might be right. "But how can I . . . hurry him along?"

"Find a place for the orphanage. That will force him to speak with the Reverend and set everything in motion. Men will always be in charge, but they can be guided, if you are clever." Her eyes sparkled with excitement, and after a moment I felt it, too, as she challenged me. "So, will you take charge of your own future, Rachel Ames?"

"I should like to," I admitted. "But I do not know how to begin to find a place."

"Nick has offered no suggestions?" She sounded surprised. "I should think he'd be eager to have everything arranged for you."

"He seems reluctant to make suggestions, but Sarah had an idea." I quickly recounted the conversation that Sarah, Nick, and I had had about the old cloister, finishing, "When I saw it on my ride to Sunrise, I thought it quite perfect, but Nick seems to feel that . . ."

"You have never visited the cloister?" Again I sensed her surprise.

"Nick seemed to feel it was unsafe."

"Pooh, 'tis every bit as safe as Sunrise or Emerald Acres. The stories are just meant to frighten children shivering in the dark. Would you like to see the inside?"

It was too strong a temptation for me to refuse. "Could I?"

"Nothing would give me more pleasure than to explore it again myself. It has been years since I was inside. There was a time when Sarah and Nick and I used to consider it our special place. I cannot imagine why he now regards it as too dangerous for children. We all haunted it." A dreamy smile softened her face, reminding me of how lovely she really was.

Envy shamed me as I imagined all the memories she shared with Nick. And all the plans for the future that they might be making. She was right, I must force Mr. Harrison to take action—and soon, for my heart was already leading me to betray all the teachings I believed in. If I remained much longer at Sunrise, I should soon resent this kind woman, who wanted only to help me.

The cloister was just as beautiful as I had remembered. The stone walls rose serenely from the flower-dotted meadow grass, its green tracing of vines gleaming in the sunlight. Geraldine stopped the trap beneath a spreading tree at the base of the small hill, securing the horse before leading me up toward the heavy brass-bound door.

My heart began to pound far more than the slight incline would cause and I felt a tingling of excitement, as though I were to meet my destiny here. "Will we be able to get inside?" I asked, trying to control my flight of fancy and reminding myself firmly that I was no young girl to be dreaming foolish dreams. I was here to take responsibility for an orphanage and all the children who would be housed in it.

"If the door is locked, I know of other entrances, but I suspect only rusty hinges will be trying to keep us out." Geraldine reached out and pulled the clinging vines away from the ornate latch and lifted it. "Give me a hand."

It took both of us to force the heavy door open and as we did, the dank air spilled out around us. A chill chased down my spine, but Geraldine was already on her way through the narrow opening. "Come on, there will be candles and matches somewhere about."

My eyes had scarce adjusted to the dim light that came from the vine-draped windows when Geraldine crowed. "Ah, here we are. I knew Nick would have left them." She struck a match and lit a candle. "Now, that is more like it."

A feeble glow slowly banished the shadows that seemed to crowd around the huge room we had entered. To my surprise, I discovered that it was not empty. Several tables and chairs were scattered about the room, and there were cabinets and shelves along the walls between the deep window wells.

"It looks much the same as I remember," Geraldine observed, lighting a second candle and handing it to me, then picking up her own and crossing the room. "But then why should it change? No one ever comes here, so . . ."

There was more, but I was too busy looking around to really listen to her complaints about the neglect of the old building. As I became accustomed to the stone walls and the dim lights, I could see the endless possibilities. What a schoolroom this would be, not only for the orphans who would live here, but for the children of those working at Sunrise and whatever other plantations or settlements were nearby.

"Come along, there's much more to see." Geraldine was already heading for the door that opened at the other end of the room. I followed her eagerly, my initial uneasiness forgotten.

Any doubts I might have entertained were gone long before we finished our tour of the huge building. It contained everything I needed: a large dining room, an ample kitchen, and plenty of small bedchambers, undoubtedly meant for the monks, but perfect for the children I should be caring for. There were even two larger bedchambers, one with a small sitting room, which would be mine. The other would serve as home for whatever island woman joined me in my task.

As we neared the rear of a second large room, I realized that the portion of the building we had explored seemed far smaller than the outer walls of the huge structure indicated. A large number of cupboards and wardrobes lined the rear wall and between them I could see no sign of an opening.

"This was likely some sort of sewing or crafting

area," Geraldine explained. "Or maybe a storehouse for the treasure that rumor claims was hidden here during the wild days of pirates and buccaneers."

"Are you saying that pirates used to live on this island?" I was shocked, for I had overheard some terrible stories from the crew of the ship on which I had sailed to St. Devina. "Nick said nothing of such . . ."

"There are plenty of tales that claim the islanders are descended from pirates who used their ill-gotten gains to settle here. Of course, I know not which are true and which were merely told to frighten me when I was a child." She chuckled, then gave me a challenging look. "Are such stories enough to keep you from moving in here?"

Her words nettled me so that my reply was sharper than I had intended. "Of course not. 'Tis only Nick's refusal that has kept me from asking about using the cloister."

"Perhaps you should speak with Jarvis instead of Nick. He would likely prove much more amenable to the idea." Geraldine moved restlessly about the room. "Unless you wish only to please Nick."

"I must speak with Paul—Reverend Michaels—before I make any plans." The implications of her words infuriated me so that I forgot proper decorum. "I am here to work with him, not to curry favor with anyone."

"You knew the Reverend before?" I could see the curiosity in her face.

"We met at Middle Brook Christian School when he came there to confer with Reverend Bennett. They are old friends." Though I had thought nothing of mentioning my acquaintance with Paul to Nick, there was something about Geraldine's gaze that made me uncomfortable. "He told all of us a great deal about the island and its need for teachers and an orphanage."

"The Reverend is a handsome man." Geraldine's sly

smile made me blush, for I remembered only too well my girlish daydreams of what might happen between us as we served God on this island paradise.

Unwilling to discuss Paul with her, I turned my attention back to the imposing wall. "What lies beyond this wall?" I asked. "The building seems much larger from outside."

Geraldine shrugged. "The closed-off area was badly damaged during one of the island insurrections. Later tenants deemed the area dangerous, so it was walled off. Now I suspect it serves as home for spiders and rats and other undesirables." She frowned. "Surely you would not need more space for your orphans?"

"No, of course not, I was merely curious."

"Well, if you have seen enough, perhaps we should return to Sunrise." She chuckled again. "If we are lucky, we should arrive in time to join the family for the noon meal."

"Are there other properties we could inspect in the afternoon?" I asked to cover my surprise at what I guessed was a ploy to spend time at table with Nick.

"Nothing to compare to this, I can assure you. There is an abandoned house near the boundary of Sunrise, but it boasts only four rooms, and the rain comes through the roof during every storm. There is a warehouse in similar condition on Emerald Acres, which could be partitioned, I suppose; but it is very near the workers' homes, and with the unrest . . ."

I nodded, realizing that Geraldine had no intention of helping me any further. As I had first suspected, her offer had been meant to please Nick, not to serve my purposes. Still, I was grateful for what she had done this day, and I realized that my question had been a mere sop to my conscience. I desperately wanted the cloister to be home to my orphanage.

My orphanage! The words echoed shockingly in my

mind. I had come to serve God's purpose and to assist Paul, not to build for my own gratification. Yet how could I deny my longing to make the old stone building live again? Even as we walked back through the long hall to the main room and out into the sunlight, I felt a connection to the weathered monument of another time.

Though I worried during the short drive back to Sunrise about what I should tell Nick, I soon discovered that I had wasted my time. He was nowhere about, and neither was Mr. Harrison. The talk at table was of fashion and the grand parties that seemed to bloom frequently on the island—a subject that fascinated me, even though I knew I should never be a part of the social whirl here.

It was no surprise to me when Geraldine left immediately after our meal; her disappointment had been obvious from the moment she'd learned that Nick would not be joining us. Hiding a smile that shamed me with the unworthy thoughts that had inspired it, I turned my attention to Mrs. Harrison. "Would it be possible for me to drive into the village tomorrow morning, ma'am?" I inquired. "I really must discuss several urgent matters with Reverend Michaels, and . . ."

"What of the children?" Her frown reminded me that my leaving today had necessitated the use of one of her servants to care for the girls.

"I thought to take them with me. They have friends in the village, since they lived here much of their lives, and I know they should enjoy a visit."

"I shall have Digger drive you in. He can see to your safety." Mrs. Harrison reached for the bell cord to summon one of the maids. "When do you wish to leave?"

The details were quickly settled and I hurried up to the third floor at once, thinking only of freeing Harriet for her duties. Still, as the afternoon dragged on, I found my attention wandering often as I listened for the sound of Nick's boots on the hardwood floor of the hall. But they never came. Nor was there an invitation to take the evening meal with the family.

Had he no interest in what had happened today? I asked myself over and over. Was he now anxious for me to leave? Or was he angry because someone had told him of my visit to the Cloister? But who besides Geraldine knew? I paced the playroom after I tucked the girls in for the night—waiting, dreading, hoping, too confused to know what it was I wanted from Nick Harrison.

I awoke early after a restless night. Only as I prepared myself for the journey into the village did I realize that I had spent the entire evening worrying about what Nick would say about my desire to use the cloister for an orphanage, when I should have been worrying over Paul's opinion. Or perhaps wondering if Paul would even be available to speak with me.

Thanks to the children's excitement, I had little time for fuming on the journey to town. Instead, I listened to Elena's endless stories about life in the village and attempted to question Digger about Paul. Neither conversation was particularly reassuring, for Elena alluded often to "the troubles" that had led to her family moving to St. Devina, and Digger had few answers for me.

"Him likely be busy teachin', Miss," he told me several times. "Or ridin' 'bout, talkin' to folks."

"Do you know where the new school is?"

To that he only shrugged. "Somebody be knowin'."

I tried to be content with his sparse information, but by the time we neared the village, I was wondering if I had made a mistake. After all, Paul might resent my coming, and my taking into my own hands such matters as finding a building. Besides, I still had no way of knowing if he meant for me to stay on Bell Harbour Island, a little fact I had been ignoring the past few days.

After I left the children with their friends, I took a deep breath and nodded when Digger asked if I wanted to go to the church. Though not imposing, the large, white-painted building was easily found, for we had driven past it on our way through the village. Now, as the cart drew near again, I caught the sound of children's voices coming from inside and my fears eased a little. If Paul was conducting classes, he might even welcome my presence, for his calling had always been to the ministry, not to teaching.

"When you be wantin' me, Miss Ames?" Digger asked, as he assisted me from the cart.

"Late afternoon, I suspect. We must be home before dark, of course, but I should like to spend as much time with Reverend Michaels as possible, so . . ." I hesitated, remembering Mrs. Harrison's attitude toward Harriet's helping me, then added, "Will that be acceptable to the Harrisons? I should not want to cause trouble for you, Digger."

"That be fine, Miss. I be doin' errands most of the day. Miz Harrison, her give me a list." His shy grin made me feel better. I definitely liked Harriet's young man and wished him well.

A familiar figure appeared in the church's open doorway just as I turned, and my breath caught in my throat. With the morning sun glinting gold in his thick blond hair, Paul was very much the man who had ruled my girlish dreams, yet now I felt nothing except anxiety. It took all my courage to produce a smile; speech was beyond me.

"Well, Rachel Ames, welcome to my humble church." He held out his hands. "Come inside."

My heart lifted with hope as he led me into the small room that opened off one side of the church. Inside it, a half-dozen children were milling about, giggling and chattering like magpies. "Have you come to help me?"

His casual question broke the dreamlike spell of finally being here and, remembering his earlier treatment, I pulled my hand free of his grasp. "Do you wish me to?"

" 'Twas why you were sent." His gray eyes were cool as they met mine.

The girl I had been shivered inside me as I met his appraising gaze, then my fear vanished and I was someone new, stronger, angrier. "I thought perhaps you had no need for my assistance, since I have had no word since my arrival."

My own words shocked me and I expected an explosion from Paul, for I had no right to make demands upon him. To my surprise, however, he was the first to look away. In fact, he moved to the window and stood staring out at the busy street scene. "I wanted to speak with you, but I had nothing to tell you, Rachel. Everything has changed since I wrote and asked Reverend Bennett to send me an assistant. With the school burned down and the islanders behaving so strangely . . ."

I waited for him to go on, but he seemed to have run out of words. Finally, I could bear it no longer; I had to know what my future held. "Are you saying that you have no need for my services here, Reverend Michaels?"

"You called me Paul when I visited Middle Brook." His voice was soft now.

"What about the orphans, Paul?"

"You are needed here, but there could be danger. Harrison was right to insist that you remain at Sunrise until the unrest eases again." His smile had vanished, and he suddenly looked older than the thirty I knew him to be. "I know you have questions, but I lack answers at the moment. That is why I stayed away."

"But I cannot remain at Sunrise with Elena and Inez. And what of the other orphans who need my care? The servants have given me a half-dozen names, and I am sure there are as many more that I have not yet heard about. There is no place for them at Sunrise." Shivers of anxiety and shock shook me, but I ignored them. Never had I spoken up this way, for I had been taught that silence and subservience were the proper demeanor for one who would serve God's purpose. Now it seemed I could not control my tongue.

"Is that why you came? To talk about the orphanage?" Paul seemed surprised.

"I saw a place yesterday, the cloister building on Sunrise Plantation. It appears perfect, Paul. There is ample room, both for the children who would live there and for a school, if one is needed. I could live there along with a woman to help me with the children, and . . ." I stopped, appalled at my own audacity. "I mean, if you would . . ."

"The cloister building." Paul appeared unaware of my odd behavior. "I have seen it, of course, though never inside. Is it much in need of repair?"

"Not really. A thorough cleaning and perhaps a bit of paint and some furnishings would be in order; but Geraldine assures me that the structure is sound and there is no sign of water damage, so I expect the roof is sound, too." His practical question gave me hope. Could it be that he would actually consider my suggestion?

Shouts of greeting from the children interrupted us, and Paul turned to welcome two young boys. As they came across the room, his smile faded. "Where are your brothers and sisters?" he asked.

"In the fields," the youngest replied. "They all be working today. Us come only 'cause we's too young to be needed."

"The others are not coming?" Paul's tone held a chill.

The boy retreated a step, shaking his head. "We be all."

105

Paul looked around. "Eight of you. That is all that can be spared from laboring in the fields? How can I be expected to teach the children of this island if they are never allowed to come to school?"

"Is there some special problem on the plantations?" I asked, hoping to divert what I sensed was a growing tide of anger.

"Nothing new. Yesterday I had but five students, and nine the day before. When I first opened my school, there were near forty in attendance and talk of more. 'Tis the planters. They fear what will happen if these children learn to read and write and do sums. They fear education. They fear me." His eyes blazed and I felt the power of his fury and his belief and it both frightened and inspired me.

"Perhaps it will change again when you have a new school for them to attend," I murmured, aware that the children were now silent and wide-eyed with fear. "Meantime, mayhap we should begin the school day with a prayer, and then you can show me which children you want me to work with."

For a heartbeat, I thought that Paul might continue his tirade against the planters, but he took a couple of deep breaths and nodded. "Come along, children," he said in a calmer tone. "I want you to meet Miss Ames. She has come all the way from Philadelphia to help me teach you to read and write. Does anyone know where Philadelphia is?"

The rest of the morning passed quickly enough and I found myself caught up in the sheer joy of teaching. The children, though largely untutored, were so eager to learn, it was fun to offer them knowledge. I was only sorry that I had left Elena caring for Inez, for I was sure she would have welcomed the lessons.

When the children left at midday, Paul led me to the small house where he rented a room from an elderly widow. While we ate the meal she had prepared for us, he returned to the subject that had been most on my mind. "Have you spoken with the Harrisons regarding use of the cloister building?"

"Not since arriving here." I hesitated, not wanting to add to Paul's anger at the planters, but aware that he had to know my choice of a building might be opposed. "When I left the ship at St. Devina, I spent the night with a couple there, George and Sarah Kasper. It was Sarah who first suggested that the cloister might be a perfect place for an orphanage; but Nick refused even to consider it. I had no opportunity to see the inside of the building until yesterday, when Geraldine Chalmers accompanied me."

"Nick disapproves?" Paul sounded amused.

"He seemed to feel that the building might not be safe, but from what I saw yesterday . . ." I hesitated, suddenly aware that I might be causing trouble rather than healing it.

"So what do you plan to do?"

Paul's question shocked me. What was I to do? I started to protest that it was not my place to speak up at all, then changed my mind, realizing that it was too late to pretend that I was not involved. "Geraldine suggested that we broach the subject with Jarvis Harrison instead of Nick."

"How charmingly inventive of Miss Chalmers. I wonder what it is she expects to gain by her kindness." Paul's tone held a note of unchristian bitterness that I had never heard there before.

More strange undercurrents? I asked myself. Had the Paul I had known changed, too? Or was I simply seeing a side of him that had never been visible in the gentle confines of Reverend Bennett's church and school? Whatever it was, it made me feel most unsettled and confused, so I hoped that all would soon be resolved.

"Tell me about the cloister, Rachel. How large is it? Could we perhaps hold classes there for the children of the Sunrise workers?"

Paul's interest inspired me to describe the huge structure in detail, and as I spoke, I found my enthusiasm growing so intense that I ached to begin converting the building into an orphanage. It was hard to rein in my excitement when Paul got to his feet and announced that it was time to return to the church for the afternoon lessons.

Frustration gnawed at me as I did my best to work with the half-dozen children who'd returned. I, who had waited patiently for assignment, never questioning the wisdom of Reverend Bennett, now ached to demand a decision from Paul Michaels. The change frightened me a little, for I sensed that such behavior would only cause me trouble. But there was so much to be done here, there were so many children who needed my care and protection, so many children eager to learn and lessons that I could teach them.

Was this how Paul had felt when he first came to Bell Harbour Island? Was that why he had been so full of enthusiasm when he visited Middle Brook last year? Looking at him now, seeing the anger and unhappiness in his face, I wondered if I, too, would change. I hoped not, for I wanted to believe in the dreams that were beginning to fill my mind, dreams only partly concerned with the orphanage and the cloister.

Chapter 7

Since we had so few children to teach, Paul ended their lessons early, then turned to me. "What time is your driver to come for you?"

I shrugged. "Whenever he finishes his errands, I expect. I knew not whether you would welcome me, so I set no special time. Why?"

"I should like to ride out to Sunrise with you. If the cloister is all that you describe, I will make it my new school as well as your orphanage. What do you think of that?" His gaze challenged me.

"I should be proud to be a part of such an undertaking." I met his gaze boldly, for the hours of working together had made me more comfortable in his company.

"Who drove you to the village?"

"Digger Blake."

Paul nodded. "He will likely be visiting his aunt. Let me ask one of the lads to stop by and tell him you are ready to return to Sunrise." He hurried after the departing children, calling several of them back. In a moment they were racing off, obviously pleased to being doing a favor for him.

I smiled as I watched him, thinking that I had been wrong to believe that Paul was called only to the ministry. Seeing him as he worked with the children had made me realize that I had admired Paul without knowing him at all. He cared about his flock, their minds as well as their souls.

Though I had hoped to discuss with Paul what he might say at his meeting with the Harrisons, I was given no opportunity, for he left me waiting at the church, while he made arrangements to be away for the night. By the time he returned, Digger, Elena, and Inez were with me.

Since the girls were hungry, tired, and cranky, Paul chose to ride alongside the cart rather than join us. I envied him as I held a sobbing Inez in my arms and listened to Elena's complaints about her time in her friend's home.

"They have nothin', Miss Rachel. No books, no toys, just sticks and bits of wood to play with. They be callin' me names when I tells them about all we gets to do." Elena's eyes grew stormy at the memory.

I winced away from this proof that I had been right about the effect of their stay at the plantation house. "Did you tell your friends that you were guests at Sunrise and that the toys belonged to the Harrisons?"

"They be sayin' we not welcome in such a grand house." Elena's pout returned.

"Well, I expect our stay there will soon be over and you shall have to leave the toys behind." It pained me to speak to her thus; but I dared not wait any longer, for I knew from experience that Elena would need time to prepare for whatever changes lay ahead. What I had not expected was the look of pure dread that stole over her face.

"You not be sendin' us away, Miss Ames? Please, I be better, I promise. Us not be touchin' nothin', if'n you say. Just don' send us away." Her voice became a wail so loud that even Inez stopped her whimpering.

Her fear broke my heart. "Elena, dear child, we shall

110

all move together. I would never leave you by choice. Have I not promised that you will be my assistant when I begin caring for more children?" I spoke quickly, using my free arm to pull her close against me.

"What is the child's trouble?" Paul asked, guiding his horse close to the side of the cart.

"A little misunderstanding," I assured him, not wanting to discuss the uncertain future in front of the children. "Elena has had a wearying day."

"As have we all." Paul's mouth closed in a grim line. "I only hope that the evening proves better."

"I, too." I met his gaze, then turned my attention back to the children, murmuring more reassurances to both Elena and Inez. At times like this, I wished that I were still a child, so that I, too, could believe that all would be well.

Perhaps if I spoke with Nick and Mr. Harrison first, I thought, as Digger drove past the mighty fortress that was the cloister and Paul left us to survey the structure himself. Surely if Nick really understood how much having the orphanage there meant to me . . . I closed my eyes, shamed by my own weakness. I had best stop my daydreaming and face reality where my future was concerned. Whatever place was chosen for the orphanage, I should have to be content, for the choice was not mine to make.

Still, I looked around hopefully when we reached Sunrise. After all, I reasoned, it would do no harm to mention to Nick all the good qualities I had noted during my visit to the Cloister. But he was nowhere to be seen, and with Inez and Elena both tugging at my hands impatiently, I had no opportunity to seek him out.

The next two hours were an eternity. I kept busy with bathing and feeding the exhausted children and preparing them for bed. Once they were tucked away, however, the hours began to crawl. Not sure what to expect,

111

I changed to one of my better gowns, then spent extra time tidying my hair.

Since there had been no invitation to the evening meal, I had once again dined with Elena and Inez; but now my patience was growing quite thin. The Harrisons might not care about my feelings, but Paul should know how worried I was. Why had he not insisted on my being a part of the discussion about our future here? After all, I was the one who had told him about the cloister . . .

A tap on my door stopped my angry pacing. I ran to open it, then nearly swooned with disappointment when I found only Harriet on the other side. "What is it?" I asked, unable to hide my bad temper.

"Please, Miss Ames, Mr. Nick asked me to come up and stay with the children. You be wanted in the library."

"Nick sent for me?" I swallowed hard.

Harriet nodded. "They all be awaitin'."

My stomach turned over, then squeezed into a tight knot of pain. What if Nick was angry? He had told me to stay away from the cloister—something I had conveniently forgotten when Geraldine offered her tour. What if they were going to order me out? Where should I go? And what of Elena and Inez?

The list of my sins grew heavier with every step as I made my way downstairs. As I started along the hall that led from the entry to the library, Nick came to meet me. He was not smiling.

"It seems you are to have your way, Rachel," he said, as he took my arm, his fingers warm against my fear-icy skin. "I only hope that you will not live to regret it."

"What . . . what do you mean?" I murmured, too shocked by his words to speak above a whisper.

"I shall let your fine Reverend tell you." He opened

the door, ushered me in, then left, closing the door behind him.

Paul greeted me with a smile. "Great news, Rachel. You are to have your orphanage. Mr. Harrison has agreed to letting us use the cloister both for the housing of the children and as a temporary school for the children on this end of the island."

"How wonderful." I forced a smile that felt stiff as I turned to Jarvis Harrison. "You are very kind, sir, and I am most grateful for the chance to help those less fortunate . . ."

He lifted a hand to stop my words. "I am pleased that the building will again be useful. It has sat empty and neglected for far too long. It will, however, mean a great deal of work for you, Rachel. Are you sure you are ready to undertake such a responsibility?"

I drew myself up to my full five feet one inch and met his gaze firmly. "That is why I came to Bell Harbour Island."

"There is much more responsibility than you realize." Paul claimed my attention, his expression grave. "You see, I cannot spend much time on this end of the island, since I am needed at the church in the village. The school and all the teaching will be left to you for the time being. Of course, once I can organize another proper school in the village, you will have only a small number of students out here; but until that time . . ." He sighed. "I fear we are asking a great deal of you."

"I have never been afraid of work," I informed them both, thinking of Nick and what he had said. Why was it no one seemed to have any confidence in my abilities? Well, I would show them all just how competent I really was. "In fact, I am most eager to begin."

Paul beamed at me, then turned to Mr. Harrison. "I told you she would be pleased."

Mr. Harrison nodded, then leaned forward, picking up

113

a pen. "Paul tells me that you have seen the inside of the cloister, so perhaps we should start by listing what you will need first. I admit it has been years since I was inside, so if there is damage, or . . ."

"Everything seemed in good repair, though it must be scrubbed from roof to floor, and once that is done, we will need some furniture. Beds for the children, tables and chairs for the schoolroom, perhaps a desk for me. And school supplies—books, paper, everything that I brought from Middle Brook. And I shall need someone to help me, a woman to care for Inez and whatever other little ones there are, while I am busy giving my lessons." The words came easily, for I had fantasized saying them many times since my visit to the cloister.

"Our staff will be happy to help with the preparation of the building; Eudora will see to that." Jarvis leaned back. "As for the furnishings, you can select what you need from the attic rooms here at Sunrise. Heaven knows we have more stored there than we shall ever use. Digger and some of the other men will gladly transport everything to the cloister and set it up for you. In fact, Digger can also do whatever repairs are needed. He is proving to be quite handy with tools."

"And I shall set about finding a suitable woman to be your companion and assistant," Paul chimed in. "How long do you think it will take before the building is ready for students and orphans?"

I just stared at him, my head spinning. "I have no idea. I had not dared to hope . . ."

Paul moved restlessly about the room, then sighed. "Well, we shall know more tomorrow after you have shown me around, I am sure. I must admit I am eager to see the place. Now, if you recall anything else you will need, please make a note of it and we can discuss it in the morning." That said, he turned his attention back to our host.

I stood my ground for a moment, stunned by Paul's casual dismissal. There was more to be said, much I needed to discuss with them, now that the decision had been made. After a few minutes, I became aware of Mr. Harrison's questioning gaze and felt the heat rising in my cheeks. "Thank you again, sir," I murmured, as I fled from the library.

Once I was in the hall, I peered around, hoping to see Nick, for I needed to explain to him how I had come to visit the cloister; but there was no one in sight. Though a part of me longed simply to climb the backstairs and retire to my peaceful sitting room to savor this miracle, I made my way instead to the entry hall, hoping that Nick might be there.

The broad expanse of polished wood was well lit, but empty of life. I caught the distant sound of feminine laughter, which told me that the ladies were still in the small parlor, their usual refuge after the evening meal. Since I had no desire to speak with them, I headed for the front door, seeking a moment of fresh air before I returned to the third floor.

The evening breeze that greeted me as I stepped outside was gentle and sweet with the scent of flowers. Starlight sparkled on the damp grass, and I moved to the rail that protected the veranda. I had no desire to sit in the shadows that crouched thick and dark between the squares of golden light that spilled from the windows.

"Everything settled already?" Nick's mocking voice came out of the darkness, startling me so that I gasped and stumbled against the sturdy rail.

He was at my side at once, his hand steadying me. "Forgive me, Rachel, I had no thought of frightening you. I forgot how dark it seems when you first come out."

"I had no idea you were out here." And seeing him

had left me quite breathless with a mixture of shock and delight, though I would never have admitted it to him.

"So you have attained your goal and now come out here to contemplate your victory." The coldness was back in his voice.

For a moment I was hurt, then my temper revived. He had no right to treat me this way. "Victory, Nick? According to your father and Reverend Michaels, I have just undertaken a great task, one that will demand all my strength and courage."

"Perhaps more than you know, Rachel." Some of the starlight penetrated the shadows, and for the first time I could see that his expression was more worried than angry or mocking.

"Why do you say that? The cloister seems a perfect place for an orphanage. There is plenty of room, and you did say that you wanted me to stay on this part of the island, so it is close at hand. Your father has offered me help with the cleaning and any repairs, and even said that we could have furniture from the Sunrise attics."

"My father has always had a lot of dreams for Bell Harbour, but some of them may not come true the way he hoped. Bringing Paul here has caused far more trouble than anyone expected, and I would hate to see you involved . . ." He let it trail off, then released my arm and moved away, turning his back to the starlit vistas, thus placing his face in shadow again.

I waited for him to continue, but he seemed quite content to ignore me. Frustration quickly overruled my sense of decorum. "Just what do you think I am to be involved in? Teaching? Caring for innocent orphans? That is my mission here, Nick, and that is all I have ever wanted to do. Why are you so sure that everything I do is a mistake?"

He said nothing, though my angry words seemed to

shimmer in the air between us. My anger fled as quickly as it had flared, and with it my confidence. How could I have spoken thus to this man? He would think me a shrew, and not without good reason. Desperately, I sought through my mind for something I might say to ease the sting of my shameful words.

" 'Tis not you that angers me." His tone was soft, kinder than I deserved. "It is only that I fear for you. There are some who might use what you are doing to further their own ends, not really caring about the cost to you."

"Your words make no sense," I protested, more frightened by his tone than I had been by any of his warnings.

"Probably not," he agreed, "but I am worried. You must be careful. The cloister may seem safe, but it has known its share of troubles."

"What do you mean?"

"I would prefer not to . . ." Nick's voice trailed off as the door opened behind me and Paul and Mr. Harrison came out.

"Rachel—Miss Ames, I had thought you long gone to tend to the children." Paul's expression as he looked from me to Nick and back again was far too easy to read. He was definitely not pleased to see us together.

"Ah, Nick, I was wondering where you had gone. Now that the planning has begun, we could have done with some of that advice you have been so free with." Mr. Harrison's expression was less easy to read, but he was not smiling either.

Feeling guilty, though I had no idea why I should, I stepped away from the rail—and from Nick. "I should be going up now; I just came out for a breath of air." I fled the tension that seemed to be simmering among the three men, closing the door firmly behind me.

What had I done? I asked myself, as I climbed the

endless stairs to the third floor. Was speaking with Nick alone so wrong? We had spent time together before, though mostly the children had been about, I had to admit. Had I committed an impropriety? I sighed. Life at Middle Brook Christian had been so restricted, I had forgotten how carefully a young lady needed to guard her reputation.

Besides, Paul's bad temper made no sense, I decided, as I moved along the third-floor hall. I had spent the day with him, and not always in the company of his students, yet he had not seen that as inappropriate behavior. Of course, Paul was a man of the cloth. I opened the playroom door with another sigh.

Harriet jumped to her feet immediately, bumping the table so hard that she had to catch the candle that flickered there. "You be startlin' me, Miss Ames," she gasped, her expression more guilty than frightened.

"I am sorry." I moved quickly to the small table, my curiosity diverting me from the perplexing behavior of the three men I had just left. A book lay open on it. "Were you reading?"

Harriet seemed to find her toes intriguing, for she refused to lift her gaze from them. "I cain't read, Miss. My Ma, her tried to teach me when I be little; but I cain't 'member much."

"Your mother could read?" I was surprised, for Paul had told me that most of the islanders never progressed beyond learning to write their own names.

"Her was maid to Miz Sarah Gardner, afore that lady married and left Bell Harbour. Miz Sarah 'lowed me Ma to study with her." Harriet's shy smile bloomed when she finally met my gaze. "Her be most proud when Miz Sarah gave her some books to keep."

"Would you like to learn to read, Harriet?" I asked, touched by her reverence for a skill I too often took for granted.

"Oh, yes, Miss, more than anythin'."

"Then I shall teach you." My heart lifted at the idea, then the pleasure fled as the real world intruded. "If you have the time. I know that the Harrisons keep you occupied . . ."

"I be findin' time." Harriet's dark eyes fairly gleamed with excitement and longing. "If'n you be havin' a bit of time now and agin, or on my day off . . ."

"I shall gladly take the time. But perhaps I could ask Mr. Harrison for permission to teach anyone on staff who . . ."

"No, you cain't tell nobody, Miss. There be island folk what fear us learnin', and they be ready to stop you." The genuine fear in her voice sent a chill through me.

"Who would do such a thing?" I asked, not wanting to believe her words, even though I clearly remembered what I had been told about Paul's school being burned down. "Surely there is no one at Sunrise . . ."

"They be everywhere. Please promise me, Miss Ames."

There was no way I could ignore her fear, so I surrendered without further argument. "Of course. It shall be our secret, Harriet. When do you wish to begin?"

"Would you be too weary now?"

I hesitated only a moment, my thoughts once again circling about the confusing events of this day, then I banished them. "I think this would be a perfect time. Let me get the reader that Elena and I have been using, then you can show me how much you remember of your mother's teaching."

By the time a yawning Harriet left the playroom, I was much too weary to worry about what had happened on the veranda. I wanted only to think of all that would happen tomorrow when I began preparing the cloister for use. My own orphanage! I smiled as I combed out

119

my hair, then braided it for the night. Tomorrow all my dreams would be coming true.

Though I had expected to awaken at dawn, the sun was well up when a series of low whispers penetrated my dreams. Annoyed, for I had been dreaming of walking hand in hand with Nick along the rocky shore beneath the headlands of Sunrise, I sat up. Elena and Inez were perched on the bench that sat at the foot of my bed.

"Be it true, Miss Ames?" Elena asked, her gaze solemn. "Are us goin' to the cloister?"

Memories from last night rushed over me and I cast a despairing glance at the sunlit scene beyond the window. How could I have slept so late? I turned my attention back to the girls, suddenly aware that they had been asleep when the decision was made. "Where did you hear that?"

"Cook be telling us we gonna be sent there."

I smiled, though I was far from pleased by the efficiency of the staff's information gathering. I should have preferred telling the girls the good news myself. "It will be a few days yet. The building must be cleaned and some repairs made before we can move in."

"Us cain't go there." Elena's lower lip was trembling. "It be full of evil spirits, Missy."

"Nonsense. There are no such things." I got up and pulled on my robe. This was the last response I had expected. "The building may look frightening, but that is simply because it has been empty for a long time. Once it is cleaned and painted and we have furniture, it will be a perfect place for the orphanage."

"No." Elena jumped from the bench and raced out of the room, disappearing into the bedchamber she and

Inez had shared. Inez gave me a frightened glance, then toddled after her sister, wailing for her to wait.

I stared to follow, then changed my mind. No doubt Cook or one of the other servants had told Elena some ghost story, so I doubted that any reassurances of mine would change her mind. But once it was ready, a visit to the cloister might. Meantime, I needed to dress and go downstairs myself. While I ate my morning meal in the kitchen, I would make sure that no more stories of evil spirits in the cloister were circulated.

By the time I finished my biscuits and jelly, my enthusiasm was fading. Everyone who came near me had a warning to offer. Even Harriet had cautious words for me. " 'Tis a dark and sorry place, Miss. Them what knows say that evil be done there a long time ago, and now them restless spirits be guardin' it."

"Don' you be goin' there, Missy." Digger had added his warning to hers as he delivered a load of freshly harvested vegetables to the kitchen. "There be other places round about the island. That cloister ain't safe for no younguns."

Unnerved by what seemed a flood of dire predictions, I left the kitchen, seeking through the huge house for Paul. Could I have been wrong? I asked myself, as I tapped on the library door.

"Come in." Mr. Harrison's voice was easy to recognize and his smile warmed away some of the chill that had come from all the stories I had heard.

"I was seeking Reverend Michaels," I explained, when he gestured toward a chair. "He suggested that I show him around the cloister this morning."

"I fear you are too late, my dear. Our Reverend Michaels is an impulsive fellow. According to Hathaway, Paul rose at dawn and decided to examine the place himself on his way back to the village. He asked Hathaway to accompany him and to report back to us."

Disappointment swept through me, quickly followed by frustration as I thought of all the questions that I had for Paul. "What did your man tell you?" I asked, suddenly afraid that Paul might have changed his mind if he heard all the dreadful rumors that I had.

"He said the Reverend appeared delighted with the place, and promised to call back in a few days to confer with you. You are to proceed with the preparations in the meantime." Mr. Harrison seemed amused by the message he was relaying.

"Oh." I was glad I had taken the chair he indicated, for my knees suddenly felt quite weak. Last night's magnificent challenge now appeared to be a gigantic undertaking for which I felt very poorly prepared.

"I have instructed Mrs. McGinty to ask among the staff for volunteers to help you with the cleaning. If you would like to speak with her, I am sure you can start whenever you are ready."

His confidence in me revived my flagging spirits and put me back on my mettle. Had I so little faith that I was willing to give up my mission here simply because a few misguided servants told me tales of evil spirits? Of course not. I had been inside the cloister, had explored it quite thoroughly and seen no haunting shadows.

"I shall speak with her at once," I assured him, getting to my feet. "There is much to be done before it can be used as either orphanage or school."

"Much indeed." His tone was thoughtful. "But I think you have the courage to make it happen, Rachel. Perhaps your good works will bring us the peace we need so desperately."

His observation confused me and I hesitated, wanting to ask for an explanation; but before I could find the right words, he got to his feet. "I shall summon Mrs.

McGinty for you. I want to be sure that Digger Blake is included among your workers."

It was after midday before I was able to lead my little band of workers to the cloister. Thanks to the wild tales being whispered about the place, I had few maids and only three men willing to go with me. Fortunately, Harriet and Digger were among them, though I sensed their uneasiness as we approached the brooding gray-stone structure.

"Look, Miss, the door be open," Harriet gasped, and the entire group came to an immediate halt.

I felt a chill in spite of the warmth of the sun, but I did my best to hide my feelings as I sought a logical explanation. "I expect Reverend Michaels left it open so that the building might air out. He was here to look around early this morning."

Knowing that they would desert me if I showed any fear, I hurried forward and stepped into the dimness of the main room. My fingers shook as I lit a candle, but I kept my tone level as I began issuing orders. I wanted the vines cut away from the deep-set windows immediately so that light could fill the room, then the scouring could begin.

At first, everyone worked slowly, glancing over their shoulders and whispering, as though they feared being overheard; but as the afternoon progressed, their mood lifted and so did mine. Digger supervised the men who cut back the wildly growing vines, then made sure that the chimneys were cleaned and inspected every inch of the roof himself.

" 'Tis remarkable sound, Miss," he reported. " 'Twill not be the damp that drives you from this accursed place."

"Why do you call it that?" I asked, suddenly weary of his somber tone. "Why should this building be cursed?"

"You not be knowin'?"

"Knowing what?" My patience was wearing very thin.

" 'Bout the massacre."

"Suppose you tell me while we look over the rear room," I suggested, suddenly aware that a silence had fallen over the other workers in the room.

"My grandmother say this place be built by the blackrobes that come here long time ago. They be gentle folk, the story say; but those that brought them were most fierce, and they tried to steal the islanders' land and treasures." He moved about the large inside room, testing the various cupboards and shelves for rot or weakness.

I waited for him to go on, but he seemed more interested in the hinges of a wardrobe door than in telling his story. "Those were Catholic monks," I said. "Probably Spanish, if I remember my history lessons. But that would have been about a hundred years ago."

Digger nodded. "The soldiers be most cruel to those that lived hereabouts, and soon there be some what chose to fight back. There be no plan to kill the blackrobes, but when the evil ones came here to hide, the blackrobes gave them sanctuary."

"This building is like a fortress," I agreed, rather pleased at the thought after what had been done to Paul's school building. "What happened then?"

"The islanders found a way inside, and when the dawn come, there be nobody left alive in here." His blue eyes met mine. " 'Tis said that the monks be slaughtered like goats, and because they done no evil, they stayed on here. 'Twere their home, after all, and no one else be welcome."

The familiar chill moved down my spine, but I managed a smile. "That is a very sad story, but not unlike others I have heard. I have no doubt that those who carried out the massacre of the monks felt very guilty.

Perhaps they even expected to be haunted by the innocents they killed. Mayhap that was how the stories began."

"But I have seen them, Miss." Harriet spoke from the doorway, her voice soft but heavy with fear.

"Seen what?" I stiffened, for I had not expected that these two, for whom I had come to care, should be arrayed against my dream of creating an orphanage in the cloister.

"The blackrobes. It be them what stalk this evil place." She met my gaze without flinching.

"Shadows. That must be what you saw, Harriet. Surely you cannot believe in spirits." I tried to sound confident, but the chill still played on my back, and when the candles flickered, the shadows shifted in the corners, growing ominously.

"Shadows in full moonlight? Stepping out through a wall of stone just as I be passin'? 'Tain't likely, Miss. I be laughin' at the stories, till that night. Mayhap that be why I seed 'um."

The feeling of dread spread through me as I looked deeply into her dark eyes and read only honest belief. This was neither gossip nor an old wives' tale; yet how could I accept something so bizarre?

Digger spoke up before I could decide what to say to refute her. "It be true, Miss Ames. Harriet come ascreamin' to the stable and her told me everythin' her saw. Me and two grooms come back here, but they be vanished. All's we heered was the night wind a whinin'."

I swallowed hard. "How ... how long ago did that happen?"

"It be last winter." Harriet seemed calmer, now that she was standing next to Digger. "I be comin' home from visitin' my auntie and her new babe. Stayed too

125

late, I did, and got caught by darkness. Never would I have come that near . . ."

I felt her shiver in my own bones as I looked around the room and realized that I should soon be living here with a group of helpless children. Fighting fear, I closed my eyes for a moment, then forced a smile, hoping that my voice would not betray my doubts. "Well, perhaps the spirits will be charmed to have the laughter of children within these dark walls. Meanwhile, we must get on with our work."

Chapter 8

I know not how I finished out the afternoon, yet somehow I managed and we all returned to the plantation house in good spirits. Mr. Harrison came out to welcome us and to invite me to stop in the library for a few moments before I went up to the children. Once there, his questions about our progress told me that he knew more about what went on among the servants than I had suspected.

"You had no trouble with your workers? No shirking because of fear?"

"There was some talk on the way to the cloister, but once we began the actual cleaning, everyone pitched in." I paused, studying him, wondering if I dared voice my own fears. I decided that I must, for the sake of the children whom I would be taking to the cloister. "They do truly believe that the building is haunted by the monks who were killed there."

To my surprise, he nodded. "I have heard the stories, but surely you do not share their fears."

"Of course not." I spoke quickly, unwilling to admit to any uneasiness.

"Good, for I do believe you have made an excellent choice for your orphanage. In fact, I want all the island to be aware of what you are doing, so I sent word to the other plantations, asking that they share in the repairs and in furnishing the place." He lifted a restraining hand as I started to protest. " 'Twill give them the feeling that it is for their benefit, Rachel, and that is important. I want your orphanage to be a part of all Bell Harbour Island, not just Sunrise Plantation."

I nodded, seeing at once the wisdom of his plan, though I also wondered if he might be alerting those who could wish us harm. After all, Paul's school had been meant to serve all the islanders, too.

"You may find that you have a motley crew to help you tomorrow, but that will do no harm. I shall spend some time there myself, making sure that all goes smoothly."

"Oh, that would be wonderful, sir," I gasped, more with relief than gratitude. With Jarvis Harrison's sturdy presence, I doubted that even the most determined ghost would dare make an appearance.

The next few days flew by. The cloister rang with laughter and conversation from near sunrise to close to sunset and there were many visitors—yet not the two I expected to see each day. Geraldine came often, and each time she brought another member of one of the planter families. Mr. Harrison was in and out daily, as were Pamela and Olivia, who professed an interest that I quickly realized was mere curiosity.

Geraldine brought several sturdy workers and a wagonload of furniture and bedding, which she helped me arrange in the various rooms as soon as they were cleaned. Digger and the men from Sunrise brought a wagonload each day, which soon had the many rooms looking less barren and more homelike.

By the sixth morning the work was nearly done, I realized, and neither Nick nor Paul had yet come to inspect the premises. In fact, I had heard not a word from

Paul since the evening meeting when Mr. Harrison had approved my choice of the cloister for the orphanage.

Should I move Elena and Inez into the cloister without Paul's permission? I asked myself, after I bade Geraldine farewell early that afternoon. By working here daily, I had come to feel quite comfortable within the stone walls of the huge structure, but now the thought of spending a night alone here with the two children sent a shiver down my spine.

Was I fooling myself with my brave talk of all that should happen once the orphanage was ready? Were the evil shades from the violent past merely waiting for the confusion of repair to die away before they appeared to me as they had to Harriet? The chill premonition of disaster deepened as I became aware that silence had at last come to the cloister.

"Digger? Harriet?" My voice seemed to echo in the large rear chamber, which I had designated as a playroom for the younger children, like Inez, who would have to be kept from the schoolroom.

The silence shifted around me, but no one answered. Was I alone here? Most of the work had been finished, of course, so the workmen had left earlier; but before she left, Geraldine and I had been busy planning for the storage of the supplies that I would need for both school and orphanage.

A skittering sound brought me around, but there was nothing to be seen except the newly painted shelves that lined the wall that separated the occupied section of the cloister from that which had been closed off. Mice, I assured myself. The unused area must be a haven for them, since Digger insisted that the roof was secure over the entire structure.

"Soon it will be filled with happy children's voices." I spoke aloud to reassure myself, then wished that I had not, for the dimness seemed to absorb my words like mist surrounding a tree. I had to grit my teeth to keep them from chattering. It was, I decided, time for me to leave, too.

My footsteps sounded like boots in the empty hall as I passed the small bedchambers, nearly half of which were now fully furnished and awaiting my charges. It took all my self-control not to keep from looking back over my shoulder. I paused for a moment in the kitchen, which was located between the sleeping area and the great room that was to serve as Paul's school until he made other arrangements.

I was halfway to the outside door, which stood open, when a shadow crossed the band of sunlight it admitted. A scream rose in my throat, but I clapped my hand over my mouth to hold it in, shamed by my own superstitious fears. Still, I shrank back until I bumped into the battered old table that Digger had brought from the attic this morning.

"Rachel, where . . . oh, there you are." Nick stepped into the room and my heart began to beat again, much faster than before. "I have come for a tour of inspection."

For a moment my relief was so heartfelt, I could only smile at him like a mindless fool; then a flicker of anger brought me back to life. "Are you sure you have the time?" I asked, my fears forgotten.

His eyes gleamed with amusement as he met my gaze. "So you have missed me this past week."

"Only because everyone else was so pleased with the changes I have made here." My own inpertinence appalled me, but when he was about, I seemed to lose control of my tongue.

"So I have heard from every planter on the island. Father has done a fine job of involving them, but you may find yourself busy sooner than you expect, for there are several preparing to bring you the orphans they have been caring for themselves." His words were delivered quietly, but his gaze moved over my face like a caress and I found it hard to catch my breath.

" 'Tis why I am here."

"Then you truly mean to move into the cloister?" He spoke so gravely, I knew that he was honestly concerned.

I turned away, afraid of what I might read in his gaze. "When you see all that we have done this past week, I am sure you will agree that this is the perfect place for a combined school and orphanage."

"Suppose you show me." His voice held a note of challenge which helped me to ignore the quiver of uneasiness that had returned to haunt me.

"Well, this is to be our schoolroom," I began, speaking quickly, listing all the virtues of the arrangement that I could recall, not giving Nick time for questions.

To my surprise, as we moved on through the dining room and kitchen, then along the hall that gave access to all the bedchambers, Nick seemed to relax. "You have done wonders, Rachel," he observed, as he peeked into one of the small cubicles that would serve the children. "I truly can understand why you were so sure that this would work."

"Then you approve?" I made no attempt to hide my surprise.

" 'Tis not my decision to make, but, yes, I believe I do." He opened the door at the end of the hall and stepped into the big rear room. "What are your plans for this space?"

"Since the older children will be using the front room as a schoolroom and I shall be occupied with the teaching, I thought this area could serve the younger ones as a place for play under the eye of an assistant."

"An assistant? Has the good Reverend produced one for you?" Nick crossed to look out the single window.

"I know not." I hated admitting it; but I knew that Jarvis Harrison was aware that I had heard nothing from Paul, so there was no use trying to hide the fact. "He has not yet come to see the changes in the building."

"I suspect he has been much too busy." Nick moved restlessly across the room, opening and closing the various cupboards and wardrobes.

"Is there something you seek?" I asked, troubled by his tone, which held a note that sounded very like disapproval.

"Only to see you smile." In two strides he was so close I could feel the heat that seemed to radiate from his strong body. The room, which had felt dank earlier, now seemed stuffy.

I wanted to step back, but when I looked up at him, I found myself unable to move. My throat grew dry, and I had to lick my lips as I sought for something to say, anything that would break the sudden tension that filled the room like the tingling before a thunderstorm.

His eyes seemed to flicker with gold and green flashes as he gently touched an errant curl, trailing his rough fingertips over my cheek as he carefully tucked it back behind my ear. His scent, a pleasant mixture of fresh air, soap, and a seductive musk, filled my nostrils and made my heartbeat quicken even more.

"I mislike thinking of you here alone, Rachel." His voice was low, almost a whisper.

"I shall have the children." A kind of dizziness made me want to lean closer, to steady myself against the broad expanse of his chest. His fingers still moved over the curl and tickled my ear, the tender skin of my neck. A shiver stole over me and I wondered if my knees would long support me.

"You are far too lovely to be alone." His fingers slipped beneath my tumbling hair to cup the back of my head as he lowered his lips to mine.

Stop him! a tiny voice shrieked inside my head, but I was too busy discovering the sweet magic of his lips as they caressed mine with infinite tenderness. I let my eyes drift shut, the better to lose myself in the new sensations that seemed to flow from my lips through my entire body. Without meaning to, I moved closer, leaning on his strength, his arm tightening around me.

Slowly, his lips pressed harder, taking command of mine. The wild delight of it increased, and I slipped my arms around him, wanting to hold on, since the world seemed to be spinning much too fast. This was definitely much different from the shy kisses that had been stolen from me during the few summer parties I had attended my last several years at Middle Brook Christian.

This was magic, enchantment, like dreaming, except that I could feel the pounding of his heart as it raced next to mine. When his mouth moved over mine, I wanted only to offer more of my lips to him. I wanted to . . .

Shock finally broke through the shimmering unreality and I stiffened in his embrace, trying to bring my arms back between us so that I could push him away. Nick lifted his head, but held me easily. His eyes seemed dark now, yet I could see the heat burning in their depths and it scared me.

"Let me go."

"Why?"

" 'Tis unseemly. We should not be alone in this place." I tried to struggle, but each move only made me more conscious of being pressed against his hard body.

"And where should we be alone?" His tone was teasing and his lazy grin made me want to forget my arguments.

"You know this is wrong."

"But it feels so right." He trailed a fingertip over my

lower lip and I trembled. "You know that, Rachel. Little innocent that you are, you feel it, too."

" 'Tis wrong."

"How can this be wrong?" His fingers caught my chin when I would have ducked my head, and in a moment, his lips claimed mine again.

I tried to resist, to hold myself rigid and unbending in his arms; but the delight that spread through me was too strong to deny. Shyly, I answered his kiss and discovered even sweeter sensations as he moved his mouth over mine. By the time he loosened his embrace and freed my lips, I was near swooning.

This was truly madness, I realized, and I must stop it now. I drew in a deep breath, then blushed as I felt the hard wall of his chest against my softer curves. I had to escape immediately or I feared I might truly do something to bring shame upon me.

Much to my relief, when I tried to pull away this time, Nick released me. I focused on the nearby open wardrobe, so that I should not betray the weakness and longing that swept over me. "I have heard dreadful stories about the past of this building," I said, hoping to divert myself as well as him from what had happened between us.

"All true, I fear. For a structure meant to house men of God, it has had a bloody history." He went again to the window, presenting his back to me, so I had no way to judge his feelings.

"I suppose 'tis not surprising that the islanders consider it haunted." This was not the conversation I wanted to have, but I was afraid to allow silence between us, afraid that Nick might ask me questions for which I had no answers—like why I had allowed him to kiss me, not once, but twice.

"The rumors have persisted through the years, so I expect there is some validity to what they say." Nick wandered again to test the back wall of the large room. "That was one reason we had this wall built."

"You had it built?"

"My father did, right after one of the servants claimed to have seen a light moving about the rooms one night. He was sure that some of the malcontents on the island were using the place for their meetings, and he wanted to put a stop to it." Nick's grim expression made me sure that he was stating facts.

"And what do you think?"

He shrugged. "I have seen neither human nor genuine haunts within these walls; but Rachel, I do want you to promise to keep the windows and the door barred at night. Take no chances."

"Against ghosts?" I tried for a light-hearted tone, wanting to believe that he was teasing.

" 'Tis not the ghosts of long-ago monks you need to fear."

"Then whom should I fear?" My voice shook slightly as I realized that he was deadly serious.

"I wish I knew." He turned away. "Now, however, I think it is time we returned to Sunrise. If you are through for the day?"

"There is little more to be done. I could move in with Elena and Inez tomorrow." The lack of enthusiasm in my voice shamed me; but how could I be excited at the prospect of living here, now that Nick had told me of his worries?

"Wait until Paul brings you an assistant. I mislike the idea of just you and the girls here." He had been heading for the hallway to the front of the structure, but he turned back with a grin. "Of course, I suppose I could volunteer to stay and guard you."

My heart accelerated wildly at the prospect, but I managed a stern glare. "I suspect that would be more

135

dangerous than any ghost or human that might decide to come ahaunting."

The moment the words were out, I wished that I could call them back; but Nick only chuckled. "In that, you may be right, Miss Rachel Ames, though I doubt you know why."

"I am quite ready to go back to Sunrise." I hurried past him, aware that my cheeks were burning and most anxious to escape his too-seeing gaze and the unsettling way it effected me.

"I expect the Reverend will be riding by tomorrow," Nick observed, as he closed and locked the heavy outside door behind us. "Now that the place is ready for use, he will have to give it his seal of approval. Then he can put his latest plans into operation."

"And do you know what those might be?" I wanted to ignore the disparaging tone of his remarks about Paul, but my curiosity was too strong. Besides, I was rather displeased with the Reverend Michaels myself. I could have used his counsel more than once these past days.

Nick shrugged. "I have no idea. In fact, I have neither seen nor had word of his actions since he rode off after winning my father's approval of your plan."

That bit of news made me forget discretion. "Where has he been?"

"That is something you will have to ask him when he comes by." Nick's tone was mocking. "Perhaps he will be more disposed to tell you what he has been doing."

"If he comes."

"Oh, I am sure he knows that the building is ready. After all, thanks to my father's invitations to the other planters, everyone on the island is well aware of your progress." Again I sensed disapproval in Nick's tone, but I kept silent on our short journey to Sunrise. Jarvis Harrison was standing on the veranda, and when Nick

136

stopped the cart at the house, he hurried forward to greet us.

"So what do you think of our Rachel now?" he asked Nick. "Has she not wrought a miracle in that old building?"

I felt the heat of pleasure in my cheeks at Mr. Harrison's praise, even as I tensed, fearing Nick's reply. He surprised me with his compliments and I was halfway up to the third floor before I realized that nothing Nick had said even hinted that he approved of what I was undertaking.

Not that I needed or wanted his approval, I told myself sternly . . . Paul's approval was what counted. Besides, Nick was probably just being stubborn because I had paid no attention to his objections when he first uttered them. Still, I had a hollow feeling as I told Elena and Inez that our new home would soon be ready. Much as I was fascinated by the cloister, the idea of moving in sent a shiver down my spine.

To combat my own fears, I began packing up my belongings the very next morning. If I meant to fulfill my mission on Bell Harbour Island, I should have to conquer my own superstition and moving into the big bedchamber at the cloister seemed the best way to do so. I had my trunk half-filled when Harriet came to summon me.

I found Paul pacing the handsome entry hall, his hair still tousled by the light morning breeze and his gray eyes glowing. "I have seen all that you accomplished, Rachel, and I am most pleased."

"I hoped you would be." The words came out a bit flat, for following my relief at seeing him came my irritation at his neglect. "I feared that I might have overstepped my authority by proceeding without your advice."

His smile faded. "I trusted that you would succeed

without my supervision. In his letters Reverend Bennett spoke highly of your qualifications for our mission here."

I winced under the implied reprimand, aware that I had earned it with my own runaway tongue. I somehow found it hard to remember that it was not my place to demand anything from Reverend Michaels. Having taken responsibility for my own life when I stepped aboard ship in Philadelphia, I had forgotten that I was meant to serve, not command.

"Forgive me, Reverend," I murmured. "I was only unsure of what I was to do. My experience has always been in an orphanage already established."

"Of course, my dear, and I have neglected my duties here. For that, I, too, am sorry; but there is much at stake on this island, and only I can make the dream come true."

When I lifted my head to ask what he meant, I was struck again by the power of his calling. His square features fairly shone with purpose, and I had no doubt of his devotion to God's will. This was truly the man I remembered from his summer visits to Middle Brook.

"Are you ready to go to the cloister?" He gave me no chance to ask any questions. "Seraphina is awaiting us there."

"Seraphina?"

"Your assistant. She is an island woman deeply devoted to our cause and more than willing to help with the care of the children. You will have need of her, since you will be spending much of your day in teaching until I have time to rebuild the village school."

Paul was already moving toward the door, so I could do nothing but follow him. "What of the children?" I asked, hoping to slow him.

"We shall take them over later. There is much that

you and Seraphina must see to before the place can be officially opened to the children."

Trusting that Harriet would see to Elena and Inez, I allowed Paul to help me into the cart that waited out front, then spent the duration of the ride to the cloister answering his many questions. It was a dizzying experience, for I had never before held such responsibility nor been forced to give clear reasons for each of my decisions.

As Paul helped me down from the cart, a tall, handsome island woman emerged from the open door of the cloister. She was, I judged, in her early thirties, her thick black hair not yet touched by silver, her golden tan skin without wrinkles; her dark eyes seemed sad as she smiled shyly at me. Paul made the introductions quickly, then led the way into the schoolroom, which was now crowded with boxes and bales—the supplies that I had brought with me, I realized.

"I asked Seraphina to wait to unpack everything until you were here, so you could decide together where everything should be placed." Paul surveyed the chaos calmly. "You shall not have any students before tomorrow."

"Tomorrow?" Shock made my question come out rather as a squeak.

"Since the children will be arriving this afternoon, I knew you would not have time both to teach and to meet your new charges." His benevolent smile told me that he was deadly serious.

I swallowed the stream of protests that rose in my mind, doing my best to remember what he had said about Reverend Bennett's confidence in my abilities. "How many children shall we prepare for?"

"No more than three or four orphans. As for students, I know not. You saw for yourself that the planters have no patience with learning. If they need the children in

the fields, they will keep them there ... for now."
Something about his final two words chilled me.

"Where shall we begin, Miss Ames?" Seraphina asked, forcing my attention back to the practical. If everything Paul said came to pass, I knew I would have no time to speculate on future problems—I would have more than enough to deal with.

By midday, the children's rooms were ready, the two narrow cots in each one covered with light blankets, the small cupboards open and ready for their few possessions. Seraphina, blessedly, had taken over in the kitchen, which was now well stocked from the larder at Sunrise.

As we ate the simple meal she prepared, Paul outlined the work that needed to be accomplished during the afternoon, then he went to Sunrise to enlist more help. I was delighted when both Digger and Harriet arrived at the cloister with the girls, bringing with them my belongings as well as those of Elena and Inez. Whether I was ready or not, I was moving in.

The orphans arrived in late afternoon, three little boys and one whimpering girl. Seraphina was the first to see them, and as I watched her greeting them, my chief worry dissipated. Her warm arms offered them a sanctuary they accepted without question, and there was no mistaking the love that filled her dark eyes as she calmed their fears. I joined her gladly, forgetting everything but the children's need to feel safe and loved and welcome.

And so it began, the great adventure I had traveled so far to be a part of. The chaos no longer mattered. The unanswered questions faded as I held little Nathan in my lap and listened to his babbling. When his skinny arms slipped around my neck in a tentative hug, I knew this was where I belonged.

It was well after dark by the time all the children

were safely settled in their beds and Seraphina and I could take a few moments for a cup of tea at the kitchen table. "What do you think?" I asked. "Will the children thrive here?"

Her shrug surprised me. "Some will, some not. 'Tis the way of the world, Miss. But we shall tend them all." She looked around the homey room. "This place has strength, and perhaps the good Reverend's power can truly drive out the darkness that has haunted it for as long as anyone can remember."

"You have heard the stories?" It was a question I had wanted to ask when we met, but there had been no time until now.

"The whole island knows what happened here in the dark past and what others claim continues even now. But your magic is strong, too. You have conquered this and made it your own. Perhaps that will be sufficient."

"My what?"

"Magic. Power. Whatever you call it. The fire that burns within and brings you here to help my people." Her serene gaze seemed at odds with her strange words.

" 'Tis my Christian duty to help those less fortunate. I was sent here to help the Reverend in his work." I spoke quickly, not comfortable with her very foreign beliefs. "Is that not why you have come here?"

"I wish to help with what Reverend Michaels plans to do, but mostly I am here because I have nowhere else to go. My two sons are wed and raising families of their own, and when my husband was killed in the fields at Emerald Acres, I was no longer welcome there. I asked at the church about finding service at one of the other plantations, but the Reverend felt I could do better helping you."

Though she spoke quietly, I sensed the sorrow behind her words and felt again very young and inexperienced in life. I reached out for her work-worn hand, taking it

141

between both of mine. "I am deeply grateful that he found you, Seraphina, for I could not ask for a better assistant. I only hope that you will be happy here at the cloister."

"Thank you, Miss Ames." Her shy smile and the glow in her dark eyes made me blink back tears.

"Please, you must call me Rachel. We shall be as sisters in our caring for the unfortunate, so we shall be friends as well."

"Rachel." Our eyes met and I felt reassured that I should have her help in all that lay ahead, for I sensed her strength.

The next few days proved me right, for Seraphina was truly a tower of strength. She cared for the little ones, fixed the meals and gave me the time I needed to set up our school. Not that it was well attended.

After five days in which I never had the same number of pupils, I began to understand Paul's anger at the planters. How could I teach a child to read and write, when he was only allowed to attend one day in three? It was as though each day he or she came was the first, for they quickly forgot what they learned.

I longed to complain, but there was no one to listen, for Paul had vanished late the first afternoon and had not returned. As for Mr. Harrison or Nick, they merely shrugged, saying they had no control over the workers from any plantation but Sunrise. Few of my pupils came from Sunrise, however, as some of the children on the plantation already knew how to read and write, thanks to Mr. Harrison's policy of educating all who expressed an interest in learning. Or maybe, like Harriet, they were afraid.

As Sunday neared, I determined that I must speak with Paul. To that end, I asked Mr. Harrison if the children, Seraphina, and I might be allowed to attend services at the church in the village. "Of course you may.

I shall order Digger to drive you in whenever you wish. 'Tis only right for you to spend some time talking with the Reverend and 'twill do the villagers good to see how well your enterprise is managing. There were some who expressed doubts about it."

"There were?"

"There are always those who doubt any change. Ask Paul, he can tell you stories . . ." He let it trail off. "Or perhaps it would be best if you refrained from reminding him of all that happened, now that things seem to be progressing more quietly."

I sighed, unable to contain my frustration. "Everyone speaks of past troubles, Mr. Harrison, but no one tells me what happened."

"We only wish to protect you."

"But if no one tells me from whom, how shall I be protected?" It was a question that had troubled me since my arrival.

"If I knew, I would gladly tell you; but I know not who stands against us. I doubt that Paul knows, either. 'Tis like fighting in one of the thick mists that come in from the sea. You know that someone is out there standing against you, but you cannot see their face."

"Are you saying that there is some person who truly wishes us ill?"

"You know that the school was burned." His gaze was sad.

I wanted to protest further, to remind him that I was here only to care for orphans; but he turned away. "You must discuss this with Reverend Michaels. He knows the temper of the people outside Sunrise far better than I. Perhaps he can help you."

"I shall ask him tomorrow," I promised him and my-self.

Chapter 9

The ride into the village was pleasant, especially as Nick was riding alongside the wagon on his dancing bay stallion. I smiled up at him shyly, happy just to be in his company, for I saw little of him now that I lived at the cloister. "I had not thought that you would be accompanying us."

"I, too, wish to speak with Reverend Michaels about several matters." His tone as well as his words told me that his father had discussed our conversation with him.

"Has there been some difficulty?" I longed for answers, but I was very conscious of both Digger and Seraphina listening to my every word. And, of course, I had no desire to frighten the children since they seemed to be settling into their new home so well.

"None that should trouble you." Nick's smile was reassuring until I noted that it did not reach his eyes.

"Anything that might affect the orphanage troubles me," I replied, perhaps a bit more forcefully than I should have. "And I do worry about the children that attend the school, too."

"As do I. Everyone on Sunrise land is under my care, especially now that my father cannot ride about the island the way he used to."

When I looked into his eyes, the laughing children

faded from my attention and I found myself lost in memories of the kisses we had shared what now seemed a lifetime ago. It had been but a week, and I could see the memory of them burning in his eyes, too. A quiver of something very like anticipation slipped along my spine and I felt the heat rising in my cheeks.

Luckily, Nick's horse chose that moment to shy away from the wagon and end our conversation, for I had not a clue as to what I might say to him. I took a deep breath, then darted a glance in Seraphina's direction, suddenly afraid that she might have observed my actions; but she was busy with Nathan and Inez, our two youngest charges.

What had come over me? I wondered, as we rode through the bright and sunny morning. What kind of woman was I becoming that I should have such wicked thoughts? True, I had giggled late at night with the other young ladies at Middle Brook Christian as we talked of boys and speculated about our futures; but never had I felt such . . . such an attraction to a man.

Not even Paul Michaels. That thought came unbidden, but I knew at once that it was true. I had entertained daydreams about coming here to do God's work with him and even considered that we might someday be like Reverend and Mrs. Bennett; but fiery kisses that made my knees weak had never had a part in those dreams.

"Rachel, are you all right?" Seraphina's gentle voice penetrated my thoughts and a glance at her told me that it was not the first time she had spoken to me.

"Forgive me, I fear I heard not . . . ?" Guilt again brought red to my cheeks.

"I was only wondering if we would have time in the village after services?"

"Of course. I must speak with Reverend Michaels and I am sure the children will want to spend a little

145

time with those who cared for them. Is there somewhere you wish to go?" It shamed me to realized that I had not asked before now. Seraphina had taken her place at my side so willingly, that I fear I took her dedication for granted.

"I hope that my sons and their families will be at services. It would be nice to see my grandchildren for a little while."

"You have grandchildren?" I was shocked. "You seem so young to even have grown children."

"I was married at fourteen and a mother at fifteen." She sighed. "Too young, perhaps, yet I should regret it had I even a day less with my man." Pain narrowed her eyes and I reached out to touch her arm. Her smile was sad, but serene. "We had good years, but I do miss him."

I tried to think of words to comfort her, but before I could, Elena claimed my attention with a question and the moment was gone. The rest of the trip passed quickly as we talked about the picnic we had planned for after the services.

As Digger neared the church, I peered ahead, seeking for familiar faces. "Where is everyone?" I asked, realizing that there was but one small cart and two tired-looking horses tethered near the church. "Are we early?"

"No, Miss." Digger stopped the team. "We be right on time."

I started to question him further, then held my tongue as Nick came over to help me down. My heart leaped as his hands clasped my waist and he swung me to the ground. Just being so close, catching his scent on the breeze, feeling each of his fingers . . . I forced myself to step back, nearly bumping into the side of the wagon. "Where is everyone, Nick?" I asked, to cover my confusion.

"There may be few in attendance these days. I have been told that many of his followers are staying away since the fire. Perhaps they fear that someone will set a torch to the church next." Nick took my arm, his calm tone nearly masking the horrible things he was saying.

I pulled free of his hold so that I could face him. "Are you saying that people are afraid to go to church?"

"Only that they might be. I told you before that our island has not been a happy place since the good Reverend began changing things here. But he refuses to listen when I counsel patience and as a result . . ." Nick let it trail off, shrugging.

"I have never heard of such a thing." The way he seemed to be blaming Paul infuriated me. "Surely a man doing God's work should not be so bedeviled."

"If you believe that, you have not studied the history of the Caribbean, Rachel. These islands may seem to sleep in the tropical sun, but nearly every one of them hides a dark past. Bell Harbour has been relatively peaceful since our families arrived, but that is only because the planters have kept control. Your own land was racked by civil war, so you must realize that nowhere is safe." Nick began urging me toward the church again.

"But Paul would have nothing to do with any kind of violence, Nick, of that I am sure. He is a man of God, his ways are peaceful. He comes to save souls and teach children, not to burn or change the people." I spoke fervently, sure that there must be some misunderstanding here.

"Do you not think that education will change the islanders?" Nick's gaze was cynical. "A man who can read and write and do sums is hardly likely to be content to work every day in the cane fields."

"Your workers seem happy enough." I met his gaze. "And you told me yourself that your father offered education to all that wished it."

147

"And we lost a number of workers. Some took better jobs, others simply left Bell Harbour for good, seeking a new life on another island. Because my father is willing to pay fair wages, we were able to hire more men to work; but some of the planters are less accepting of progress. At least, that is what I suspect is behind the trouble. No one knows for sure."

"Perhaps if you explained to Paul . . ." I began, then let the sentence trail off as we entered the church.

"You try," Nick whispered, as he led us all down the aisle.

There were, I noticed, more people inside than I had thought. The lack of carts and wagons outside must mean that the villagers attended services even though the plantation workers did not. I swallowed a sigh and did my best to compose myself—no easy feat with Nick sitting so close beside me that I was aware of every breath he took.

Paul spoke eloquently and the children were, for the most part, quite well behaved. Or awed by it all, as Nick said when we walked outside after the service ended. To my surprise, he offered to help Seraphina—whose family had not come after all—supervise the children for a little while, giving me a chance to speak with Paul.

"I was delighted to see you here today, Rachel." Paul beamed at me. "And with all the children. You set a good example. I only hope word of it will reach the other plantations so that some of them will make the effort to attend."

I was in no mood to be distracted by compliments. "Nick seems to think they may be afraid to come."

"Regrettably, he could be right." Paul's smile vanished. " 'Tis a troubled island, I fear."

"Why?"

"Oh, many reasons." He started to turn away. "But I

want to hear about the school. How many students do you have?"

"I want to know what those reasons are, Paul. Everyone tells me that I must be careful, that there are dangers here. I have a right to know where they come from, do I not?" I met his gaze firmly.

For a moment, I thought that he might deny me the knowledge I sought, but he finally sighed. " 'Tis the planters, of course. They suspect my plans and wish to drive me from the island."

"What plans? Surely they cannot fault you for wishing to have a school or an orphanage. What is going on, Paul?"

His frown should have frightened me, but I was too angry to be intimidated. He glared for what seemed an eternity, then finally turned his attention to the scene beyond the church. "The school and orphanage are only the beginning, Rachel. The island folk are little better off than the slaves that we just fought the southern states to free. The education we offer is their emancipation. My plan is to use Bell Harbour Island as a training ground. I will educate the young here and they will go to the other islands to teach. Soon everyone will be able to read and write, and then the planters will no longer be able to control them."

He stopped as though expecting me to say something, but for once I was speechless. When I finally managed to find my tongue, all I could do was ask, "Then what shall all these islanders do?"

"They will do what they choose as men do in Philadelphia. They will become clerks and shopkeepers, and some will be teachers and ministers. It will be a new society for them."

"And the planters?"

"They will have to give up their high living and work like other men. But that is far in the future. Now I want

149

only to have the children in my classroom instead of the fields." His face hardened. "That is what I wanted, when I still had a school in which to teach them."

I heard Nick's suggestion that I try to convince Paul to go slowly echoing in my mind, but I knew that it would do no good to try. "Just be careful," I whispered, feeling a coward. "You are their hope, so you must survive."

"God will protect me, for I do His will." Paul's smile was radiant with his belief. "And you are helping me. Tell me now, how goes the school?"

At my suggestion, Paul joined Digger, Seraphina, Nick, the children, and me for the picnic Nick had ordered packed for us, and we spent a happy hour beneath a flower-laden tree, chatting like carefree friends on holiday. It was only when we were packing up the food that Paul gestured to Nick and the two of them strolled off together, talking earnestly. I watched them, frustration chewing at me, wondering if they were discussing my future, too.

Since I had no chance on the ride back to Sunrise to ask Nick what they had discussed, I invited him to stay a bit when we reached the cloister. "What may I do for you?" he asked, as he dismounted and tied his horse to one of the trees a short distance from the building.

"I should like to know more about the part of the cloister that I have never seen." The idea had come suddenly as we drew near the immense structure, but as soon as I uttered it, I knew it was more than an excuse to be alone with Nick so we could talk. "The building is so large, it seems a shame that only our part of it is being put to use."

"Much of the rest was damaged during an island uprising. Walls were weakened and in some cases even breached. It was deemed unsafe, so it would be best for you to forget any plan for exploring the area." Nick's gaze was surprisingly stern. "Promise me that you will not venture outside the part you have so cleverly adapted for your needs."

Protests rose in my mind, but when he stared down at me that way, I could deny him nothing. Besides, I knew well that he still had the power to have us evicted from the building, should he believe that we were, indeed, in danger. "I should never want to endanger anyone. It is only that I am curious. Could you not show me a little of the area?"

For a moment, I thought that he might refuse, but after what seemed an eternity, his teasing grin returned. "You are like a kitten, Rachel, always wanting to poke your pretty nose in where it might catch the scent of trouble. But how can I refuse the opportunity to be alone with you in that spooky old cloister?"

My heartbeat quickened as he took my arm and led me not into the cloister, as I had expected, but around to the side of the building. His remark about being alone with me had definitely tempered my determination to explore. My anticipation was now much more personal and a little disturbing.

The wild island plants made our walk almost a battle, for they formed their own barricade between the grassy hillside and the stout stone walls they disguised. In fact, I should have passed the heavy wooden door without ever seeing it had Nick not pushed aside the heavy bushes. He tried the door, which proved to be firmly locked, then took a key from a hidden niche. To my surprise, it turned easily enough.

Though I wondered why the lock was not rusted beyond use, I held my tongue. I had long ago learned that asking too many questions could keep me from finding out the answers. Nick stepped into the darkness first, pausing just beyond the door sill to feel around. I heaved a sigh of relief when he struck a match. A moment later, an old lantern bloomed with light and I was able to join him.

Looking around, I felt a chill that came only partly from the dank air that surrounded us. The rooms I had explored in the front of the cloister had been barren and dirty, but this room was in ruins. Broken furniture, timber from the walls, debris from the tumbled ceiling were strewn about the filthy floor.

"Oh, Nick, what happened here?" I made no attempt to hide my horror.

"This area of the cloister served as sanctuary to the men who were fighting to subdue the islanders. It was here they fled when their cruel treatment of men who had been free finally drove the would-be slaves into a violent rebellion. When the furious islanders broke in, they killed everyone, then began looking for the treasure the invaders were said to have."

"They killed everyone?" I was grateful for his arm, which he now slipped around my shoulders. "What of the women and children? Or were these invaders only soldiers?"

"In the beginning, they were only men, but once they began to build plantations, most brought their families from Spain or from the other islands that were settled earlier. Where they actually came from was never very clear, since no records were left by the time my family and the others arrived here." Nick kicked a piece of wood out of the way and picked up the lantern in his other hand.

"What happened to the women and children?"

I felt his shrug. "If any of the invaders survived, they never spoke of it wherever they fled. The islanders said only that the island was cleansed of the evil invaders. I have heard, however, that there were a number of people buried in what is now a small fenced-off area not far from here. There are, of course, no headstones or markers, but it is said that the monks and the innocents were put to rest properly. The rest were burned in a fire that could be seen from all parts of the island."

A shudder shook me, for I could almost hear the screams that must have filled this room and all the others in the old building. What had only been a story to me before now was all too real. I was rapidly losing my interest in exploration.

Nick seemed to sense my feelings, for his arm tightened and I was grateful for the warmth of his strong body next to mine. "Now you see why this place has its reputation for ghostly presences."

I nodded, then forced the ugly images from my mind. "Is that why this part of the building was never cleaned up or repaired?"

"According to legend, attempts were made by the islanders; but each time the work crews ventured back here, a horrible accident would end their efforts. By the time we arrived, it seemed sensible to simply wall off this part of the building. Once we did, the worst of the haunting stories ceased and the place seemed to be at peace." He spoke softly as he led me slowly across the room to what was either more devastation or a proper opening in the wall.

I peered ahead fearfully as the glow of the lantern illuminated even more signs of destruction. I shuddered again, no longer eager to see any more. "Did they find the treasure they sought?"

"The stories vary. I have heard that they found a vast fortune and lived like kings for a time; but there were no signs of it when the families arrived. The village was nothing but shacks, the boats were scarcely able to make it from one island to the next, there were no plantations, few small farms. People simply existed, feeding themselves from gardens and the sea. We brought civilization." He sighed, holding the lantern high so that he could study the damage. "Do you really wish to see more?"

I shook my head. "You were quite right about venturing back here. 'Tis like another world, and not one that I should ever choose to visit." I hesitated, then added, "Have you come here often?"

"As a boy I adored exploring the area." He chuckled. "My father swore I would end up lost in here, but when you are playing at being a pirate or an islander defending his home, it can be a wonderous place. And, of course, when all else paled, we could search for the treasure."

"And Sarah?"

"She was as wild as the rest of us. Even Geraldine spent a few summer days in here. Mostly, of course, we were sent away to school, but when we were on the island, we tended to gather here to escape the eyes of our parents." He sighed, then went on, but I scarcely listened, for I was picturing him here with Sarah and Geraldine and I was envying them.

I suddenly became aware of the fact that Nick had stopped speaking and was now looking down at me curiously. I spoke quickly to cover my lapse of attention. "Well, I shall have to take care to keep the orphan children from such adventures."

"I doubt you will have trouble with any island child. They were all raised on the tales of the evil spirits that haunt the place. 'Tis more likely that you will have trouble keeping them inside the building." His teasing grin was back. "That is probably part of the reason your students are reluctant to come for their lessons."

"Do you really think so?" I frowned. This was a reason for the many absences that I had never considered and I suspected that it would not have occurred to Paul, either.

"Perhaps you should talk with the children about the

154

stories and reassure them." Nick blew out the lantern, then set it on a ledge that had been built into the outside wall itself, thus left intact. The air felt warm and sweet as we stepped out into the sunlight.

"I shall," I promised. Then, belatedly remembering my reason for seeking to be alone with Nick, I tried to find a graceful way to approach the subject of what he had discussed with Paul. It took me only a moment to realize that I had no gift for guile, so I simply faced him and asked, "Did you and Reverend Michaels make any plans for the orphanage during your talk today?"

Nick had been busy locking the heavy door as I asked, but when he turned to me again, I could see that my question surprised him. "Should you not be discussing this with Paul?"

I sighed. "Of course, but I never know when I will see him, and I thought that you might guide me while he is busy with his other concerns."

Nick's eyes gleamed with wickedness. "I should love to guide you, dear Rachel, but I suspect the good Reverend and I should never agree on where you should be taken. The fact is, the only thing Paul and I seem to be able to agree on these days is that you must be protected. That was what we discussed."

Frustration knotted my stomach and before I could stop myself, I was glaring at him. "Why will no one tell me how I can protect myself?"

Our glares clashed for a moment, then he reached out and gently stroked his finger down my cheek. My anger fled as quickly as it had flared and the heat that replaced it set my heart to pounding and made my knees so weak I was glad when he slipped his arm around me. He was going to kiss me. I could see his desire in his eyes and was powerless to resist.

"Perhaps it is because protecting you is so enchanting," he whispered, just before his lips claimed mine.

During the days since our first kiss, I had told myself that it was just a one-time bit of magic that should never happen again; but Nick quickly proved me wrong. The same wildly exciting sensations swept over me and the dizziness seemed worse this time, for I had to cling to him or swoon. Yet mad as it was, I never wanted him to stop—a weakness of will that made me feel a fool when Nick finally lifted his lips from mine.

He held me even tighter so that I could feel the thunder of his heart beneath my own heaving bosom. His breath stirred my tawny curls like a gentle breeze and I felt his lips brush my hair. "Ah, Rachel," he sighed, "perhaps it is I who need protection from you."

For a moment I heard only the longing in his tone, then the import of his words struck me and drove the clouds of illusion from my mind. I pulled free of his arms, burning with shame and hurt. I glared up at him, wanting to deny the accusation implicit in his words; but how could I? I had wanted his kiss and answered it. What had I become?

Unable to find words to answer him and fighting tears that threatened to flood my eyes, I turned and ran. I heard him call my name once, but as I stumbled around the corner of the cloister and headed for the open door, I realized that he was not pursuing me. Though I should have been grateful, all I felt was bereft as I went inside.

Fortunately, the big schoolroom was empty, as was the hallway beyond. I escaped into my rooms without seeing anyone—or being seen. Once there, I bathed my face with the cool water in the pitcher on my washstand, then met my own gaze in the mirror. I scarcely recognized the dark-eyed stranger with the slightly swollen lips who stared back at me.

I had never truly considered myself attractive, for such frivolities were frowned upon at Middle Brook

Christian. We were taught to be good, clean, and pure of heart; beyond that, the shape of face or nose, the wideness of eyes and length of lashes, had no meaning. Now, however, I studied myself.

My face was rather ordinary, except that my cheekbones were high enough to give my dark eyes a slight slant, and my lashes, though only a few shades darker than my light brown hair, were thick and quite long enough to hide my gaze when I lowered them. And Nick had called my nose "pretty" . . . The quiver came back inside me, especially when I studied my mouth and remembered how his had felt on mine.

Was I wicked? I longed for someone to ask, but whom? The only person who came to mind was Sarah Kasper, and she was but an acquaintance, for all her kindness during my short stay on St. Devina. Geraldine Chalmers should have been a possibility, for she was both older and more experienced around men than I; but even thinking about discussing anything personal with her chilled me. Besides, I could not shake the feeling that she had some special affection for Nick.

I turned from the mirror, disgusted with my lack of will. I knew well what Mrs. Bennett would say: she would tell me that I must stop this foolishness at once. I had no one here to protect me from my own weakness, and Nick Harrison was a powerful man. We could be friends, nothing more.

A shiver traced down my spine and I touched one finger to my tender lips. Friends? I knew that what I felt for him had already gone beyond such a gentle word. Yet how could I change my feelings? What should I do? Or was it already far too late?

A tap on the door was a welcome interruption, and I hurried to open it. Seraphina stood on the other side, her usually serene face creased by a frown. "What is it?" I asked, beckoning her inside, then waving her into one of the mismatched chairs that Digger had brought from the Sunrise attic. "Has something happened to one of the children?"

"Oh, no, 'tis not that, Miss . . . Rachel. Everyone be fine." Her expression made her last words a lie, as did her hands, which twisted in her lap as she perched on the edge of the chair.

"Then what is it?" I did my best to keep my tone calm, even though my mind insisted on calling up what Nick had said about accidents following any attempt to invade the boarded-off areas of the cloister. Could my venturing there . . . I pushed the very thought away. "What has happened, Seraphina?"

" 'Tis something strange, mayhap even nothing, but . . ." She met my gaze, then looked away. "I had thought not to disturb you, but now I have to tell you."

"Tell me what?" My patience was beginning to wear thin, mostly because my imagination was producing more and more worrisome images.

"It appears that someone has been in the rear room."

"Someone?" I was not sure of her meaning. "You mean, while we were away at services someone entered? But how . . . Has something been taken?"

"I think it would be best if you saw what I did." Seraphina got to her feet at once, looking far calmer than when she had come in.

I followed her along the quiet hall, then asked, "Where are the children?"

"I put the little ones down for naps and left the others playing in their rooms. I thought a bit of quiet was called for after such a busy day."

I nodded, feeling guilty as I realized how I had turned everything over to her after our return from the village. I had been so intent on being alone with Nick, I had actually neglected the children placed in my care. Further proof that what had happened was wrong. It shamed me

158

to realize that I still longed for Nick's company, his arms around me, his kiss . . .

I forced that thought away and focused on the dim rear room. It looked blessedly normal, though tidier than usual, since the children had been away most of the day. "What is it that you wished me to see, Seraphina?"

She led me across the room to the largest of the wardrobes, the one I had chosen to use for storing all the old clothing that had been brought to us from the various plantations, and opened the door. For a moment, it appeared empty, then I realized that all the garments were now lying in an untidy pile on the floor of the wardrobe.

"Why did this upset you so?" I hurried to examine the first few garments, which seemed wrinkled, but intact. "Everything seems all right."

"But it was all thrown on the floor."

"Perhaps one of the children . . ." I began, but she shook her dark head firmly, stopping my words.

"I came to get a clean shirt for Ben after he spilled milk on himself this morning. 'Twas just before we were to leave, and everything was hanging neatly."

I started to respond, but there was something about her gaze that made me change my mind. "What do you think happened?" I asked, suddenly sure that there was more that she had to tell me.

"I'd not be knowin'." Her gaze skittered away from mine.

"Has something else happened?"

There were several minutes of silence before she sighed and again met my gaze. " 'Twas day before yesterday. I baked four loaves of bread and left them cooling while I took the little ones out for a bit of sun while you were giving lessons. You remember?"

I nodded, though I had scarce noticed their passage through the schoolroom, so intent had I been on my teaching. I waited for her to go on, but she seemed to have forgotten what she was going to tell me. "Then what happened?"

"When I returned, there were but three loaves."

"What?"

"One was gone. I searched everywhere, even in the rooms that are empty, but I found nothing, Rachel. Then I thought perhaps one of the students . . . Sometimes, if a child is left hungry . . ." Her eyes mirrored an understanding of hunger that touched my heart and at the same time opened my mind to worry.

"You thought one of the schoolchildren took it?"

She nodded. "Who else could it be? You were in the schoolroom, so you'd have seen anyone enter from outside, and I had all the little ones with me. Though it matters not, since none of them would have been able to reach the cooling shelf."

The air in the quiet rear room seemed to shift around me and I had to control a strong urge to run as I stared down at the tangle of clothing on the floor of the wardrobe. I swallowed hard. "I remember no student leaving the schoolroom, Seraphina. At least, not to go into the kitchen. I'd have noticed. And there certainly were no schoolchildren here today."

"But the bread was gone and the clothes are on the floor." Seraphina's expression told me she was feeling the same chill that made me shiver in the warm room.

To my shame, I was the first to look away from the questions in her eyes. "What we must do is put them back on their pegs," I said. "They will never do this way." I picked up a dress and carefully shook it out. I was conscious of the shocked way Seraphina just stood and watched me, but I knew nothing else to do, nothing that I could say to ease her fears—or my own.

Chapter 10

The rest of the day passed quietly enough, at least outwardly; but there was no peace for me. Every time I entered the rear room, either to get an item stored there or to check on the children who played and studied there, I felt a strange sense of menace. Though I knew the room was unchanged, it would never be the same to me.

My conscience also troubled me, for I continued to find myself remembering what had taken place between Nick and me. Too often, when I closed my eyes, I found his fascinating face before me, and when I thought of his lips touching mine ... Had I not been raised to be a lady, I should have used some of the words I had heard so frequently aboard ship. Sleep was hard to find that night and my dreams were troubled.

Still, the days passed. As I had promised Nick, I spoke with my students about the supposed haunting of the cloister—something I now understood much better—and found that he had been partially correct. They had not stayed away simply because of the old stories, but all were relieved when I assured them of their safety in this part of the violence-tainted structure. I only wished I could believe my own reassurances.

Near the end of the week, my class had dwindled to

only two children, so I let them leave shortly after mid-day. I gathered up the almost unused slates and chalk and stacked the books that I had so carefully selected, what seemed a lifetime ago. I could sympathize with Paul's frustration. Not one child from Emerald Acres had attended since midweek, which meant they were being forced to work instead of learn, something I considered wrong.

"Ah, dear Rachel, you must not frown so, you will get wrinkles." Geraldine strode through the open door, stripping off her riding gloves. She halted and looked around, a slight frown touching her elegant features. "My goodness, what has happened to your little school? I thought by now you would be teaching half the island children here."

"Perhaps I should be asking you that question," I snapped, not liking her slightly superior tone. " 'Tis mainly the children from your plantation that have been missing this week."

"Is that so?" She seemed surprised. "Perhaps Duquanne had urgent need of their help in the fields these days. As overseer, he has the right to order them about, you know. But what of the other plantations? Have they not sent their students?"

"A few." Guilt at my show of bad manners forced me into a rueful smile. "They have been missing much of the time, too. I am beginning to appreciate the difficulties Reverend Michaels told me about. But enough of my problems. What brings you to the cloister this lovely afternoon?"

"Why, I wished to visit you, of course. I have missed seeing you, now that the orphanage is a reality. So I thought I should come and discover for myself if everything is going well for you and your charges."

"We are managing, thank you." I watched as she strolled across the room to the window that gave a

162

slight view of the third floor of the Sunrise plantation house.

"Did you enjoy your visit to the village last Sunday?" Her tone was casual, but I knew her too well to be fooled. Geraldine had heard that Nick had accompanied us to church and had come to find out what had happened.

"It was most pleasant. The children enjoyed seeing their friends in the village and the diversion of the trip."

"And Nick, did he enjoy his role?" When she faced me again, her smile in no way melted the frost in her gaze.

"You should ask him." I smothered a highly unworthy smile at this proof that I had been right in my suspicions about her motives for helping me.

"He has been so busy of late . . ." Geraldine wandered around the room again. "I thought perhaps he had been helping out here."

"We also see little of him these days," I admitted, weary of the game of guile she was inspiring me to play. I put the last of the books away, then gave her a genuine smile. "Would you like some lemonade and cookies? Seraphina just made a fresh batch for the children."

"I should love to meet her and see how everything is progressing here. Did I tell you? There are two more children who may soon be needing your care. The father was lost at sea over a year ago, and now the mother is very ill. Will you have room for them? The boy is nine, I believe, and the girl six or seven."

"Of course we will have room. 'Tis why we are here." I led the way to the dining room, suddenly ashamed of my earlier suspicions. Thanks to Geraldine's help, my orphanage was well able to take on more orphans, and I had no reason to be jealous. Nick could never be mine, and he might well have given his heart

163

to her long before my arrival on the island. "Are these children from Emerald Acres?"

"No, they are at Sea Cliff. Baxter Travis just told me about the family yesterday. Have none of your students from there mentioned the Wartons?"

I swallowed a sigh. "I fear I have not yet attracted any students from Sea Cliff. There was one young boy the first few days, but he never returned, so I just assumed that the distance might be too great."

"Sea Cliff workers live a bit closer to this area of Sunrise than our workers do." Geraldine acknowledged the introduction of my assistant, then accepted the cool glass of lemonade from Seraphina, before helping herself to one of the molasses cookies. "I should have thought they would be most eager to make use of the education you offer here."

"Perhaps they are unaware of what we offer," I suggested. "If I can find the time, I shall ask Digger to drive me out that way to talk to whoever is in charge. Reverend Michaels has taken care of all that and I fear my knowledge of the geography of your island is still woefully inadequate."

" 'Tis a pity that you have no horse here. We could ride over together today." Geraldine eyed me, then frowned. "You do ride, do you not?"

"Not since I was a girl. My grandmother kept no riding horses, and once I went to Middle Brook Christian ..." Her tone and expression reminded me forcefully of all the ways we were different, the glaring deficiencies of my upbringing in this world of money and privilege.

"Well, next time, I shall drive over and give you a tour of the plantations. 'Tis about time you met some of the other planters; it seems you spend all your time with the Harrisons. I am surprised that Nick has kept you such a secret."

"I truly have little time for visiting, Geraldine. With the school and the children to care for . . ." I let it trail off, aware that she was no longer listening to me. I followed her gaze and saw Nick cantering away from the plantation house on his handsome stallion.

"Of course you are busy." Geraldine turned back to me with a dazzling smile. "And here I sit, wasting your valuable time. Do forgive me, dear Rachel. I will ride over to Sea Cliff myself today and speak with Baxter. If he is planning to bring you two more mouths to feed, he should at least pay a call first."

She finished her lemonade, called out an airy "Thank you," and was gone before I could think of anything to say. Somehow, I was not surprised when I glimpsed her galloping in the same direction Nick had taken. What bothered me most was the anger and envy I felt. Could I be jealous? Even the question shamed me.

When I turned from the window, Seraphina was standing at the dining table. "What is it?" I asked, sensing from her expression that something was troubling her. I thought at once of the missing loaf of bread and the fallen clothes, but could find no words to ask if something else untoward had taken place.

"Is Miss Chalmers a friend to you?"

The question startled me, but I tried to be honest in my answer. "She was most helpful in the beginning, even brought me to the cloister the first time; but I doubt she has any calling to care for the island children." I hesitated, then my curiosity overwhelmed my sense of proper decorum. "Is there something that I should know, Seraphina? I realize that you once lived at Emerald Acres, so if you . . ." I could not voice my own shameful suspicions about Geraldine and Nick, so I simply let the words trail off, unsure of what to expect.

"That overseer, Duquanne, be evil. Him never let the

165

children come here to listen, 'less Miss Chalmers order it. And that not be likely."

"What do you mean?" I was struck by the bitterness in her voice even when she spoke of Geraldine.

"Afore I talked with Reverend Michaels, I be hearing how you would mistreat the children. That they would be locked away in the cloister. I be afraid to come, but he say the stories wrong, that you be kind and he be right." Seraphine's dark eyes shone with a loyalty that made my throat tighten and made tears burn in my eyes.

I reached out to take her hand. "I am so grateful that you did come. I could never get along without your help. But why would the overseer at Emerald Acres try to keep you from coming? I understood that you needed to leave there."

"It not be him what started the stories. It be her."

"Geraldine said I would hurt the children?" I found that hard to believe. "But she was the one who helped me find this place and encouraged me to ask Mr. Harrison's permission to start the orphanage here. Why would she . . . ?"

Seraphina shrugged. "I not be knowing why, Rachel, but I would never lie to you. Those that urged me to refuse the post here told me what she whispered about you."

"But I thought she was in agreement with the Harrisons about the need for a school and an orphanage on Bell Harbour Island. She even spoke of offering to help Reverend Michaels in his plans."

Seraphine lifted her head and started to turn away. " 'Tis only that I thought you should be warned," she murmured, as she started toward the kitchen.

"Wait." Realizing that I had hurt her feelings by voicing my questions, I hurried around the table to face her. "I have no doubt that you told me the truth, Seraphina.

166

I only wonder why she would say one thing to my face and another behind my back."

Her stiff posture eased as our eyes met. "I know not."

"I thank you for the warning. I shall have a care wherever Geraldine Chalmers is involved. And please, you must do what you can to assure the islanders that the children are safe here. I should hate it if any orphan suffers alone because of some ugly rumor."

"You have little to fear with Digger Blake going about the island speaking your praises. Him carries messages everywhere for Mr. Nick and be talking to everyone."

"He is a good friend."

Seraphina nodded and I thought she might say more, but at that moment a mournful wail came from down the hall and she hurried away to tend to one of the babies. I started after her, thinking to help; but my steps were slowed by the feeling of betrayal and my head spun with confusion. How could I comfort a child when I felt deeply in need of comfort myself?

Could Seraphina be wrong? It made no sense for Geraldine to support me with one hand and destroy me with the other. Perhaps one of the islanders had misunderstood something Geraldine had said, or might it not be the overseer Duquanne who had started the ugly rumors, maybe even attributing them to Geraldine without her knowledge?

That possible explanation eased away some of my hurt and confusion. I might question the depth of Geraldine's interest in the orphanage, but I was loath to believe that she was capable of such duplicity. Still, there was much more I must sort through before I could know whom I should trust and whom I must watch carefully. Taking a couple of cookies to fortify me, I slipped out of the cloister, hoping that the answers would come to me on the breeze that sighed through the palms and tugged at my hair.

Remembering what Nick had said about the burial place of the innocent victims of the island uprising, I chose a barely visible path that led in the opposite direction of the road to Sunrise, shivering as I rounded the corner of the building and stepped into the shadow of the cloister. I looked up at the jade vines that festooned the gray stone of the mighty fortress walls. How strong it appeared, how invincible; yet I had seen the destruction inside, the devastation that still remained after so many years.

How had those long ago women felt when their husbands and fathers brought them here? Had they come with hope, expecting protection from the walls and the monks, who represented an even higher Protector? But the thick walls had not stopped the vengeful islanders.

Frowning, I studied the structure, suddenly wondering why they were still standing, if they had been breached. Nick had made no mention of how the islanders had found their way inside. I continued walking, studying the walls as closely as I could, seeking some sign that a portion might have been rebuilt; but all seemed the same, weathered by time, but intact.

Sighing, I forced such dark speculation from my mind, well aware that my interest was strong only because it was easier to wonder about the past than the present. My concern should not be how the islanders had entered the cloister; I needed to decide how to deal with what Seraphina had told me about Geraldine Chalmers.

The tiny thread of a path lead me down the hill behind the cloister and into the shade of some very old trees. I paused near a thick growth of flowering bushes, my attention caught by what appeared to be a section of a low stone wall. A tiny shiver traced down my spine as

I pushed through the thick growth to reach the wall and then looked beyond it, not sure what I expected to see.

For a moment I was disappointed as I studied the area, for there was nothing to be seen, just a tiny meadow, still partially surrounded by remnants of the stone wall. No trees grew in the circle, no bushes; the afternoon sun caressed only thick grass and a scattering of wildflowers. I started to turn away, then gasped, struck by the implication of the very emptiness of the space. From what I had seen on my journey to and from the village, such lack of heavy undergrowth was not natural here. Obviously, someone had kept the bushes and trees from growing inside the stone wall, someone who knew about those who slept beneath the grass.

That thought eased my sadness a little, for it proved that Nick had been wrong about one thing. Someone *had* cared about the dead; not all the residents of the cloister had died unmourned. Evil had been done there, but perhaps there had also been good.

I settled myself on the top of the wall and looked back up the hill at the dark bulk of the cloister, so proud and strong against the intense blue of the sky. In school I had been told unpleasant things about the monks who had come to the Caribbean with the Spanish conquerors, but I was no longer sure that I should believe everything. Perhaps there were new facts to be learned about the history of the cloister.

Meanwhile, for the sake of the children entrusted to me, I must do my best to bring some peace to the present. In order to do that, I should have to speak with Paul regarding Seraphina's revelations about Geraldine and the overseer at Emerald Acres, I decided. He would know best how to deal with whatever game they were playing and how to keep the children safe, which was, after all, most important.

I smiled at the sunlit meadow. "You can rest in

peace," I whispered, my thoughts again returning to the monks, who would, I suspected, have been men rather like St. Devina's Father Sebastian. "I shall do my best to make you proud of what was once yours. The cloister will be a place of safety and laughter and innocent joy for those who have known too little of it." A gentle breeze caressed my cheek as though in thanks as I got to my feet again and started back up the hill.

As I neared the cloister's walls, I caught the distant sound of hoofbeats, and my thoughts turned to Nick. Should I tell him what Seraphina had said? It would be easy to confide in him, to ask if he really believed Geraldine would behave so deviously; but I knew I must not. It was not my place to come between old friends or question the motives of one who had helped me. Besides, in my heart, I knew I would always suspect my motives, if I did. Still, I hurried around the huge building, hoping that I would find Nick's horse tied near the entrance.

The front of the cloister appeared just as deserted as it had been when I left. Shamed by my disappointment, I stepped inside, determined to put my foolish fantasies aside and tend to my duties. What would Reverend Bennett think, had he seen me idling away my time dreaming about past residents of this troubled structure—or wondering about the handsome man whose kisses had somehow addled my senses?

"Ah, Miss . . . Rachel, there you be." Seraphina came hurrying through the doorway from the dining room, her usually placid expression now marred by a frown. "I was beginning to fear that something . . ."

"I went for a walk, that is all." I fought back my flare of irritation, suddenly remembering the child that had cried out before I left. "Has something happened? Is one of the children unwell?"

"No, all are safe." She spoke quickly, but without a change in her expression.

"Then what troubles you, Seraphina?" I softened my tone at once. "Has something else happened?"

" 'Tis Elena, Rachel. She was getting that old rag doll from the playroom, the one that little Inez is so fond of. Anyway, she came screaming to me, claiming that she saw someone in there."

"Whom did she see?" My stomach tightened at the thought of someone in our sanctuary.

"Her say it be one of the black robes come back." Seraphina's grim expression told me that she took Elena's words seriously.

"A monk?" For a heartbeat, I shared her chill, then the sheer ridiculousness of the child's claim eased my fears. "Where did she see this ghostly image?"

Seraphina shrugged. "In the playroom, be all I know. She refuses to talk about it now, just huddles on her bed, holding Inez and crying. 'Tis why I be seeking you, Rachel. The child is terrified."

"Have you looked in the playroom?"

She nodded. "I saw nothing."

"Shall we look again, together, just to be sure?" I moved ahead of her, leading the way along the hall, then stepping into the silent room at the end of it.

I took my time peering around, studying each shadowy corner, then I crossed and opened each of the wardrobes so that I could look inside. There was, of course, nothing to see. The room was empty of life, yet as I turned back to Seraphina, I felt the chill of watching eyes prickling on the nape of my neck. A shiver chased down my spine in spite of the warmth of the day.

"What is it?" Seraphina seemed to sense my discomfort. "Did you see something?"

"Nothing. 'Twas just a shadow that Elena saw, I sus-

171

pect. Undoubtedly the result of all the tales that are told about this place. Shall we go and reassure her?"

It proved more difficult than I had expected, for Elena clung to her story with a tenacity that made me wonder, even as I assured her she had seen only a shadow, if she might be speaking the truth. But how could someone disappear through a solid wall? I had no desire to believe in ghosts, but I knew the shelf in the far corner to be sturdy, and there was not enough space between it and the other shelves for a man to hide.

Finally, Seraphina persuaded Elena to help her with the preparations for the evening meal and I took the rest of the children to the playroom to dispell the gloom that I had felt there. Watching the little ones racing about, giggling and enjoying the toys that Nick had brought from the Sunrise playroom, eased away the shadows for me, and I felt almost light of heart as I hurried them off to wash before taking them to the dining room.

Only later, when the children were all in their beds and Seraphina had retired to her bedchamber, did my troubling thoughts return. What if Elena had seen someone? Not a ghost, for I had no belief in such things; but a person. I had heard often enough that someone wished us harm, and how better to cause it than by making the ghosts of the cloister seem real? But how?

For a moment, I considered asking Nick for help in finding out what might be going on; but memories of what had happened between us in the devastated section of the cloister made me sure than I dared not turn to him. Should I ask Paul? I could go to him, of course, but would he believe me? Would anyone believe me? Would I have believed it myself had I not felt the presence of someone or something in that room? I really could not be sure.

So what should I do? The answer was disturbingly simple. I needed to find some proof that a person had slipped into the room. My stomach knotted in protest as I picked up a lamp and headed resolutely for my door. If I was going to ask Paul for help, I would have to search the playroom first.

My footsteps echoed in the hall and the lamp cast eerie shadows about the playroom when I stepped through the door. It took all my courage to hold my ground until the uneasy darkness settled into recognizable shadows cast by the sparse furnishings and bulky wardrobes. Remembering the fallen clothing, I headed for the big wardrobe again, opening the door and studying the interior with great care.

Everything seemed to be in place. I closed the door and moved along the wall to the inside corner where Elena had said the ghostly shape had vanished. Again, I could see nothing new or different. The books and blocks on the shelves were tumbled in untidy confusion, but that was hardly surprising, considering the children used them often. Feeling foolish, I set the lamp on the floor and began to straighten them.

I had nearly finished when I caught a glint of metal in a spot at the rear of the shelf that had been hidden by the books. I reached past them to pull out whatever might be hidden there. My fingers closed over a small handle, and when I tugged on it, the whole shelf eased away from the wall. Shock sent me staggering backward.

Once I had steadied myself, I gazed at my discovery. For a moment I saw only darkness where the shelf had been, then the lamp's glow reached past me and I saw that the bottom of the shelf had hidden an opening in the floor. Swallowing my fear, I lifted the lamp and I could see that carved stone steps descended from the opening into the darkness below.

"Rachel, what have you found?" Seraphina's gasping

words startled me so that I almost dropped the lamp into the abyss.

It was several minutes before I could get enough breath into my lungs to answer her. "The shelf moves out. There is a hidden handle."

Slowly, fearfully, she crossed the room to join me, and together we held our lamps over the stairway and peered down into the darkness. "What do you think it be?" she asked.

I shrugged. "Could the cloister have a cellar?"

"There is one beneath the big house at Emerald Acres, but here?" She gazed fearfully at the darkness. "I not be going down there."

I closed my eyes, feeling the same reluctance that she was, but unable to deny my curiosity. "I shall go down." I was proud that my voice sounded steady. "You stay here and hold your light over the opening and make sure that the shelf stays where it is now." I showed her the handle I had discovered, then took a firm grip on my lamp.

"Don't go!" Seraphina's voice was high with fear. "You not be knowing what might be down there."

Though I shared her fear, I fought it back, taking a deep breath so that my voice should not betray me. "We shall never know what lies below unless I do go."

"Perhaps we should just close it and wait for Mr. Nick or the Reverend or even Digger." Her hand was shaking so that her lamp flickered ominously.

"And if there is someone hiding down there, would they not slip away or worse this night?" I stepped carefully on the first of the stone stairs, wishing that I could just close my eyes to this discovery and return to my peaceful bedchamber.

"Take care, then." Seraphina's voice steadied, and so did her hand. More light spilled ahead of me, and as it did so, I became aware of something I had missed before. The steps were thickly covered with the debris of time and mice. I was relieved to note that my foot seemed to be the first to disturb this collection of dust.

Taking heart, I moved more quickly down the stairs, my attention now focused on the darkness beyond the bottom of the steps. As my lamp's feeble light pushed back the blackness, I noted the earthen floor and solid rock walls of a quite ordinary, though large, cellar.

"What be down there?" Seraphina's voice followed me as I stepped into the huge room.

"A cellar. Very large and, it appears, completely empty." I gazed around again, both relieved and disappointed. A hidden staircase seemed to hint at something important, like possibly the hiding place of the treasure so often mentioned in the tales of the cloister's violent past. I shook my head, embarrassed at my own too-vivid imagination. Still, I progressed a bit further into the room, wanting to be sure that no rooms opened off this chamber.

"Are you all right? Be there any sign of an intruder?"

Turning back, I cast my gaze to the floor, which bore clear traces of my passage. "I doubt anyone has been here in years. If Elena truly saw an intruder, this was not his destination."

As I climbed back up, I studied the rear of the shelf, seeing for the first time that there was a handle there, too. Looking at the wall against which the stairs had been carved, I could see that there would be a space between the closed shelf and the stone side of the building. A person could have slipped inside and hidden there, then left again once the room was empty. Not a consoling thought, but one I determined to keep to myself. Seraphina was already frightened enough; I had no desire to risk her fear driving her to leave the cloister.

"Did you truly find nothing?" she asked, as I emerged.

"Why not go and see for yourself?" I urged her to explore, hoping that she would be reassured by the normal appearance of the old cellar.

She took far less time down there than I had, but returned to me with a look of relief. " 'Tis as you said, just a cellar. But why should it be hidden this way?"

Luckily, I had used my moments alone at the top of the stairs to delve into that question myself and I had come up with what I hoped was an acceptable answer. "Perhaps those who walled off the rest of the cloister felt it might attract anyone who wished to hide and so kept temptation from those who might take refuge in this part of the building."

Seraphina nodded. "What do you intend to do about it now that we have found it?"

Another tricky question, but one for which I had also prepared an answer. "I think it best that we forget our discovery for the present."

"But Mr. Nick and the Reverend . . ."

"Would wish to explore it." I interrupted her protest. "And they would do so during the day, when the children are about. Think of the danger to the little ones, should they discover the lever and decide to open it themselves."

Her dark eyes grew grave as she pictured the possibilities. "It would be dangerous for them."

I nodded. "So long as no one else knows, they are safe. Also, it is quite possible that Nick knows about the staircase. After all, his family were the ones to wall off the rest of the building to protect those who might use this part of it. If he chose to keep the secret, why should we not?"

"No one will learn of it from me."

Relieved by her promise, I closed the shelf again, then marveled at the perfect way it disguised what lay behind it. Whoever had constructed the device had been

176

clever. But not so clever that I had missed it, I thought, reveling in my discovery.

My good humor lasted until I bade Seraphina good night and retired once more to my small sitting room. Only then did I realize that though I had made an interesting discovery, I still had no idea whom or what Elena had seen in the playroom. That realization made sleep a long time coming and filled my dreams with shapeless, but threatening, shadows.

Chapter 11

Though I had expected the haunting images of the night to follow me about through the day, I quickly discovered that I had no time to worry about Elena's shadows or the hidden cellar. Trey and Carol Warton, the orphans from Sea Cliff, arrived in a battered old wagon driven by a most unfriendly man shortly before noon the next day.

Having been alerted about an approaching wagon by one of the children, I hurried out to welcome whoever it might be with a smile. "Good day," I greeted the cold-eyed man who reined in the skinny mule. "How may I help you?"

"You be the one what takes in orphans?" He made no move to get down for the wagon, forcing me to look up at him.

"This is the orphanage." Though the morning was bright, I felt as though a cloud had covered the sun. "I am Rachel Ames. And you are?"

"I come from Sea Cliff. You be takin' them two?" He jerked a thumb at the children who huddled together in the wagon bed, not even looking over his shoulder at them.

"We should welcome them." I smiled at the children,

my heart aching for them as I pictured their long ride with this surly driver. "I was told that Mr. Travis . . ."

"Get out." His order was directed at the children, but the rudeness of his interruption was like a slap in the face.

"Let me help you." I hurried to the side of the wagon to offer my arms to the boy and girl, who appeared to be about Elena's age; but they both jumped from the wagon without my assistance. "Where are your belongings?" I peered into the wagon bed, which seemed to hold only straw.

"Them gots nothin'." The man slapped the reins on the mule's back and the wagon creaked away scarcely missing my toes with its rear wheel.

Anger made me want to run after the man, to demand some details about the children; but seeing the anguish in their dirty faces, I pushed him from my mind. He could be dealt with some other time; these two needed me now. I forced a smile that I was far from feeling. "So tell me, what are your names?"

Their shyness had them speaking only in whispers until Seraphina and Elena came out to join me. Having lived her entire life on the island, Seraphina recognized the children and introduced them to me, then spoke to them of their parents, easing the moment.

Elena, bless her caring heart, did the rest, for she quickly requested that Carol, the seven-year-old, be allowed to share the room with her and Inez. Then, seeing Trey's worried expression, she assured him that he would be right across the hall with Ben and Nathan.

By midday, the children were bathed and dressed in clean clothing from the supply that filled the wardrobes. They ate as though starved, though I doubted that they had been, for they appeared healthy enough. Later, since there were no lessons, they were soon caught up in the games that the other children had devised and I was free to take a moment to discuss them with Seraphina.

"Who was the man who brought the children?" I asked, thinking that I should like to speak to Nick or Paul about him.

"He be the man what works for the overseer at Sea Cliff. Blaine, I believe, he be called. A nasty one, as you could tell. You keep clear of him, Rachel. He be no gentleman." Her frown made her worry obvious.

"I thought I might walk to Sunrise and discuss his actions with Mr. Harrison."

"'Tis unlikely him be able to do anything." Seraphina sighed. "Mr. Travis be that set upon keeping his overseer. He claims Mr. Humbolt be the best on the island at raising crops and keeping his workers in line."

"But if this Blaine only works for the overseer . . ." I began, then stopped, realizing how little I knew of how the plantations were operated. "Has he power, too?"

"He carries out Humbolt's night orders." Seraphina looked away from me. "That be what cannot be done in daylight."

I waited for her to go on, but she only continued to stare at the dining room floor. Finally, I could bear the silence no longer. "What do you mean?"

"Things go on that nobody in the big house knows about." She moved nervously. "And that be all I kin say. It not be safe to know more."

My outrage made me want to press her for details, for I was sure that there must be redress for whatever wrongs were being done; but something about her expression stopped me. I realized that I had no right to force her to risk her own safety just to satisfy my curiosity. Swallowing my frustrated anger, I nodded. "I shall tell Mr. Harrison only of the man's rudeness and ask that we be told more about the children who are brought to us."

Seraphina's relief worried me more than her warning. What power did these overseers hold? And why was it that Sunrise was the only plantation on the island that had none? I longed to discuss this with Nick, for I was sure he could explain it to me. But then I remembered my decision to keep my distance from him. It would, I supposed, be better to ask Mr. Harrison my questions.

"Will you be able to see to the children for a time?"

"Have no worry, I shall keep them safe." Her serene smile was back in place, and as I turned away, it struck me that she had become my right arm. Without her to help me, I should have been lost here.

The walk to Sunrise was quite long, but pleasant, for the afternoon was sunny, yet not too warm. As I looked at the fields and meadows that bordered the roadway, I realized how much I had come to love this island—and how desperately I wanted to stay here.

Would I be allowed to remain? Though all was going smoothly at the orphanage, I still had almost no students to teach and no knowledge of how to gain more. Should Paul decide that what I was attempting was not what he wanted . . . I pushed the thought away, suddenly less sure that I should speak with Mr. Harrison about the newest of my charges. If my anger at this Blaine caused trouble for Paul . . .

I slowed, then finally turned away from the road to Sunrise and headed instead toward the path that led down to the shore. Mayhap I should be better served by complaining to Paul after service tomorrow. It was, after all, his orphanage, though it rested upon Harrison land. That resolved, I detoured to the headlands, preferring to stare down at the restless sea now that I had made my decision.

As I crossed a bit of meadow, I caught the distinct sound of hoofbeats and my heart leaped. Surely if what I heard was Nick approaching, it would be Providence that brought us together and none of my doing. I turned toward the sound, dizzy from my longing and anticipation.

The rider broke out of the trees and my excitement quickly ebbed, for he was a stranger. Feeling very much exposed in the open grassland, I took a few steps toward the nearest band of trees, hoping to slip into their shadows and thus escape his notice. My earlier encounter with the surly man from Sea Cliff had taught me the value of caution.

"Miss Ames." The man guided his mount in my direction. "Please wait."

I stopped, my uneasiness growing as the man approached me. His mount and his clothing marked him as a gentleman, but Nick and Paul's warnings still echoed in my mind. If they were unsure of who might want to hurt me, how was I to know whom I could trust?

"You are Miss Ames, are you not?" He reined in the big white horse, then dismounted, taking off his hat so that I could see his face clearly for the first time.

I nodded, tongue-tied under the impact of his silver-blue eyes. The man was handsome enough to be the subject of a painting; he lacked only shining armor or perhaps the golden glow of sainthood that marked the pictures I had seen. Black hair waved back from his forehead, and his perfect features easily formed a smile that once would have set my heart to pounding.

"Forgive me for startling you, Miss Ames, but I just came from the cloister. The woman there told me that you had gone to Sunrise, but I saw you walking this way, and . . ." He extended a hand. "I am Baxter Travis, come to apologize for the way the Warton children were dumped on your doorstep."

"Mr. Travis." My voice sounded odd even in my own ears, never a good sign; but I was too addled to do more than just give him my hand.

182

"I had planned to pay a call on your orphanage this morning, but there were difficulties, and Blaine left with the children while I was occupied with plantation business. I hope that you were not too deeply inconvenienced by not having been told to expect them."

"I ... ah ... actually, I knew that they were coming, though not when. Geraldine Chalmers mentioned ..." I found myself having great difficulty forming proper sentences, perhaps because he was still holding my hand.

"Dear Geraldine, she is so helpful." His lazy smile curled around me as I gently freed my fingers from his grip. "You will be able to keep the children, then?"

I met his gaze and the illusion of caring charm that had so dizzied me vanished, for I found no warmth in his eyes. It became much easier to speak as my sanity returned. "We have already welcomed them. Did you not see them when you stopped at the cloister? I am sure, had you asked, Seraphina would have been pleased to ..."

He stopped me with a gesture. "'Twas not necessary. I came only to apologize for any inconvenience caused by their arrival. From the good reports I have heard, I have every confidence that you will take excellent care of any child you take in."

"You are most kind."

"And you are a very lovely young lady, Miss Ames, something no one bothered to tell me. I believe I now understand why Nick has been keeping you so close to Sunrise." His admiring gaze brought heat to my cheeks, but I felt little pleasure in the compliment or his mention of Nick.

"I have been occupied with my work in the orphanage." This would never do, I decided, forcing myself to meet his gaze. I had to take control of this conversation before the man said anything more about Nick and me.

183

Remembering what Seraphina had told me, I decided to see if I could put him on his mettle. "And, of course, I have been trying to offer lessons to the children of the nearby plantations. But perhaps you were unaware of that, since I have had no students from Sea Cliff."

Had I not been watching for it, I should have missed the odd flicker of anger in the depths of his icy-blue eyes; but I saw it and knew that my words had touched a sore spot. His smile still came easily, this time with a chuckle. "The whole island has heard of your school, Miss Ames. I only regret that none of the Sea Cliff children seem disposed to take advantage of what you offer. Perhaps they are just not ready for education."

"They have no desire to learn?" I was too shocked to hide my skepticism. "But on that first day . . ."

"Were some of my workers at your school?" His tone and expression were both casual, but something about the way he had interrupted sent a chill of warning through me.

"I thought there was one young boy . . . or was it a girl?" I stared down at my shoes, finding prevarication difficult, but sure that it was necessary to protect the child who had come to my schoolroom but once. "But perhaps I misunderstood. I know so little about the island, I could have been confused as to where the child came from. I know only that there are no students from Sea Cliff."

"Perhaps that will change when Reverend Michaels rebuilds his school in the village." Mr. Travis took my arm, gently urging me forward, toward the bluffs that rose above the pounding waves. "Where were you bound this afternoon, pretty Miss Ames? Surely you know this is not the way to Sunrise."

His tone was teasing, but I felt only the sharp twinge of guilt followed by a stab of anger at his casual assumption that I welcomed his company or owed him an explanation. I choked back my temper firmly, remembering how much I could lose by angering the wrong person. "I had thought to speak with one of the servants at Sunrise regarding transport to the village for church tomorrow, but the day was so lovely, I decided to walk this way first."

"Has Nick not warned you of the dangers of wandering about the island alone? Or did you expect to meet him out here?" His friendly smile seemed securely in place as he looked down at me, but it did nothing to disguise the coldness in his gaze.

"What?" I stopped, pulling my arm free of his grasp. "How dare you suggest such a . . ." I had no word to describe what he seemed to be saying. I pushed impatiently at the wildly curling tendrils of hair that blew across my eyes with a hand that was shaking. "Never have I been so insulted."

Baxter Travis caught my hand, perhaps sensing that I was ready to flee. "I meant no insult, lovely lady, I assure you. 'Tis only that I had heard that Nick was quite besotted with you." He seemed genuinely contrite. "I humbly beg your forgiveness, Miss Ames, 'tis only that our Nick has quite the reputation with the ladies, and since he had the opportunity of meeting you first on St. Devina . . ."

"He was there to help the Verdugo children and to bring me to Bell Harbour as a favor to Reverend Michaels." I held myself stiff, though I could feel the impact of his most attractive smile and the charm he seemed able to produce at will.

"And he brought you directly to Sunrise."

The injustice of that observation fired my temper. "Where would you have had us stay—in the church? Or in the village without a chaperone? Nick brought us to his family home, where the children and I remained until Mr. Harrison arranged with Reverend Michaels for

185

the cloister to become our orphanage. To infer anything from those circumstances is to insult my host, Reverend Michaels, and myself, as well as to question the work I came here to do."

"You must forgive me, dear lady, but I fear that you have been the subject of the island's gossips. I must warn you, tongues have been wagging."

Though I had lived much of my adult life in the peaceful confines of Middle Brook Christian, I was aware enough of the ways of the world to believe him. "I feared it might be thus," I admitted, touched also by my guilty knowledge that such gossip might not be totally unfounded, not after the way Nick had kissed me. "But I know not how to make it stop except by going about my calling and doing the best that I am able."

Mr. Travis tucked my hand beneath his arm again. "Perhaps it would help if you were seen about the island with someone other than Nick, someone such as I? Would that not stop the talk?"

"You?" I was too stunned by the suggestion to hide my shock.

"Am I so repulsive that you would not consider it?" His eyes were full of laughter as he looked down at me. "What if I offered to escort you into the village for services tomorrow? Would you accept?"

Though I felt no desire to spend any more time in his company, I could see the wisdom of what he was offering. Yet how would trading one escort for another benefit my supposely already tarnished reputation? Still, this was an opportunity to become better acquainted with Mr. Travis, and perhaps to win him to our way of thinking about education. If I could convince him to let the children of Sea Cliff attend my classes . . . "What of the orphans? They will be expected at worship also."

"Bring the whole wagonload. I have no objection." His grin deepened, reflecting concern and warmth. "In

186

fact, if you wish, I can save you the walk to the plantation house. Just tell me what you will need and I shall inform the servants there when you wish them to arrive at the cloister."

Even as misgivings twisted inside me, I yielded to his urging and answered his questions about the arrangements, then allowed him to escort me back to the cloister. Perhaps it was better that I not chance seeing Nick today, I reasoned, as I gazed longingly toward Sunrise.

Mr. Travis bade me a pleasant farewell at the door, then mounted his horse and cantered away. Yet I hesitated outside, frowning as I watched him disappear behind a grove of trees. I should be pleased with what I was doing, yet I felt only dread when I thought of tomorrow.

"Be you safe, Rachel? He did you no harm?" Seraphina's soft voice brought my attention back to the present, and I finally stepped inside the cloister.

"What?" I was shocked by the concern I could read in her face. "Why should you think Mr. Travis would harm me?"

"He be no friend to what we do here." Her gaze became veiled as though my sharp tone had made her doubt the wisdom of speaking out.

"He sent two children to us, and that was why he came, to apologize for not having asked our permission first." I managed a reassuring smile. "I am sorry that you were concerned, Seraphina. Was it because of something he said when he stopped here?"

"He was most polite, Rachel, merely inquiring where you might be found. Since I could not be sure, I suggested that he try asking at Sunrise. I hope that caused no trouble."

Her words reminded me that I had left without advising her of where I was going, something I knew I should not have done. "It was perfectly proper, and I

187

apologize for not having told you that I was just taking a walk to clear my head."

Seraphina nodded, then turned away, but not before I caught a glimpse of the disbelief in her expression. Suddenly, I wondered if she, too, had heard the gossips' tales. Could she have suspected I had an assignation with Nick? The very possibility sent a chill through me. One thing my years at Middle Brook Christian had taught me was that anyone who cared for innocent children must be above reproach.

"I was disturbed by the way that man Blaine behaved and thought to speak with Mr. Harrison about it; but as I walked, I changed my mind. Mr. Travis found me strolling on the bluffs above the sea. He was quite pleasant and has offered to escort us into the village tomorrow, so perhaps he is changing his mind about the work we do here." I offered the explanation as casually as I could, hoping that it would convince her that there was no basis to any story she might have heard about Nick and me.

"He is going to services?" Her shock was complete as she turned back to face me.

"Is that so strange? I understood that Reverend Michaels was brought here to serve the spiritual needs of all the island residents, not just the workers and orphans." I spoke quickly, hoping to learn something, for I had noticed that Nick had been the only member of a planter family attending last Sunday's services.

"'Twas the planters that built the new church, but since Mr. Harrison was taken bad last year, there been few who have attended. 'Tis said Reverend Michaels offended them by insisting that the students should put their schooling ahead of working in the fields."

"The Reverend can be quite outspoken," I admitted, happy to accept this explanation for the animosity that I sensed surrounding Paul, "but I think in time the

188

planters will have to realize that their workers would be more valuable if they were educated." I thought of Harriet and her desire to improve her reading skill and wondered how many of the older islanders shared that longing. If there were several, perhaps I might add a weekly lesson in the early morning or late evening when they had completed their duties.

I was about to make such a suggestion to Seraphina when a crash followed by the wails of several children sent us both racing along the hall to the rear playroom. By the time the squabble was settled and the toys picked up, the moment had passed and I was once again caught up in my duties.

As I had been concerned about spending time in the company of Baxter Travis, I was shocked and appalled when he arrived not on horseback, as Nick had, but driving a smart little carriage. His charm was much in evidence as he explained, "Since I knew the children and your assistant would be traveling in the wagon from Sunrise, I thought we might have a chance to talk on the way to the village, Miss Ames. There is much I should like to know about this venture of yours.'

It was an irresistible invitation, and talking about my dreams for the cloister's future made the drive to the village seem short. By the time we arrived, I had grown quite fond of Baxter, as he asked me to address him. His interest seemed quite genuine, and as we spoke, he even offered a few suggestions for winning over the other planters.

He was easy to laugh with, full of witticisms and slightly wicked observations about the planters I had yet to meet. I was feeling most light of heart when he helped me from the carriage and took my arm as we crossed to the church. Everything changed, however, the moment we mounted the steps and met Paul in the open doorway.

Paul's smile seemed to congeal, and his gray eyes were suddenly as dark and stormy as the sea during a squall. "Rachel, I had thought . . ." He stopped and his smile returned, tight and stiff now. "Welcome to our poor church, Mr. Travis." His tone was formal and chill as a northern winter.

"I look forward to attending, Reverend." Baxter's tone was warm and slightly edged with amusement. "Miss Ames has told me how movingly you speak."

I swallowed hard at his lie, for we had spoken little about Paul or the church; but I could do nothing but nod to Paul and allow Baxter to lead me forward. Even reminding myself that my mission was to convert Baxter Travis to our way of thinking did nothing to restore the joy I had felt on the drive in. Paul's attitude made it clear that there was animosity aplenty on both sides of the controversy that seemed to be tearing the island apart and it seemed I had made it worse, not better, by my impetuous acceptance of Baxter's invitation.

Fortunately, the wiggly children kept me too busy to worry during the service. I was also relieved that Paul appeared to have regained his composure as he spoke in glowing terms of spiritual grace and mentioned nothing about his dreams for the islanders.

This day, I had no intention of lingering as I had last week with Nick, but Paul stopped me at the door. "If Mr. Travis will excuse us, we need to have a few words, Miss Ames. There are several matters regarding the children . . ." The formal politeness of Paul's request told me that his anger had not dissipated after all, and my stomach was knotted with anxiety as I followed him back through the church to a small room I had not seen before.

Paul turned on me the moment the door closed behind us. "What are you doing in the company of a man like Baxter Travis?"

"Bringing the children to services." His tone banished my doubts and I stiffened my spine to face him without wincing. "You asked no questions when Nick Harrison escorted us last Sunday, so I thought it wise to bring others among the planters into our fold."

"You what?" His vehemence eased slightly, perhaps tempered by shock, for he appeared quite stunned by my words.

I hurried to recount what had happened yesterday, beginning with the unheralded arrival of the Warton children, then continuing with Baxter's apology and kind offer. Naturally, I omitted any mention of his words about the gossip that had followed my visit to church last Sunday. "Since he expressed an interest in our work at the orphanage, I thought that I might convince him of the value of allowing the children of his workers to attend my poor school." I paused, then added, "Was I mistaken, Paul?"

His silence made clear his difficulty in answering, but I managed to wait without showing my impatience. For the first time, I felt that I might be making an important contribution to our future on Bell Harbour Island, and I desperately wanted to know if he would accept it.

"I can see that your reasons were noble, Rachel, but I must warn you that Baxter Travis has been outspoken in his animosity toward our cause. Forgive me for my show of anger, but I have good reason to suspect his motives in befriending you. You would do well to guard yourself when you are in his company."

"He has been a perfect gentleman, Paul. And most interested in everything about how we changed the cloister into an orphanage. I suspect that he was simply uninformed before. It may be that he will become a supporter, and could that not aid our cause with the other planters?" Relief made me effusive.

"If you manage that, dear Rachel, I shall believe you

devinely inspired." His smile was gentle and sweet, reminding me of the man who had once filled my heart with dreams, and I felt a surge of happiness when he took my hands in his. "Meanwhile, I ask only that you be careful in your attempts to make peace. I should be deeply wounded if it brought you grief."

"I am always mindful of my responsibility to the children, Paul. I take no chances." I waited, expecting to feel the delight that had surged through me when Nick had touched me; but my happiness faded as quickly as it had come, leaving only the warmth of friendship between us. A pleasant sensation, but not one to fill my nights with tender romantic dreams.

Paul nodded, then released my hands and began asking about the needs of the children, mentioning several other orphans who might be sent to the cloister. I answered his questions proudly, basking in the glow of feeling a real part of what he was doing here. No longer was I the outsider, confused and frightened; I was in charge of the cloister, and of my own fate. It was a feeling I treasured and wanted more than anything to keep.

When our discussion was ended, I hurried back outside, worried that I had inconvenienced Baxter by keeping him waiting. As I stepped into the sunlight, however, I discovered that Baxter was well entertained. He and Geraldine Chalmers were deep in conversation as they stood in the shade of a handsome old tree.

Geraldine was the first to see me, and her greeting seemed warmer than I expected. In fact, she chatted with me for several minutes about "our charming orphanage" and all her efforts to assist me. All the while she batted her eyelashes at Baxter Travis. I found her behavior most unseemly and was hard put to keep my smile pleasant.

"'Tis a shame you missed services," I observed, when

she paused for breath. "Reverend Michaels was most inspiring. Did you not think so, Baxter?"

"Definitely. I had thought to compliment him, but his business with you appeared quite urgent . . ." Baxter's curiosity was charmingly obvious.

"He wished to inform me that I may have more charges soon, and . . ." Mentioning the children reminded me that I had been neglecting them and I glanced around. The wagon was gone! "Where are Seraphina and the children?" I was shocked and ashamed that I had been so tardy in my notice.

"The little ones were growing restless," Geraldine informed me. "I suggested that Digger start back with them. I knew you would have no trouble catching up. Baxter drives that little carriage like a man possessed."

"Now, you must not be telling Rachel such tales," Baxter protested. "She knows how carefully I drove on the way here."

Their teasing continued for several moments, making me feel an outsider, so I was glad when Geraldine announced that she must be on her way. I had had more than enough of her company. It was only after she rode off that I wondered if she had come to the village specifically to see if I was again being escorted to church by Nick. And if she might be riding off now to find him—a possibility that did nothing to restore my good humor.

"We should be off, too, since I must be at the cloister to help Seraphina with the noon meal. The children will be very hungry after such a long journey." I turned toward the waiting carriage.

"Must you return immediately?" Baxter assisted me into the highly polished conveyance, then took his place beside me. "I had hoped that we might stop by Sea Cliff on the way. I should like to introduce you to my family."

193

I hesitated a moment, tempted by the opportunity of meeting more of the planters, but I realized that I could never neglect my duties. Besides, I had a strong suspicion that Paul would disapprove of such a visit. "That is a charming prospect, Baxter, but I fear I must hurry on back to the cloister. The children need me."

"Another time, perhaps. Would you be free to take the evening meal with us one day soon? Or perhaps I could escort you to one of the parties that serve our local society?" His smile showed no hint of anger at my refusal, which was a relief.

"I am not sure what would be proper," I murmured, shocked by his casual invitation.

"You should make dear Geraldine mightily happy if you accepted my invitation." Baxter's eyes held a glint of mischief.

"Whatever do you mean?"

"I suspect she might be one source of the rumors about you and Nick. After all, she has the best reason to resent all his attention to you." His expression had become serious, and I felt a chill as I looked into his eyes, then away.

"I fear I do not understand what you mean." Or was I really afraid that I did understand? It was a question I had no desire to answer.

"They have been promised to each other since childhood. Both their fathers desire a union of Sunrise and Emerald Acres. A prospect I personally find uninteresting, but they are both devoted to the betterment of their plantations. 'Tis surprising to me that they are still unwed. But then, you would know all about that, having spent so much time in Nick and Geraldine's company." There was a mocking note in Baxter's voice.

The words struck me like a blow to the stomach, robbing me of breath and bringing the sting of tears to my eyes. For a moment, I feared I should be unable to speak, then a healing anger spread through me. That was exactly what he wanted, I realized. He had delivered the facts in just that way so as to wound me, but why? Could it be that he still suspected my involvement with Nick and chose this method to find proof that he was right?

The very suspicion stiffened my will, and I managed what I hoped was a credible smile. "Since my contact with both Nick and Geraldine has always involved only their assistance with the orphanage, such personal matters were never discussed. I do, however, see what a well-suited pair they are, and I hope that Geraldine's foolish imagination does nothing to jeopardize the arrangements their families have made."

Once I finished speaking, it took all my self-control to keep from crying out at the pain that came from my lies. Still, the shock that washed over Baxter's handsome face as he digested my words was some reward, as was the grudging respect in the glance he sent my way before he whipped the horse into a fast trot and headed along the narrow road in pursuit of the slower farm wagon. It was not, however, much balm to my shattered heart, nor would it help me rebuild all my broken dreams.

Chapter 12

I was so sunk in my own despair that I scarce noticed anything beyond the rough jouncing of the carriage as we raced along the rough track. It took my full concentration to blink back all the tears that filled my eyes when I thought of what might have been. Finally, however, Baxter slowed the beast to a more respectable pace.

"Are you all right, Rachel?" His voice was surprisingly gentle. "You have been so silent since we left the village."

For a moment, I was tempted to plead illness; but my strict upbringing kept me from using such a lie. Instead, I straightened my shoulders and turned to face him. "You must forgive me, but I find myself a bit weary from the long drive. And it was hard to speak when we were moving so rapidly."

"Are you sure you cannot change your mind and accept my invitation? I know my mother and aunt would delight in spoiling you the rest of the day." He took my hand.

He seemed so kind, I was drawn to him, tempted to let him ease away my feelings of betrayal with his compliments and light words. If he was willing to take me to meet his family, it must mean that he was free to . . . to what? To kiss me as Nick had? To make me feel the delightful sensations that . . .

I forced the scandalous thoughts from my mind, suddenly aware that Baxter was watching me expectantly. Swallowing the lump in my throat, I shook my head. "'Tis sweet of you to offer, and I do thank you for the invitation, but I came to Bell Harbour Island to care for the children, and that is what I must do."

"Every hour of every day and night?" He lifted my hand to his lips, then turned it over so that my palm was against his mouth. His teeth nibbled at my skin, and his tongue tickled the spot before he released my fingers. "I think not, dear Rachel. You are too much woman to be always shut away in that dark and fearful cloister. When you have forgotten your feelings for Nick Harrison, I shall be more than willing to show you the joys of living on Bell Harbour Island."

I opened my mouth to protest, fury and shame heating my cheeks as I buried my trembling hand in the folds of my gown. Unfortunately, I was too unsettled by all that had happened this day to find the words to tell him what a cad he was. For that reason, we made the last of our ride to the cloister in stony silence, arriving just as Digger was lifting the last child from the wagon.

I tried to scramble from the carriage on my own, but my shock had left me clumsy and Baxter was too quick. As he clasped his hands about my waist, he winked at me. "I shall be coming by from time to time, dear Rachel, for I know you will soon be ready for someone who can give you the attention you deserve."

My fury blazed, and the strength of anger kept me on my feet. I had to bite my tongue to keep from shouting at him. Instead, I gave him a polite little smile. "I thank you for escorting me to services, Mr. Travis. It has been . . . interesting. Good day." I turned and, scooping up Inez, headed for the sanctuary of the cloister's stout stone walls.

Once inside, I leaned against the cool wall, trying to draw strength from it as I waited for the shudders to stop. Never had I been so shamefully treated by a man pretending to be a gentleman—or so shamed by my own weakness. Not that I was tempted by Baxter Travis, for I knew now that Paul was quite right to warn me against him; he was truly not my friend. It was my weakness for Nick Harrison that made me ache, for even after what Baxter had confided, I still longed to feel Nick's arms around me, his lips on mine.

"Is something amiss, Rachel?" Seraphina ordered the children on their way, even lifting Inez from my arms and sending her with her sister. "Are you all right?"

"Just a moment of weakness." I straightened up. "We had to hurry to catch up with you and all the jouncing ..." I let it trail off, wishing mightily that I could confide in this kindly woman, but afraid to trust anyone now.

"'Twas no need for such speed. I can see to the children. Why not just lie down for a bit? Elena and Carol can help with the midday meal. They both fancy themselves my assistants." Her genuine concern shamed me.

"Nonsense." I patted her arm. "I am right as rain now. 'Twill do me good to be busy. You know what the Reverend said about idle hands."

Her soft chuckle made me feel better. "You are in little danger of doing the devil's work. Your hands are never still."

I managed to laugh with her as we hurried to the kitchen, well aware that our charges were hungry and likely to be quarreling among themselves if they were not soon fed. Still, whenever my mind wandered, I stared at my hand, remembering Baxter's touch.

Why had he been so sure that I was attracted to Nick? And what made him believe that I would turn to him? After growing up without serious suitors, it was confusing for me to find myself pursued this way. Especially when I wanted only Nick's attention and, according to Baxter, that was already promised to Geraldine.

How had this happened? Could I be falling in love? The very idea frightened me, for it was something I had considered only during giggly night conversations with my closest girl friends at Middle Brook Christian. As an adult, I had realized that I was unlikely to marry. Only since I came here had I begun to dream again.

And now I must set those dreams aside, I told myself firmly. Nick was an honorable man, and I was wedded to my mission here. If we could not be friends, then I must keep my distance from him. There must never be any scandal whispered about me, for it would destroy everything that Paul had accomplished here and the children would lose the sanctuary of this orphanage.

Though I had been grateful for the diversion that caring for the children offered, I was relieved when midafternoon found most of them sleeping or playing quietly and I could escape to my rooms for a brief respite. I needed to be among my belongings, to draw strength from the memories of Middle Brook that they would evoke. I needed to . . .

The moment I closed my sitting room door behind me, the chill touched me. Someone had been here! I looked around, trying to discover exactly what it was that unsettled me; but I saw nothing out of place. My books rested on the table near the small rocker. My discarded shawl still lay over the back of the battered sofa. Yet something was wrong; I could feel it in my bones.

I prowled the room, touching each of my possessions, trying to reassure myself; but nothing dispelled the core of ice within me. Was my family Bible in a new spot? Had the small painting of my parents been moved? Still trapped by my strong feeling of being violated, I stepped into my bedchamber, hoping that it would fade.

My chill deepened. Here, too, I sensed an unseen

hand. Each drawer seemed to bear invisible marks, and as I shifted my neatly folded clothing, I shuddered at the idea of some stranger touching them. But who would do such a thing, and why? What could anyone hope to find here? It made no sense, yet no amount of denying my feelings could change them. Even sitting in my little rocker with my Bible open in my lap could not dispel the dark shadows—my sanctuary was gone.

Still, there were no outward changes in the next few days. Seraphina appeared unaware of the intruder, and the children were unaffected. It seemed that only I sensed the shadows, only I felt the weight of watching eyes whenever I was alone in the cloister. It was a fearful burden, especially since there was no one with whom I could share it. Paul made no visit, and I saw Nick only from a distance as he rode about the plantation.

That was undoubtedly for the best, I told myself; but my heart grew heavy. Was he angry with me for attending services with Baxter? I wondered. Or was he grateful to have someone else paying attention to me so that he was free to concentrate on his intended? That thought brought even more pain, especially since I had seen nothing of Geraldine after our encounter at the church.

My plan to convince Baxter Travis to allow his workers' children to attend my school seemed to have come to naught also, for my students grew fewer and fewer. Finally, by late Thursday morning, I was near tears with the frustration and a haunting sense of failure.

To my surprise, Seraphina came bustling into the schoolroom with a bright smile and dancing eyes. "I be thinking you need a walk, Rachel. You have been too long inside this day."

"'Tis too close to midday," I protested, though I could scarce ignore the bright sunlight that sparkled just beyond the open door. "I should be in the kitchen helping you prepare a meal for the children."

"Not today." Seraphina almost pushed me toward the door. "'Twill do the girls good to help me. They have little enough to occupy them these days."

Since her urging was only slightly stronger than my own desire to escape, I allowed myself to be persuaded, though I did insist on returning to my rooms to freshen up before my walk. I promised myself I would use the time alone to think about what I should say to Paul on Sunday, for I had no doubt that he would ask me what was happening with the school and my grand plan for winning the patronage of Sea Cliff

Such thoughts were far from pleasant company as I walked, so I turned toward the distant headlands, thinking that I might skip the midday meal and feed my heart by making the long walk down to the wave-washed sand. Perhaps the endless march of the sea could soothe the turbulence that seemed to be tearing at me whenever I thought of Nick—something I did far too often for my own good. Sometimes, I feared that he had bewitched me.

That thought tickled my fancy, especially when I tried to picture a down-to-earth man like Nick hunched over a cauldron, whispering incantations. Suddenly I found myself lifting my face to the sun and laughing. Perhaps my grandmother had been right when, so many years ago, she had warned me of the dangers of taking life too seriously. At the time, I had been unable to understand, but now . . .

A rustling sound off to my left forced my mind away from my musing and I slowed, suddenly aware of the loneliness of the area. Remembering the strange feelings that had been haunting my days and nights at the cloister, I turned toward the thick brush, not sure whether I should call out or run.

"'Tis about time you got here." Nick stepped out of the shadows. "I was beginning to think that Seraphina had failed me."

I opened my mouth to speak, but just the sight of him dried my throat and robbed me of my breath. He was so handsome, the sunlight kindling flame in his thick auburn hair and dancing in his eyes. I felt like laughing and crying and seemed incapable of doing either as he hurried across the thick meadow to take my hands. "Cat got your tongue, Rachel?"

His teasing broke through my paralysis and I managed to catch my breath enough to ask, "What has Seraphina to do with our meeting?"

"Did she not insist that you needed a walk?" His grin gentled into a smile that set my heart to pounding so that I was sure he must be able to hear it above the sighing of the ever-present breeze.

"Well, yes, but . . . It was your idea?" I suddenly understood the reason for her amusement in the face of my depression. "You told her to . . ."

"How else was I to separate you from that great pile of stone and all those children?" Nick showed no sign of guilt.

"That 'pile of stone' is an orphanage, and I am here to take care of those children, you know." My protest lacked any heat and there was no way I could keep from smiling like a giddy girl.

"But not all day, every day. Surely one little picnic would not constitute failing in your duty, would it?"

"A picnic?" I tried to feign doubt, but I suspected he knew that I could never refuse him, not when he looked at me that way.

"The basket waits just the other side of those bushes, and I have a perfect spot in mind for our meal. Will you join me?"

"How should I refuse when you have already taken such pains to arrange it?" How could I refuse when he was offering me exactly what I wanted most in the world—time alone with him?

"This way, pretty lady." He tucked my arm beneath his and led me from the sunlight into the shadows of a stand of trees, stopping only to retrieve an impressive hamper, then guided me along a narrow path that I had not seen before.

For several minutes, I simply basked in the joy of being near him, then reality made me aware of the magic of the moment and I was suddenly afraid of what might happen, of my own weakness in his presence. "Where are we going?" I asked, hoping to dispel the illusion and establish, at least for myself, that we were just two friends.

"If you listen, I think you can guess." Nick glanced down at me and a quiver of anticipation shivered inside me, for I could see from the longing in his expression that I had company in my foolish dreams.

For several heartbeats I was too lost in his gaze even to think about what he had said, but finally, the words penetrated the veil of my desire and I realized that he was right. I could hear the crashing of the waves clearly. "The headlands?"

He nodded. "'Tis just a bit further, and well worth the walk."

When we left the shelter of the trees, I gazed around, fascinated. Though Nick had taken the girls and me for several walks along the heights during the days when we were all staying at Sunrise, this place was unfamiliar. Where other areas of the bluffs were rocky and barren, this small outcropping dipped into a tiny depression that was surrounded on three sides by the tough island trees. Only the outer edge was open, and when we reached it, I discovered a breathtaking view of the restless sea below us.

"Is it not special?" He let go of my arm, but only so that he could set down the hamper, then he slipped his arm about my shoulders as we stood together above the frothing waves.

"'Tis enchanted." The word was out before I thought, yet I knew at once that it was the only one which described this place. From the multihued sea below us to the flowers that grew in abundance in the little grassy bowl where we stood, it was perfect, and the wind-twisted trees stood guard against any intruder to our paradise.

"Truly." He turned from the view and when I looked into his eyes, I felt enchanted, too. I lifted my lips and closed my eyes as his mouth claimed mine.

The world seemed to fade as his lips teased and nibbled, then ravished mine so thoroughly that I clung to him to keep from swooning to the soft grass. My heart pounded in rhythm with the crashing surf as I buried my fingers in the silken depths of his hair. His lips left mine to nibble a trail of kisses across my cheek and down the side of my throat beneath my ear.

"Oh, Rachel, I have missed you so these past days. All I could think about was holding you, kissing you . . ." His lips retraced their path and claimed mine again.

Dizzy with the wild sensations that quivered and shivered through me, I yielded eagerly to his demands, glorying in the strength of his embrace as he pressed me close against him. Nothing in my life had prepared me for such feelings. I felt almost a part of him and I loved it. I loved him!

The words shimmered in my mind, rich and sweet with promise, then shattered the fragile illusion as I returned to sanity. I dared not love him; to do so would be folly, for he belonged to another. Tormented by shame and guilt, I forced myself to let him go and tried to pull away. His arms were like bands of steel and his lips sought mine again.

Since I could not free myself, I turned my head so that his hungry mouth caught on the corner of mine. "No, Nick, we must stop." The words sounded more like a plea than a commandment, but then, a part of me had no desire to be free.

For an eternity he simply held me, then slowly, his embrace loosened and I was free. The warm air chilled me and I was hard put to stay on my feet without the wonder of his supporting arms. Even as I knew that I had done the right thing, my traitor heart ached to be pressed once more against his chest.

"What troubles you, Rachel?" His voice sounded a little rough, but when I looked into his face I saw only concern. "Did I frighten you? 'Tis only that I have spent so much time longing for this moment that I . . . forgive me, please. I should never want to cause you pain."

The gentleness of his apology brought the stinging of tears to my eyes and I could not let him take the blame that should have been mine for allowing him to take such liberties. "'Twas not fear of you, Nick, but of what we were doing."

"My kisses frightened you?" A frown marred his golden forehead. "But I thought you wanted . . ."

"It is wrong for us to behave thus." I turned away, unable to meet his gaze, for I was having a terrible time finding words to explain my feelings. My gaze fell upon the deserted hamper and I moved toward it eagerly. "Now, let us have our picnic and talk of all that has kept you so busy these past days."

"If that is what you want." His tone was so devoid of feeling, I dared not look at him for fear of what I might read in his face.

What if he should hate me for leading him on? I had not thought of it before, but I did remember hearing the young men whisper disparagingly about such girls at one of the few parties I had attended during the holidays at Middle Brook. I shrank inside at the idea that my momentary weakness might have made him think I cared only for the thrill of his kiss.

Nick took a cloth from the hamper and spread it, then I helped him unpack the food that Cook had prepared for us. It was a charming repast, but I had no appetite, my heart was too heavy. Nick ate without speaking, his gaze resolutely on his plate as though he misliked even looking at me. A fact for which I was grateful, for I was having a difficult time keeping back my tears.

We were near finished, when he set aside his plate, then took mine and set it down, too. He took my hands, which were cold and shaking in spite of the warmth of the day. His touch forced me to meet his gaze and I was shocked by the pain I read in his face.

"I cannot bear this, Rachel. You wanted me to kiss you, I know enough of women to be sure of that. And you enjoyed it as much as I did. There is another reason you pulled away and I must know what it is. I care too much about you to just let you go."

"I cannot deny my feelings, but they are wrong. We are unsuited, and to indulge in such behavior lightly . . . I have responsibilities, Nick. Reverend Bennett sent me here as his representative. I cannot risk my reputation by spending time with you, since you are already promised to another." I spoke quickly, ignoring the pain my words caused me as I tried to free my hands from his grasp.

"Since I am what?" His fingers tightened.

"Are you not betrothed to Geraldine Chalmers?" My lips felt numb just forming the words.

"Where did you hear that?"

"Baxter Travis told me." I gritted my teeth as I held his gaze. "Is it not the truth?"

His grasp eased slightly and he sighed, looking weary now. My heart dropped within me as I anticipated the horrible confirmation that we could never share another kiss. Somehow, until this moment, I had clung to a tiny shred of hope that Baxter might be wrong.

"There was a time when my father and Geraldine's talked of such an alliance, and I admit that a few years ago I might have allowed the match to be made, but the time has passed. I have no such feelings for Geraldine, she is no more than a third sister to me. We could never wed."

"Never? But if your father . . ." I had to fight my own relief, the joy that seemed to be singing inside me at the thought that there might be a chance for us.

"My father would never insist upon a match that I had no heart to make." He spoke firmly, but it was his touch that truly reassured me, for he caressed my fingers with great tenderness.

"What of Geraldine?"

Nick chuckled. "She was so uninterested that she left the island shortly after our fathers made the proposal. Went to stay with some cousins in the Bahamas for nearly a year. She has only been back to stay a bit over a year, and nothing has been said about our alliance since her return."

"Still, she might be planning that someday you two would be married as all the island seems to expect." Why was I pressing this way? I asked myself. Why could I not just accept his words and enjoy his kisses again?

"I doubt it, but if some folk still harbor such ideas, I know a perfect way to put an end to all the speculation." His eyes gleamed green-gold with excitement and a touch of mischief.

"What?"

"You shall be my partner at the ball that we will be holding at Sunrise a week from Saturday. Would you do me that honor, Rachel? 'Twas one of the reasons I asked

Seraphina to help me spend some time alone with you. I wanted to ask you before Baxter did. 'Tis not too late, is it?"

"A ball?" I swallowed hard. "Oh, Nick, I don't know if I should accept. It might not be seemly, since I am here to care for the children, not to . . ." Longing halted my words as I pictured what it would be like to attend a ball at Sunrise. I had seen the immense ballroom and both Pamela and Olivia had told me numerous tales of the parties given there.

"Who would begrudge you a night of revelry? Especially since it will be at Sunrise, so near the cloister that even the children will hear the music once the dancing begins. You must say yes, Rachel. The invitation comes from my whole family, I assure you." He lifted my hand to his cheek, thrilling me as he rubbed it against his face. I felt the prickling of his barely sprouting whiskers and the intimacy of such a touch sent a flood of heat through me.

"I should adore to be your partner, Nick," I whispered, unable to deny my longing.

"Then 'tis settled. I shall call for you at midafternoon a week from Saturday. I can have one of the servants fetch your gown, if you like, since I know most ladies prefer not to crush them in the carriages. Mother always sets aside several changing rooms for the convenience of our guests."

I swallowed hard, suddenly aware of what I must do now that I had accepted his invitation. My wardrobe was sadly lacking in festive gowns of the sort I had seen Pamela and Olivia trying on, yet I refused to allow that fact to dampen my pleasure. Thanks to my mother's patient training, I was skilled with a needle and the evenings at the cloister offered few diversions. I lost myself in the molten depths of Nick's eyes, content to savor this magical moment.

By the time Nick escorted me back across the fields toward the cloister, I was too happy to care about anything beyond the thrill of holding his hand and listening as he talked of the coming ball. It was, I realized, going to be the event of the island social season and would be attended by all of the planter families. And Nick had chosen to invite me as his personal guest! That had to mean something; I only wished that I could be sure exactly what.

As we neared the cloister, Nick slowed. "I shall escort you into the village on Sunday." His tone made it clear that this was a pronouncement, not a question. "Should I expect to encounter Baxter?"

Could he be jealous? My heartbeat quickened at the thought, but I carefully kept my gaze directed at the building ahead so that he would not be able to read my feelings in my face. "I truly don't know. He said he would be calling from time to time, but I have seen no students from Sea Cliff this week."

Nick snorted. "Nor are you likely to. The Travis family prefers not to have educated workers. According to old Mr. Travis, 'A bit of learnin' makes a man uppity' and I expect that Baxter agrees."

Since his words seemed arbitrary and perhaps unfair when applied to Baxter, I felt impelled to defend him. "Baxter seemed most interested in the school and what his people would learn if they attended."

"Interested in the school, or in the teacher?" Nick's question confirmed my suspicions thrillingly. He truly was upset that I had allowed Baxter to escort me to Sunday services.

"He behaved as a perfect gentleman, though he did invite me to take the evening meal with his family." I was having difficulty keeping my tone properly demure, especially when I felt like giggling with delight at this proof that Nick cared about me.

"You refused, of course." Nick had come to an abrupt halt, and since he had hold of my hand, I was forced to stop, too.

"I felt my duties at the orphanage came first."

"Well, I trust that you will continue to refuse." Nick still sounded angry, which surprised me.

"Why?"

"It would not be safe for you to travel to or from Sea Cliff after sunset. Surely you remember the warnings that you received when you moved into the cloister."

My amusement at the situation faded as quickly as it had come, for his words and expression seemed to have more behind them than the jealousy I had been enjoying. "I am sure that Baxter meant for me to be accompanied."

"Even so, it would be best if you remained here, where you are safe." Nick glared at me, then looked away as though uncomfortable with what he saw. "Promise me, Rachel."

For just a heartbeat, I wanted to refuse. I had little patience with the continued warnings that I got from both Nick and Paul, yet I remembered the mysterious occurrences at the cloister, the intruder whose presence I still felt in my rooms. For that reason, I surrendered my recently acquired sense of independence and nodded. "I shall ask your father's permission before accepting any invitations."

His eyes flashed with a flare of anger, then his gaze softened and he chuckled ruefully. "But not mine."

"You have been absent much of the time, so how could I be sure to find you in residence?" Just meeting his gaze and speaking so boldly made me quiver with anticipation. Being around Nick was changing me, making me feel more alive and . . . perhaps "womanly" was the word. It was a heady emotion.

"Perhaps I shall have to spend more time watching

over you, pretty Rachel." He released my hand and touched my cheek with his fingers. "Now, however, I must leave you. Otherwise, I shall cause a tiny scandal by kissing you right here, for all the world to see."

The heat that spread through me made it clear that I should offer him no argument if he tried, but I was relieved when he stepped back. Bolder I might be, but I must remember that I was here to care for innocent children and thus must be above reproach in all things. Swallowing a sigh of longing, I thanked him for the picnic and fled into the quiet shadows of the cloister, ready to dream about the ball I would be attending.

Not that I was given much chance, for Elena met me at the door, babbling excitedly about new arrivals. I regretfully set aside my dreaming and followed her to the playroom where Geraldine introduced me to the three children whom she had just brought from Emerald Acres.

"'Tis a sad occasion," she explained. "They have been with their grandmother for near two years, having lost both parents during a fierce storm that caught them out in their boat. The woman seemed well and happy to care for them, but she fell day before yesterday, and today . . . she was gone."

I picked up the youngest, a girl not much older than Inez. "We shall do what we can to comfort them, though I suspect it will take time."

"I's already been helpin'," Elena announced. "I be tellin' 'um how you took in me and Inez. And how this gonna be their home now. Sassy say she be wantin' to learn to read like me."

Sassy was, I assumed, the older girl who stood across the room near Seraphina with an older boy. I hugged Elena with my free arm, grateful for her generous heart. "I know how much you help, dear. And Sassy shall

211

read. All of you will learn to read and write and do numbers, that is part of being here."

I talked briefly with the two older children, and conferred with Seraphina regarding the rooms they should occupy and other matters of their care. Then I turned to Geraldine. Her cold gaze froze in my throat the pleasantries I had been about to utter. It took me several seconds to recover enough to ask, "Is something amiss, Geraldine?"

"If we could speak in private?" Her tone was calm, but I sensed the turmoil beneath the mask she wore.

"We can go to the schoolroom. Would you like something cool to drink?" I did my best to appear unruffled by her odd behavior, though too late, I wondered how Seraphina had explained my long absence.

Geraldine refused any refreshment, hurrying along the hall and closing the door that separated the big front room from the dining room and kitchen area. I braced myself as she turned to face me, not sure what to expect.

An uneasy silence spread between us as she just stared at me, her lips so tightly pressed together that I could see a pale rim around them. Not sure what I might have done, I endured the glare as long as I could. Finally, however, I could bear it no longer. "Is there some problem you wish to discuss, Geraldine?" I asked in my most professional tone.

"I want to know where you were all afternoon. I have been waiting since shortly after midday." Her anger spilled around me. "If this is the way you care for the children entrusted to you . . ."

The attack caught me off guard, and for a moment I wanted nothing more than to inform her that I had spent most of the afternoon joyously kissing Nick Harrison; but fortunately, sanity returned before I did so. Not that

I had any intention of keeping my whereabouts a secret from her or anyone else.

I stiffened my spine and met her malevolent gaze with what I hoped was a casual smile. She would know about Nick's invitation soon enough, so I might as well tell her enough to prepare her for what was happening between Nick and me. "It has been a difficult week, so when Seraphina suggested that I go for a walk, I accepted. I went further than I intended and ended up sharing a picnic lunch with Nick."

"You were with Nick? But I thought that you and Baxter Travis had . . ." She let it trail off, seeming to recover her poise at least enough to give me a polite smile. "A picnic, how charming. Nick and I used to do that often, but of late he has been so busy running the plantation for his father . . ."

"How is Baxter?" I asked, not because I cared particularly, but because I hoped to divert her attention from Nick and the kinds of questions about the picnic that I had no desire to answer.

"He does stay as busy as the rest of us. You have no idea the difficulties involved in keeping these plantations running smoothly. 'Tis a wonder any of us have time for a social life." Her smile changed. "But perhaps that is why the balls and parties are so important to us. They give us a chance to have fun together and forget the problems that . . ." She shook back her dark hair, her smile becoming patronizing. "But that is of no interest to you, I suppose, since this is your world."

"I am interested in everything about Bell Harbour Island," I informed her, controlling a desire to strike back in retaliation for the snub inherent in her last words.

She seemed to sense my feelings, for she moved to the table near the door to collect her hat and gloves, which I had failed to notice when I drifted in. "Well, I really must be on my way now. I had thought to be home before this."

"It is a delight to see you again, but you could have entrusted the children to Seraphina, you know. She is my good right hand here." I was in no mood to accept guilt for having taken a single afternoon for myself.

"I wanted to be sure that the children would offer you no problem. I know that the school must keep you busy, and with so many orphans already . . ."

"At the moment, I have few students, so the newcomers will be a welcome addition. Besides, I am teaching only until Reverend Michaels takes over once again."

"That may be a long time." Geraldine's sniff made it plain that she felt no sorrow at the prospect.

"Has there been more trouble?" My stomach knotted as I realized that I had heard nothing from Paul since I attended the Sunday services. And I had not thought to ask Nick how Paul fared either, a shameful realization.

"It seems Reverend Michaels paid a call at Sea Cliff and was ordered off the property by Mr. Travis. Baxter said his father swore that he would put the dogs on him if he set foot on his land again, so I doubt that you will be getting any students from Sea Cliff for your lessons here." Geraldine told the story with a certain degree of relish, adding, "But I thought that Baxter would have told you all about it."

"I have not seen Baxter since Sunday."

"How odd. He seemed quite taken with you when we talked on Sunday. He claimed to be most interested in everything you are doing here. I do believe he even mentioned that he might like to help in some way." She stood in the doorway, the light behind her making it impossible for me to see her expression.

"Perhaps his father made him change his mind," I suggested, not really caring.

"'Twould be a shame if he did, for you two seemed

214

well suited to each other. A delightful pair, as my father would say." The purr in her voice was unmistakable.

For a moment I considered telling her that I had no interest in Baxter Travis, but I was given no opportunity. She turned on her heel and disappeared in the direction of the little stream, where she must have left whatever conveyance had brought her and the children to the cloister.

Curious, I remained where I was and in a moment, a carriage crossed my narrow view. Somehow I was not surprised to note that it was headed not toward Emerald Acres, but directly for Sunrise. I winced as a sharp pang of jealousy tore my tender heart, for I was well aware that Geraldine must be on her way to see Nick. What would he say to her? Would he tell her that he had chosen me to be his guest at the ball?

I took a deep breath, suddenly unsure about my acceptance. I had no doubt that I wanted to be with Nick, but did I have the right to cause such pain to Geraldine Chalmers? I had never been faced with such a moral dilemma before. Did I have the right to find my pleasure at the expense of another person's pain?

"Rachel?" Seraphina's gentle voice forced my attention back to the more practical demands of life.

I felt a small sense of relief as I turned to her. Though I found Nick's kisses wildly exciting, trying to understand the emotions that flowed between men and women was proving most perplexing. I closed my eyes for a moment, wishing once more for the counsel of a mother; then opened them as I remembered that it was my duty to assume the role of mother to the children here, for they had none to protect them.

Chapter 13

By the time the children were all in bed that evening, I was fairly bursting with the need to talk about what had happened. Besides, I reminded myself, Seraphina was not exactly an outsider, since she had sent me to meet Nick.

"Shall we have a cup of tea?" I suggested, as we finished putting away the toys in the playroom.

"I should like that." Seraphina's shy smile reflected a delight that shamed me. While I was busy worrying about my social life, she must be very lonely here, I realized. After all, until Paul had brought her here, she'd lived with her sons nearby and all her friends; now she had only the children and me for company.

"I want to thank you for what you did today," I began, as I got the cups from the cupboard and watched while she set about brewing the tea. "It was good to have some time away from here. I just want you to know that you are entitled to the same privilege. Whenever you wish to go visiting, you just let me know and I shall see if Digger is free to drive you to Emerald Acres to see your friends and family."

"You are very kind." Her eyes sparkled. "I have missed my sons and my grandbabies, but I know you need me here . . ."

"We can find a way."

We settled companionably at the well-scrubbed kitchen table, a plate of Seraphina's cookies between us. "Did you have a pleasant picnic?" She was too shy to meet my gaze, but I sensed that her interest went beyond idle curiosity, a fact that reminded me of what Baxter had told me about the island gossip.

"It was lovely. We went to a spot along the headlands that I had never seen before. The waves seemed to be washing at our very feet, and the water was heavenly shades of blue and green."

"Mr. Nick said that he needed to talk to you, that it was important; but he was afraid that you might hesitate to spend time alone with him."

Her words gave me the opening I wanted. "I have been avoiding him because I was worried about gossip, Seraphina. Since the orphanage is my responsibility, I must be very careful of my reputation. 'Twould never do to have people gossiping about my behavior."

" 'Tis a small island, Rachel, and there be little else to talk about." Seraphina seemed unworried. "Everyone knows that you are here under the protection of the Harrisons, so why should you not spend time with Mr. Nick?"

I took a deep breath, knowing that now was the time to say the words I most wanted to shout from the cloister rooftop. "Well, there will be more talk after the Harrisons' big ball, I fear. One of the things Nick and I discussed was my attending as his guest."

"Oh, Rachel, how thrilling." Seraphina clapped her hands with delight just as one of the girls from Middle Brook would have. Her smile was warm and open, without censure. "What shall you wear?"

Relief eased the knot in my stomach so that I felt free to help myself to the cookies. If it seemed right and proper to Seraphina, then it would likely appear the

217

same to most of the other islanders. Or at least, I prayed that it would. "My choice of a gown is what I was hoping to talk to you about. I certainly have nothing proper in my wardrobe. I had no idea when I was packing to come that I should be . . ." I trailed off, embarrassed by my own enthusiasm.

"So what shall you do?"

"Well, I do have a royal blue satin gown. 'Tis rather plain in cut, but I was thinking . . ." I began describing all the ribbons and laces that I had brought with me. To my delight, Seraphina immediately offered suggestions, and I realized that she knew much more about the way the island ladies dressed for balls than I did. When I asked her how she knew, her smile faded.

"There was a time when I served in the house at Emerald Acres. I was Mrs. Chalmers's maid, took care of her clothes and dressed her hair." The sadness in her eyes faded slightly. "She used to tell me that no one was better at managing her hair than I; but that was long ago."

My curiosity was piqued, but I held my tongue, knowing well that I had no right to demand her confidences. If she wished me to know why she had been banished from the house staff at Emerald Acres, she would tell me. I reached out and patted her hand. "Then I shall treasure your advice."

"And I shall adore helping you to get ready. 'Twill be a grand ball, I am sure. I used to hear them talking about such things, and they always said that the best parties were held at Sunrise." She spoke without a trace of regret or envy, for which I was grateful.

"Shall we go and look now?" I suggested. "Or are you too weary? I know it has been a long day for you, all alone with the children and with Geraldine."

Seraphina's gentle chuckle surprised me. "She was a bit upset when I informed her that I had no idea where

218

you might be found. I think she suspected that you were with Mr. Nick."

"Does she care deeply for him?" I hated myself for my need to ask, yet I knew I must be sure before I went any further with my own dreams.

"Mr. Nick is by far the best catch on the island, and I have no doubt that she would like to be mistress of Sunrise someday; but I fear Miss Geraldine cares little for anyone but herself. It has always been so. Broke her mother's heart, it did; but her father fair dotes on her, so 'tis unlikely to change." Seraphina spoke with a casual honesty that thrilled me, for it told me that she trusted me not to betray her.

"She seems determined to spend time with him."

"Mostly since your arrival, I wager."

"Well, I have no way of knowing . . ." I grinned at her as I left the sentence unfinished. " 'Tis only that I have no wish to cause trouble to anyone on the island, since I know that feelings are already strained because of the school."

"No one could be displeased with you, Rachel. The orphanage is thriving, and you have nurtured the children as well as anyone could have." Her words were fervent, but even as I led the way to my rooms, I wondered if other people would be as generous.

Still, it was delightful to pick through the ribbons and laces, to try first one and then another around the modest neckline of my blue satin gown. By the time we said goodnight I was beginning to believe that between us we would create a gown I could wear with pride.

All day Saturday I found my concentration distracted by each distant sound, for I hoped that Nick might ride by. But the sun disappeared below the tree-crested hills that formed the center of the island without my catching even a glimpse of him. Once the children were safely tucked away, I retired to my room.

Had he changed his mind? What if Geraldine had convinced him that my attending the ball would be a mistake? I pricked my finger and barely managed to avoid dripping blood on the white lace that I was trying to stitch along the seams of the skirt.

Cursing in an unladylike fashion, I carefully hung the gown back in the wardrobe. If I kept this up, I was sure to ruin it, and then what would I do? The room seemed to be closing in, smothering me. I needed a breath of fresh air.

Not really thinking, I picked up my shawl and slipped out into the deserted hall. I would just step outside for a few minutes, I decided, only long enough to feel the evening breeze and watch the moon rise. I had taken but a single step when a soft sound made me turn around. Someone was moving about in the rear playroom!

For a moment I hesitated. I had no desire to talk to the children or even Seraphina, but at the same time, I could not avoid my duty to all of them. Swallowing a groan of frustration, I hurried along the hall, thinking that I would escape as soon as I had sent whoever was in there off to bed. After all, we would be rising early for services tomorrow.

That thought offered little solace, for I knew that I would have to inform Paul of my upcoming social engagement. After his response to my being escorted to services by Baxter Travis, I found myself unsure of what he might say about my attending a purely frivolous occasion like the Sunrise ball. Unless, of course, he had also been invited; a prospect I had not considered before.

I was so busy with my thoughts when I opened the rear playroom door that it was several moments before the scene beyond registered. The big wardrobe door stood open and much of the clothing within was scattered about both on the floor of the wardrobe and outside it, too. The flickering light of my candle cast eerie shadows in the thick darkness that seemed to sigh and shift away from the feeble glow.

"Seraphina?" My voice sounded high and frightened, even in my own ears. A faint click was my only answer. "Who is in here?" I demanded, sounding a bit stronger as anger at the mess overrode my shock. "Come forward now."

I forced myself to step further inside the room and used my candle to light one that waited on the table near the door. The additional light only intensified the shadows that lurked between the massive wardrobes and in the corners.

"What is it, Rachel?" Seraphina's voice came from behind me, and since I had not heard her approach. I started, nearly dropping my candle.

"I thought I heard someone in here." My voice was shaking so that I had to stop and take a deep breath before going on. "I just assumed that you . . ."

"I was telling the older girls a story when I heard you call." Seraphina added her candle's light and gasped as she saw what I had. "Someone has been here."

I nodded, then moved forward to explore the room, hoping to find one of the children perhaps hiding for fear of punishment for the naughtiness we had found. My apprehension deepened when no guilty child emerged, and when I met Seraphina's gaze, I could see that she felt the same way.

"You are sure that you heard someone?" Her expression begged me to lie and deny the memory.

I waved a hand at the chaos. "This was done by someone, Seraphina. We both know that the room was tidy when the children were put to bed."

"But who could . . ." She stopped, and her gaze fol-

221

lowed mine to the shelves that concealed the hidden stairway.

I closed the door and went over to open the concealed spring, trying hard not to think what I might discover on the other side. It was a relief to find absolutely nothing. The dust that swirled up, teasing my nose, bore no trace of footprints.

"It be spooks, Rachel. Maybe the black robes be angry with all the children playing in their haven. 'Tis their way of telling us to . . ." Seraphina stopped, shuddering.

For a moment my stomach knotted with a terror that matched hers, then sanity overwhelmed the superstition and brought a flood of righteous anger. "Not likely," I snapped. "Why should a ghost choose to knock clothes from their pegs? Why not appear to us and speak?"

Seraphina's wide-eyed gaze told me that I had shocked her with my suggestion. "But who . . .?"

"Someone who wishes us gone, perhaps. I have been told often enough that many on the island resent what Reverend Michaels and I are doing here, so this might be their way of trying to send us screaming from here." The words came easily, though I truly had not contemplated such a thing before.

"But where are these people?" Seraphina held her candle high, making the shadows dance menacingly on the walls.

"I have no idea," I admitted. "But if they keep returning to trouble us, perhaps one day we will catch them. Meantime, I suggest we put things to rights, then try to get some sleep. We must leave early for the village, you know."

Though her doubts and fears were obvious in her face and posture, Seraphina offered no argument as we quickly returned the room to its normal tidy appearance. Once finished, I retired to my sitting room, my need for escape forgotten, now that the night outside seemed somehow as threatening as the willful chaos we had found in the playroom.

Could I be right about our intruder's intent? I asked myself. And if so, what should I do about it? Ask Nick or Paul for help? That seemed the best plan, but even as I considered it, I realized the dangers. Nick might very well demand that we leave the cloister and Paul . . . His duties kept him much too busy for him to be of any help or protection.

I straightened my shoulders and shook back my thick, unbound hair. This orphanage was my dream, so why should I not handle this myself? If I could settle the matter without asking for help, would that not prove that I was worthy of the trust Paul and Nick had placed in me? Besides, if someone thought I could be frightened away by a few wrinkled clothes or bumps in the night, it was time to let them know that I was made of sterner stuff. That decision made, I prepared myself for bed, smiling at the realization that tomorrow I would, at least, have some time with Nick.

The morning dawned gray and for a time I feared that rain might keep us from making the long drive into the village, but once everyone was dressed and fed, the sun was beginning to burn away the worrisome clouds. Like my feelings, I thought wryly; for I had spent much of the time since I woke alternating between excitement at the prospect of seeing Nick again and fears that he might have changed his mind about my attending the ball.

Digger arrived with the wagon as expected and I was pleased to note that Harriet had been allowed to accompany him. I saw far too little of her since leaving the main house. Thanks to the chaos the children created, it was several minutes before I thought to look around for Nick. Since the wagon would be full with Seraphina, the children and me, I expected him to come on horseback; but he was nowhere about.

"Are we to go unescorted?" I asked Digger when most of the children were settled in the wagon.

"Mr. Nick said for you to wait upon him, Miss Rachel. He be comin' right along."

My heartbeat quickened with anticipation, then slowed with dread. Had Nick arranged for privacy so he could tell me that he would be escorting Geraldine to the ball? I forced myself to nod to Digger, then waved them on their way, feeling very much alone as the wagon creaked and rattled along the road, disappearing around a stand of trees. I glanced toward Sunrise, then stepped back inside, not wanting to appear impatient, though I was.

Within moments, I heard the sound of hoofbeats, and after a few deep breaths to settle the butterflies that appeared to have taken up residence in my stomach, stepped back outside, closing the door firmly behind me. Should I lock it? I wondered, remembering what had happened last Sunday. Then I smiled wryly. Locking it had not protected us from last night's intruder, so I suspected it would make no difference today, either. Resolutely promising myself to banish all thoughts of last night, I stepped out into the weak sunlight to greet Nick.

The moment our eyes met, I knew that my fears of rejection were groundless. His grin made my heart beat so fast I feared I might become dizzy from it. Nick leaped from the light carriage and caught me in his arms, his lips finding mine willingly parted, though I had not expected such a passionate greeting.

"I have missed you. It seems a century since our picnic." His whisper sent shivers through me as he trailed kisses across my cheek.

"Nick, we must have a care," I protested, mostly because I found that I was enjoying his embrace so much. "Someone might see us."

His groan echoed my feelings, but he obediently stepped back slightly before helping me into the small carriage. "Have you not missed me at all?"

"Of course I have, but for the sake of the children, I cannot risk any gossip. A woman who cares for the innocent must be above reproach." How often I had heard that phrase from Reverend Bennett, but never before had I resented it.

"I know you are right, but I find your sweet lips irresistible." His heated gaze moved over my face like a caress. "Besides, my feelings for you will be well known soon, anyway, thanks to Geraldine. She paid a call Thursday, and Pamela happened to mention that I had invited you to the ball, so . . ."

"Pamela knew?" I could not hide my surprise.

"I informed the family that morning of my intention. I told you that the invitation came from all of us."

So he had, I recalled, but in the throes of all my new emotions, I had paid little attention. "Was she angry?" I had to ask, though I doubted that I should like his reply.

"Angry? Why should she be?" His look of confusion reassured me. "Actually she seemed to find the idea quite amusing, said it would surely cause a flurry among the other planter families. Which, I daresay, it will." He sounded almost pleased at the prospect.

"I hope it will cause Paul no trouble," I murmured, trying to focus on that instead of the warm sensations that moved through me when Nick took my hand.

"He manages to cause enough of his own, 'tis unlikely he will be disturbed by your actions." Nick clucked to the horse and we set off in pursuit of the farm wagon.

I leaned back, content to listen as Nick told me about the various crises that had kept him from calling at the cloister yesterday. For the first time in my life, I felt special and proud and truly happy, and it was because Nick was holding my hand, because he had chosen me. Could this be what it was like to be in love? The very thought sent a shiver of anticipation down my spine, and I lifted Nick's hand to press it against my cheek before we reached the wagon and I had to let it go.

The church was already half full when we arrived and I was conscious of all the curious eyes that followed our somewhat noisy entrance with the children. Was Paul's ministry finally attracting the crowds he deserved, or had many come only to confirm what the gossips were saying? Even thinking such base thoughts shamed me, but I found them difficult to escape.

Paul's demeanor as he spoke did little to lessen my fears, for there was no joy in his face or in his words. I wondered that the children were not frightened into tears as he thundered his message of retribution. I could only hope that it was his treatment at Sea Cliff that had triggered this fury, and not my behavior.

As he had last Sunday, Paul requested a private meeting with me as soon as I emerged from the church on Nick's arm. Since his grey eyes had bored into me often during the sermon, I followed him to the small room on knees that trembled. Once there, however, I lifted my chin and braced myself, vowing that I would face him without showing my fear.

"Is it true?" He looked disturbingly like an avenging angel from a drawing in one of Reverend Bennett's books.

"Is what true?" I met his gaze without wincing.

"Have you accepted an invitation to the ball at Sunrise?"

I nodded, ignoring the tremor in my stomach. "The family invited me, and I accepted. It seemed an excellent way for me to meet the rest of the planter families and for them to get to know about me and the orphanage." I should have been ashamed of this little stretching of the truth, but I was truly sick to death of having my every action questioned by a man who had never taken the time to explain to me exactly what he expected me to do.

"You should have refused the invitation, as I did. 'Tis wrong to be mixing socially with the planters, Rachel. The islanders will feel that you are aligning yourself with them instead of serving those whom we came here to help." He moved restlessly about the small space, no longer glaring at me, but obviously agitated.

"Since I spend each day caring for the orphaned children of the islanders, I doubt that my spending one evening at a ball will be so perceived. Besides, do we not need the planters' consent to educate the children of the islanders?"

Paul's frown made me step back a little. "You seem to have learned a great deal about how this island is governed since last week. Did your friend Baxter offer his advice, too?"

"Perhaps you should have asked him while you were at Sea Cliff." The words were out before I could stop them, proof positive that my tongue was in urgent need of control. Shamed, I dropped my gaze to the floor. "Forgive me, Paul. I had no right to say that. I have not seen Baxter since Sunday, and I have no intention of spending time with him in the future."

I braced myself for the tongue-lashing I knew I deserved, but the silence only deepened. Finally, I chanced lifting my head. Paul was staring at me, but not in an-

227

ger. He looked thoughtful and a bit surprised, nothing more. I swallowed hard. "Will you forgive me?"

He sighed. "We serve the same master, and perhaps your way will prove helpful. Just have a care, Rachel, and trust no one. You are still an innocent, and vulnerable to those who might appear to have our best interests at heart. 'Tis important that you remember that everyone has their own reasons for what they do and many are far from honorable." He took my hand, gave my fingers a quick squeeze, then released me, turning away to open the door. "Now I must let you get back to the children, for I have other duties to perform."

I think I murmured a few words of thanks, though I cannot be sure, for I was still too stunned by his abrupt change of mood. Of all his responses, this caring and protectiveness was the last I would have expected from Paul—especially considering the defiant and rude way I had behaved toward him. I shook my head as I walked through the empty church, wondering if I should ever be able to understand the ways of men, for truth to tell, they were very much a mystery to me.

I paused just outside the church, drinking in the scene before me. Nick was leaning against the wagon, teasing Elena and making her giggle. The sun, now high in the sky, sparked flames in his russet waves and glinted from his white teeth as he laughed with her and the other children. How at home he seemed with them, and how much they appeared to enjoy his company. Even the three new children were shyly joining in. I should have been jealous of the attention he lavished on them had I not loved them deeply myself.

Digger must have said something, for Nick looked my direction, then came to meet me. His eyes were full of mischief as he held me at arm's length and pretended to examine me. "It appears that you have survived without injury, so I assume Paul has given his blessing to your attending the ball."

" 'Blessing' might be too strong a word, but he no longer objects, anyway." I blushed at his words, realizing that I had not been the only one to guess the reason for Paul's bad temper this morning.

"How generous of him." Nick's tone was mocking. "Too bad he cannot bring himself to join us. It might be that he would learn something of what he faces because of his eternal impatience."

Guilt made me uncomfortable. I felt that I should defend Paul, yet I could think of little to say in his defense. "He is concerned only with how the islanders would view his spending time with the planters."

"And so the planters continue to view him as a firebrand running amok through the dry tinder of the workers." Nick shook his head, then tucked my arm beneath his as he led me over to where the others were gathered by the wagon. "Is everyone ready for a picnic?"

The happy shouts filled the air and dispelled my momentary gloom. Trust Nick to have arranged for a treat the children could enjoy, I thought, contrasting today's merry group with the silent children of last Sunday. Love for Nick swelled inside me, and I wondered how I should contain such a powerful emotion without bursting into either tears or joyous laughter.

To my delight, Nick spent the entire day with us, insisting that he wanted to see how life was lived at the cloister. During the afternoon, he solemnly inspected the garden that the children had planted, offering advice to Ben, who had been given the responsibility, since he was the oldest boy in our care. Later he read stories to the children, then listened with infinite patience as Elena displayed her newly acquired reading skills.

With the children tumbling after him like eager puppies, it was much later, when the silence of bedtime settled over the huge structure, before we finally were able to slip away for a few moments alone. Nick suggested that we take a short stroll before he returned to Sunrise.

"Well, what do you think of the orphanage, now that you have seen how 'tis run?" I inquired, as we left the building behind, heading down the hill toward the old burial ground I had found, what now seemed a lifetime ago.

"I am impressed. The children seem so happy. Somehow, I expected it to be a bit grim, since they have all lost so much." His solemn expression surprised me.

I tried to explain the situation to him with the same thoughtfulness his words had reflected. "There are some who still cry at night, but most are learning to look ahead, not back. I try to encourage them to make plans, to take responsibility for their own futures as much as they are able. I think it makes the loss easier to bear."

"Like teaching Elena to read? Did you know that her dream is to be a teacher, just like you?" His smile was visible in the soft moonlight that spilled around us.

"She is very bright and brave, and a great help to Seraphina and to me. I expect she has a true calling, and I hope I can help her make her dream come true."

He stopped in the shadow of a rustling palm tree, pulling me gently into his arms. "I will do my best, darling Rachel, to see that you have the opportunity to try. But you must be careful. Please promise me that you will take no foolish chances. I fear there are dangerous days ahead for us."

His lips covered mine before I could reply, and once the magical caress began, nothing else mattered. Only the two of us existed, our hearts pounding in perfect rhythm as we savored the sweetness of our kisses and celebrated the passion that swelled excitingly between us. I was quite breathless when Nick finally lifted his head.

"I must be going soon, Rachel."

"And I should return to the cloister. Seraphina will wonder what has become of me." I spoke quickly to keep from protesting, for I wished to remain as we were forever. I was becoming truly shameless in my desire to be in his arms.

His chuckle rumbled beneath my blushing cheek. "I have no doubt that Seraphina knows exactly what has become of us. And I think she approves."

"She is very dear to me."

"Keep her close to you, Rachel. She is a good friend." His voice has lost its humor, and I felt a chill in spite of the warmth of his arms.

"Are you trying to frighten me, Nick?" I pulled free of his sheltering embrace, fighting my own weak need to cling to him.

"I worry about you. The cloister seems far from the house, especially for women and children living alone." He made no move to hold me again, and I could see that he was frowning. "I wish that I could bring you all back to Sunrise."

I closed my eyes for a moment, picturing what it would be like, then laughed. "I fear that you would soon be wishing us much further away then the cloister. The children were on their good behavior today, but they can be quite a handful."

He had the grace to join in my amusement as we started back up the hill toward the cloister. "I suspect you are right, but I do wish that Seraphina's husband was still alive so that there would be a man living at the cloister."

"If he was still alive, she would be living at Emerald Acres, not here, and I doubt that would help your worrying." I kept my tone tart, but with difficulty, for I remembered the intruders that had plagued us and the hidden stairway I had discovered. I truly wanted to tell him, but his protective attitude made me sure that if I did, he would drag us all back to Sunrise, no matter what the result.

"Next time I speak with Paul, I shall suggest that he seek among his congregation for an older couple who might be interested in working with the children. That would free you for your teaching duties, and . . ."

I lifted a hand, stopping his words. "Please let me speak with Paul. He has placed me in charge of the orphanage, and I should be the one to request changes of staff."

"But will you do it?" His frown deepened.

"When the time is right, I will."

"And when will that be?" He sounded angry now.

I stopped, turning so I could meet his gaze. "When I need more time for teaching. I have so few students at present, I have quite enough time to tend to the needs of the children."

"And what of your safety?"

"We bar the doors and windows each night, as I promised. And what danger would we be in during the daylight hours with Sunrise so close at hand? Besides, you said yourself that we are just two women tending a group of orphans. Who would wish us ill?"

"I can imagine no one wanting to hurt you, but there is a kind of madness in the air, Rachel. I cannot put my finger on the cause, nor even tell you who might be behind it; but I know that it is out there, and I cannot deny that it frightens me. I keep remembering the stories of other times and uprisings."

"You treat your workers well on Sunrise. Those I have talked with seem most fond of your family, and I would trust their loyalty." I spoke firmly now, convinced that I was stating the truth.

"We may all be wagering our lives on it." Nick paused as we reached the door of the cloister. "Just remember to be careful, love ... for all our sakes." He brushed a final light kiss on my lips, then turned and headed for his carriage. Once he was inside, he waited until I had retreated into the building and barred the stout door before he drove off. I leaned against the door, wishing that I were with him, though not because I was afraid.

Chapter 14

Though I had hoped to see more of Nick, now that he had invited me to the ball, the next few days proved disappointing. No matter how many times I checked the path from Sunrise, it remained ominously unused. Still, during the day I kept busy with the children, and my evenings were devoted to the preparation of my ballgown as the decorations grew steadily more elaborate.

By Thursday afternoon, it was finished and resting in quiet elegance in a box in the corner of my wardrobe. It would be far from the most expensive gown at the ball, but it would not shame Nick, of that I was sure. Feeling restless, now that the task was complete, I wandered down the hall to the playroom, where several of the older children were gathered around a battered table, playing a card game that Seraphina had taught them.

I watched them for a moment or two, then, under the spur of my own impatience, I left the friendly gathering and went to what I had expected to be my schoolroom. It was, as it had been for much of the week, deserted. The older orphans were now my only steady pupils and that fact grieved me, for I remembered the eager children who had attended the first few days.

Would I be able to change the planters' minds at the

ball? I wondered. Or would they be like Baxter Travis, full of interest in all that I did, but still refusing to send their youngsters to school? Resentment gnawed at me, and I understood well Paul's frustration. There had to be a way . . .

"What has become of all your students, dear Rachel?" Geraldine appeared in the doorway, her mocking gaze making a lie of the concern in her voice.

"They seem to be occupied elsewhere, perhaps in the fields at Emerald Acres and Sea Cliff." I met her gaze calmly. "I remember several promising young ones from your plantation, but now none of them seems able to make the trip."

"'Tis a busy time of year." She moved through the room with a swish of her elegant riding costume. "What about Baxter's young workers? Have they not come around?"

I merely smiled at her, sensing from her sarcastic tone that she was aware of the answer.

Her stiffening posture told me that my silence irritated her, but her mocking smile was still firmly in place as she offered a suggestion. "Perhaps if you had chosen to attend the ball on his arm, Baxter might have been more willing to allow his workers an education."

The insult was more than I could bear, so I answered her in kind. "And on whose arm must I be to win students from Emerald Acres?"

Silence shivered in the warm room and I lifted a hand to my lips in horror as I realized what I had said. Though I felt she deserved the sharp retort, I had once again forgotten my fragile position here. Yet how could I apologize? I could think of no words that would undo the damage I had just done, so I braced myself for an explosion.

Geraldine stared at me for several moments, her expression unreadable, then slowly she relaxed into laughter. "So the pretty, shy kitten has claws like the rest of us. I, for one, am pleased to know it, Rachel. It will make the rest of your stay on our island much more entertaining."

With that, she turned away and left without a backward glance. I stood alone in the silent schoolroom, shaking a little in the aftermath of her visit, wondering fearfully just what she had meant by her cryptic words. I suspected that whatever it was, it boded no good for me.

"Was someone here?" Seraphina stepped into the room.

"Geraldine stopped by for a moment."

"What did she want?"

I sighed. "I have no idea." But as soon as I said the words, I knew they were a lie, for I did know what Geraldine sought: she wanted to be rid of me so that she could be on Nick's arm Saturday night at the ball. She might have fooled Nick with her sweet words, but I had seen behind the charming facade to the jealousy that swirled inside her and it frightened me even more than the intruder who had left his mark on the playroom last week.

Though I sometimes feared Saturday would never come, the moment I had both longed for and dreaded finally arrived. It was time for me to leave the cloister for Sunrise. Thanks to Seraphina's and Elena's constant chatter about the ball, all the children had become involved. I had tried on my gown several times for the children to see, and their excitement had added to my own.

Still, I was far from prepared for what happened when Nick drove up to the cloister Saturday afternoon. A dozen willing hands carried the boxes containing my gown and all that was to be worn with it. Everyone followed me from my room to the door, then Elena shyly produced a garland of fragrant white blossoms from one of the trees.

"Us be thinkin' these do for your hair, Miss Rachel. The boys picked 'um, but I wove 'um myself." She presented the gift with a credible curtsy, then shyly stood with her eyes downcast.

For a moment, I saw only the uneven chain of wilting flowers, then I recognized the love that had gone into it and set it reverently with all my other belongings on the carriage seat. "I shall wear it with pride tonight," I promised, hugging each child in turn, scarcely noticing the tears that rolled down my cheeks.

"Remember everything so you can tell us tomorrow," Seraphina whispered when I hugged her, too. "And have a wonderful time."

"I plan to enjoy every moment." As I spoke, I looked over her shoulder to meet Nick's gaze and my heart leaped with joy. It would, I was sure, be an evening to long remember.

"They truly love you." Nick's tone was surprisingly sober as he guided the horse around and headed back for Sunrise.

"And I them." The words came easy.

"'Tis a shame they cannot all be hiding at the top of the stairs to watch the guests arrive the way Pamela and Olivia used to."

"Did you ever hide there to watch?" I felt a great longing to know more about Nick, for I found it difficult to picture him as a boy of Ben's or Trey's age.

"Never. I was far more interested in sneaking out to the stable to listen to the men from the other plantations as they talked. That was how I heard all the bloody details of the various uprisings, since my father forbade such discussions in our household. I used to adore hiding up in the loft, spying on the men as they drank and gambled in one of the empty stalls below me."

"Did your father ever find out?" I tried to appear shocked, but I was really more amused by the picture his words created.

"For years, I was sure that I had fooled him, then one day he asked me if I really believed all the tall tales I had heard during those nights. He had known all along, but because he had done much the same thing when he was a boy, he had let me enjoy my secret." Nick's grin told me how much he loved his father for that, and my feelings for him deepened.

"And what about you? Did you ever sneak out of bed to spy on a ball when you were a little girl?"

"My parents never gave a real ball, but I used to spy on their parties. I adored seeing the lovely gowns and listening to all the laughter. I always dreamed that one day I should be going off to such parties myself, but by the time I was old enough, I was at Middle Brook Christian, and . . ." I faltered, embarrassed by my own words.

"Then tonight you shall be attending your first ball." Nick took my hand. "I shall be honored to have on my arm the most beautiful girl there."

I felt the heat rising in my cheeks. "You are being too kind, but I thank you for saying it." I studied my hands, fighting a sudden rush of anxiety at the thought of the evening ahead. What would it be like? How should I behave? What if everyone felt as Geraldine did—wishing me away?

Luckily, Nick seemed to sense my uneasiness, for he asked me about the children, distracting me from my troubling fears. By the time we reached the house, I felt almost ready to face whatever the evening might bring. At least, so I thought, until Nick lifted me down from the carriage and I turned to find a cold-eyed Geraldine

Chalmers descending the steps from the veranda, a false smile of welcome on her beautiful face.

"My dear Rachel, how nice that you could leave the cloister early to enjoy the afternoon with us." Her fingers were cool as she clasped my hand. "It must be pleasant to escape from your responsibilities once in a while. Such heavy burdens for such a young lady."

I met her gaze calmly, matching her smile with one of my own. I had no intention of being reduced to "poor dear Rachel, the charity case" by her words. "I adore the children and never consider them a burden, Geraldine, but it is a delight to be back at Sunrise, and for such a festive occasion. I feel honored to be a part of it."

"It will be our pleasure to present you to local society tonight." Nick had come up beside me, and his arm rested lightly around my shoulders. Though he spoke softly, I detected the fine edge of steel in his tone, and my heart leaped with joy at the way he was taking my part. "Come along inside, now; Harriet can get your boxes. I want to introduce you to some of our other guests."

I was swept up the steps on his arm, leaving Geraldine to follow at her leisure. For a moment, I felt uncomfortable in the grandeur of the fancifully decorated entry hall; then Harriet winked at me as she passed on her way to the backstairs with my boxes, and the sense of being an outsider faded. Her welcome was as genuine as Nick's, that I knew.

From that moment on, I had little time to worry about my reception, there were far too many people to meet. At first I was dizzy with the strain of trying to remember all the names and faces; but as the afternoon progressed, I began to sort them out. And with the sorting came a chilling realization—with the exception of the

Harrison men, not one of the people I met offered more than lip service to welcoming me.

I was relieved when I was finally able to retire to my old rooms on the third floor to change for the ball. Though all the guests had been polite, even the air up here felt more friendly. I slipped through the sitting room door, closed it, then leaned back against the solid wood.

"Be you all right, Miss?" Harriet appeared in the bedchamber doorway. "I just came up to make sure that your gown be hangin' out right, and to help you dress, if you like."

"'Tis nice to feel the warmth of friendship, Harriet." I held out my arms to her. "The chill downstairs is fierce."

"Miss Pamela say that the gentry be real disturbed 'bout you bein' with Mr. Nick." Her dark eyes gleamed with malice. "But us be most happy."

I hugged her again. "It pleases me, too, though I wish that the planter families would give me a chance. I came here only to help those they employ, so why do they resent me so?"

"I not be knowin', Miss." Harriet turned away. "You be the kindest lady I know."

"At the moment, I feel most confused. I had hoped to convince these people that I mean them no harm, but how can I, when they barely speak to me?"

I had not expected her to have any answers for me, and so was not disappointed when she began telling me that Digger had asked her to be his wife. Actually, I rather welcomed the change of subject, especially to such a happy topic. It was a joy to hear her plans and dreams for the future. It made it easier for me to ignore the precariousness of my own.

Still, as she talked of the future that she and Digger hoped to share, I found my sense of resolve reviving.

240

Knowing the two of them so well, I ached as I realized the limits the island's system cast upon them. They were both intelligent, and capable of far more than the menial tasks that were all they were given. If they could read and write, they could hope for . . .

"What about this, Miss?" Harriet claimed my attention by holding up the now sadly wilted coronet of flowers that Elena had made for me. "Did you wish something done with it?"

"Elena made it for me to wear." I sighed, remembering my promise to her.

"'Tis beyond savin', Miss." Harriet turned it in her hands. "There be no more than two, three blossoms with life left in 'um."

"Could they be freed and placed in my hair?"

"Let me try." Harriet moved quickly to create a swirl in my carefully arranged curls, then neatly pinned the healthy blossoms in the nest. Their creamy color contrasted nicely with my dark honey hair. "There they be, Miss."

"Splendid. I should hate to disappoint Elena; she and all the children worked so hard to make this, and I promised them that I would wear their creation to the ball." And I needed to feel them close about me, I realized. By wearing their gift, I should not have to face the cold-eyed planter families alone.

"Them would be most proud, Miss." Harriet adjusted a curl and smoothed back an errant tendril, then stepped away, adjusting the looking glass so that I could see. "You look a picture. All them fancy ladies gonna be green with envy behind their fans."

I giggled, more with nervousness than humor, but Harriet joined in. For a moment I felt as I had with my friends from school and I longed to be back in Philadelphia. Then I remembered that Nick would be waiting downstairs for me and I knew that I would trade places with no one tonight.

Feeling a little like the princess from an old fairy tale, I made my way down the front staircase alone, aware of all the eyes that followed me, but meeting only one gaze. Nick came to the bottom of the stairs to take my hand. He whispered compliments, but I scarce heard them over the pounding of my heart. I was already responding to the passionate heat of his gaze.

More people had arrived while I was changing, and this time my reception was a bit warmer, especially when I talked of the children and the orphanage. It was only when the school was mentioned that the tenor of the conversations changed. For the first time I became deeply aware of just how much these people feared education of their workers. At the mere mention of it, the women became pale and the men's faces turned red with fury.

Still, I had to try, for I believed every well-thought-out argument I offered. It was Digger's face or Harriet's that filled my mind as I spoke and their right to a better future that I wished to make these people understand. It was, unfortunately, a battle I had no hope of winning, and by the time the small band of musicians struck up the first tune, I was delighted to give my full attention to the dancing.

Though the tall windows of the huge white and gold ballroom stood open to the night breeze, the island heat soon had me feeling wilted, and after a rather sprightly dance with Baxter Travis, I excused myself to freshen up in one of the rooms Mrs. Harrison had set aside for guest use. I had just bathed my flushed cheeks with the cool flower-scented water when the door opened and Geraldine came in.

"So are you enjoying your taste of our island society?" Her blue-eyed gaze chilled me more than the water.

"'Tis a marvelous ball." I returned my attention to blotting my face and smoothing my tousled curls. I had thought to remove the blossoms, which were not surviving the dancing well at all; but now I hesitated, my hand shaking so that I feared I might ruin the hairstyle Harriet had worked so hard to achieve.

"Too bad it may be the last for a time, thanks to you."

"What?" I dropped the bit of cloth and faced her again. "Whatever are you saying, Geraldine?"

"Have you really no sense of what you are doing?" Her polite smile had vanished and the hardness of her expression aged her, making me aware that though she was but three years my senior, she was far more experienced in the ways of the world than I.

"I have been dancing."

"You have been making a fool of Nick Harrison. Forcing him to defend your radical ideas. I care not for how much danger you place yourself in, but have you no feelings for his safety? Can you not see the temper of the other planters?" Her voice rose as she spoke, and for the first time, I realized that she was genuinely upset.

"'Tis well known that Mr. Harrison brought Reverend Michaels here," I protested. "And I have only spoken of my feelings about education. I meant no . . ."

"Pretty, simpering little girl, prattling on about things she can never hope to understand. This island is teetering on the edge of an uprising and you run about with your matches. Well, let me warn you that if trouble comes, the cloister cannot save you any more than it could save the monks from the results of their meddling ways." With that she turned and stalked from the room, leaving me alone with the echoes of her dire predictions.

I closed my eyes, not wanting to believe her words. Surely she was just speaking from her own fears. But her emotion had been all too real, I realized. Though I was aware that because of Nick she had no love for me, I was equally aware that she did love Nick. And he had been defending me. I had been flushed with pride at his vehement defense of my teaching; but now . . .

What if his friends turned on him because of me? Fear swelled inside me so that I worried that the seams of my gown would be strained. How could I go back out there and face him now? For a heartbeat, I considered simply going up to my familiar rooms on the third floor. I could plead illness or weariness and ask to be driven back to the cloister . . .

And Geraldine would have exactly what she wanted—Nick all to herself for the remainder of the evening. I should become a laughingstock as she whispered to her many friends how easily her words had sent me running. I stiffened my spine and carefully repaired my appearance. When I went back out to face the hostile crowd, I was determined to look my best.

I found Nick waiting in the hall. "I was beginning to think you might be ill." He took my hands.

"I feel wonderful," I assured him, with a smile that probably glowed with the flames inside me. So long as he wanted me here, nothing Geraldine Chalmers could say would make me go.

"Shall we return to the dancing?"

I nodded, my breath caught in my throat at the prospect of being in his arms once again. Geraldine was mad; this night was full of magic, not malice. I hoped it would go on forever.

For a time, it seemed that all was well. We danced, then sat laughing and talking as we feasted on the elegant repast that the servants had set out for us. Refreshed, I allowed Nick to lead me back to the ballroom, ready for more dancing. This time, however, the musicians had hardly begun when a great hubbub from the entry hall interrupted.

"I must see to that," Nick said, frowning as he led me off the floor. "You wait here."

He was gone before I could protest, so I simply followed him, stopping only when I reached the edge of the huge entry hall. A number of people were already gathered in a knot near the door, but they parted as Nick approached, and I gasped as I realized that they had been standing around a man who lay stretched out on the floor.

As Nick approached, the man struggled to sit up and I was horrified to see the bright spreading stain of blood on his pale shirt. "Nick, Nick, you must send help! There be trouble at Emerald Acres."

"Allen!" A shriek from behind me forced me to look away just as the man collapsed back on the polished floor. Geraldine raced by me, then dropped to her knees beside the man, screaming his name over and over. He made no sound, and a moment later, Nick pulled her away, shouting for the island physician, who was among the guests.

I took a deep breath and forced my feet forward, aware of my duty. As part of my training at the school's orphanage, I had cared for injured children many times. It was not a skill I enjoyed, but when I'd learned that I was coming to this far-off island, I had been pleased to have it.

"May I be of assistance?" I asked, as Dr. Hogarth, whom I had met earlier, began his examination of the ominously still man.

He glared at me, obviously impatient with my interruption. "What can you do?"

"I can help you free his shirt from the wound and if one of the servants could bring us soap and water and cloths, I can help clean it." I met his gaze without wincing away.

"Fetch what they need," Nick ordered, half-dragging Geraldine toward the parlor. "The rest of you, stand back and give them room to help Allen."

The doctor moved aside to make room for me as I knelt beside him, heedless of the spreading puddle of blood that was seeping from the man's side. Nausea burned in my stomach as we eased the shirt away and I could see the ugly gash in his torn flesh, but I was too busy following the doctor's orders to do more than swallow hard.

My knees had gone numb by the time we had the bleeding stopped and the doctor had bandaged the wound. "He can be carried to a room now." Dr. Hogarth sat back, his face weary from the strain. As soon as several men came to gently lift the man, he turned to me. "Where did you learn such skills, Miss Ames?"

"At the orphanage where I worked before I came here. Our children were always injuring themselves by falling from trees or in rough play. 'Twas a part of my duties to help them, since there was no doctor near at hand." I tried to get up, but sank back as my numb legs refused to hold me.

"Are you feeling faint?" He peered at me, his dark eyes worried.

"'Tis only my legs," I assured him. "From the kneeling."

He nodded, offering a tired smile. "Mine also."

"Will the man be all right?"

"If we stopped the bleeding soon enough, he should be. The wound is ugly, but not likely to be fatal. He was lucky, the knife struck nothing vital."

I swallowed hard, not liking to remember the gaping

wound. Bandaging scraped knees and cut hands had been poor preparation for what I had seen tonight. I wondered that I had managed it without swooning.

"Rachel, let me help you up." Nick held out his hand to me. "And you, Dr. Hogarth, are you all right?"

The doctor grunted a reply, then got slowly to his feet as Nick lifted me to mine. The room dipped and swirled sickeningly for a moment, but with Nick's warm body as my anchor, it quickly settled back to normal and I could open my eyes. I drew in a deep breath, seeking the strength to free myself from Nick's wonderful but highly improper embrace. Before I could do anything, however, Geraldine exploded through the parlor door, scattering the few remaining onlookers like pigeons fleeing a rampaging cat.

"Where is he? What have you done with Allen? Please tell me he's not . . ." She shuddered to a stop in front of Dr. Hogarth, but I felt her blazing glare when she glanced toward Nick.

"I have had him carried to a bedchamber, Miss Chalmers," the doctor replied. "And he is doing quite well, considering. He will require a great deal of rest, good food, and care; but if no fever comes from the wound, he should heal in time."

"I should like to be with him." Geraldine looked now to Nick. "If you can tear yourself away from your little . . ."

"Rachel needs me at the moment, Geraldine. She went a bit faint after assisting the doctor in treating Allen's wound." Nick's tone was emotionless, but I felt his tension in the tightening of his arm. "Perhaps one of the servants could show you where Allen was taken."

Her stormy gaze bored into me for another moment, but I noted that her lower lip was trembling as she turned to accept the arm of one of the men who had helped carry the unconscious man up the broad staircase. I looked up at Nick. "Was this Allen someone dear to her?"

"A cousin. He came to live with them several years ago." His expression became thoughtful. "I had not realized that they had become so close."

"Are you about ready to go, Nick?" Baxter Travis emerged from the rear of the house with a large group of men. His gaze touched my face, and his lips thinned as he frowned. "Or were you planning to remain here with Miss Ames?"

I should not have wanted to be on the receiving end of the furious glare that Nick sent his way, but Baxter merely smiled. "Not that I should blame you, she is obviously a woman of many talents." His gaze moved to my skirt, and when I followed it, I saw that my lovely white lace was now dyed red with Allen's blood. It took all my self-control to keep back the swirling sickness that rose inside me.

Gritting my teeth, I forced myself to step away from Nick's side. "Where are you going?" I asked.

Nick gave me a distracted look. "To Emerald Acres. Did you not hear Allen say there was trouble there?"

A chill passed over me as I remembered the man's gasping words and realized fully what they might mean. My first thought was of Geraldine's warning. If there was trouble, the children and Seraphina might be in danger, too. "I think perhaps I should go back to the cloister. If you can spare Digger . . ."

Nick frowned down at me. "You are to remain here, where you will be safe. Digger can go and warn them at the cloister." He started toward the door, then turned back. "Did you hear me, Rachel? I want you to stay here with my family until I find out exactly what is afoot."

I opened my mouth to protest, but before I could find the words, a second group of men came in from the ve-

248

randa, shouting that the horses were ready, and demanding weapons. In the resulting flurry of activity, I was unceremoniously pushed into the parlor, where most of the women were now gathered. Within moments, the shouting men went galloping off.

Silence settled over the room like a pall. I looked around and found myself the center of attention. Mrs. Harrison rose from where she had been seated on a couch and came over to pat my arm. "You were very brave, my dear, to help that way. If you would like to change, I am sure that one of the maids would be happy to try to get that stain out of your lovely gown."

"Thank you, I should like to change, and then I really need to get back to the cloister." My knees were shaking so that I wanted more than anything to sink down on the nearest chair, but the hostility in the eyes of most of the women made it clear that I was unwelcome in their midst.

"I believe Nick would want you to remain here with us, Rachel," Mrs. Harrison said. "Let me ring for someone to go up with you."

"Please, I can . . ." I let it trail off as Harriet came into the parlor. Tears burned in my eyes at the sight of her friendly face. I offered no more arguments as Mrs. Harrison ordered her to escort me to my rooms and to see to my needs.

It was heaven to lean on her strong arm as we climbed the stairs and even better to answer her eager questions about what had happened. Stories had been rife in the kitchen, but no one had known the real story as I did.

"I hope they got that old devil Duquanne," Harriet said, as we neared the door to my old sitting room.

"Harriet!" I gasped at her words, for I had always considered her a proper young girl, sweet and kind.

"Beggin' your pardon, Miss, but I be speakin' the

truth. You can ask Digger, if him not be a devil." She lifted her little chin and met my shocked gaze.

"I should like to speak with Digger. I need him to drive me to the cloister as soon as I change. If you could fetch him after you undo my buttons . . ."

"I be pleased to help you change, Miss." Harriet hurried ahead of me to light a candle. "And I be glad to try to get out that awful stain afore it sets bad."

I sensed that she was evading my request. "What about Digger?"

"Mayhap I could ask someone else." She glanced at me, then looked away, her expression troubled.

"Where is Digger, Harriet?"

She shrugged. "I not be knowin'. Likely he went with the men to Emerald Acres." Her nervous movements told me that she was lying.

A sudden horrible suspicion swept through me. "Is he in trouble, Harriet?"

She moved behind me to undo the buttons and it seemed an eternity before she spoke. "I not be knowin', Miss, for true. Him not been 'round since afore sunset. I be most awful worried 'bout him, but I dasn't ask nobody, if'n you know what I mean."

Unfortunately, I understood perfectly, and my heart ached. "I shall say nothing, you know that. Digger has been a good friend to me, too."

"Do you really need someone to drive you to the cloister?" Harriet finished the buttons and helped me with the dress.

"Is there a small wagon or buggy that I could drive myself?"

"Oh, Miss, this not be a night for a woman to be out on her own." Harriet let the gown fall as she met my gaze. "Mr. Nick would have my head, if'n I should . . ."

"He shall never know. Just tell me if there is such a

conveyance available." I picked up the gown I had worn this afternoon and slipped it over my head.

"There's likely several near the kitchen door. Folk came in all manner of wagons, and most left on horses from the stable."

I fastened my gown, then smoothed the skirt. Urgency goaded me like a spur, and I looked around the room. "You stay here and see to the gown and pack up my other belongings; that way you can honestly say you have no idea where I went."

Harriet came to put her arms around me. "Have a care, Miss. Stop for no one and nothing. Take a big whip."

"I shall be perfectly safe. The cloister is within sight of Sunrise, after all." I spoke with confidence, but as I made my way down the backstairs and slipped out into the night, my heart began to pound. Suddenly I felt a sense of menace that I had never known before. Had I not been desperately worried about those I had left at the cloister, I should have gladly turned back.

Gritting my teeth, I headed for the closest conveyance—a pony cart. I snapped the whip and sent the sturdy sorrel on its way out of the familiar stable area and into the shadows that stretched between Sunrise and the cloister . . . shadows that might hide all manner of evildoers.

Chapter 15

At first, I was worried that someone might come after me; but as I left, there was no sign of anyone coming from either the well-lit plantation house or the dimly lit stable. Had all the men gone with Nick and the others? But who would defend the women left behind? I was sure that only Dr. Hogarth and perhaps Mr. Harrison had remained at the house.

My stomach clenched as I realized just how much danger there might be . . . and where I was. The shadows closed around me, hiding the rough path from my eyes, so that I had to allow the horse to slow to his own pace, trusting that he could see better than I.

All at once I became aware of a rustling in the trees and brush that grew beside the narrow road. Was there someone there? I pictured some huge, faceless man with a long knife, perhaps already dripping with blood from the ugly wound I had helped to clean. Shuddering, I lifted the whip, ready to set the horse to running. But I set it back down as the breeze tugged at my hair. Panic was my enemy, too.

Swallowing hard, I forced myself to peer beyond the screen of the encroaching vegetation. My fears eased as I glimpsed the reassuring bulk of the cloister against the starless sky. Dark and grim it might be, but it was the sanctuary to which I'd fled, and I was glad that it appeared so peaceful.

It would also take me much too long to get there if I followed the road, I decided. Far better to take the shortcut that Nick had used earlier today—or was it past midnight, making our short ride to the ball something that had happened yesterday? I almost giggled at my wayward thoughts, then shivered, though the night was far from cold.

Fear was making me foolish, my fear for all the innocent inhabitants of the cloister and, even worse, my heartfelt fear about what might be happening to Nick even now. What had they found at Emerald Acres? What horrible thing had happened there tonight? Worse—what might still happen there?

I shook my head, willing the terrible images to leave my mind so that I could concentrate on finding the break in the thick brush that bordered the road and follow the path that crossed through the cane field that spread between Sunrise and the cloister. Even though I peered intently at the dark wall, I nearly missed the opening between the bushes.

The horse seemed reluctant to turn, but I held firm to the reins and he finally obeyed, plunging into an even darker area. I shuddered as a palm frond trailed its cold fingers along my cheek, then swallowed a scream as some night creature scurried away from the cart. I was beginning to regret leaving the road.

There was a small open area between the bushes and the beginning of the cane field and I nearly turned back. This time, however, the horse seemed more willing, for he plunged without hesitation into the narrow track that bisected the field. The thick growth seemed to close in around me, shutting off my view of both the cloister and the plantation house.

I closed my eyes, fighting my growing panic. 'Twas

only the sugar cane whispering, I assured myself. The scurrying sounds came from the small creatures who lived in the field. No one else would be here in the middle of the night. The brassy taste of blood filled my mouth, and I realized that I had bitten my own lip to keep from screaming.

"This is madness." I spoke aloud, seeking reassurance from the sound of my own voice. "There is nothing to be afraid of. In a moment I shall be at the cloister, and . . ."

The cart jolted to a stop so suddenly I nearly fell from the seat. I peered ahead, then seeing nothing, slapped the reins on the sorrel's back. The beast stamped his feet, but moved only sideways, snorting at something in front of him.

Were there snakes in the cane fields? I wondered, as I tried to see what was frightening him. The blackness was too complete, thanks to the overcast that obscured both moon and stars. I picked up the whip, ready to lash the poor animal into action, but a low groan stayed my hand.

"Who is there?" I whispered, my heart pounding so loud in my ears that I feared I would not be able to hear an answer.

"Miss Rachel?" The words were more gasp than speech, but I recognized the voice nonetheless.

"Digger." I dropped the whip and jumped down from the pony cart, nearly stumbling in the dark and rutted soil of the narrow track. The horse shied away as I moved past him toward the dim shape that lay across the pathway. "Is that you, Digger?"

His groan was my only answer, and when I reached out to touch him, his shoulder was wet. Memories of the bloody man who had stumbled into Sunrise sent a shiver of apprehension through me. "Digger, what happened to you? Are you hurt? Please, you must talk to me."

He took a deep breath. "I be hurt, Miss. I were tryin' to git to the cloister, only I fell and . . ."

"Can you stand if I help you?" I longed to reach out to him, but in the dark I had no way of knowing where he might be injured and I feared hurting him more.

"I kin try."

My eyes had begun to adjust to the dimness and I was able to discern his wavering form well enough to offer my shoulder for support. I was panting from the exertion by the time he was safely in the cart and it was no surprise to me when he immediately collapsed. I climbed up beside him and urged the horse forward. "Once we are out of this field, I shall take you back to Sunrise," I promised, as soon as I caught my breath. "Dr. Hogarth can tend your wounds, and . . ."

"No. Please, Miss, I can't go back. If'n they sees me, they kill me. You gotta hide me, Miss Rachel, or I be a dead man." His words came in gasps, between moans.

"But you are injured, Digger, you need someone to care for you, and . . ."

"I'd sooner die in the fields than be strung up by the planters. Nobody be listenin' to me, if'n they sees me now."

Remembering the wild fury of the group who had ridden out from Sunrise, I had a chill feeling that he might be right. "Were you at Emerald Acres, Digger?" I asked, though I doubted that I would be pleased by his answer.

"No, ma'am. I be halfway there when the black robes got me. Out of the night they come, screechin' somethin' fierce. Beat me half to death, afore I got away, then them rode off laughin'." His voice was growing weaker, but I could hear the ring of truth clearly.

"Why were you on your way there?"

He barely stirred, his silence telling me that he had slipped into near unconsciousness. Fearing for his life, I picked up the whip and snapped it, urging the horse to hurry the last endless distance through the cane field, then up the hill to the cloister.

I stopped the cart at the door, then checked to make sure that Digger was still breathing. He moaned at my touch, which reassured me. I hurried to the door and was relieved to discover that Seraphina had obeyed my orders and barred it. Fighting panic, I pulled the ancient cord and heard the distant sound of the bell. What seemed a lifetime later, the bar was lifted and Seraphina's lamplit smile welcomed me home.

It took Seraphina and me near an hour to clean and bandage Digger's many wounds. I was truly grateful that he remained unconscious throughout the ordeal, for there was nothing I could offer him for the pain our ministrations caused. Deep cuts on his shoulder, forehead, and back were the worst injuries; but he was bruised near from head to toe and I wished mightily that Dr. Hogarth was here to make sure none of his injuries were life-threatening.

When we had done all we could, Seraphina brewed some strong tea and handed me a cup. "What do you plan to do with him, Rachel?" she asked. "Are you sure 'twould not be best to take him to Sunrise?"

Having had plenty of time while we worked to consider just those questions, I had my answers ready. "If evil was done at Emerald Acres this night, I fear the planters would be likely to blame Digger. They were in no mood to listen to reason when they rode out. I think he must stay hidden until the temper of the planters cools."

"Where?"

"He would be safe in the cellar and it would be easy

enough for us to feed and care for him." I met her gaze. "'Twould have to be a secret from everyone, and I know that it could cause us serious trouble, should he be found; but if you are willing to help me . . ." I let it trail off, knowing that she deserved a voice in this decision since she would suffer, too, should our actions be discovered by the wrong people.

"I would turn no man over to Duquanne and his ilk." Seraphina drained her cup and got to her feet. "'Twill not be easy to get him down there, but if we can rouse him . . ."

It was near dawn before I sent Seraphina to her room, then made my weary way to the front room of the cloister to make sure that I had barred the door after we dragged Digger inside. I was about to blow out the lamp, when a tap on the door stopped me in my tracks.

"Rachel? Are you in there, Rachel?" The voice was Nick's.

I opened the door, bracing myself for anger, sure that Nick had come to scold me for leaving Sunrise against his orders, but the man outside was wavering so that I merely slipped my arm around his waist and helped him inside.

I gasped when I saw him in the lamplight. His white shirt was stained with blood, as were his fine trousers. "What happened to you? Dear God, you are injured, Nick."

"Trifling wounds." He waved his hand and immediately collapsed into a chair. "I just rode by to make sure that Seraphina and the children were safe, then I saw the cart outside and . . ." He looked as though he wanted to chastise me, but he was obviously too weak.

"Take off your shirt," I ordered, turning my weary steps toward the kitchen. "I shall take care of your wounds while you tell me what happened at Emerald Acres."

257

"My injuries can wait until we . . ." He started to rise, then stumbled back, this time nearly falling to the floor, before I reached his side and eased him down into the chair again.

"Will you just be still and do as I ask?" I was far too tired to be patient. "You cannot go anywhere in this condition."

For a moment his eyes flashed with rebellion, then it ebbed and he began to make a clumsy attempt at unbuttoning his blood-soaked shirt. I looked down and noted that an equal amount of blood was seeping from a long slit just above the knee of his trousers. I closed my eyes briefly, thanking God that I had a large supply of soap, bandages, and the healing ointment that I had brought with me from Philadelphia. If anything should happen to Nick . . .

Unwilling to even entertain such a horrible possibility, I straightened up and hurried to the kitchen to get my supplies. As long as there was breath in my body, I would care for Nick and protect him from the fever that could come from untreated wounds. I brought my scissors with me when I returned.

"What happened?" I asked, as I gently bathed the deep gash in his shoulder. "Who did this to you?"

"I don't know." He winced.

"How can that be? I thought you knew everyone on the island."

"'Twas a band of masked men, all wrapped in black capes. They came riding out of the night and were about to set fire to the sugar mill at Emerald Acres. We tried to stop them and there was a battle. Several of our men were seriously injured. Still, we drove the attackers off. Did them some damage, too." He sounded pleased at that.

"Anyway, then we took our casualties to the plantation house. 'Tis chaos there, too. Duquanne was killed and so were several other men. The Chalmers servants were terrified, but once they saw us, they were ready to help."

"What of the rest of your group?" I smoothed the salve thickly over the gash, then began making a bandage to protect it.

"Once we were sure Emerald Acres was secure, we thought to make sure that the attackers struck nowhere else." Nick shifted in the chair and I saw the lines of pain deepen in his face as he moved his injured leg.

"And you decided to ride over here instead of having your own wounds tended." It was not a question. I secured the bandage and picked up the scissors.

"What the devil do you think you are doing?" Nick demanded, as I placed my hand on his muscular thigh just above the welling wound.

"I was about to cut away your trouser leg," I informed him tartly. "Unless you wish to remove them so I can treat the wound on your leg."

His scandalized gaze would have been amusing, had our situation not been so serious. I met his gaze firmly, ignoring the heat that blazed not only in my cheeks, but from deep within me, as I felt the muscles tense in his thighs. After what seemed an eternity, he looked down. "Cut away."

My hand shook slightly as I tried to be gentle, freeing the sodden fabric from his skin with great care, using my scissors gingerly for fear of nicking the pale, hairroughened skin I was exposing. Once the cloth was gone, I was relieved to see that the gash was not as serious as the one on his shoulder. Likely 'twas the strain of riding here that had made it bleed so freely.

Relief made my head light, or perhaps it was the madness of the night, for I found myself taking extra pains with my cleaning of the wound. A strange compulsion seemed to grip me as I smoothed the salve on his muscular thigh. I wanted to stroke his pale skin, investigate the odd sensation caressing him caused. I felt mesmerized . . .

"Just bandage it, Rachel." Nick sounded as though he might be strangling, but when I looked up at him, my heart was seared by the blazing fire of desire in his eyes. I had to look away.

Shattered by the realization of what I had been doing, I found myself shaking too much to manage the bandaging. Shame and longing swept over me in alternating waves, and tears burned in my eyes. Never would I have believed that I could have behaved so wantonly. My humiliation was complete when Nick took the strip of cloth from my hands and fashioned the bandage himself.

He struggled to his feet, bracing himself against the back of the chair as he tested his leg. When he was satisfied with his strength, he turned to me again. "Now, I want you to get Seraphina and the children. I shall take all of you back to Sunrise until this foolishness is under control."

A part of me wanted to do exactly that. I was weary of fear and worried about the children; if they were safe at Sunrise . . . But Digger's face filled my mind. And I remembered the way everyone in the parlor had looked at me after the men rode off. Nick might want me in his home, but I suspected no one else in his family did. Even Jarvis Harrison must be wondering if he had made a mistake by bringing first Paul, then me, to the island.

"Rachel?"

"I cannot leave here, Nick. We have too many children to care for now. Surely we are safe here, for what danger are we to anyone?" I spoke quickly, trying hard to believe my own words.

"If there is a revolt, no one will be safe, Rachel." His face was grim, all signs of his desire having vanished.

"Remember that the men who built this place died within its stone walls."

I shuddered, but held my ground. "We shall be careful, and Sunrise is near at hand."

He straightened and whispered a soft oath. "You are a stubborn woman, Rachel Ames. If I were not so infernally weakened by loss of blood, I should . . ."

Not wanting to hear what he might do to me, I interrupted him. "What you should do is take the pony cart back. I fear that I took it without permission, and I have no idea to whom it belongs. At least that way, you can keep from opening the wound on your leg again."

I made the mistake of looking into his eyes, and what I saw there took my breath away. His anger melted under a heat that flamed within me. Suddenly I was in his arms, and in spite of his wounded shoulder, he held me close for a kiss that bruised my mouth and turned my world upside down. When he stepped back, it was I who staggered, weak and dizzy.

"For the sake of your reputation, I shall go now, but I will be back, Rachel. 'Tis not safe for you here. In fact, it might be best if you spent the next few weeks on St. Devina with Sarah. At least there you would be out of danger."

I opened my mouth to protest that I should never leave Bell Harbour Island and the children entrusted to me; but he gave me no chance, for he was already limping toward the door. Once there, he stopped only long enough to order me to bar it and keep it barred until I heard otherwise. Then he was gone and I was alone with my confused and aching heart.

What did he feel? I had seen the desire in his eyes, felt it when he ravished my mouth; but was there more? Was it only wanting that he felt, or could he care for me, even love me as I now realized I loved him?

His anger had flared so quickly and his desire to send

me away had come so soon after his kiss. What did it all mean? Too weary even to think about it, I blew out the lamp and picked up my candle. It was time for bed. I paused at my sitting room door, leaning against the wall as I squinted at the clock on my desk. No, bedtime was long past; it was already close to dawn. I groaned, realizing that the children would be stirring soon.

The next few days were the longest I had ever known. In obedience to Nick's orders, I kept the children inside, which made it nearly impossible to care properly for Digger. Still, according to Seraphina, who ventured down during the babies' nap time while I kept all the older children busy in the schoolroom, he seemed well enough to eat the food she carried and asked only if everyone at Sunrise was safe.

I watched each day for Nick, but no one left the road to approach the cloister, so I had no idea how he fared. I could only hope and pray that he had reached the house safely and that his wounds were now being cared for by Dr. Hogarth. And that he would come by soon— both to lift his restrictions and to let me know how he felt about me. My need to know that ached inside me every time my thoughts wandered from the tasks at hand.

Why had no one told me that love could bring pain as well as joy? And how should I ever learn to live without him, if he had no feelings for me? And even if he did care about me, was there really a chance for us when it seemed that near everyone on the island blamed me for the trouble that had erupted?

A pounding on the door brought me from the kitchen late the third morning and I was delighted to throw open the door, sure that, at long last, it must be Nick. I was stunned to find Paul standing on the other side.

"Why is the door barred?" he demanded, as he

stepped inside. "Where are all the children? Have you no students to teach today?"

I found the final question the easiest to answer. "I have been without students for days. And, no one would be coming after the trouble at Emerald Acres. As to the children in my care, they are in the playroom."

"And the door?" His displeasure was obvious.

"Nick suggested that I keep it barred, so—" I stopped abruptly, not wanting to invite questions about the circumstances under which Nick had given that order. "Do you think it would be safe to let the children out during the daylight hours?"

"Of course. No one wishes harm to the children. Besides, I expect the trouble has passed. 'Twas just a natural uprising. Duquanne, the overseer who was killed, was an evil man. His death could be considered divine retribution for the horrors he visited upon the innocent." As Paul crossed the room, I got a good look at him and saw the lines of weariness in his face.

"What else has been happening?" I asked. "I have heard nothing since the night of the ball, when a man came from Emerald Acres to report the attack."

"All has been peaceful. There was some talk among the planters of punishment against the islanders, but since they have no idea who might have attacked Duquanne and his henchmen, that has died down." Paul looked pleased. "Now I think the planters might be ready to listen to me, so I have been riding about making visits. Which is why I expected to see some results here." He glared around the empty schoolroom. "Perhaps the barred door has discouraged them."

"I should have heard any knock, and there is the bell," I reminded him, smarting from the censure in his tone. "Would you like to see the children?"

He shook his head. "Not this time. I was on my way to speak with Jarvis and Nick, then I must ride on to

Sea Cliff. Perhaps this time they will be more willing to listen to my warnings. 'Tis plain that their ways are only making the islanders more restless."

"Oh, Paul, are you sure you should . . ." I stopped under the weight of his gaze, realizing immediately that I had no right to question his judgment. I was still the outsider here, whether I felt that way or not. "I only want you to be careful."

"The islanders would never harm me." His tone held no doubt. "Nor would they trouble you, so there is no need for you to worry about Nick's warnings. You are doing God's work, and the folk we came to help respect that, in spite of what the planters wish us to believe."

"What do you mean?"

"You said yourself that Nick warned you to keep the children inside and the door barred. 'Tis what comes of mixing socially with them, Rachel. We must be above their ways."

I nodded, though my heart refused to accept his implied condemnation of Nick. Nick and Mr. Harrison were different from the other planters, I had to believe that. Just as I had to believe that Nick would come by soon to make sure that we were faring all right. I was relieved as Paul rode off, but his words continued to disturb me.

Still, I was grateful for his visit, since it allowed me to release the unhappy children into the bright sunlight. My only concession to Nick's warning was to insist that they stay close to the cloister. As all the children were anxious to work in their newly planted garden, no one offered any argument, and I was able to slip down into the cellar to spend some time with Digger.

In spite of our neglect, he was recovering fairly well and already growing impatient for news of the outside world. I relayed everything that Paul had told me while I checked and rebandaged his wounds, then faced him as I asked, "Is he right, Digger? Was this just a small uprising of the people that Duquanne had abused?"

His frown deepened. "I not be knowin' for sure, Miss, but 'tweren't no men from Emerald Acres what attacked me. I be knowin' most folk on the island and ... They come outta the night like devils, wrapped all in black and wearin' masks. And they be ridin' fine horses."

I swallowed hard, aware of his meaning. "Could they have been borrowed or stolen?"

He shrugged, then winced. "If'n I could get out of here and go about ..."

"You need more time to heal." I hesitated, then added, "And where would you go, Digger? It might be best if I spoke with Nick about you before ..."

"No! You saved me, Miss, there be no way I be puttin' you in danger. One night I be slippin' away and no one ever be knowin' that I been here." His gaze was proud and strong.

"But not yet," I countered, sure that he would only get into more trouble if he left, something I very much wanted to prevent. I wanted Harriet's dreams to come true, and for that to happen, Digger must somehow be able to return to Sunrise unchallenged.

"The longer I be stayin' here, the more danger you be in."

I lifted a hand to stop his words. "There is no way anyone could find you here, Digger. Only Seraphina and I know about the hidden stairway and no one but Reverend Michaels has ever come by since the night of the attack."

"You be sure of that?"

"What do you mean?"

"I be hearin' stuff, late at night. Shuffling sounds and some bangin'."

"Perhaps it was the children, or ..."

He shook his head, stopping my words. "'Twere long after they be in bed." He got up and limped slowly toward the stairway. "I be moving 'bout, gettin' my strength back. Seems like it be comin' from over there." He indicated the area beyond the sturdy wall at the top of the stairs.

I swallowed hard. "That would be the walled-off part of the cloister. There should be no one over there. 'Tis little more than a ruin."

Digger said nothing, and shortly after that, I had to leave, for it would never do to open the secret door while one of the children was in the playroom. His words haunted me through the rest of the day. Could someone be hiding in the rest of the cloister? It seemed very unlikely, yet what else could the noises mean?

Other memories stalked me after the children were settled for the night. Could our intruder and food thief have come from the other side of the wall? And what of the times I still had the chill feeling that I was being watched? For the last week or so I had tried hard to believe that it was just a reaction to the island superstition, but now . . .

I paced my sitting room, too restless to prepare for bed, though I was still weary from the strain of the past few days. I should do something to protect the children, but what? Perhaps when Digger was well, I could show him the door that Nick had taken me through, and he . . .

I shook my head, well aware that I might be putting him in danger. What I should do was tell Nick. If I mentioned that I had heard noises in the night, he would be sure to investigate. Right after he ordered all of us to Sunrise. I closed my eyes, unable to imagine the misery such a move would create for the children and for the

Harrisons. I hugged myself, feeling closed in and smothered by my doubts and fears.

Perhaps I should go and talk to Digger, I decided. I might even hear the noises myself, if I was in the cellar. I opened my door quietly, not wanting to disturb Seraphina, who was as uneasy as I, having heard nothing from her family in the days since Duquanne's death. I tiptoed along the hall, wishing that I had thought to ask Paul to make inquiries for her.

The playroom door was closed, but we kept it well oiled now so that we could slip in and out without waking the children. I opened it slowly, still unsure of exactly what I was going to do. If Digger was sleeping, might I not be rousing him unnecessarily? He needed his rest, too, for I knew he would not agree to remain hidden much longer.

As my candle glow invaded the darkness, I heard a soft sound. Had Digger chosen tonight to make his escape? Wanting to stop him, I pushed the door open and stepped through it. Something black swirled out, enveloping me for a moment. I stumbled, losing my grip on the candle as I tried to keep my feet. A hard hand pushed on my back and I crashed into the wall, screaming as I fell to the floor.

I must have lost consciousness for a moment, for when I was again aware of my surroundings, I heard a creaking, followed by a soft click. Struggling to sit up, I was shattered to discover I could see nothing. Where was I? Why was it so dark?

"Rachel? What is it? Where are you?" Seraphina's frightened voice came from a distance.

"Seraphina!" I tried to scream, but my voice came out a squeak as ripples of terror swept over me, holding me prisoner.

In a moment, the wonderful glow of a candle flame appeared and I could see that I was lying on the playroom floor. My own candle lay several feet away, having been extinguished when I fell. Seraphina dropped to her knees beside me. "What happened? Are you hurt?"

The touch of her hands dispelled the worst of my terror, and I managed to catch my breath. "I'm all right, but someone was here. I heard something, and . . ."

Her expression stopped my words and I saw her gaze turn toward the hidden stairway. Without a word, she closed the door to the hall, then righted my candle and lit it before she went to open the panel. As she disappeared down the stairs, I forced myself to get up.

My shoulder hurt, as did the side of my head, which I dimly remembered striking against the wall before I fell. Right after I had felt someone push me! My stomach knotted, and it took all my courage to go toward the opening. If someone had pushed me down, might they not be waiting for Seraphina. . . ?

Seraphina appeared as I reached the opening. She held her finger to her lips as she emerged and closed the panel behind her. "He's sleeping sound, snoring even. Likely he never heard your cry. I doubt I would have, had I not been coming from the kitchen."

"You were in the kitchen?" I shook my head, trying to make sense of what had happened. "But someone was here." I described what had happened as best I could.

"I saw no one, Rachel, and I was just coming into the hall when I heard your scream, so . . ."

She stopped, but I could finish the sentence myself. No one could have run from this room without her seeing them. Yet someone had been here, someone who had pushed me into the wall. I shivered at the memory of the hard hands and the swirling material that had momentarily blinded me. Black cloth, like a black robe or cape. I shuddered, remembering what both Digger and Nick had told me of those who'd attacked them.

Not speaking, we both looked around the room, now fully illuminated by our two candles, but there was nothing to be seen. "Perhaps we should lock the door," she suggested.

I shook my head. "Not while Digger is hidden here. He would be a prisoner."

"But if someone was in here . . ."

"Clearly no one is here now, so where could they have gone? Perhaps it was only my imagination. I must have stumbled in the darkness, and . . ." I met Seraphina's gaze, wanting to believe my own words, hoping that she would accept them. I saw only the reflection of my fear.

Chapter 16

I had expected to lie awake the whole night after such a fright, but my weariness proved stronger than my fears and I slept late the next morning. When I awoke, however, my bruises were a sharp reminder of what had happened. Someone had to be told, I decided as I washed and dressed for the day, someone who would believe my description of black cloth blinding me.

Since I was unable to confide in Nick without risking dire consequences, I was determined to tell Digger. After all, he had seen the black-robed riders, so he was sure to believe me. I only hoped that he would be able to come up with some idea as to where my attacker had gone and how we might be able to find him again.

Though the thought of confronting my mysterious visitor filled me with anxiety, I knew I must face him soon or risk madness, for I could no longer bear wondering if he truly existed. Besides, no one would be safe here until we knew who was slipping into the cloister and what it was he wanted from us.

Because I had overslept, I had no opportunity to talk to Digger in the morning, though Seraphina reported that he had appeared to be in good spirits when she'd taken his food down before dawn. I had to content myself with a thorough search of the playroom under the guise of tidying it. To my chagrin, I found not a sign of our mysterious visitor.

Since no students appeared after the midday meal, I had hoped to have a short time alone while the children were busy helping Seraphina or working in the garden; but as I started down the hall, Elena came running inside, shouting that a wagon was approaching. Heart pounding with hope, I hurried to the school room, praying that it might, at long last, be Nick.

Within moments, I was kneeling on the grass outside the door to greet the five children as Nick lifted them from the wagon bed. Skinny, bruised, and far too quiet, they stared back at me with wide, frightened eyes, too timid even to tell me their names. I had to blink back tears as I gently lifted a little girl and saw the burns on her legs.

"What in heaven's name. . . ?" I looked beyond her to Nick.

"I found them in the woods last night. We started looking for them not long after the attack. Their home was among those that burned, and 'twas feared that . . ." He let it trail off, his expression warning me that what he had to say was not meant for the ears of the children.

"Could you wait while I get them settled?" I asked. "There is much we need to discuss."

"I can come back later. I need to stop by the house and make sure that everything is all right there. My father has been feeling poorly the last few days, and . . ." He sighed, his worry evident.

"Oh, I am sorry. If I had known, I would have . . ." I stopped, realizing how foolish my words were. I was probably the last person Jarvis Harrison would wish to see.

"Perhaps I could drive you up tomorrow." Nick's gaze was like a caress. "I know he would be pleased to see you, but you must not risk walking so far alone."

"But Paul said . . ." I began, then shook my head. "You go to your father and we will see to these little ones."

Nick reached out, brushing my hand with his fingertips. "Later, Rachel, I promise."

My heart leaped with joy, but I could only nod, for just looking into his eyes stole the breath from my lungs. Though I would have stood and watched him until he disappeared from sight, the needs of the battered children forced me to follow them inside, and once there, my heart and my full attention belonged to them, for they were in dire need of care and love.

It took several hours to gently bathe them and treat their wounds; but by the time they were clean, fed, and dressed in fresh clothing, all but the little girl with the burns were smiling and talking. Her injuries were the most serious, but even as I gently smoothed the healing salve over her reddened skin, I was sure that much of her pain came from something other than the fire that had burned her.

"Can you tell me how this happened, Lilly?" I asked, having been told her name by one of the older children.

She shook her head, her big blue eyes darkening with fear.

"Is it that you don't know what happened?" I hated to press her, but felt I must, for I had seen before how fear could seal a child's lips and keep them a prisoner. Only if she could speak of it would she be free.

"Not tell! Never tell!" The whimpered words pierced my heart like a scream, for the child was rigid in my arms.

"Did you promise someone that you would never tell?" I brushed back her golden curls, then swallowed hard as I uncovered a welt hidden beneath them. What could have been done to her?

Her solemn gaze as she nodded told me that, though

she was no more than four, she was truly determined not to speak. I hugged her gently. "You are safe now, Lilly. No one will hurt you here."

"Not tell, never."

"All right, it can be your secret for now. Mayhap someday, when you feel like it, you can whisper it in my ear. What do you think? If I promise never to tell, would that be enough?"

She slipped her thumb into her mouth and regarded me seriously for several moments, then she slid from my lap and limped away to join the other children. I watched her go with a heavy heart, suddenly feeling like a stranger here. What sort of person would frighten a child so terribly?

Though I hoped that Nick would return soon, the long afternoon crept by as I did my best to keep the children busy and content. It was only an hour from sunset when I heard the welcome sound of an approaching wagon. A quiver of anticipation stole my breath as I hurried out the door.

It was the wagon from Sunrise right enough, but Harriet was driving, not Nick. My heart broke when I saw her tormented gaze, for I knew at once what troubled her. Guilt swept over me for not finding a way to let her know that Digger was safe.

She jumped down from the wagon seat. "Mr. Nick be askin' me to bring supplies, Miss. Him been called off again. Trouble be brewin' over to Sea Cliff, they be sayin'." Her dark eyes met mine, then she looked away. "Things be bad, Miss."

I caught her hand as she started to reach into the wagon bed. "Digger is safe, Harriet. I cannot tell you where or how, but he is well." I kept my voice soft, so as not to be overheard, for the children were spilling out of the building, eager to see Harriet.

"For true?" The hope that filled her face banished the

ten years she had aged since the ball. "You not be just sayin' . . . ?"

"Say nothing to anyone for now, but 'tis true, I swear." I peered over the side of the wagon. "Now, what have you brought us?" I turned to the children. "Shall we help her carry everything in?"

Their enthusiastic attack on the stack of boxes, baskets, and even huge pots of food effectively diverted Harriet so that she was able to cover her abrupt change of mood. I did my best, too, by asking her for the details of Mr. Harrison's illness and about the condition of everyone at Sunrise. Still, as we sorted the various items, I was constantly aware of the happy excitement in her gaze and I began to wonder if I had made a mistake. Yet how could I allow her to suffer her fears a moment longer?

Once the children had scattered, I turned to Harriet. "Has there been more trouble since the night of the ball?"

She nodded. "Mr. Nick be gone more'n he be home. Ridin' from one plantation to the next, talkin' to folk, tryin' to keep the peace, but . . ." She shook her head. "The burnin' still be goin' on."

"Burning?" A chill finger slipped down my spine. "But who would do such a thing, Harriet?"

"Nobody be knowin'. Burnin' folk in their beds, it be evil, Miss. That Lilly and her brothers and sisters— why'd anyone be wantin' to destroy their little farm?"

"They came from a farm, not Emerald Acres?"

"'The land be near Emerald Acres, right enough. 'Twere a reward the first Mr. Chalmers gave to 'um for savin' some family treasure durin' the first uprising, years back. Folk say them got burned after the attack on Duquanne, but them not be talkin'. Mr. Nick be sayin' mayhap the older folk seen too much, but nobody be knowin' for sure."

"Were they the only ones burned out?"

Harriet shook her head. "Be new smoke most every night."

I swallowed hard, realizing how wrong Paul's reassuring words had been. "And now they are at Sea Cliff?" The thought of Nick riding out to fight such violence terrified me. I had seen his wounds from the first battle and I knew what the night riders had done to Digger. If they should catch Nick . . . I fought the images that filled my mind, aware that I should go mad if I gave my imagination free rein.

"'Twas what the rider said. I reckon Mr. Nick will be by to tell you, if'n it not be too late when he be back." Harriet's gaze was full of compassion and understanding, telling me that I was doing a poor job of hiding my feelings for Nick. "You best not be worrin'."

I drew her away from the others. "Have the Harrisons been looking for Digger?" I had decided that I must find out what sort of welcome Digger might expect should he return to Sunrise.

"In the beginnin', but now most folk be thinkin' him dead." She swallowed hard. "I be scared, Miss. Thinkin' most awful things 'bout him."

I patted her arm. "Rest easy, you will be seeing him again, when the time is right."

"Soon, Miss?"

"I hope so." I wished that I could say more, but I was afraid to promise her anything else, since I had no idea what Digger would do when he left the cloister. I had been hoping that the anger of the planters would have dissipated by now, but if the burning was still going on, he could be in even greater danger now than he would have been the night of the attack.

Harriet left soon after, not wanting to make even the relatively short drive to Sunrise after dark. I could understand her fears; I still had nightmares about the night

I found Digger. I watched her drive off with a heavy heart, wishing that I could go with her and talk to Mr. Harrison about Digger. I was sure he would believe me and protect Digger.

Thinking about Digger reminded me of what had happened last night and my need to discuss it with him. I longed to slip down to the cellar, but there was no opportunity. Thanks to our growing family, I was rarely alone and the playroom was never empty. Only after all the children were finally in bed was I able to open the hidden panel and carry Digger's food down into the quiet cellar.

I stopped at the bottom of the steps, suddenly realizing that no lamp burned in the darkness beyond the open doorway. "Digger?" I called softly, aware that he might be sleeping, since day and night were little different in his windowless room. Silence was my only answer.

Fear gripped me so tight, I could scarcely breathe. Where was he? My fingers ached with the tightness of my hold on the small basket we used to transport his food and water. I stepped cautiously through the door into the cellar proper, lifting my candle in a hand that shook so much it set the flame to dancing wildly.

The pallet of blankets, the dirty dishes from his morning meal, even the lamp, were all visible; but not Digger. Still shaking, I set the basket down and lit the lamp. It gave a reassuring glow, dispelling the last of the shadows; but the room was still empty of life. Unwilling to trust the evidence of my own eyes, I made a circuit of the room; but there was nothing to see. Digger had vanished without a trace.

Not sure what to think, I placed the basket on the floor and blew out the lamp. Digger had told me that he would leave when the time was right, but how could he have escaped today of all days? No one had seen him, and I knew well that the playroom had been full of people most of the day. How could he have left? I returned to the playroom, closing the panel with care.

Seraphina looked up as I entered the kitchen. "Where are the dishes?"

"I forgot them. He left, Seraphina. No one is down there."

Her gasp told me she was as stunned as I had been. "But how could he . . . ?"

I shrugged. My curiosity faded as I considered what Harriet had told me. I cared less about how he had managed to escape unseen than how he'd fared in the dangerous night. Harriet had mentioned patrols from the plantations—what if one of them should happen on Digger? My stomach knotted with fear. If only he had waited until I'd had a chance to tell him all that I had learned this day.

"What should we do, Rachel?" Seraphina offered me a cup of tea, though I had not even noticed her preparing it.

"I fear there is nothing we can do until Nick returns. I had hoped to speak to him today, but . . ." I hesitated, fighting frustration and weariness. I wanted desperately to do something, yet I was a prisoner within the stone walls of the cloister. I could not even be sure that Nick was safe—wherever he was.

"Perhaps in the morning . . ." Seraphina's sorrowful gaze told me that she shared my fears, but neither of us put them into words. Instead, we sipped our tea in companionable silence and I wondered if she dreaded the night ahead as much as I did.

Because of Digger, I hated barring the door, but I knew I must. My thoughts were constantly on Nick and Digger as I made my nightly rounds, checking the children, inspecting the schoolroom and the playroom, making sure the windows were secured. Only then could I go to my own rooms.

I was sitting in my nightdress, brushing out my hair, when a tapping sound drew me to my own shuttered window. "Who is out there?" I whispered, hating the way my voice quivered.

"Come unbar the door, Rachel. We have to talk."

My heart skipped a beat as I recognized Nick's voice. I snatched up my robe, drawing it close about me, then picked up my candle. What could bring him so late? Had there been trouble? But if there was, would he not ring the bell to rouse us all? Could he be wounded again? That thought gave my feet wings as I ran barefoot through the quiet hall and into the schoolroom.

The moment the door opened, I realized that Nick was not alone. He shoved Digger inside rather roughly. I swallowed hard as I noted the misery in the young servant's face. "I had to tell him 'bout you hidin' me in the walled-off part of the cloister, Miss. Forgive me."

"Is it true then? Did you hide him here, Rachel?" Nick's gaze bored into me, sending a chill down my spine. He appeared to be furious.

For a moment I was simply paralyzed by my conflicting emotions, then I realized what Digger had said. He had felt he must lie to Nick to keep the cellar a secret. A healthy anger at his treatment of Digger swelled within me, banishing my weary longing for Nick's approval. "Of course I did," I snapped. "I found him beaten half to death between here and Sunrise, what else should I have done? You were all off chasing those who attacked Emerald Acres, and I feared that Digger might be blamed before he had a chance to recover enough to speak."

My words were a slight exaggeration, but I was in no mood to be subservient and apologetic. Digger had obviously been a victim of the same men who had wounded Nick, so why was he attacking us this way?

"He was that badly beaten?" Nick's frown deepened.

I turned my attention to Digger. "Did you not tell him about the masked men who attacked you?"

Digger nodded, straightening up in response to my belief in him. "I tole him everythin', Miss. 'Bout the black robes and the fine horses them rode, even how you found me comin' through the cane field."

I shifted my gaze to Nick. "What would you have had me do? Should I have turned him over to those at Sunrise who were ready to shoot anyone who appeared unannounced?"

Nick closed and barred the door, then leaned against it, his frown fading into weary lines. "Forgive my questions, Rachel, but why did you not tell me when I came by that morning?"

I suddenly found his gaze difficult to meet. If I told him that Digger had feared and mistrusted him, might that not prejudice Nick against helping him? I already had proof of how fragile Nick's trust of Digger was, I had no desire to test it. "You were injured and exhausted, I thought it better not to add to your worries."

"So you hid him in the ruined area of the cloister. Who else knew?"

Though I also wished to shield Seraphina, a look into Nick's eyes made it clear that he was already skeptical. Besides, I was a dreadful liar and, because of my feelings for Nick, it was difficult to keep anything from him. "Just Seraphina. I needed her help to get him safely inside and to see to his needs."

I had hoped for some warming in Nick's hard face, but instead of meeting my gaze, he turned his attention to Digger. "Where were you going tonight, Digger? Who were you to meet?"

"I not be meetin' nobody, Mr. Nick. I just lookin' for

a new place to hide on accountta I be 'fraid of makin' trouble for Miss Rachel."

Nick studied him closely for what seemed an eternity, but Digger no longer squirmed beneath his scrutiny. It was obvious that he had moved beyond either fear or hope. He was merely waiting for Nick to decide his fate.

"Do you trust him, Rachel?" Nick's question startled me.

"Of course."

"Well, after being missing for so long, he cannot return to Sunrise without risk. Every plantation owner on the island is questioning everyone else's workers. I shall have to speak with my father and see if he can find a way to assure Digger's welcome back under our roof. Until that can be accomplished, I would like Digger to remain here, in hiding, to protect you."

"Protect me?"

Nick nodded, rubbing his stubbly chin. "Paul has been riding about the island, pressing for education of the children, claiming that what has happened is proof that the workers will no longer suffer what he calls 'our island's brand of slavery." He refuses to listen to reason and I cannot guarantee to keep the other owners from attacking him much longer. When they do, I fear this orphanage could come under attack as well."

"I'd guard her with my life." Digger's fervent vow touched my heart, for I had no doubt that he meant it literally.

"I truly doubt . . ." I protested. "We do nothing but care for children here, Nick. There have been no outside students in the schoolroom for weeks and . . ."

Nick's sardonic gaze stopped my words. "If logic ruled this island, the trouble would have ended long ago, Rachel. People who are frightened and angry behave in ways that would horrify them in other times. Trust no one except me. These are ugly times, and I want no more victims." He turned to Digger. "I have an extra gun and ammunition in my saddlebag. Can you use it?"

Digger nodded, his eyes glowing with pride. "Nobody be hurtin' Missy while I breathin'."

Nick looked to me for approval, then nodded. "Come along then, I shall give you the gun and see you safely into the ruins."

As Digger turned away, I realized that I wanted him here, not somewhere in the ruins beyond the wall. "Have you had anything to eat today, Digger?" I asked, hoping to keep him inside our part of the cloister until I could think of a better excuse.

"No, ma'am." His quick glance told me that he recognized what I was trying to do. "I be powerful hungry."

"I shall fix you something." I turned to Nick, offering what I hoped appeared to be a genuine smile. I found it painful to practice subterfuge around him. "You, too, if you can spare the time."

"I must get back to Sunrise, my father will be waiting to learn about conditions on the other plantations, but I really think that . . ." He seemed troubled at the idea of leaving Digger alone with me.

"Surely you can trust Digger to return to his hiding place on his own," I assured him. "He has been there since the night of the ball."

Nick's frown stayed in place and he took my arm. "Wait in the kitchen, Digger." He waited until we were alone, then opened the door, leading me out into the moonlit night. He drew me into his arms once the door was closed behind us. I lifted my mouth in happy anticipation, but he only brushed his lips lightly on my forehead.

"You must keep him hidden, Rachel. If it becomes known that you have harbored a man here, there will be little I can do to shield you. The island is near the point of explosion, 'twill take only one more spark to set it off."

"But if he is to guard us . . ." I could not hide the fear his words ignited.

"I only hope such a precaution is unnecessary." His arms tightened. "I wish . . ." Something very like a shudder shook his big frame, then he let me go so abruptly I had to lean against the door frame to keep my feet. "Let me give you the weapon and ammunition, then you had best get back inside. 'Tis hard to know what eyes might be watching."

I looked around, his words reminding me forcefully of all the times I had felt the prickly sensation of being spied upon. For a heartbeat, I considered confiding in him; but I was given no chance, for he was already thrusting the deadly weapon into my cold hands. He left without touching me again, only warning me to bar the door at once. Thanks to his dire predictions about the future, I had no need for his orders.

I hurried to the kitchen, my mind already busy with all the questions I wanted to ask Digger. As I entered, he looked up from the plate he had heaped with food from the various cupboards and storage places, his gaze begging for understanding. "I hope you be forgivin' me for gettin' this, Missy, but 'taint right for you to be doin' it."

Realizing that he had likely spoken the truth about not eating today, I smiled at him reassuringly. "I should not mind preparing food for you, but take whatever you need, Digger, you know you are welcome to it." I laid the gun on the table, then shivered. It seemed obscene in this place that was dedicated to the care of children victimized by just such weapons. "Please sit down and eat while we talk."

His gaze became apprehensive, but he did as I ordered and as he began to eat, I could see that he was shaking. Not wanting to add to his suffering, I began telling him about Harriet's visit, then I described what had happened to me last night. To my surprise, he only nodded when I mentioned the way my phantom attacker had disappeared.

"What do you know of this?" I demanded, suddenly wondering if I had been wrong to trust him. Could he have been my attacker?

"Only how he be gettin' in, Missy." Digger met my gaze for a moment, then looked away. "It be how I left."

"What do you mean?"

"I heered them noises again late last night, so's I came up to see who be doin' what." Digger paused for a drink of water, then frowned. "I seen the door of that big wardrobe closin' when I come outta the stairway, so's I poked around a bit. It be a doorway into the ruins."

A chill slipped down my spine. "Could someone be hiding in there?" I found that his words explained a great deal, yet at the same time they opened up some frightening possibilities.

"Not likely." Digger shook his head. "I be explorin' most of the day and I not be findin' much. 'Taint like the cellar. It be spooky and fallin' down."

I nodded, well aware that he was right. "But someone has been using that opening to get in here." The knot in my stomach tightened into an ache of apprehension. "Why?"

Digger shrugged, then returned to his eating as I described all the various instances of someone invading our part of the cloister. When I finished, he reached out and gently caressed the gun. "Mayhap I could wait in the playroom and stop 'um with this."

The thought made me shudder. Violence, here? It

seemed very wrong. There had to be a better way. "Perhaps I could fashion some sort of lock for the wardrobe door," I mused, liking that idea better. "That way whoever is using the opening would not know he had been found out."

"'Twould not be caught, either." Digger's frown deepened. "Mr. Nick not be likin' that."

"At the moment, 'tis more important to know who might be spying on us and why. Stopping them can come later." I glanced at his now empty plate. "Fill another jug with water and come along. I want you to show me how that panel works." I got to my feet. "I left a basket of food and water down in the cellar, along with your blankets and the lamp. I hoped that you would return."

His grimace told me that he felt guilty about his abrupt departure. "I were wrong to go like that, not sayin' nothin' to you or Seraphina; but I be worryin' 'bout bein' found by whoever be usin' the wardrobe."

"I understand, Digger, but you have to promise me that you will never do such a thing again. If you want to leave, it should be through the front door, and because you are on your way back to Sunrise and Harriet."

"Yes, miss." He followed me along the silent, shadowed hall to the playroom.

My heartbeat quickened as I reached the door. Last night the intruder must have been just on the other side waiting to attack me. I took a deep breath and opened the door, then waited until the candle's glow pushed back the shadows before I stepped inside. "Do you know what caused the banging you mentioned?" I asked, as my anxiety faded.

"Mayhap someone be lookin' for the treasure."

"Looking for what?"

"The treasure the black robes kept hidden here. There

be stories . . ." Digger began, then shrugged. "Not that I be believin' 'um."

"Did you find any signs of such a search?" I remembered that Nick had mentioned the tales to me when he'd showed me the hidden entrance to the ruined part of the building.

"It be hard to tell, Miss. 'Tis an evil muddle beyond the wall. 'Taint a proper place for a lady like you."

I opened my mouth to inform him that I had already visited the area, then closed it without speaking. Nick's concern for my safety was cause enough for gossip, there was no need to make it clear that we had spent time alone together in such a place.

"So how does the panel work?" I asked, opening the wardrobe door.

"Most the same as the other one, 'cept the handle be hidden better." He moved some of the clothing to one side, then ran his fingers along the seam where the back and side of the wardrobe met. He slid a small section of wood to one side and I could see the handle that had been hidden beneath it.

I stared at it, my curiosity quickly overcoming my fear. I reached past Digger and gave it a tug. It moved away from me with a click that I recognized as the sound I had heard last night. Darkness stretched endlessly beyond the narrow opening. I took a single step forward.

"No, Miss." Digger caught my arm. "Mr. Nick would kill me, if'n I let you go in there. 'Tis an evil place, haunted by them what died there. 'Twould be best to keep this closed forever."

His vehemence surprised me, but I was glad to step back. The musty air that stirred on the other side smelled of death and sadness and, yes, evil. The panel swung back into place and I realized that the handle had vanished, too. Curious, I copied the exploration I had watched Digger make and found the small depression in the paneling. I eased it open, then closed it again.

"You be wantin' me to nail the wardrobe door shut?" Digger broke into my concentration.

"We cannot."

"Why not?" He seemed surprised at my refusal.

"How should I explain it? No one except Seraphina can know that you are back, and even she must not know about this."

"What 'bout Mr. Nick?"

"I have not yet decided. You kept the cellar a secret from him, did you not?"

He nodded. "I would never betray you, but if there be someone wantin' to harm you, Mr. Nick should know."

"We have no way of knowing what they might want, so I think it best not to tell anyone until I can discover what all this means." I met his worried gaze as calmly as I could, hoping that I was doing the right thing. Nick had more than enough to worry about without this little puzzle. I closed the wardrobe door and studied the simple catch that held it. "Meanwhile, can we not secure this with a piece of wood?"

Digger examined the catch, then nodded. "If'n it be wedged, it be right secure. I think there be something' I kin use in the cellar."

I watched him go, then turned my gaze back to the wardrobe. Two secret panels in this room, panels that had to have been built at the time Nick's family closed off this part of the cloister. Had Nick known about them? It was hard to believe that he would have missed them in his boyish explorations. Yet he had never told me about them.

A chill traced down my spine. Could he be the one using the wardrobe entrance? But why? To seek Digger or check on our safety? That made no sense, for he knew I would always welcome him. Besides, he would never have pushed me down that way, would he? All my doubts and fears swirled around me, but my heart shrieked: "Not Nick! Never Nick!"

Chapter 17

Though I had expected some dire emergency to follow Nick's warning and Digger's return to the cloister, the next two days proved to be the most peaceful since the ball. I was able to devote myself full-time to helping the new children become a real part of our little family, an undertaking that proved quite challenging, for they were all still withdrawn and shy.

Fortunately, I had Elena's devoted assistance, for she rarely left my side. The fact disturbed me at first, but I soon came to appreciate it since her very presence seemed to help the new children trust me. I could only admire the way she put her own grief behind her to comfort those whose sorrow was more recent.

Only Lilly seemed immune to our offers of warmth and caring, often turning away when Elena or I tried to talk to her. She refused to listen to the stories I told the children and showed no interest in the toys that Elena tried to tempt her with. She even refused comfort from her brothers and sisters, preferring to sit alone in a corner, her thumb in her soft little mouth, her eyes seeming focused on a distant scene that none of us could see.

"What be happenin' to Lilly?" Elena asked, as sunset neared and I gave up on still another attempt to reach the child. "You be good to her and her just turns away."

I met Elena's worried gaze and smoothed back her tangled dark curls. "She must be too hurt to even know how much she needs us."

"You not be sendin' her away?" Elena's worried gaze went from me to the oblivious little girl.

"Of course not. We shall just have to give her more time." I sighed. "If only I knew what happened to her that the others escaped. Have any of them told you anything more?"

Elena shook her head. "They not be knowin'. Them just say her come outta the trees after the fire burned out. They be glad 'cause they be afeered her were in the cabin."

"Perhaps she was." I studied the healing burns on Lilly's legs. "Mayhap when she closes her eyes she sees the evil men who burned her home and killed her parents."

Elena's soft whimper stopped my speculation, and my heart ached for her pain as I pulled her into my arms. My own thoughtlessness appalled me. How could I have spoken thus to her with her grief not long past? Just because she sometimes seemed older and stronger did not mean it was so. I hugged Elena tight, wishing that she were my own child, for I could not have loved her more.

"I be sorry, Miss Rachel," she sniffed. "I wants to help, not cry like a baby."

"Crying can be good, Elena. Lilly would be better off if she could cry over what is hurting her so. And you do help. I could never take care of all these children without you by my side."

"Can I stay forever? I wants to be a teacher and help you always. Please say I can." Her longing touched a chord deep within me, for I remembered that need. Though I had not spoken up at the time, I had felt it the first day I had been allowed to help in the Middle Brook Orphanage.

"You can stay with me as long as you want," I promised her, praying that nothing would happen to force me to break my word. "And I think you will make a fine teacher. Did you not read the story to the children after the midday meal?"

Elena snuggled closer, but her eyes were dry and I could see the determination in her little face. I had no doubt that she meant every word she'd said. I looked across the room to where Lilly sat alone and swallowed a sigh. If only I could find a way to help her.

Elena's gaze must have followed mine, for in a moment, she asked, "Shall I read Lilly a story afore her goes to bed?" When I nodded, she slipped from my lap and made her way to the shelf that concealed the entrance to the cellar. "I know the one be right."

I smiled my encouragement, but deep down I was afraid that it would take more than a story to reach Lilly. As I got to my feet, my thoughts turned to Paul and I realized how long it had been since he had come to the cloister. Frustration curled tight inside me. I definitely needed to speak with him about Lilly and the other new children. After all, this orphanage was his concern, too, yet he seemed interested only in getting students for the school.

As I left the playroom to help Seraphina prepare the babies for bed, I tried to calm myself by deciding that such neglect was really a mark of Paul's confidence in my abilities. A part of me remained unconvinced, however, and I wondered wearily if I should ever understand any man. Which, of course, brought Nick's compelling image into my mind.

Where was he? Why had he not returned? Did he care nothing for me, now that he knew I had hidden Digger here without his blessing? Or had I misunderstood everything that had passed between us since our meeting on St. Devina? I had to admit it was possible, since my knowledge of men was so limited. Yet my heart cried out that Nick was too much a gentleman to toy with my feelings and take advantage of my innocence. I forced the doubts away and turned my attention to the children.

I had been sleeping deeply for several hours when the distant sound of pounding roused me from a dream of Nick. Frightened and unsure of whence the sound had come, I slipped from my bed and pulled on my robe. Could this be the noise Digger had heard coming from the far side of the dividing wall? Only when I stepped into the hall did I realize that it was coming from the front of the cloister, not the rear.

As I hurried along the hall, Seraphina opened her door and I could see my fear echoed in her face. She started after me, but I waved her back. "I shall see who it is," I told her; then, not sure what I might find, I added, "Keep the children in their rooms if they wake. And summon Digger if anything appears amiss."

"Have a care, Rachel."

I nodded, my heart already pounding with fear as I hurried through the darkened rooms, my candle barely staying lit. By the time I reached the heavy door, there was only silence. I pressed my ear against it and tried to sound as commanding as an angry Mrs. Bennett. "Who is out there?"

The silence deepened until I felt it surrounding me like a chill mist. "Speak," I ordered, my tone reflecting the anger that flooded in to fill the hollow my fear had created.

A soft scraping sound was the only answer. I strained my ears for several more minutes, not sure what to do. Caution told me not to open the door, but other images rose in my mind. I remembered Digger as I had found him lying in the cane field, and Nick, bleeding and weak. What if some poor soul had spent the last of his strength pounding on the door and now lay . . .

Knowing I could never return to my bed without being sure no one needed me, I lit the lamp, then got the heavy poker from the fireplace. Holding it at the ready, I unbarred the door and eased it open. As the shadows receded, a low groan greeted me and a scream rose in my throat.

"What be it?" Seraphina called from the doorway on the other side of the room.

"Get Digger, quick." I dropped the poker and moved the lamp so that I could see the battered person who lay, like a bundle of bloody rags, on my doorstep. "Paul!"

"You gots to hide 'um." An unfamiliar male voice came from beyond the bush that grew to the left of the door. "Us found 'um near Sunrise. Hide 'um or the planters be finishin' the job."

"He needs a doctor," I gasped, appalled. "I cannot care for someone so badly injured. Please summon help."

"If'n you want 'um to live, tell nobody him be here." I heard a soft rustling.

"Wait. Who are you?" I peered into the darkness, but I saw only a faint movement, a shadow drifting along the side of the building, then nothing. Paul groaned again, forcing my attention back to him.

He struggled to lift his head, his eyes wild with fear as he gripped my hand. "Hide me, Rachel! They want me dead. The hooded ones . . ." A shudder racked him and he collapsed again, his fingers slipping from my hand.

"Paul, Paul, speak to me. Wake up! You must tell me what happened." I was still frantically trying to rouse him when Digger and Seraphina came.

The next few hours were a continuing nightmare. The

three of us carried Paul to the dining room and laid him gently on the big table, so that I could tend his wounds. As Seraphina lit extra lamps, my horror grew, for his injuries were indeed grievous and I knew not how I should treat them.

Digger paled and stepped back at the sight. "Shall I go for help?"

"Where?" I asked, though I suspected I already knew the answer.

"Mr. Nick could summon the doctor." Digger's eyes met mine and I knew that he would risk his life to get help for Paul.

Though I wanted more than anything to have the doctor here, I swallowed hard and told them what the person who had brought Paul to us had said, finishing, "If they found him near Sunrise, could it be that he has an enemy there?"

Digger evaded my gaze, but I saw a glance pass between him and Seraphina. "Can you help him, Miss? Him be safe 'nough in the cellar and I be there to watch over him."

Since I could not bear to even think of the implications of his question, I merely nodded. "I can try." I gritted my teeth as I carefully smoothed Paul's blood-soaked hair back from an ugly cut on his forehead; then, whispering a prayer, I began issuing orders.

At first I feared Paul's silence; but later, while I clumsily imitated Dr. Hogarth's movements as I cleaned, then stitched up the ugly gashes in Paul's side and back, I was glad he had escaped the agony in unconsciousness. I only prayed that he would survive my treatment. And that I should not swoon and injure him as I fell.

By the time the last of his wounds was covered with salve and clean cotton bandages, I was shaking with fatigue and the strain of such demanding work. I slumped against the wall, my legs quivering so that I feared I might collapse.

"What now, Miss?" Digger asked.

"We must get him to the cellar," I murmured, wondering how we should ever manage it, for Paul was a heavy burden, even for Digger, who was near his match in size.

"How?" Seraphina looked from me to Digger.

"Mayhap him could help, if'n him were to rouse." Digger met my gaze.

I hesitated, hating the thought of forcing Paul to endure the agony I knew waking would bring; but I knew there was no other way and time was running out. Once dawn arrived, the children would be leaving their rooms, and if they saw Paul . . .

I shivered, aware that one word to an outsider would be all it took. Someone had already left Paul for dead, so I had no doubt that, should they learn they had failed, they would come here to finish the job. I took the smelling salts from my medical supplies.

We roused him enough to make the perilous journey to the cellar, but he quickly slipped back into unconsciousness. The next two days and nights dragged by as I did my best to nurse Paul back to life. 'Twas a painful process, for he woke only marginally—enough to swallow water or Seraphina's strengthening broth, but not enough to speak coherently or stand by himself.

Still, I told myself, he was alive, and his wounds were healing without much fever. 'Twas only the blow to his head that troubled him. And the nightmares. Since I felt I must stay in the cellar with him through the nights, I heard his screams, his babbling about the hooded attackers, his moaning cries for help, and my anger at the men who had done this grew stronger and deeper. I needed answers.

Though Harriet once again brought us a wagonload

of much-needed supplies, I saw nothing of Nick. It was as though he had forgotten me, a possibility that made my heart ache. Another lack added to my worry and fears; no one had come by the cloister to ask me where Paul might be. That fact chilled me more than any other, for I knew that his absence from the church and the village must have been noticed.

Did no one care? And what of the Harrisons? They had brought Paul to Bell Harbour Island and supported his dreams of a school. Did they care so little about his safety that they refused even to mount a search for him? Or, worse, did they have reason to believe him dead?

By the third morning, I knew that I must try to find out who was behind what had happened to Paul, yet how? There was no way I could go to Sunrise or the village and ask questions. Another source of information occurred to me. If I could discover the identity of the intruder, perhaps that would tell me who our enemy was.

Since I had kept the wardrobe door blocked, no one had come into the cloister to trouble us; but that meant nothing. They could still be prowling the ruins at night. Digger had claimed to have found no clue to whom it might be, but perhaps I could find something. Determined to try, I asked Seraphina to keep the children inside while I sought the outside entrance Nick had showed me what now seemed a lifetime ago.

Finding it proved more difficult than I expected, though I had no trouble gaining entrance once I did. The ruins stretched before me, just as intimidating as I remembered them. As the shadowy destruction loomed around me, I wished mightily that I had asked Digger to accompany me. If I should encounter the intruder here . . . The very thought was enough to send me fleeing back to the sunshine, so I forced it away.

At first, it appeared just as it had when Nick brought me here, but after I mastered my fear, I realized that there was a slight difference. As I moved deeper into the ruins, I had no need to pick my way with care—someone had cleared the worst of the debris from a narrow passageway. Taking a deep breath, I followed the cleared path.

As I moved through the rooms, I realized how much they resembled those on the other side of the wall, at least as far as size was concerned. I even managed to judge my location with some degree of ease, so I was unsurprised to see the thick boards of the wall that Nick's family had erected just ahead of me. This was, of course, where the path had taken me.

I peered around the area, not sure why this particular spot might have been chosen for the wall. Had the destruction been less on the other side? Or had they simply cleared and repaired a part of the building, then given up? And where was the entrance Digger had discovered?

Knowing that the stairway to the cellar was located near the outside wall of the structure, I tried to judge the distance from the stone wall to where I believed the wardrobe was located; but I found nothing. The wooden barricade seemed solid and no amount of poking about led me to a break in the boards.

Had I found a different wall? Or was I so disoriented by the debris and shadows that filled the rooms that I had made a mistake? I peered around, glad that the high windows on each side had not been covered, for they gave some light as I tried to make sense of what seemed an impossibility. I had seen the darkness beyond the hidden panel, so I knew that there had to be an opening, unless, of course, I had truly been driven mad by living here.

No, I could not be wrong. Besides, the cleared path had led this way, so . . . Gazing around, I suddenly realized that it had not ended at the wall, as I'd supposed.

Indeed, it seemed to continue on along the length of the boarded-up area toward what on the other side would be the corner of the room opposite the hidden stairway.

As I walked, I held my candle low, searching the dusty floor instead of the wall. It was, I could see, well marked and scuffed by other feet, at least a part of the way. Where the scuffing ended, I stopped. This time it took me only a moment to locate the tiny seam in the wall.

I looked back across the width of the room, sure this could not be the panel I had seen Digger open. The location was wrong. Still, I had to know what was on the other side, so that meant finding whatever device opened this panel. It proved far more difficult than I expected, and in the end I located it purely by accident when my skirt snagged against the bottom board.

In the process of trying to free the fabric without tearing it, I discovered that there was a recessed niche between the bottom board and the one above it. A light tug and the panel opened, startling me so that I nearly dropped my candle as I stumbled back.

Darkness yawned beyond the open panel. I swallowed hard, then tugged a piece of broken wood out of a nearby stack of debris, placing it so that the panel could not close by itself. Only then did I venture through the opening, gripping my candle holder so tightly my fingers ached.

Though I could touch both wooden walls by extending my arms, the area was like a tunnel and a single candle's light was woefully inadequate to penetrate its length, for it plainly ran the entire width of the cloister. And it was not empty, I discovered, as the light cast ominous shadows about piles of boxes or bales or some such debris.

I started toward the first stack, thinking to learn more about those using this hidden entrance by studying what they had left behind, but the sound of Seraphina's voice stopped me. "Please stay, Mr. Nick, I be sure her be returning from her walk soon and I know her be eager to speak with you."

"And I with her. There has been more trouble, and she has to be warned. Unfortunately, I must attend the meeting of the planters at Sea Cliff later today, so I cannot remain much longer." Nick's weary tone awakened a familiar ache of longing within me.

"Have you time for a cold drink and some cookies? We have been baking, and the first are just out of the oven." As I headed back to the open panel, I could hear the children's voices, Elena's chief among them, urging Nick to stay. His rumbling agreement came as I removed the wood and allowed the panel to close once again.

It took me less time than I had expected to make my way back through the ruins to the hidden outside entrance, and after pausing to tidy my dusty clothes as well as I could, I hurried around to the orphanage door. My heart pounded with happy anticipation, but my stomach knotted with apprehension as I thought of Paul, hidden in the cellar. What should I do if Nick asked after him? How could I lie to the man I loved? Yet how could I expose the man who might have been his victim?

Not sure now that I truly wanted to talk to Nick, I paused in the kitchen to bathe my face and hands with cool water and to try to decide what I could say. For the first time in my life, I wished that I had a gift for deception. Though I should never lie by choice, I now held secrets that could harm those who had trusted me, and I knew I could never betray Paul.

Still unsure of what I would say, I stepped into the hall and nearly collided with Nick. "Rachel!" He caught my arms, steadying me. "I was about to go looking for you."

The joy in his eyes warmed me for a moment before my doubts returned to chill my pleasure at his touch. "Nick, what are you doing here?" I had no trouble feigning confusion, for my own emotions supplied more than enough of it.

He released my arms, then glanced over his shoulder. I followed his gaze and saw that several of the children had come with him. "Perhaps we could step outside?" He took my arm, giving me little choice but to move through the dining room and school room. He closed the door behind me.

"I mislike your wandering about the area alone, Rachel. It could be dangerous even in daylight."

"I was not that far away." I spoke without thinking, startled by what seemed very like an attack.

"Then why did you not hear me ride up?"

Stung that he should question me and suddenly fearful of what his suspicion might mean, I pulled away from him, moving into the shade of a nearby tree. "Perhaps I wandered further than I thought. Forgive me, I had no wish to worry anyone."

"And you must forgive me for chiding you. 'Tis only that Paul has gone into hiding and I fear that those who seek him might be spying upon the cloister, thinking him here."

"Paul has disappeared?" My shock was genuine, for I had not expected him to interpret Paul's disappearance as voluntary. I decided to see what I could find out. "Why should he go into hiding?"

"He has been causing a lot of trouble among the workers, Rachel. Some have left the fields untended, others refuse to obey the overseers. Many of the loyal workers are frightened that they will all suffer for the actions of a few. Families are divided by what he is doing and the planters are losing patience. I know not how much longer I can keep the peace."

Peace? I thought of Paul's battered body and the words of the man who had brought him to the cloister. Hooded figures riding fine horses, that had been what Digger had seen, and the same images apparently haunted Paul's nightmares, for he screamed in terror of them. "What do you wish from me?" I asked, suddenly aware of the silence stretching between us.

"Only that you remain safe. If you would all move into the house . . . You could have the entire third floor, I am sure. And then I would be able to keep watch over you."

"I thought that was to be Digger's job."

"Where is he?"

"Somewhere in the ruins, I expect. He has to remain hidden, or the children might see him." I kept my gaze on the distant gleam of Sunrise as I spoke the lies. I ached to trust Nick, to tell him that Paul was not hiding, but a victim of the same men who had injured both Digger and Nick during the first attack; yet I dared not. What if my heart was wrong? My love blind?

"Why do you turn away from me, Rachel? Have I done something to anger you?" His voice softened, and the tenderness in it tore at my already bruised heart.

"'Tis only that I see you so seldom." I met his gaze, unable to deny my feelings for him, the longing that haunted me day and night.

"Do you not know that I hate being separated from you? 'Tis only that my father's health is worse, and I have to be his eyes and ears throughout the island. I cannot remember the last night I spent at Sunrise or the last morning I woke to good news."

I lost myself in his eyes, letting the cares that weighed so heavily on me slip away as my heart swelled with love. All I wanted was to be in his arms, to feel his lips on mine, to belong to him as I had never belonged to anyone.

He seemed to read my thoughts, for he pulled me close, then covered my lips with his. His kiss was tender at first, gentle and questing, then as my lips parted, a shudder shook his powerful body and he deepened the caress. Now his mouth took command, demanding an answer that I gave without question. This proof of his hunger quickly satisfied all my doubts as his passionate lips covered my face with kisses and his arms crushed my willing body to his.

He groaned as he loosened his embrace and stepped away from me. "I have to go, Rachel, but I shall return, never doubt that. I will keep you safe, no matter what comes."

I wanted to throw my arms around him and hold him here or at least beg him to stay. I needed to warn him that he, too, could be in deadly danger, but I was given no chance to find the right words as he hurried to mount his horse. In the end I could only blink back my tears and call, "Take care, Nick," as he rode away. The hollow in my chest told me that he took my heart with him.

Feeling weary far beyond words, I went back inside to help Seraphina with preparations for the midday meal, then tried to lose myself in the details of our everyday life. This time, however, I was not successful. All I could think about was Nick's fervent promise to return and protect me. That, and the mysterious area I had discovered on the far side of the wall, which I feared was somehow connected to the danger that seemed to surround us here. What did it all mean? I had to find out or go mad.

Since the children had been inside all morning, Seraphina took them outside to play or work in the garden after I finished with the older ones' lessons. I used their absence to take water and food to the cellar so I could check on Paul. I found him sitting in the corner, frowning, his eyes ablaze with anger.

"Why am I being kept prisoner here?" he demanded.

"We are simply keeping you safe." I met Paul's glare without flinching. "Why?"

"I must leave. I have people to help, plans to make."

"I be tryin' to tell 'um 'taint possible, Miss," Digger began, his weary tone making it clear that this argument had been going on for sometime.

"You have to stay, Paul. You were nearly killed. If your friends had not brought you here, you would surely have died of your wounds. It will be at least a week before you can hope to go anywhere."

"You cannot keep me here. My mission is . . ." Paul tried to stand, staggered wildly, then collapsed back on his blankets.

"Your mission is doomed if you are killed." I controlled my temper with an effort. "Nick was just here to warn me that those who are seeking you may be watching the cloister. How far do you think you would get? You can barely stand."

I watched him wilt as though my words were blows, but I ignored the twinges of pity. At the moment, he was in no position to care for himself. "Let Nick talk to the . . ."

"Did you tell Nick I was here?" Paul was suddenly so still I wondered if he was all right.

"Of course not. Digger and Seraphina are the only ones who know. Why?"

"Because I have reason to believe that he might be behind the attack. Those who have been keeping watch on all of Sunrise tell me that he rides about the plantation at night. And they say that the black robes gather in the ruins. These ruins." He waved a hand at the stone walls that enclosed us, then gripped his head with both hands, obviously fighting pain.

302

"The black robes that attacked you?" My mouth was so dry I wondered that the words came out clearly enough to be understood.

"The same." Paul dropped his hands and straightened, though I could see that the movements cost him. "They are the ones who would keep the workers enslaved on their plantations. They fear education, for it would give their workers a choice, a chance to escape their control."

"But they attacked Nick, too, that first night. He was wounded just as you two were. Nick could never ... His father is the one who brought you here, Paul, how can you ..."

"Jarvis Harrison brought me here because he wanted me to keep the poor sheep content, not to lead them out of the flock. He has no share in my dream, and as for Nick ..." His contempt was obvious. "He talks peace, but I have no doubt that he means to keep it with guns, not books."

I wanted to argue, but I kept remembering all I had seen on my morning explorations. For a moment I considered telling Paul and Digger, but when I looked into Paul's eyes, I held my tongue. He would only say that my discoveries proved that Nick was involved, for he knew how much Nick loved the cloister. And I had no way to refute his belief—at least, not yet.

"You seem to be feeling better, Paul," I observed, suddenly eager to change the subject of our conversation. "Have you remembered more of what happened the night you were injured?"

"Only that I was riding from Emerald Acres to Sunrise when I was set upon by a half-dozen hooded riders. They said nothing; perhaps they feared that I might recognize their voices. They had clubs and cane knives. One swung at my head, and ..." He shuddered. "I remember nothing after that."

"Were you alone?"

He nodded, then winced again, and in spite of the poor light, I could see that he had grown pale. "You need rest, not conversation." I set my baskets on the floor and picked up those that they had emptied. "I shall try to come back tonight, but if I cannot, Seraphina will bring you more food and make sure that you are both safe."

"Stay away from Nick Harrison, Rachel, he can only bring you harm." Paul's warning followed me as I climbed up the steps and paused at the panel, listening to be sure that the room beyond was empty before I opened it.

Once out, I set the baskets on the table and hurried over to the wardrobe, wondering if I dared enter from this side to inspect the boxes I had seen there. I would not have to return through the wardrobe, if I could discover how to open the second panel from this side. The temptation was too great to resist. I removed the wedge that secured the wardrobe door, then picked up a lamp and matches. I had to find out what was going on before the danger swamped us all.

Chapter 18

I kept the panel open with my foot while I lit the lamp, but once it bloomed to life, I allowed the panel to close. Only then did I realize that I had no idea how to operate it from this side. Panic swelled through me, making my hands shake so that I had to set the lamp down for a moment or risk dropping it. When I did so, I saw the glint of metal and my terrible fear ebbed. There was a handle on this side. Hoping that I would not need to use it, I lifted the lamp and looked around.

This part of the man-made tunnel ended not too far from where I stood, but not in a stone wall. Which explained the space at the top of the steps to the cellar. I checked the wooden wall carefully, rather hoping that there might be an opening into that area, but there was none.

Disappointed, I turned my attention to the other end of the dark passage, hoping that I might find some clue there. Using the pile of boxes I had seen earlier as a landmark, I searched for and located the handle that opened the panel into the ruins, which brought a sigh of relief. Once I had finished my search here, I had only to let myself out that way. I could stroll around the building and quietly join the others near our garden.

That decided, I turned my full attention to the boxes,

eager to see what they might contain. I lifted the top from the first box and gasped as my fingers brushed the black fabric. A black cloak! I shuddered, remembering how it had felt as it, or one like it, had covered my face to keep me from seeing my intruder the night I had nearly encountered him.

For a moment, I wanted only to leave this accursed place; but a couple of deep breaths calmed the tide of panic and I turned my attention to the next box. More cloaks and other dark clothing, even masks; a lot of masks, enough to cover dozens of faces. I fought back a strong desire to drop a match in the pile. Perhaps without their masks . . .

I forced the thought away and carefully smoothed the cloaks, before I replaced the lids I had removed. Soon, I promised myself, but not until I knew who donned these masks. Only then would those I loved be safe. I held the lamp high and looked at the next stack.

This one appeared to be debris, broken bits of board, some cloth, nails, and off to one side, the tools that might have been used to build the wall. I bent closer, studying the hammer and saw, then frowned. Nick had told me that the wall separating the repaired part of the cloister from the ruins had been built years ago, but the tools showed no sign of rust.

"Elena, Elena, be you in here?" Seraphina's voice sounded so close that I started nervously, then steadied myself as I realized that she must be in the playroom. My heart pounded as I waited for her to answer.

"I suppose she must be somewhere else, Sassy," Seraphina continued after a moment or two. "Did she tell you she was coming in here for something?"

A chill slipped down my spine. Could Elena have been in the playroom when I came up from the cellar? I swallowed hard, then shook my head. The room had been quiet, and if Elena had seen me, surely she would have spoken. I rested my head against the solid wood as I tried to catch the child's soft reply. "Her come for Lilly's raggy."

I smiled, thinking how like Elena it was to think of taking the old rag doll out to Lilly.

"Well, do you see it about?" Seraphina sounded impatient, and I suspected it was because she had noticed my abandoned baskets and was wondering where I might have gone.

"'Tis over there." Sassy's words brought back all my uncertainty. If the doll was still in the playroom, what had become of Elena?

I stayed by the wall, listening until Seraphina sent Sassy off with the doll, probably so she could remain long enough to retrieve the baskets of dirty dishes and empty containers. A moment later, I heard the door of the playroom closing.

Impatient to discover what might have happened to Elena, I considered slipping back out through the wardrobe; but realizing the danger of discovery, I rejected the idea. If Elena was wandering around somewhere, others of the children might be as well, and if any one of them saw me . . . I reached for the handle I had located earlier and made my way quickly through the ruins.

Only when I opened the outside door did I realize that I still carried the lamp, and aware of how strange it would appear should the children come this way looking for Elena, I blew it out and hid it behind a pile of debris. I would have to retrieve it later, but that was the least of my worries. Right now, I wanted to know what had become of Elena.

My rush around the huge structure left me gasping by the time I reached the edge of the garden the children had planted. I leaned against the cool stone wall as I studied the busy group and tried to catch my breath.

Much to my relief, I located Elena's dark head immediately.

"What happened, Rachel?" Seraphina came up behind me. "I found the baskets, and I ..."

Guilt swept over me as I looked into her worried eyes. For a moment I considered telling her everything I had discovered, but before I could speak, Elena gave a shriek of joy and came racing to me, throwing herself, sobbing, against me. "Oh, Miss Rachel, I thought you left me!"

"What?" I dropped to my knees so I could hold her close and was shocked to discover that she was trembling. "Why would I leave you, Elena?"

"You were gone. I looked everywhere and you were gone." She lifted her face from my shoulder, her eyes full of pain. "Like Mama and Papa. You were here and then you were gone."

Her words sent a chill through me. Could she have seen my exit through the wardrobe? Her expression was troubled, but surely if she had seen me disappear she would have questioned me more closely. "I was busy inside, dear, and you were helping out here. Where did you look for me?" I held my breath, dreading her answer, but she spoke not a word. "Well, we must have just missed each other, I was moving about a great deal."

Suddenly, she looked away from me as though she had just noticed all the children that had come to gather around us. When she turned back to me, she no longer met my gaze. "I be sorry, Miss Rachel. I just be scared of losin' you."

My guilt intensified and I hugged her close again, trying to soothe her suffering. "You must never be afraid of that, Elena, or any of you. We are a family now, and we will all take care of each other. That means that no one goes away."

"For real?" Elena's tear-damp gaze searched my face. "Never?"

Though I wanted more than anything to make that promise to reassure her and the other children, it was impossible, for it would be a lie. "I should never want to leave you, but no one can know the future. I can only promise that I would never choose to leave you. I want the cloister to be my home and yours. Will you believe that and trust God to make it happen?"

There was a moment of silence, then the murmurs of assent began and soon everything seemed to return to normal, much to my relief. No matter what, I had to protect the children from the evil that haunted the ruins of the cloister. But how? That question tormented me through the rest of the afternoon as I tried to go about my normal routine.

As the shadows lengthened, I remembered the lamp and, knowing that it would be needed in the playroom after the evening meal, I decided to retrieve it before it was missed. It seemed an easy enough mission, for everyone was busy with their chores and I had only to slip out the door and around the building to the hidden entrance. Unfortunately, the moment I stepped outside, I felt the weight of watching eyes.

Could Nick have been right about there being spies? I studied the various stands of trees and bushes that marked the uncultivated area on that side of the cloister. There could be a dozen people concealed out there, I realized, as I stayed in the shadows close to the wall. I wanted to turn back, to claim that I had broken the lamp, then I realized that one lie would doubtless lead to another and I was so poor at prevarication.

I paused again outside the hidden door, surveying the area as best I could. Nothing moved but the palm fronds and the leaves that stirred in the breeze. Perhaps I was only imagining a watcher. I tried to convince myself, but the prickling feeling remained with me on my return walk. My fear grew—if someone was out there now, might they be planning some evil for this night? My stomach knotted with fear, yet I realized that I had to find out who it was—our very lives might depend on it.

By nightfall, I had made my decision. I would spend the night in the ruins. That way, if the men came for their hooded disguises, I should see their faces—the faces of our enemies. A shiver of foreboding slipped down my spine as I wondered if Paul could be right—that I would find Nick among them.

No one was pleased with my plan. Digger wanted to be the one hiding in the ruins, but Paul's restlessness was growing; I feared that he would try to leave if he was left alone, and neither Seraphina nor I had the strength to restrain him when he struggled in the throes of his nightmares. Seraphina was fearful for my safety, but I allowed neither of them to change my mind. I had to know if I could trust the man I loved, and I had to protect those entrusted to my care.

Once Digger had returned to the cellar and Seraphina was safe in her room across the hall from mine, I changed into a dark gown, then wrapped myself in my old brown cloak, thinking that I could use its folds to hide my face and hands if and when the men came. Armed with a stub of a candle, I made my way to the playroom and carefully opened the wardrobe panel.

Fortunately, no lights greeted me, so I proceeded through the walled-off passageway and on into the ruins. Once there, I paused, unsure of where I should take up my vigil. A particularly sturdy pile of debris about halfway between the entry to the room and the wall caught my eye. Feeling very much alone, I took my place behind it and extinguished my candle.

The darkness suffocated me. I had trouble catching my breath as panic washed over me in waves. I closed my eyes, fighting my need for light; this terror was something I had not considered when I made my plan. After a moment, a rustling noise distracted me and I opened my eyes.

The room seemed lighter, and I realized that the moon was shining through the high windows. Though I could see only the dim outlines of the debris that surrounded me, I felt better, even when the rustling continued. A mouse, I told myself firmly, or some other night creature whose world I had invaded. Taking a deep breath, I settled myself more comfortably, determined to wait, to see what the night would bring.

It brought discomfort and boredom and, as my weariness overcame me, a restless sleep. I know not when I drifted off, but I was dreaming of Nick's arms when a sudden sound interrupted. Startled, I opened my eyes, wondering fearfully where I was. When I saw the debris around me, I remembered and prayed that I had not cried out in my sleep, for I was no longer in the dark. A flickering glow came from just beyond the doorway between this room and the next.

"'Tis about time you got here. I have been waiting forever." I had no trouble recognizing Geraldine Chalmers's voice. I held my breath, expecting them to come closer, but they stayed just out of my sight.

"Keep your voice down." The male voice was a whisper.

"Who do you expect to hear us, the ghosts? All the orphans are long in their beds. And dear, trusting Rachel, too, no doubt." Geraldine's bitter tone chilled me. "No one suspects anything. Since we disposed of that thief Duquanne, everyone is convinced that it was Paul behind the attacks. Defending his precious workers from the cruel overseer."

"Maybe, but I wish I knew where he went to ground after we left him. I could have sworn he was too near death to move." The familiar voice sent a shiver down my back.

"One of you should have cut his throat while you had the chance, Baxter. If Paul manages to survive your little attack, he just might be able to dispel the rumors that all our trouble comes from the restless workers."

"After tonight, no one will be in a mood to listen to the Reverend's ranting. Once our band of raiders reduces Sunrise to a charred ruin, even that fool Jarvis and the rest of the diehards will have to admit that educating the islanders was a mistake. Such an attack will prove that no one is safe from their wrath." Baxter chuckled.

"You will be careful?" Geraldine's tone changed. "Nick will want to fight, you know."

"If you do your part, he should be properly distracted. Who knows, you may even be able to make him forget his interest in Rachel."

"So you can take over?" She mocked him. "Or have you and your friends lost interest after all your prowling and spying?"

His curse burned my ears, but Geraldine only laughed at him. "When do the others come?" she asked after a few minutes.

"They will not be meeting here this night. I fear 'tis too dangerous with Michaels and that servant of Harrison's still missing. I came to get the disguises." Baxter sighed. "I shall miss all this. Still, our new wall and the false back on the wardrobe served us well, and who knows, perhaps we will find other uses for this building once the orphans are placed in service, where they belong."

"I shall be glad to avoid it forever." I heard the sound of movement and a shadow blocked the light, then Geraldine went on, "Give me a candle, I must be on my way. 'Twould never do to be caught out this night."

"So far as anyone knows, all of us are home, safely sleeping in our beds. 'Tis only the evil islanders who ride about in the dark, burning and stealing from their betters." His voice crackled with excitement.

"Have a care, Baxter, 'twould be a shame if you became too fond of leading your little group of raiders. Once we have won our way, they will have to disband." Geraldine's trill of mocking laughter reached me even though the light dimmed as she moved away, heading no doubt for the hidden entrance.

Almost at once, the light brightened again and I shuddered, pulling my cloak over my head as I crouched behind the rubble. Baxter must be on his way to the tunnel that he had created. And I had to get out of here! The moment he was inside that wall, I had to run. Nick and his family must be warned.

It seemed an eternity before the click and sudden darkness told me that Baxter was inside the passage. I struggled out of my enveloping cloak and swallowed a wail of despair. The room seemed darker than ever, yet I dared not take time to light my candle. I began inching out from behind the debris, feeling my way with my feet until my eyes adjusted enough so I could see the vague outline of the cleared path. Then I picked up my skirts and hurried as fast as I dared, praying that Geraldine had not tarried once she left the building.

I was nearly to the door when something crashed off to one side. I skidded to a halt. Could Geraldine still be inside? But where was her light, and what would she be . . . A child's soft whimper broke through my chaotic thoughts.

"Who's there?" I whispered.

"Miss Rachel, be that you?" Elena's joyous cry sounded clearly and was near at hand.

I hurried toward the sound, caught between anger and concern. "What are you doing here, Elena?"

"I be lookin' for you." She scrambled to her feet, then whimpered again. "I seen you earlier with the lamp, and you be gone from your room tonight . . ." A sob rose in her throat, stopping her words, and at that moment I heard a sound from the other room.

"Hide," I whispered. "Did you hear what Geraldine and Baxter said?"

She nodded, her face a pale blur in the faint light.

"Whatever happens, you go to Seraphina and tell her all you heard. Tell her to send Digger to Sunrise to warn them."

Elena opened her mouth, but I pushed her roughly behind the debris. The glow of Baxter's candle was already visible through the heaps of rubble. He would be sure to see me, or hear me, if I tried to bury myself in the chaos of fallen wood and burned furnishings that crowded the area. And if he found me, he would also capture Elena.

Without taking time to think further, I headed for the door and raced out into the night, leaving it open. I heard a shout from behind me, but I dared not look back. I dove into the shadows beneath the nearby trees, praying that Baxter would look for me nearer the building. He burst through the door just as I rolled under a protective hibiscus bush.

"Rachel, my dear, come out. We need to talk." Baxter's voice was soft, almost caressing. "You must not hide from me, pretty Rachel. I can help you, protect you from the evil that is stalking our poor island. I know that what has happened is none of your doing, Rachel. All you care about is protecting the children and I can help with that."

I shuddered, watching as Baxter moved away from the open door, but not really seeing him. Instead, I pictured a hooded Baxter chasing poor Lilly or setting fire to the cabin where she was hiding. Threatening her so that she feared to even speak of what had happened to her. I lay very still, praying that Elena would have sense enough to wait before . . .

Even as the fear crossed my mind, I saw a faint movement in the doorway. If Baxter saw her, he would not hesitate to kill her, that I knew. Killing me would be much more difficult, if there was any truth in what Geraldine had said earlier. Not daring to wait any longer, I scrambled to my feet and began running away from the cloister, not really sure where I was going, but confident that Baxter would come after me and give Elena a chance to slip away and get help.

A curse shattered the night and I heard a crash as Baxter plunged into the trees after me. He sounded ominously close, far too near for me to hide again. But where could I go? An image of the lonely burial place at the bottom of the hill filled my mind. I had often visited the area on my walks, so I knew that if I could reach it ahead of him, there were a number of places where I could hide.

I dodged through the trees, stumbling over the vines and roots that covered the soil. My cloak snagged on the bushes and my shoe was nearly torn from my foot, but I kept going, fighting to stay on my feet. There was some open land between the grove I was in and the trees that surrounded the burial place, but if I could cross it before Baxter saw me . . .

I slowed, suddenly aware that I could hear no one behind me. Had he given up his pursuit? Or had he seen Elena? Fear for her slowed my steps even further. I paused at the edge of the meadow, shaking with fatigue as I tried to control my gasping enough so that I might hear his approach.

The breeze caressed my cheeks as I peered back into the shadows. Nothing. I held my breath, listening. Silence, except for the whisper of the palms and the soft sighing of the distant sea. There was a chance. Maybe he had fallen or given up. I took no more time to think as I started across the meadow, my eyes trained on the line of welcoming trees.

He came galloping out of nowhere, grinning, his teeth gleaming in the moonlight. He scarcely slowed his horse as he leaned from his saddle and pulled me into his arms. I tried to scream, but landing on my stomach across the saddle in front of him turned it into a gasp of pain.

I think perhaps I lost consciousness for a time, but when I opened my eyes, I was still across his horse's withers, my face bouncing painfully against the beast's hard shoulder. Dizziness swept over me as I tried to use my hands to protect my face and I shuddered as Baxter slowed his horse and tightened his hold on my waist.

"So you are awake. Good. I want you to listen to me, for I have a plan, dear Rachel, and you can have a part in it, if you are willing to cooperate." His hand moved from my waist to caress the curve of my breast and his low chuckle sent a shiver of terror through me.

Furious protests rose in my throat, but thanks to my lack of breath, there was nothing I could do or say. I tried to look ahead, but my hair hung in a thick curtain against my face and I could see little beyond the horse's dark body. Baxter's touch had left me few doubts as to what he meant to do to me and shivers of revulsion raced through me.

Never! I vowed, as I fought nausea and a fresh onslaught of dizziness. I would die before I allowed Baxter Travis to put his hands on me. The chill within me deepened as I realized that I might actually have to make such a choice. Yet what could I do? How could I fight when I could not even lift my head from the sweaty hide of his horse? I would have cried, but my misery was too deep for tears to wash it away.

Suddenly, the horse stopped and I became aware of the pounding of the surf near at hand. Baxter shifted away from me, then dismounted. "My poor darling, I hope you are not too distressed to enjoy our time together here. 'Twould be a shame, since I plan to teach you all the secrets of love before I go to settle things with that fool Harrison."

I felt his hands at my waist and thought to kick out at him; but he was too quick for me, dragging me roughly off his horse. I braced myself to run the moment my feet touched the ground, but my knees refused to support me and I sagged against Baxter, my skin crawling at the feel of his hard body so near mine.

"Are you unwell?" He steadied me, a frown narrowing his eyes as he peered at my face. "I had no choice, you know. We had to get away from the cloister. Harrison might have set someone to watch over the place."

Hope flared within me and I found my voice as my strength flowed back. I tried to step away from him. "Nick will kill you when he finds out what you have been doing."

"Nick Harrison will not survive this night." His hands tightened on my arms, his fingers biting into my flesh. "That idiot Geraldine believes that she can save him, but I know his kind. He and his father will never change. If we let them live, they will continue their molly-coddling ways and the unrest will grow until we have a real uprising."

Shock paralyzed me for several moments, then a fresh rush of fear broke me free of it. He meant for the night raiders to kill everyone at Sunrise, I realized. That would be the perfect way for him to take control of the island. With the other planters fearing for their lives, they would do whatever he suggested. Including killing Paul, once he was strong enough to emerge from the cellar. And I . . . when I looked into his burning eyes, I had no doubt the price I would be forced to pay if I wished to go on living.

Unable to bear looking at him, I turned my gaze away, scanning the area where we now stood. The headlands were nearby, I felt the mist wafting up from the crashing waves. Sunrise was not far away. "If you think to run from me, forget it." His lips twisted in an ugly grimace. "You are mine, Rachel, and I shall not leave here until you know it as well as I do."

He released one of my arms and stroked his fingers along my cheek, then down my neck and along the edge of the modest neckline of my gown. When he reached the line of buttons, he began to undo them.

Though terror twisted through me like a maddened serpent, I held myself still. I lifted my head, feeling the breeze as I looked beyond him to the line of trees that edged the headland. I braced myself, praying that he would think me submissive and let go of my other arm. When he did, I would run for the cliff. Better the cruel rocks below than his filthy, blood-soaked hands touching me.

I was ready to close my eyes when something moved in the shadows beneath the trees. A rider! It took all my self-control not to respond to the hope that surged inside me. Instead, I dropped my gaze and let my body sag as his questing fingers sought beneath the fabric of my gown, groping roughly . . .

Suddenly he released my other arm. Without thinking, I spun around, flapping my skirt at the head of his grazing horse as I raced past it. Startled, the beast leaped back, crashing into Baxter, giving me a chance to escape his reaching hands. I ran toward the cliff, but instead of plunging over, as I had planned, I stopped to look back over my shoulder.

"Rachel, be careful!" Nick's voice carried to me easily as he raced his horse across the open field, straight toward Baxter, who was fumbling beneath his coat for something. Nick hurled himself directly at Baxter just as he produced a gun. The fearsome explosion of a gunshot shattered the night, and in a moment the two men were struggling on the ground.

My heart stopped as Baxter fought his way free of Nick and struggled to his feet. He still had the gun! I screamed as he leveled it at Nick, but Nick was already moving. Something flashed in the moonlight and Baxter toppled backward, the gun firing loudly once again.

"Nick, oh, Nick!" I was shouting and sobbing as I ran back across the open headland. I fell to my knees beside Nick, terrified of what I might find; but determined to be at his side, no matter what. He lay frighteningly still, but his eyes were open, and as I bent over him, he smiled at me.

"Help me up," he whispered. "I have to be sure that Travis is . . ." He winced as I slipped an arm beneath his head, and I felt dampness on my fingers as they caught in his thick dark hair, but he was already on his knees.

"Did he hurt you?" I gasped the words even as he crawled the few feet to where Baxter lay on his back. I scrambled after him, then nearly choked as I saw the hilt of a knife protruding from Baxter's chest. Nick pulled the gun from Baxter's hand and tucked it into the waist of his trousers, then sagged back against me.

"Where are you hurt?" I asked, holding him tight against me, vowing that I should never let him go again.

"Don' know." He sounded weak, distant. "Din' feel anything."

"Let me look." I eased him back on the tough grass and moved my hands gently over his shoulders and chest. I found nothing. "Perhaps your back," I suggested. "If you could sit up so I can see . . ."

He sat up slowly, but without any help from me. His pale shirt was marked with dirt and grass, but I saw no bloodstain. I swallowed hard, relieved, yet confused by his odd behavior. I reached up to gently smooth back a lock of his russet hair and found my fingers damp. "Your head!" I gasped.

Nick lifted his hand and gingerly touched the spot that I had brushed, then winced. "He must have hit me when I jumped him. Only I cannot recall . . ."

"The gun went off as you hit him." I tried to lift his hair away to see what damage had been done, but there was too little light for me to see.

"I never saw the gun until it was too late." Nick sighed, then glared at me. "What the devil were you doing out here with Travis, Rachel?"

"What was I . . . Did Digger not tell you?" Shock at the question changed to anger as I realized the implications of his words. How could he think that I had chosen to come here with Baxter Travis?

"Digger? I last saw him when I left him to guard you. What are you talking about?" His frown deepened, but he straightened up, seeming much stronger.

"The attack. Elena was to rouse Seraphina and send Digger to warn your family that the raiders . . ." I let the sentence trail off, another question distracting me. "How did you find me, if no one told you what happened?"

"I was on my way to the cloister when I saw a rider racing this way and decided to follow him. I had no idea . . ." He stopped, shook his head as though to clear it, then met my gaze more firmly. "What happened, Rachel? What did you say about the raiders?"

I took a deep breath, fighting my longing to dissolve in tears, then stood up. This was no time to think of love or to resent Nick's lack of trust. Not when the very lives of his family might be in danger. "Baxter was their leader. We have to get to Sunrise now. They were to attack before dawn, and your family could be in terrible danger if no one has warned them."

"How do you know this?" Nick got to his feet. "Did Baxter tell you? Or was it Paul Michaels?"

Stung by the suspicion in his tone, I left him to catch the two horses that grazed so peacefully only a few yards from where Baxter lay. "I shall tell you as we ride." I turned away, pretending that I was readying myself to mount, not wanting him to see the pain his question brought me. He sounded as though he actually believed that I might be in league with the raiders. I leaned against the horse, well aware I could never make it to the saddle, not with my heart weighing me down.

"Let me help you." Nick's hands clasped my waist and he lifted me easily onto the back of Baxter's dark horse, then vaulted into the saddle of his own bay stallion.

I felt the quivers of longing move through me and my heart broke. How could I ache for his touch when he suspected me of who knew what evil involvement? How could I love a man who refused to trust me? And what should I say to him? Would he even listen to what I needed to tell him? Or would he call me a liar when I informed him that Geraldine was in league with his enemies?

I had no chance to find out, for even as I was seeking for a way to begin, we heard the sound of gunfire. Nick swore. "Stay here, Rachel," he ordered, then spurred his horse into a full gallop.

I gritted my teeth, wound my fingers in the horse's mane, and sent him after Nick. This was my fight, too.

Chapter 19

Nick headed into the trees and the low branches nearly swept me from my precarious seat on the racing horse; but I merely slumped lower, pressing my face to the horse's neck, trusting him to follow Nick's stallion through the thick growth. So intent was I on keeping my eyes closed against the stinging strands of mane, I was nearly thrown when the beast suddenly stopped.

"Blast it, Rachel, I told you to stay back on the bluff."

Nick's furious voice brought my head up, once I had settled back on the saddle. Instead of answering him, I peered ahead and my heart nearly stopped beating. We were in the shadows at the edge of the trees, and the buildings of Sunrise were just across a small field from us.

Though dawn had not yet come, the scene was brightly lit by several small fires that blazed in the out-buildings. Dark-clad riders galloped round and about the main house, but none ventured too close, for rifle fire came from several windows. Relief swept over me. "Digger must have gotten here in time."

"Digger?" Nick glared at me, his expression a mixture of anger and confusion.

"I sent Elena to wake Serephina and tell her what we

overheard in the ruins." This was not the way I had wanted to tell Nick, but my time had run out. "Baxter and Geraldine were there discussing the planned attack on Sunrise. It was to be the final one, for they were sure if you and your father were victims of the supposed islanders, the rest of the planters would insist that Paul and his school be driven from the island."

"I should have guessed that Baxter was a part of the trouble, but Geraldine?" The shock in his face hurt, but I had no time to wonder why.

"There never was an uprising among the islanders, Nick. Those men out there are from the planter families."

"Well, they must be stopped, no matter who they are." Nick pulled out Baxter's gun and offered it to me. "Do you know how to use this?"

I swallowed hard, a treasured memory filling my mind. One long ago summer my father had taught me to shoot, much to my mother's disgust. "I can shoot it, but I never hit anything."

"You can if you must, believe me." He took his own gun from the pouch on his saddle. "Anyway, 'tis likely that a warning shot would be enough to keep them away. Can you reload?"

I nodded, hoping that my memories were clear enough—or better, that I should not have to find out. I only wanted this horrible siege to end. Still, I took the bullets and placed them in my skirt pocket.

"What do you want me to . . . ?" I stopped as Nick turned away and took aim at a masked rider who was heading for the stable with a torch in his hand. The explosion of the shot made my horse shy and I nearly dropped Baxter's gun as I tried to keep the beast in the shadows. When I looked back, the rider lay motionless on the ground.

"Go to the cloister," Nick ordered. "If we drive them

323

away from here, they might decide to take revenge on the children."

I wanted desperately to argue, to make him see that he needed my help here; but deep down, I knew that he was right. "Be careful," I whispered, not sure that he could hear me over the shouts and gunfire that erupted from the house as another rider tried to approach the big building.

Nick swore, then spurred his horse out of hiding, firing as he went after another of the raiders. Knowing that this would be my only chance to escape unseen, I reined my horse back into the trees, though I wanted more than anything to keep watch until I knew that Nick was safe. Not that I could allow myself to think that he might not be; for that I could never bear.

I paused at the edge of trees that sheltered the road, feeling better just being able to see the cloister on the far side of the cane field, its dark bulk silhouetted against the paling sky. Suddenly, I heard the rattle of approaching hoofbeats, and my blood chilled. If they were coming now, what should I do?

The rider showed no inclination to turn off the road to head my way, however. Indeed, the hoofbeats grew even faster as the horse neared Sunrise. My heartbeat quickened. Could it be Geraldine on her way to warn Nick and his family? If so, she was much too late.

That thought chilled me into action. My heart might have been with Nick, but my protection was pledged to the innocent children who could also be in danger. I guided the horse along the narrow path through the high walls of cane, then up the hill to the cloister door. I jerked the weary beast to a stop, then froze as I realized that the door was standing open!

What if they had come here first? My knees turned to jelly as a realization struck me the moment I slipped from the saddle. They must have come here first, for

Baxter had left their hooded disguises hidden in the ruins. For just a heartbeat, I stayed where I was, clinging to the horse to keep my balance.

Once I caught my breath, however, I forced myself into action, calling out, "Seraphina? Elena? Is anyone here?"

Silence was my only answer. Trembling, I lifted the gun and stepped through the door. It was dim inside, but nothing moved, so I set the gun down long enough to light a lamp. Then, carrying the gun in one hand and the lamp in the other, I moved cautiously through the rooms.

Though each door I opened brought a fresh wave of hope and fear, I found nothing. The rooms appeared much as I had left them, except that all were now empty of life. No babies slept in the tiny beds, no children dreamed on their cots. Every bed was rumpled, as though its occupant had been roused from sleep and taken ... taken where? And by whom?

Visions of knife- or gun-wielding men in black hoods rousting the children from their beds set my stomach to rolling and bile rose in my throat. I forced it back. Such a horrifying possibility made no sense. Men on their way to attack Sunrise would have no reason to burden themselves with crying children. But if they had not been taken, where had they gone?

As I opened the playroom door, I felt a rush of hope, even though the room appeared empty. I crossed to the shelf and opened the hidden panel. Light bloomed below and I heard the soft sound of Seraphina's voice above the wild pounding of my heart. I nearly tumbled down the steps in my eagerness to see them.

They were there, children sitting or sleeping in a circle around Seraphina. Relief filled me, even as I realized that Ben, our eldest orphan, was missing. Elena was the first to see me and she scrambled to her feet, running into my arms, nearly making me drop both lamp and gun.

"I done it, Miss. I tole 'um all. Digger say he go and the Reverend say us gotta stay here till him come back." Her dark eyes pleaded for approval.

I dropped the heavy gun in my pocket and set the lamp on the floor, then hugged her. "You did exactly what had to be done, Elena. I am proud of you and I thank you."

"What is happening?" Seraphina came to my side. "Did Digger and Paul reach them in time?"

"Paul went, too?" I was stunned, though I realized that I should have known, since he was nowhere in the big room.

"Him be sayin' 'tis him fault," Elena supplied. "Him be mutterin' somethin' fierce."

"And Ben?" I had to know what had happened to the quiet older boy whose quick mind and love of books I had come to treasure.

"Digger be sending him to tell his friends." Seraphina's dark eyes met mine. "Him say them be needed."

I nodded, well aware that Digger had been right. Nick would need all the help he could get against his well-armed and clearly desperate neighbors. I shuddered, remembering the rattle of gunfire that had followed me as I rode away. Nick had to be safe!

"Where you been?" Elena asked, and I saw the question echoed in Seraphina's gaze.

"I tried to lead Baxter away so you could get inside. I thought I had escaped him, but he found me and took me to the bluffs. Nick saw us and followed. Baxter . . ." The ugliness of the memories clogged my throat for a moment, but I forced them away. "He is dead."

"And Mr. Nick?" The alarm in Elena's face told me that she cared for him, too.

"I left him at Sunrise trying to help fight off the raiders. He feared that some of them might come here, if they were driven off."

"'Twas what the Reverend feared." Seraphina met my gaze. "Be it safe to venture up? We be needing food and water."

Knowing that she wished to question me about the situation at Sunrise out of the children's hearing, I nodded. "Elena, will you keep the children down here, while we go up and get what we will need?"

Once we were in the playroom with the panel closed, I told Seraphina everything that had happened, including my use of the second hidden panel and what I had overheard between Geraldine and Baxter Travis. She shook her head, her expression sad. "'Twill tear this island apart. Planter against planter, islander against islander."

"Not if the Harrisons survive." I spoke from my heart. "Nick can make it right. I know he can."

Her gaze was full of compassion, which did nothing to lift my flagging spirits. Could I be wrong? Was there more about the island that I had not yet come to understand? I had no chance to ask, for a wayward breeze brought the distant rattle of gunfire, sending us both hurrying to the kitchen. As we gathered supplies, I wondered how long we might need to keep the children hidden . . . and how we should know when it was safe to come out.

There was no way I could hide, I realized, as I helped Seraphina carry everything back to the playroom. They would be safe down there, but Nick . . . Nick was fighting for his life, for the life of the island, really. And that was my fight, too.

"I shall have to go back to Sunrise," I told Seraphina as we settled the last of the supplies on the cellar floor. "If you stay down here with the children until I come back, you all should be safe."

"But the danger . . ." She touched my arm.

"I have Baxter's gun."

"If anything should happen to you . . ." She looked deep into my eyes, then straightened. "I shall keep them safe."

"I knew I could trust you." I hugged her impulsively, then gave Elena a wave and raced back up the steps before they saw my tears. I had come to love them all deeply, and I hated leaving them, even though I knew they were safe—for now. Their future as well as mine was being decided at Sunrise, and I had to know what was happening.

Though I had been here less than an hour, it was full daylight when I stepped outside, a lovely cool morning that would have been perfect had the wind not brought the scent of smoke. Since I had simply abandoned the beast when I arrived, I was relieved to see Baxter's horse was calmly grazing near the trees. He would get me to Sunrise much more quickly than my feet.

It took me several minutes to catch the trailing reins, for he seemed quite wary of me—perhaps remembering the way I had flapped my skirt to frighten him when we were on the bluffs. Finally, however, I was able to lead him to a nearby rock, which gave me enough height to mount. With the gun bouncing against my thigh, I guided him down the hill toward the cane field, my heart already pounding with fear about what I might find at Sunrise.

A rather frightening silence seemed to have fallen over the area as I emerged from the cane and started up the hill toward the road. Was the battle over? I hoped so, yet fear fluttered inside me like a trapped bird. Who had won? And at what cost? I had just started through the trees, wondering how I should approach the house, when a shadow moved and my horse shied.

I clung desperately to the reins, trying to hold the

328

beast so that I could free a hand to reach into my pocket for the gun. Why had I not taken it out before? I wanted to cry or curse ...

"Miss Ames, oh, Miss Ames, thank God it be you." A boy's voice broke through my dark thoughts just as the horse stopped his nervous dancing.

"Ben!" Relief made me tremble as he stepped out of the bushes, then my fear returned as I saw the number of people behind him. A half-dozen or more men followed him, and all of them were armed, some with the deadly looking cane knives, others with old guns or rifles. I swallowed hard, suddenly not sure what was going on.

"Us be skeered, Missy," Ben continued. "Us gots prisoners, but 'taint sure what to do with 'um."

"Prisoners?"

One of the men nodded and signaled someone behind him. A moment later two black-clad men were pushed forward. A shiver traced down my spine as I recognized them both from the Sunrise ball. They were quite battered from the battle, and one wore a makeshift bandage about his thigh.

"Miss Ames," the taller one said, "you must help us. These men are part of the uprising, and they have done terrible harm to those at Sunrise. If you could just take us to Sea Cliff ..." He winced as one of his captors poked him with the tip of a knife.

"What has happened at Sunrise?" I asked Ben, ignoring the others. "Are the Harrisons safe?"

Ben shrugged. "Firin' stopped. Us be afeered to go near."

"The islanders have control there, Miss Ames, you would be in deadly danger." The bandaged one spoke up now. "Get us away from here and we shall all be safe."

My heart lifted at his words. If these men were afraid

329

of those in control at Sunrise, that must mean the raiders had lost their battle. I studied Ben. "Why are you afraid to go to Sunrise?" I asked after a moment.

"Them could shoot us."

His look of mingled sadness and pride told me far more than his words and I understood his fear. Thanks to the activities of the raiders, no one in the area was much inclined to trust. "I doubt anyone will shoot me, so perhaps I should lead the way."

"Bless you, Miss Ames." Ben looked up at me with gratitude. "us be mos' worried 'bout Digger."

My heart contracted as I realized how little time I had given to worrying about all those for whom I cared. "Is he at the house?"

Ben shrugged. "You be wantin' us to bring them?" He jerked a thumb at the prisoners.

"By all means. They should face those they have wronged."

The two men in black began to curse me, but a quick jab from one of their captors stopped their words. I rode Baxter's horse past them onto the road and headed for Sunrise, my heart pounding with anxiety. Still, I kept my head high, not wanting those who followed me to sense my dread of what might lie ahead.

The carnage of the battle was clearly visible the moment we left the shelter of the trees. A dead horse lay just beyond a flowering tree, there were several burned areas on the lawn and two of the once lovely trees were now charred stumps. My horse snorted and shied away from rusty puddles, fighting my hold on his reins, and my throat burned as I wondered whose blood had been spilled.

We were halfway to the house before the front door opened and a man carrying a rifle stepped out onto the shadowy veranda. "What you doin' with them, Miss Ames?" I easily recognized Hathaway's voice.

"These men fought the raiders, too, Hathaway. They have two prisoners that they wish to turn over to Mr. Harrison or Nick." My voice sounded strong, but I could hardly breathe, so tight were the bands of fear that constricted my chest.

"That be true?" Hathaway advanced to the edge of the veranda.

"Is Digger here?" I asked, wishing that I dared to demand answers about Nick's safety, but afraid to press Mr. Harrison's most trusted servant. "These are his men."

"Wait here." Hathaway stepped back, then disappeared into the house, closing the door behind him. Though nothing was said, I was conscious of movement behind the drapes that covered the broken windows on the lower floor of the house. I shivered as I noticed still another small spot of charring on the veranda rail. The raiders had come dreadfully close to achieving their goal here.

"Miss Rachel, what you be doin' here?" Digger emerged, still carrying the gun Nick had given him when he'd brought him back to the cloister to guard us.

"I had to come and make sure that everyone was all right. Where is Nick? And Mr. Harrison? And Paul?" The sight of Digger's friendly face set my tongue free. I slipped from the saddle, nearly falling as my knees refused to support me.

"You be hurt?" Digger came down the steps.

"Just worried."

"Us be fine. Mr. Nick, him gone to fetch the planters here. Mr. Jarvis, him be restin'. The Reverend be inside. Us gots everythin' under control." His head was high, and I could see the blazing pride in his eyes. "I kin take them." He pointed to the prisoners. "Us gots more under guard inside."

Ben and the others came forward, all talking at once,

eager to know what was happening now that the battle had ended. While they talked, I moved past them and up the stairs. I could hear the battle stories later; now I simply wanted reassurance that Nick was in no more danger.

Paul rose to his feet slowly as I entered the parlor. He looked pale and ill, but he straightened up, his head high. His expression, however, was unfriendly. "What are you doing here?"

I met his gaze without flinching. "Everyone was safe at the cloister, so I came here to see if I could help."

"'Twould be better if you stayed away. There will be trouble once Nick brings all the old planters here. 'Tis unlikely they will be willing to admit their part in what happened this past night and all the days since the ball."

"They may not admit their guilt, but I can quote from the mouths of their own to accuse them." My anger flared hot, renewing my strength.

"You would do that?"

I reached into my pocket and pulled out Baxter's gun. "This came from the leader of the raiders and I was nearly his victim."

"Rachel!" A gasp from behind me brought me around to face Geraldine Chalmers. She shrank back at the sight of the gun, appearing almost as disheveled as I, her face pale, her hair streaming about her face, her clothes stained and torn.

I glared at her. "What are you doing here, changing sides again?"

A shadow flickered in the depths of her eyes, but her smile never wavered. "My dear, whatever do you mean? I heard a rumor of the impending attack and came at once to warn the Harrisons; but I arrived too late, it had already begun."

"That is because your dear friend Baxter had no intention of allowing you to save Nick for yourself. He laughed at your plan because he knew that only the death of Nick and his father and the destruction of Sunrise would rally the families against the islanders and put him in command."

"Baxter would never . . ." She caught herself, seeming to realize what her admission told those listening about her involvement. "Baxter would have no part in what was happening here. When he arrives, he will tell you himself. This was all the work of a few malcontents in league with the islanders."

"When he arrives here?" I frowned at her. "What do you mean?"

"Nick rode off to Sea Cliff to fetch Baxter. There is to be a meeting of the planter families to decide what is to be done with those who were captured in this morning's attack." Geraldine swished by me, head high, her expression as haughty as ever.

"Is that what he told you?" I was having a hard time hiding my confusion. Whatever was Nick about? Why had he not told Geraldine of Baxter's death? Was there still another plot, one that I had no knowledge of?

"I doubt Miss Chalmers had an opportunity to speak with Nick." Paul's tone was devoid of emotion. "She arrived only a short time ago, well after the battle was over. By that time Nick was gone."

"But I thought . . ." I let the sentence trail off, deciding on another tack. "I heard a rider approaching as I left earlier, Geraldine. I thought it was you."

"You were here?" Her smile was gone now.

"I was with Nick."

For a moment, her fury blazed at me, then as quickly as a blink, it was gone and she produced a slight smile. "You rode away?"

"Nick wanted to be sure the children were protected." I made a show of putting the gun back in my pocket, though truth be told, I should gladly have given it to

333

someone else. Just touching the cold metal reminded me of how near Nick had come to death at Baxter's hands.

"And now you are here to report. How sweet."

"I am here to help with the wounded, if there are any." I cast a glance at Paul. "I have had quite a bit of practice recently."

"There are quite a few who could benefit from your expertise," Paul said. He had seated himself again, his movements slow and awkward. "We had them taken to the second floor. Any of the servants can direct you."

"It appears that you could use some rest, Paul." I moved closer to him, seeing for the first time that there was a fresh bloodstain on his shirt and a bulky bandage beneath his sleeve. "You were hurt again."

"Again?" Geraldine's gaze moved from Paul to me and back again. "You were the one hiding him, were you not, Rachel?"

"Someone had to care for the victims of your evil scheme." I met her gaze, then offered my arm to Paul. "Come along, I am sure Hathaway or Mrs. McGinty can find you a bed. 'Twould not do for you to be too tired to face the planters when they arrive."

I had expected an argument, but my final words seemed to convince him. Paul struggled to his feet and even allowed me to help him up the elegant front staircase.

"So Geraldine really did have a part in all this," he mused. "I found it hard to believe when Elena was babbling her wild story. The woman was always offering to help me secretly, claimed that her father would never approve of my work, but she did."

"She was probably trying to get information for Baxter Travis." I hated the anger that flooded through me and the cynicism I heard in my own voice. I had been far happier before I'd seen so much of the world's evil and duplicity.

"I was riding here from Emerald Acres when I was attacked, yet I never suspected that she might have told the raiders where I could be found." He sighed. "Sometimes I wonder if the Lord expects too much of us poor mortals."

"Reverend Bennett says He never asks more than we can give." I tried to keep my tone calm, though his seeming collapse was frightening. Paul had been the rock on which all my dreams for the orphanage had been built. If he should give up now . . .

"Dear Rachel, to think that I considered you a fragile vessel for such a hard task." His chuckle was devoid of humor. "And now I learn that you have courage enough for all of us. Were you really with Nick?"

"He saved me from Baxter Travis." I paused, looking both ways to make sure we were not overheard. "Baxter was the leader of the raiders, but he is dead. They fought, and Nick killed him."

Paul sighed as I guided him to the room that Hathaway had assigned him. "So much terror and death. I fear I shall never understand it, Rachel. All I wanted was to make the lives of the islanders better. 'Twould cost the planters so little and mean so much."

"We will do it, Paul," I whispered, as I helped him lie down on the bed. "You just rest now. I shall come for you when the meeting starts."

"So tired . . ." His soft snores followed me to the door, which I closed firmly behind me.

When I looked up, Ben stood a few feet away. I signaled him to come to me, my worry stronger than my reservations about involving anyone else. Besides, I reasoned, Ben had already played a part in this battle.

"Ben, would you sit with the Reverend? I am worried about him. He is still very weak, and there are people here who might not want him to survive his wounds."

His eyes brightened immediately, and he took his

knife from its sheath. "I be guardin' him with my life, Miss."

"Just send someone for me if he takes a turn for the worse. Otherwise, I think sleep will help him recover."

Ben nodded, then slipped through the door when I opened it for him. That settled, I hurried back along the hall to the rooms where Hathaway said the wounded had been taken. Weary though I was, I knew I could never rest so long as Nick was somewhere in danger and my poor skills could help ease the suffering of those who had been injured in the battle.

Pamela and Olivia, who had been sitting with the injured men in one of the rooms, actually greeted me with welcoming smiles. "We thought Nick would send someone for Dr. Hogarth," Pamela muttered, as she laid a cooling cloth across the forehead of a young man I remembered dancing with her at the ball, "but he said everyone had to stay until this was settled."

"Sometimes I think 'twill never be settled." Olivia sniffed, then gently replaced the thin cover a feverish patient had kicked off. "'Tis all so ugly and frightening."

"Can you help them, Rachel?" Pamela met my gaze. "I have no idea what to do, and Mother refuses to leave Papa's side."

"Is your father worse?" I felt a chill.

"He was taken ill after the battle and Nick made him lie down. We have been here ever since." Olivia glared around the room. "There was no one else to care for them, since Harriet and the other servants are watching over those in the other room."

"Well, we must do what we can." I bent over the first man, probing gently at the wounds visible on his back and shoulders. My instincts took over and I began issuing orders, which, much to my surprise, Olivia and Pamela and the servants obeyed without question.

The hours passed almost unnoticed. The two rooms, each crowded by a half-dozen cots holding the injured, grew hot and stuffy. Then, later, the outside world dimmed as clouds filled the sky, hiding the sun and threatening rain. At some time during the endless day, Mrs. McGinty sent up a huge tray of food, which we shared with those injured who were strong enough to eat. And still Nick did not return.

By mid-afternoon, I had reached the end of my strength. Having slept only briefly in the ruins, I could no longer keep my eyes open or my head up. Harriet, seeing me stagger as I straightened up after changing the dressing on one of the men's wounds, caught my arm and steadied me.

"You be needin' sleep, Miss," she whispered. "If'n you stays up much longer, you be needin' doctorin' yourself."

I tried to find the words to deny my weakness, but burst into tears instead. Harriet slipped an arm around my waist and gently led me up to my familiar quarters on the third floor. "You be safe here," she assured me.

"When Nick comes, or if any of the men need me . . ." I began.

"I know where you be." Her warm grin touched me like a comforting hand. "You sleep."

Though I wanted to argue, just looking at the bed was enough to draw me down on it, and I think I was asleep before my head touched the pillow. After the terror of the past twenty-four hours, escaping into sweet dreams of Nick was pure heaven.

The room was shrouded in shadow when I opened my eyes. Where was I? As I tried to remember, I heard it—a stealthy sound, like someone moving cautiously outside the room where I lay. Heart pounding, I eased up into a sitting position and looked around. I was at Sunrise. A sweet sense of homecoming filled me, then

337

memories of all that had brought me here swept it away and set my mind to whirling with anxiety.

Had someone come to hurt me? Geraldine might have guessed that I knew more about the attack than was safe for her. And there were others who ... I slid from the bed and tiptoed to a shadowy corner near the door from the sitting room. If anyone came in, I wanted to be ready to run.

For several minutes, I heard nothing, and I was beginning to think that my mind was playing tricks. Then I heard a soft sound and the doorknob began to turn. I braced myself, fighting my fear with anger at all that had been done to the innocent victims of Baxter Travis and his band.

The door slowly edged open and a glow of candlelight spilled in. A flicker of hope chased through me. Surely no killer would come with a candle. But what sort of friend would simply open the door without knocking or calling out to me?

I held my breath, shrinking behind a chair, readying myself for a confrontation with whoever came through the door. "Miss Ames, be you in here?"

Relief nearly undid me. "Ben!" I gasped. "You frightened me half to death."

The boy jumped back, nearly extinguishing the candle by his sudden movement. "Miss Ames." His wide, frightened eyes told me that I had returned the favor by scaring him in turn.

Recapturing my dignity, I managed a shaky smile. "What are you doing here, Ben?"

"I thought you be needin' to know. They be questionin' the Reverend." His worried expression sobered me.

"Who is questioning Reverend Michaels?"

"Them—the planters what Mr. Nick brought back with him."

338

"Nick is here?" For a heartbeat the joy of knowing that he was safe banished my icy fear, but it returned quickly. If all was well, why had Nick not come seeking me? He had to know that I had all the answers he needed. If he wanted them.

Chapter 20

I did my best to marshall my fear, not wanting to alarm the boy, since he already appeared frightened. "When did they send for him?"

"Mr. Nick came hisself. I thought it be all right, Miss, but then I 'members you sayin' I's to stay with him and . . ." He studied his bare toes. "Harriet tole me where you be."

My mind whirled with the dire possibilities his words suggested. "Thank you for coming up to tell me. Do you know where Digger is?"

He shrugged.

"I shall be down as soon as I can. Meanwhile, I would like you to find Digger and have him waiting for me at the top of the staircase. Could you do that?"

"I kin try, but I bein't 'lowed in the halls no more."

My apprehension deepened, but I refused to give in to it. "Where are they questioning Reverend Michaels?"

"I don' know." He suddenly looked very young and frightened, reminding me forcefully that he was but a boy who had undertaken a man's tasks this day.

"No matter. I shall find out. You just go where they tell you for now and I will take care of everything." I spoke with far more confidence than I felt. I kept remembering Geraldine's condescending smile and her powers of deception. I had no doubt that hers had been the first voice Nick heard upon his return to Sunrise and I knew she would have nothing good to say about me.

I washed my face and tidied my hair as best I could, but there was nothing I could do about my gown, which was streaked with dirt and sweat from the horse, and spotted with bloodstains. Then, taking a deep breath, I made my way to the front stairs. This was no time to creep down the backstairs like a servant; it was time to face my enemies.

I felt the tension in the air even before I reached the grand staircase that led from the second floor to the entry hall. Hathaway stood near the top of the stairs. I stopped in front of him. "I must see Nick immediately. I have urgent information about the raiders."

"They are in the library, Miss Ames, but I was told that they were not to be disturbed." Hathaway's tone lacked its usual command.

"They will want to hear from me." I moved past him without hesitating, keeping my back straight and my head high, though all I wanted to do was run down the stairs shouting Nick's name.

The library door was closed, but I could hear the loud voices behind it. Taking a deep breath, I lifted a hand to knock, but before I could, the door opened and I was face to face with Geraldine Chalmers. For a heartbeat, I could see the blazing hatred in her eyes, then she smiled cruelly. "Well, well, the lying little turncoat is still here. I thought she had decided to flee from the punishment she deserves for siding with our enemies." She stepped around me and went down the hall, her head high.

"Miss Ames, please come in. We have some questions for you." The voice was unfamiliar, but as soon as I saw the man who has spoken, my heart dropped. The resemblance was uncanny; he had to be Baxter's father.

I hesitated for a moment, seeking among the faces of

those who sat in the chairs that seemed to crowd the room, hoping for a friendly gaze; but I found none. Paul sat on the far side, slumped in a chair, looking even worse than he had earlier, and Nick ... Nick was looking out the window, half turned away, as though he had no desire to see me.

"Please sit down, Miss Ames." Mr. Travis seemed in command of this meeting, and Jarvis Harrison was nowhere to be seen. "And then I should like to hear your version of what happened this past night." He hesitated, then in an ominous tone added, "In detail."

I sank down in the chair indicated, then took a moment to compose myself. Though I had little hope that anyone would believe me, I faced the unfriendly men without flinching and began my story with my discovery of the disguises in the passage between the playroom and the ruins.

It seemed to take forever and some parts of the story were very hard to tell, especially when I had to face Mr. Travis as I spoke of his son's duplicity and repeated everything I had overheard. As I described the way Baxter had captured me and taken me to the bluffs, Mr. Travis jumped to his feet, his face near purple with his fury. "'Tis all lies! Geraldine explained to us that you tempted my son, led him into your evil plans. He would never ..."

I cowered back, shocked by his words and frightened as he lifted his hand as though to strike me.

"Enough." Nick stepped forward. "Sit down, Travis. You have no right to threaten Miss Ames, she is a guest in our house and she has come to tell you the truth, whether you would hear it or not."

Mr. Travis returned to his chair, but his fury still boiled over in the words he continued to spit at me. "She has you under her spell as well, Harrison. You heard Geraldine Chalmers. This woman is a schemer in league with that preacher you brought here to stir up trouble. Everything was peaceful before he came with his damned school."

"I am sorry about your son, Mr. Travis," I murmured. "But I speak the truth, and Geraldine is lying because she was a part of what the raiders did. Those were her exact words that I repeated. She arrived here too late only because Baxter lied to her. He wanted the Harrisons dead and Sunrise burned; she simply wished to ingratiate herself with Nick."

The gasps from the other gentlemen in the room told me how deeply my words shocked them, but it was Nick's gaze I sought. His face was marked with weariness and sorrow, but I could read nothing in his eyes. I might have been just another stranger and it broke my heart.

"You must not blame Rachel for my actions." Paul's weak voice startled me. "She has done nothing but protect the orphan children I put in her care. She risked her life so that Elena could tell us what was to happen. If she had not, the raiders would surely have . . ."

"Who is this Elena?" Mr. Travis interrupted, his gaze going from Paul to Nick, then coming to rest on me. The naked hatred in his eyes sent a chill through me.

Though I had wished to spare Elena, there was no way I could avoid his question. "She is but a child who followed me into the ruins and therefore overheard what was said."

"And where is she now?" Travis was on his feet again.

I met his gaze with matching anger, already aware that he meant to terrify Elena with questions. "Safe hidden, out of fear of the raiders."

"I would . . ." Travis began, but Nick moved between us.

"We shall have to question Elena, Rachel," he said,

343

his gaze suddenly softening, "but I shall do it. The others may listen and suggest questions, if they wish; but I promise, she will not be bullied." His tone changed on the final words and I sensed the cold steel of determination beneath his veneer of kindness.

"Shall I go and get her?" I asked.

"That will not be necessary." Nick turned away. "You and Paul may return to the cloister. Elena has already arrived. I sent Digger to fetch her as soon as I heard the whole story of what happened. I thought it best to hear her recollections of the conversation as well as yours. Digger will drive the two of you to the cloister."

Nick had never trusted me! The fact that he had sent for Elena made that obvious. For a moment, pain overwhelmed me. Then a sharp flare of shame and anger stained my cheeks. I had willingly trusted him with my heart, and now it appeared he hesitated to believe me, even though I had risked my life to try to warn him.

It was my worst nightmare. I got to my feet slowly, feeling as though my body and my head had become disconnected. I was dimly aware of Paul leaning heavily on my arm as he guided me from the library. Behind us, the room erupted into chaos as the planters shouted questions at Nick. A part of me wanted to wait, to linger long enough to hear his answers, hoping, of course, that they would somehow prove that he did care about me. But I had no opportunity, for Paul kept me moving toward the front door where Digger waited.

He hurried toward us, taking Paul's other arm, his worried gaze forcing me to see what I had overlooked in my pain over Nick's lack of trust. Paul was pale as death and scarcely able to walk. My nursing skills revived. "Perhaps you should lie down for a while before we make the journey to the Cloister, Paul."

He merely shook his head and kept moving forward. "I glanced at Digger. "Where is Elena?"

"Her be with Harriet."

I felt relieved, grateful that she would have a friendly face to turn to in this terrible time. "Nick said you would drive us to the cloister."

"You be safer there."

I winced, not liking the implication of his words; then I remembered what I had been doing earlier and hesitated at the side of the wagon. "There were injured men upstairs . . ."

"Mr. Nick brought Dr. Hogarth." Digger assisted Paul into the wagon bed, where he collapsed on the straw. Once he was settled, Digger helped me up to the seat, then climbed up beside me. Only then did I realize that he looked as weary as I felt.

"Is it not over, Digger?" I asked, realizing that he might know more than anyone what had happened. "Will there be more fighting?"

His shrug did little to ease my fears. "I be thinkin' we gots all them raiders, but them be planter folk. 'Tain't likely they be payin' for all them done." He sighed. "Not even if'n Samuel brings folk from St. Devina."

"Nick sent Samuel for help?" I was stunned. It seemed a lifetime since I had seen the blond giant who had sailed back from St. Devina with us. Yet I knew at once that Nick would have trusted him with such a mission.

"Soon's the shootin' stop, Mr. Nick say him gots to go."

Paul groaned. "'Twill be difficult for everyone after all that has happened, but the proof is indisputable, if only those men will listen."

I sighed. At the moment, that seemed a lot to expect. The men I had spoken to seemed far from willing to believe my words and if Nick could doubt me . . . I slumped in the seat, too weary and dispirited to continue the conversation.

Once we reached the cloister, Digger helped Paul into bed in one of the rooms, then left to return to Sunrise for Elena and Ben, whom I felt might need him more than we did. Paul showed no sign of fever, so there was little I could do for him, except ensure his rest and order some foods that might strengthen him when he awoke. That done, I yielded to Seraphina's suggestion that I get some rest myself, insisting only that she wake me when Elena returned.

It seemed I had slept but a moment when a hand gently shook my shoulder and I opened my eyes to see Seraphina, wrapped in a robe, holding a candle. Elena, already in her nightdress, stood beside her. The moment our eyes met, tears began to stream down Elena's cheeks. Without thinking, I lifted the cover and patted the bed.

Elena slid in beside me without hesitation, wrapping her thin arms around my neck as though she feared I might disappear. Seraphina waited a moment, then left when I nodded. It was clear that Elena needed to spend this night in my arms; truth be told, I had no wish to be alone.

"What happened, Elena?" Though I was eager to know, I asked mainly because I knew she would never be able to sleep until she had told me. Her answer was punctuated with sobs and hiccups, but in the end I had the whole story and I knew that Nick had protected her from the anger that had so filled the library when Paul and I were there.

"Mr. Nick, him say I come back here. Him be most angry, Miss Rachel. Him say they all be blind fools."

I smiled as I stroked her dark hair. I could picture him so easily, his eyes flashing green fire, his head high as he faced them all and defended my story . . . my story as told by Elena, I reminded myself as my moment of happiness faded. And what did his defense prove? Not that he loved me. Not that he wanted me to stay and . . . And what? Run the orphanage? Assist Paul with the teaching?

My heart grew heavier inside me. That could well be all that he wanted from me. And if it was? The ache inside me deepened. Could I bear it? Could I see him every day and not ever again know the wonder of his kiss, the wild delight of being in his arms?

Elena sighed and snuggled closer as she drifted into sleep. I shifted my embrace, knowing that I should have to learn to live with whatever lay ahead. There was no way I could abandon Elena and the rest of the children. Or Paul, who would need my help more than ever during his recovery. I closed my eyes, but the tears still seeped between my lashes and fell softly to my pillow. I had never realized that love could be so painful.

The next two days were the longest of my life. I rose at dawn and kept busy through the day, tending the children, helping Paul as he slowly began to regain his strength. But the emptiness never went away, and I was glad when Digger came back to the cloister late the second afternoon. He brought little news, just telling us that the planters had left Sunrise and that Jarvis Harrison was back on his feet at last.

"What of Nick? Is he well?" I hated myself for the weakness that made me ask; but I could not deny my need to know.

Digger's answer surprised me. "He left with the prisoners at dawn. Them be gonna stay in the village."

"Not at Sunrise?" Though it made no sense, the news made me feel even lonelier.

Digger nodded. "Likely him be afeered someone come to break 'um free."

"Oh." A chill passed over me as I had to once again face the fact that he might still be in danger.

"Him say I be stayin' here again now."

"Is Nick expecting more trouble?"

Digger only shrugged. "Him not be sayin'."

I swallowed a sigh, sensing that Digger was not telling me everything that had taken place at Sunrise, but unsure how to get the details. "You are always welcome, Digger. We owe you a great debt."

"And I owe you my life." His bright blue eyes met mine with quiet sincerity. "Mr. Nick knows I not be lettin' nobody hurt you or the Reverend or the little ones."

I wished that I could hug him as I had hugged Ben when he returned, but Digger's stance told me that he was fully a man now, too grown up to accept such affection. I took his hand and squeezed it instead, then went into the kitchen so no one would see my tears.

Another day and night passed before Elena summoned me to the schoolroom, announcing that a small carriage was approaching. Heart pounding, I raced to the door, praying that it would be Nick, come at last. I needed to see him, to read in his eyes what he might feel toward me. Even if it meant more pain, I had to know.

A stranger stepped down from the carriage. "Would you be Miss Ames?"

I nodded. "How may I help you?"

"I just came from Sunrise. Mr. Harrison wishes me to transport Reverend Michaels to a meeting there—if he is well enough?"

"Just Reverend Michaels?" I tried not to allow my disappointment to show.

"Those were my orders, Miss Ames." His polite smile left me no room for argument.

"If you will wait here, I shall tell him. I know he is

eager to speak with Mr. Harrison." Though not as eager as I was, I added to myself. Not that it seemed to matter. If Nick had no desire to see me, I would never press my unwelcome presence upon him.

I had thought to put my anger and resentment behind me once Paul left with the stranger, but I was far too restless. Unable to tolerate the four walls of the cloister, I decided to escape for a walk. It seemed an eternity since I had sought the tranquillity of the old burial site. Perhaps if I went there today, I would find the courage to accept the fact that I was here only to serve God and care for the orphans, not to fall in love.

The afternoon was sweet and cloudless, the air heavy with the scents of flowers, and the only sounds came from the buzzing insects and the chirping of the birds that fluttered through the trees. Building nests, no doubt, I thought bitterly. Finding love.

A chill chased down my spine as I crossed the meadow where Baxter had captured me, but I gritted my teeth and continued walking until I was safely sheltered by the old trees that shaded the crumbling stone wall. Feeling lonely, but at peace, I climbed up on the wall and stared at the flowers that bloomed in the thick grass that filled the area encircled.

For a time, my thoughts drifted, but then the questions that had haunted me since the day after the attack returned to torment me anew. Was I destined always to be alone, to love only children that had been born to others? They enriched my life and I loved them deeply, but Nick's kisses had made me hunger for more. Because of him, I had dared to dream of loving a man and being loved in return, of bearing a child of my own and . . .

I was so lost in my contemplation that the rider was nearly upon me before I heard the creak of saddle leather and the faint jingling of the bit. Frightened, I nearly fell from the wall as I turned to see who might be approaching.

"Seraphina told me I might find you here." Nick slipped from the saddle and dropped his reins so his horse could graze free. He took a step closer, then stopped. "I need to speak with you, Rachel. There is so much that we . . ."

"Have you and Paul finally decided what is to be done with me?" The hurt I felt at his neglect these past few days added an edge to my voice that surprised me even as it startled him.

"What do you mean?" His tentative smile was now replaced by a frown.

"You summoned him to discuss something." I slid off the wall so that I could face him on my feet. Whatever he had to say, I was determined that he must never see my pain or guess how deeply I had been hurt. If I was to stay here as his friend, I would wrap my pride around me and rise above the weakness of loving him.

"We had some details to settle about the future, now that those responsible for the raids have been dealt with." He closed the distance between us in two strides and I was once again forced to deal with the overwhelming attraction that turned my knees to jelly and my heart to flame.

"What details?" The breathlessness of my voice was obvious, yet I could not hide my longing to be in his arms.

"Your living conditions." His frown softened, and I was suddenly conscious of the wicked golden flecks that danced in the depths of his hazel eyes.

"I am quite content at the cloister." I spoke without conviction as a sudden fear overwhelmed me. "You would not send me away?"

"On the contrary, I wish to add a permanent member to your household, if you will agree." He was touching me now, his hands moving very slowly up my arms, his fingers stroking my skin through the thin fabric of my gown. "Would you allow someone to move in to protect you?"

"Digger is already staying there." I had a dizzy feeling that I was being pulled closer to him, though I had not moved.

"I have other plans for Digger." His hands reached my shoulders, then one hand slipped beneath my tumbling curls to cup my head.

"Then whom did you wish to . . . ?" My mind was beginning to drift as I lost myself in the sweet magic of his touch.

"Your husband." His lips caught mine, capturing the gasp that came as his words registered in my fuzzy mind.

For a moment, I was too stunned to react to his kiss, but his mouth commanded and my lips opened to his without question, just as I leaned into his strong, hard body. My arms closed around him, holding onto him as the only security in the wildly spinning world. It was a wonderous eternity before he lifted his lips from mine.

"What did you say?" I gasped, looking up at him, still unable to believe my ears.

"I asked Paul to Sunrise because he is the nearest thing you have to family here on the island and I felt I should have his permission to ask you to be my wife. He was less than pleased at the prospect, but once I convinced him that I intended to wed you with or without his permission, he decided to listen. When I told him I intended to move into the cloister and help you run the orphanage, he gave me his blessing." He stopped and his lazy grin faded a little. "You will accept my proposal, will you not?"

My head was whirling too much for me to fully comprehend his words. Besides, there were still some things that needed explanation. "When you never came, I . . . I thought that you mistrusted me. That you believed Geraldine's lies. I thought you no longer wanted to see me."

"I had to protect you, love. Travis was mad with grief once he learned the circumstances of Baxter's death. He chose to believe it was your fault, and I had to keep a close eye on him until Samuel brought the authorities from St. Devina." He kissed my eyes, my cheeks, then my nose. "I knew if I came over here, I should forget everything but the magic of holding you, loving you." He found my lips again, and this time I answered him without words.

When he finally stepped away, I could see that he was as shaken by our passion as I. "Will you marry me, Rachel?"

I was beyond artifice. "Of course. When?"

He sighed. "If I had my way, 'twould be this night; but I suspect we shall have to wait at least a week or two. There is much to be done, and I hope that the celebration of our wedding will help to bring all the people of the island back together."

Seeing the love in his eyes made me want to laugh and cry at the same time. "You really mean to live in the cloister . . . with the children and Seraphina?" I also wanted him to kiss me again.

"I want to live with you and from what I have seen, you come with a rather large family, so I think the cloister will make a perfect home. I shall start repairing and restoring the rest of the building at once. After all, we shall have our own family, too, some day."

My quiver of anticipation became a startling flood of desire as I hugged him. "Soon," I whispered as I lifted my lips to his. "Very soon."

A
Season Abroad

by

Rebecca Baldwin

FAWCETT COVENTRY • NEW YORK

For Sam Berlind

A SEASON ABROAD

Published by Fawcett Coventry Books, a unit of CBS Publications, the Consumer Publishing Division of CBS Inc.

Copyright © 1981 by Rebecca Baldwin

All Rights Reserved

ISBN: 0-449-50215-5

Printed in the United States of America

First Fawcett Coventry printing: October 1981

10 9 8 7 6 5 4 3 2 1

One

Madame Contessa d'Orsini had prospered sixty years through a series of increasingly advantageous marriages, and according to her impatient heirs, would probably continue upon the same principles for yet another sixty.

She had once been a Beauty, in a lush, darkly Neopolitan fashion, and although she was inclined to *embonpoint*, she was still an attractive female, dressed tonight in murex watered silk and all of her diamonds, a lilac turban placed upon her dark curls and several plumes nodding above her head as she moved through the ballroom of Villa d'Orsini, speaking a few words to each of her guests in their own languages, for the company at Lake Como was very international that summer after the war, and very much in keeping with the unsettled quality of the times. Since nothing amused the contessa more than making up unlikely gatherings, throwing all conditions of per-

5

sons together and watching the results, *con brio*, she had chosen a *bal masque* for the theme of tonight's entertainment, and she was deriving a great deal of entertainment from her guests' confusion over which of their disguised fellows they should ignore and which should be awarded their first considerations.

This summer had been particularly delicious, for in addition to the usual Milanese and Roman families, the exile of Napoleon, and the restoration of the unfortunate (and very dull) Bourbons to the French throne had added both the exiled, and slightly down-at-the-heel Bonapartists, the suddenly re-affluent Royalists to the company, and their careful avoidance of one another was a delicious thing to behold.

The suggestion to throw such confusion into the other summer dwellers of the villas along the lake by summoning them to a costume ball had been that of Madame's good friend the Princess of Wales, and how right dear Caroline had been, for unable to recognize anyone not of their own set, everyone was forced to stand upon terms with everyone else, and that, together with the very good wine flowing in abundance, was serving to make the evening far more of a success than one might have thought possible. Only the two families of *inglese* stood a little apart from the general merriment, and that, Madame thought, could easily be attributed to their discomfort over the sight of the estranged wife of their Prince Regent, wearing her black wig decked with curls, a dress cut far too low over her ample bosom and far too short over her ample legs, making a perfect fool of herself with her friend, that droll Signore Bergmani,

6

dancing the waltz as if her years numbered just half to the forty she had upon her plate. The Princess of Wales, rumored within her Brunswick family to be a little odd, was certainly proving the rumor tonight, her friend thought indulgently, but that was what summers at Lake Como had been provided for. It was only a great deal too bad that the *inglese* were doubly discomfited by the appearance upon these tranquil shores of a second English exile in attendance tonight as a member of the Princess's entourage.

It was not a very good recommendation for a country, the contessa pondered, when they ostracized not only their future Queen, but also drove their best poets and their most fascinating men into exile. She could not really recall the exact nature of Lord Robert Marchman's scandal and his subsequent flight from his native land, nor did she really care. The English, she had long ago decided, were an efficient but rather hypocritical lot, and she was really quite fond of the gentlemen who were endowed with cryptic smiles and the most subtle hints of danger in the depths of their manners.... What had the scandal been? She tried to recall. Something about a woman and a duel? She shrugged her elegant shoulders. In sixty years, one saw a great many scandals, and even perhaps created some oneself, if truth were to be known.

Indeed, she thought, her eyes surveying the room's masked and costumed figures, she could count upon her fingers the number of liaisons Marchman had been rumored to have initiated only over the course of this summer, in the best Continental tradition, all of them with voluptu-

7

ous, sophisticated ladies married to men very much their seniors in age and...desire.

"A most charming—and most interesting evening, Contessa," a Dominican friar in the robes of the Inquisition whispered into her ear, and beneath her bird-mask, Madame's eyebrows rose.

"Lord Robert! I was just thinking upon you!" she replied, tapping the Inquisitor's arm with her fan.

"Indeed," said Lord Robert Marchman, procuring a glass of champagne from a passing waiter and presenting it to Madame with a bow. "Nothing unflattering, I hope?"

The contessa laughed. "Of course not, although I think perhaps your countrymen and their families might be torn between their shock over meeting you and seeing their future Queen done up like a bareback rider in the circus!"

From beneath his hood, Lord Robert chuckled. "Lord, ma'am, perhaps you have missed her taking the air in her white shell-shaped barouche, drawn by white horses and driven by a cherub in spangles? It is as if one were at Astley's Amphitheater all over again! For the life of me, I cannot understand why Her Highness and Prinny do not come along! Their tastes are remarkably similar. But please, I beg of you, relieve me! Her Highness has indicated that she wished me to dance the waltz with her, and I promised that I had engaged you for that dance! I have no wish to be called out by that man-milliner Bergami!"

The contessa clucked her tongue, but laughed nonetheless. "So very improper of you to be speaking of your future Queen in such terms!" she said, unable to suppress a little laugh.

8

"I have engaged enough mistakes in my own lifetime not to wish to be held responsible for those of the Prince Regent!" Lord Robert drawled. "Pray, dear ma'am, save me from becoming a member of the Order of St. Caroline!" The hooded head moved from side to side. "Although I find the Princess Original, Contessa, even *my* reputation should suffer damage if I were to set her up as one of my flirts—quite above my touch!" Lord Robert held out a mockingly pleading hand. "Pray, madam, save me from an honor I have no wish to win! I beg of you!"

From across the room, Her Highness nodded and smiled, her cheeks flushed beneath the rouge with which she had liberally adorned her plump cheeks, and Lord Robert bowed. Signore Bergami, in the costume of a Crusader, frowned very severely upon Lord Robert, and drew a little closer to the side of his companion.

"*Facciona!*" The contessa exclaimed, tapping Lord Robert's arm with her fan again. "You are very, very naughty—and very, very diventanta, Robert! It would be hard to say who is the greater *ammazzasette*—you or Her Highness's companion! However, I shall contrive to rescue you—ah!"

The contessa's attention was diverted from her companion toward the grand stairs, where two unexpected and rather late arrivals were making a somewhat timid entrance.

The resemblance between the young man and lady who were surveying the gathering with ill-concealed distress proclaimed their ties of kinship. Both were dressed in a style which proclaimed to Italian eyes a simplicity of taste and a great deal of wealth; to Italian eyes, a most unfortunate com-

9

bination, for both the lady and her relation could have done with brighter colors and a bit of ornament. But Italian eyes had never seen Quaker costume before. Lord Robert, however, was not unacquainted with the preferred dress of those members of the Society of Friends, and his lips curved upwards in appreciation of the jest, for jest it must be, to appear so plainly dressed in a riot of colors and glittering jewels.

Each of the couple was a little above the medium height, with a long, fine-boned face and wheat-colored hair. The young man, who could not have been much above his nineteenth year, was slightly inclined to plumpness, however, and had a slight cast about his eyes and mouth which betrayed a trace of that invalidish self-indulgence so common to those who have lately emerged, unscathed but very much cosseted, from childhood illnesses. The young lady was some ten or so years his senior, to judge (and Lord Robert was an expert in such matters) from her appearance. Where her brother looked a trifle peevish, her large and serious blue-gray eyes surveyed the gathering with a lively, if somewhat awed interest, and—could it be possible? There definitely seemed to be a hint of amusement beneath her timidity. Even in the first flush of her youth, she could not have been ajudged any great beauty, Lord Robert thought, but despite the severe bands of her hair, tucked neatly beneath a plain white lawn cap and the fact that the Princess of Wales could have spared her some of her rouge (with more than enough left for her own royal cheeks!) there was something that cynical rake, in general a connoisseur of voluptuous, dark-eyed charms, found compelling—

10

and disturbingly attractive. Perhaps it was the way in which those blue-gray eyes met his own, certainly not boldly, but with a sort of frank appraisal that left him with the uneasy feeling that she would be able to see beneath his cynically chosen costume into his very soul, and was only mildly interested in what she had discovered in those secret regions.

"Theresa, if you please, who are these Quakers you find upon your steps?" he asked his friend, and was rewarded with a deep chuckle of amusement.

"Americans, Robert. Americans! Is it not a novelty? That, my friend, is Mr. and Miss Wingate of a place called New York City, in America, sent here by their *nonno*—how do you say?—grandfather, a very rich man, for the young boy to recover his health in sunny climates! Signore Wingate, *le nonno*, builds the great boats which he sends everywhere to trade, and makes a great deal of money; Signore Jonathan is the heir; Miss Lydia his sister, is the *inferiera*, the *bambinaia* of her family—so very many of them, she tells me, she is aunt many, many times over! So, Signore Wingate, *le nonno*, sends Miss Lydia to look after her brother. *C'est très drôle, ça,*" the contessa lapsed into French. "But they have taken a villa for the summer, across the lake, and although they are— naive, and not what you would call *up to snuff*, Robert, I find them vastly *dolce* and quite amusing! Is that the word I seek? It does not matter! I must make them welcome, however, for they are my guests, and so many *different* people must overwhelm them, no?"

"Contessa!" Lord Robert caught his friend's

arm. "I beg you, do me the double service of rescuing me from Her Highness and make me known to Miss Wingate!"

"Ecce!" the contessa said, frowning slightly, her sense of propriety not so far gone as to cast an innocent female into the path of so notorious a womanizer as Lord Robert Marchman; it was a struggle between that and her vast sense of mischief. In the end, and after only a very few seconds of debate, her sense of mischief won over. Miss Wingate after all, was well past her first youth, and for all of her seeming naiveté, possessed a very sharp tongue and a very shrewd sense of herself! It would be amusing to watch her depress any of Lord Robert's practiced flirtations in her straightforward, Yankee way. And after so many triumphs, it would also be amusing to see Lord Robert a little cast aback. Heaven forfend, she added as she crossed the room, her hands out in greeting to the Americans, that the boy would rescue his sister; if he noted anything beyond himself, she had yet to see it happen.

"Miss Wingate! Mr. Wingate!" she said in her low voice, greeting them happily. "I bid you welcome to Villa d'Orsini! I am so pleased that you chose, after all, to come! And such *clever* costumes!"

Upon seeing at least one familiar face in all the crowd in that vast marble hall, both Wingates relaxed slightly, and Lord Robert, at his hostess' side, was pleased to note that Miss Lydia Wingate had a very charming smile.

"Lord Robert Marchman, may I present to you Mr. And Miss Wingate of New York City?" The contessa was saying, prodding him just a little with her fan, "Lord Robert has, I believe, visited your country, and that should provide you with something in common!"

"You must forgive us for our lateness, Contessa," Miss Wingate was saying, "but Jonathan had a slight cough, and I wanted to be sure that he was able to stand the winds across the lake before we embarked! How do you do, Lord—Robert?" she added, coolly offering him her hand.

Mr. Wingate surprised Lord Robert by shrugging his shoulders at his sister's remarks. "Lydia always wants to wrap me in cotton wool, even though I tell her that I am quite recovered! It was a grand sail, Contessa! We were forced to tack nearly the entire length of the lake, but what a night for the water!" He nodded at Lord Robert and offered his hand, surveying him with eyes as indifferent as his sister's were speculative. "How d'you do, sir?"

"Very well, I thank you," Lord Robert returned. "It is a ripping night, is it not? I myself live only five hundred yards down the coast from the contessa's landing, yet it took all of my powers to bring my boat into port!"

Mr. Wingate's eyes alighted. "Do you sail yourself, sir? How capital that must be! We have rented the most *hogged*, least yar piece of float I have ever seen! How I yearn for a decent little ketch—"

"You have been in our country, Lord Robert?" Miss Wingate cut over her brother gently but firmly.

He nodded. "I happened to be in New Orleans in '15," he said gently.

Both Mr. and Miss Wingate stiffened slightly and the contessa looked from one to the other in

13

some puzzlement. "I was with Sir Francis Pakenham," he added. "Attached to his staff. My admiration for the bravery and intelligence of your General Jackson is sincere—witnessed as it was firsthand! I can only hope that in any future conflict, America and England will find themselves aligned."

"Quite so," Mr. Wingate said stiffly.

"But now there is peace everywhere," Miss Wingate put in calmly, "and for that we must all be glad, and endeavor to forget the past."

"Quite so," Lord Robert repeated, and received a sharp look from Mr. Wingate.

The contessa, sensing more danger than she had bargained for, and from quite a different source, swiftly interposed. "Mr. Wingate, you had expressed a desire to view the Roman foundations! Seen from the balcony by the *chiaro di luna*, one might almost imagine the *apparizione* of Pliny lingering there!" And so saying, she firmly hooked one bejeweled hand into the crook of Jonathan's elbow, steering him away before he could protest.

Miss Wingate looked after her brother and the contessa for a second, her lips curving upward in amusement. Lifting the black silk mask to her face, she fanned herself with it, then regarded it ruefully. "Oh, dear! I have forgotten to disguise myself! And we did particularly mean to attach them before we made our entrance!" She sighed.

"I, for one, am very glad that you did not!" Lord Robert replied, very smoothly relieving Miss Wingate of the strip of silk. "If you will allow me to assist you in disguising yourself from the incurious view of this rather ill-mixed lot, perhaps you will return the favor by allowing me to lead you out into the set they're forming. That is—I am not totally certain if a Quakeress dances?"

Miss Wingate's expression was hidden by the mask, but her voice was calm enough. "My brother and I are not members of the Friends, Lord Robert—and despite being an American, I can assure you that I do dance!"

"Ah," Lord Robert replied, tying the strings of the mask beneath Miss Wingate's cap. "Then forgive me if I sounded to depress that sect. The Friends, I believe, are most admirable folk, for they believe, at least, in peace! And upon that score, they and I are much in agreement!"

Miss Wingate nodded, but the look that she cast upon her companion was completely disguised by her mask. "It is perhaps fortunate that I should have to wait until midnight to behold your face, sir. A Quakeress and an Inquisitor must needs make an odd pair upon the floor! Let alone an Englishman and an American!"

As he placed his hand upon her waist, Lord Robert was pleased to note how slender her figure was beneath her simple gray and white dress, cut low to the floor and high about the neck, her charms hidden beneath a severe white lawn fichu. As the gay music of a waltz poured out upon the dance floor, he was also pleasantly surprised to find that his Quakeress not only waltzed, she waltzed gracefully and well, as if anticipating his every move, spinning lightly and easily within his arms as if she had always been there.

But she conversed not at all, contenting herself with humming, not unpleasantly, with the music, her lips curving upward in that faint, amused

15

smile, as if she were not at all aware of the stares of the curious upon such an incongruous couple.

Lord Robert had become so inured to his own reputation as a hardened libertine that he found himself a bit disappointed that this lady seemed oblivious to her own danger. If she had any cognizance of his character at all, she had chosen not to betray it, and instead of acting like a frightened apeleader, uncomfortable in the society of a worldly man, she actually seemed to be—could it be?—faintly bored. Lord Robert, from whose lips practiced compliments fell so easily and upon such fertile ground, could think of nothing but clichés to utter to this enigmatic female, and he was slightly taken aback by his own unwonted silence; but she seemed not to note this at all. All of their communication seemed to pass in the harmony with which they glided across the floor, striking by their very plainness of costume amidst so much that was fantastic and feathered, jeweled and glittering.

"Did I offend you by my disclosure of serving with Parkenham in New Orleans?" Lord Robert asked at last.

"The truth, sir, must never be offensive," Miss Wingate replied absently. Collecting herself, however, she bit her lip and added, "Of course there are some truths that one should never ever breathe, in consideration of the feelings of others, such as the fact that that very peculiar lady in the plumes and the very short white dress is staring at you in such a way!"

Lord Robert spun Miss Wingate about, and nodded to the Princess, who looked a little put out, despite the attentions of Signore Bergmani. "That peculiar-looking lady, Miss Wingate, is none other than the Princess of Wales!" Lord Robert said in his most dry tones.

"Really!" Miss Wingate replied, not at all discomposed. "To be sure, Jonathan and I have seen her villa, and knew she was here, but we never expected to actually *see* her! Dear me! I do wish Mrs. Madison were here—she would be absolutely in hysterics!"

Assuming that Miss Wingate referred to the First Lady of the United States, a female also known for her elegance of dress and gracious hospitality, if not for such flamboyance as exhibited by Her Highness, Marchman's brows rose beneath his hood. "Does Mrs. Madison cut such a dash then?" he asked.

Miss Wingate shook her capped head. "Oh, no! It is only that people will say so—those who have not known her—and if they were to be served such a lady as Her Highness for First Lady, I fear we should have a second revolution—this time from within!"

"Such might well be the case if Her Highness chooses to return to England," Marchman said. "For she is as nothing compared to Prinny."

"If by that you mean the Prince Regent," Miss Wingate replied thoughtfully, "I can well see the virtues in elected rather than inherited government. To be sure, if a president cut such a figure, he would never be elected!" She frowned. "Not that I mean to cast aspersions upon your country, sir—"

"My country, Miss Wingate, has cast its aspersions upon me!" Marchman replied a little bitterly, perhaps more than he had meant to convey. "But let us not speak of politics tonight—"

"In truth, sir," Miss Wingate replied evenly, "it is the nature of this gathering which puts me so firmly in mind of politics, for a larger grouping of persons disguised as one thing and no doubt being quite another can resemble nothing so much as a group of politicians, be they Parliament or Congress!"

One of Lord Robert's rare laughs escaped from his lips, and he regarded Miss Wingate with a new degree of respect. "But," she continued, "at the risk of appearing much ruder than my curiosity would permit, I wonder what sort of aspersions your country has cast upon you! It sounds dreadful! Are you like our Mr. Burr? Or are you like poor Byron, whom I understand to have been driven into exile by the most peculiar circumstances concerning his sister?"

Marchman laughed ruefully. "I did set myself up, did I not?" he asked. "In truth, Miss Wingate, I cannot believe that you have been here all summer and not heard some rumor of me." Having said it, Lord Robert could have willingly bitten off his own tongue. It was hardly, he thought, as if he wished to *brag* about the scandals with which his name was associated. It was, he suddenly understood, as if he wished to warn this female, above all others, away from damaging her reputation by too intimate a contact with such an unsavory person as himself. Miss Wingate was no flirt, and though she might conduct herself as if she were well past the age of contracting a marriage, there was still some aura of innocence about her, an innocence he felt she was deliberately

18

seeking to disguise behind her air of self-composure. This totally new emotion with regard to the damned female sex annoyed him after all. With some thirty-eight years upon his dish, he had ample time to develop a cynicism toward her sex which had, he thought until this moment, deliberately hardened him to all of their wiles. "Why," he heard and hated himself for saying, "I am a hardened rakehell, Miss Wingate, a seducer dressed up in a sheet to affright young females as yourself! Do you not listen to the gossip? Merely by dancing with me, you put your good reputation into dire peril, ma'am!"

Although she could not see the cynical smile behind his hood, Miss Wingate greeted this remark without the horrified reaction he had expected, instead merely looking a little thoughtful and not missing a beat of the dance. "Dear me," she finally said thoughtfully. "What a very odd thing to tell me, to be sure!" Her voice, he noted, had that curiously drawling cadence of American English; it was not unpleasant in his ears. But her next words very profoundly shocked even Lord Robert. "Don't you think," she asked quite seriously, "that the proper dramatic moment to reveal your hardened character would have been *after* you had lured me into an assignation with you in some secluded and very romantic spot, completely despoiling me of all character and virtue? That would have been very much more the thing, you know."

Marchman was struck dumb for several beats; Miss Wingate seemed not at all discomposed, merely abjuring him to remember her feet and keep to the music.

"Perhaps," he said at last in a very strangled voice, "I merely wanted to deprive all the old gossips of this place of the pleasure of giving me their versions of my black character!"

Lydia gave what sounded suspiciously like a giggle from beneath her mask. "To be sure! For everyone gossips *so* here, and knows *all* about everyone else—and what they do not know, they are sure to invent! But, Lord Robert, I fear you find yourself dancing with a female every bit as *outré* as yourself—for exactly opposite reasons! I sir, am a bluestocking of the most abandoned and unfeminine nature, and to be seen dancing with *me* can scarcely add to your consequence! I am an Authoress, sir! A female scribbler!"

"Good Lord!" Marchman said in mock horrified tones.

"There you have it," Miss Wingate responded complacently. "Now I fear, the shoe is on the other foot! Only consider what depths your reputation is sinking into for being seen dancing with a female who *writes*! I am sure that it will prove quite insupportable, and you will have to hide in your villa for at least three days before some new scandal takes their wind!"

For the second time that evening, Lord Robert laughed and such an event was quite without precedent. "I am sure, Miss Wingate, that we must both be quite cast down into the depths—to find that our reputations have not preceded our meeting!"

"I feel quite *neglected*," Miss Wingate sighed. "I did not expect my reputation to be exactly international, but I did feel that it would cause *some* comment. Jonathan is forever prosing on about it, you see! Dear me, Lord Robert, can it be that neither of us are as black as we are painted?"

"Or as we have chosen to paint ourselves! To tell truth, Miss Wingate, I have never before encountered a bluestocking—a female intellectual—"

"Oh, I imagine we are not quite in your line of endeavor, sir. But then, I have never before chanced to encounter a hardened libertine, either."

They regarded each other with laughter in their eyes. "You must forgive me for being unacquainted with your works, Miss Wingate. I am not a bookish man, I fear," Lord Robert ventured.

"And you must forgive me for being unacquainted with yours!" Miss Wingate shot back. "Are there any of your conquests in this room? Pray discreetly point out to me which female's jealousy I must avoid at all costs!"

It had been many years since Lord Robert Marchman had been shocked, and now he was very much taken aback for several seconds while Miss Wingate surveyed the ladies in the ballroom. "I collect Her Highness might be among your, ah, conquests? For she is certainly making no secret of her interest in you...."

Lord Robert was swift to assure Miss Wingate that the Princess of Wales was by no means any more than a friend, and quickly diverted the conversation back to herself. "But we were speaking of your work, Miss Wingate. Procuring books in English is very difficult in these parts! Newspapers and periodicals from England take months to arrive, and ordering books—well, that is another story entirely!"

"My work, as you put it, Lord Robert, has only appeared in America. I suppose you would find it very dull, for it is nothing but a collect of sketches—satirical sketches for a magazine in New York. I have been exiled abroad with Jonathan until the scandal died down!" She added in woeful terms, "Is it not a great deal too bad? My grandfather, when he discovered my authorship, was thrown into a taking of such magnificent proportions as to quite put The Family into a fright. All I had done was to set down a very few accounts of some parties and balls in New York, and Washington—and a few other observations upon what passes in America. Mr. Irving is a very good friend of The Family, and he pressed me to publish them—he was the only soul I permitted to view them, you see—and now I am a Success and a Disgrace to the Family and an Exile!"

"If your sketches are one half as humorous and insightful as Washington Irving's," Lord Robert replied, "then you must be a success with your pen! But there, you see, we have yet another commonality between us, for I too, am in exile by the wish of my Family!"

Miss Wingate nodded in sympathy. Beneath her mask, Lord Robert could almost see her eyes, peering up at him from beneath her lashes. "Family can be such an oppressive thing, can it not? The Wingates are very, very respectable, you see, and they were so shocked to find that Aunt Lydia had gone behind all of their backs and written such provoking things about everyone—I confess I did not spare any of my cousins or my brothers and sisters, any more than the wildest frontiersman come into the city for the first time, or the poltroons or anyone!"

"My sins," Lord Robert said gravely, "were far, far worse. Despite the reputation of my country's peerage, there are still a few Families, like my own, who are depressingly concerned with Respectability!"

"Sin!" Miss Wingate said, shaking her head. "To be sure, Jonathan and I have been looking earnestly for it, but you sir, are the first vestige of it that we have managed to uncover! Oh, sir, you look quite shocked, but allow me to explain! Of course there is sin in America—there is poverty, and slavery and injustice and hypocrisy and cruelty and all matter of evil—and those things one must not only deplore, but endeavor to set to rights! But there are other sins—luxury and sybaritism, and, well, all manner of romantic intrigues! These are the sins we particularly wanted to view—oh, dear, I am not explaining myself at all, and prosing on in the most boorish manner!"

"But look all about you, Miss Wingate!" Lord Robert said drily. "Do you not see a Bacchanalia that would be certain to shock your good family?"

Miss Wingate shook her head. "No. All I see are exactly the same sort of depressingly ordinary people I may see at home. America is a rather polyglot nation, you know, and we have our share of exiled Bonapartists and Milanese counts hanging out for a good American fortune and—to be sure, I have found much to fill my letters to the Family—Jonathan never writes a line, you know—he is far too ill to pick up a pen! We have seen great cathedrals, and magnificent châteaux, and so much ancient beauty and so many miles and miles of Great Art

23

that I am quite dizzy with it all, but worldly sins
have quite disappointed me! All that I may squib
in my pen is the behavior of our fellow tourists!
And since Jonathan and I walk and gawk and
wonder as much as any of them, I am quite and
all at a standstill to present my editor with anything!"

"Your Family must be pleased," Marchman
ventured.

"To be sure!" Miss Wingate returned. "I do believe that I was sent abroad with Jonathan as a
punishment, you know, for they would never con-
ceive that anything that does not occur between
Wall Street and Madison Square would ever be of
the least interest."

"The same might be said of my Family of Coldstone Place and Grosvenor Square," Lord Robert
sighed.

"Then you understand what I speak of!" Miss
Wingate said with an unconscious bitterness. "It
was supposed that a trip abroad, into sunnier climates, would restore my poor brother's health, and
so we have been obliged to travel to every spa and
watering hole in Europe to drink the most vile
waters and bathe in the most noisome springs im-
aginable. I do believe that until we came upon the
villa at Como, that we had not chanced to encounter a soul beneath the age of sixty, and all of
our letters of introduction have been to the dullest
set of people you can imagine—consuls and ambassadors and shipbuilders like grandpapa—all of
them anxiously willing to steer us away from anything that even faintly hints at worldly intrigues!
It is because Grandfather is a Quaker, I suppose,

24

but Jonathan and I are *not*, and if Mrs. Van Schuyler had not happened to know Contessa d'Orsini, we might never have chanced upon Como, which has been a very good thing, for at least it is beautiful here, and we have an excellent villa leased cheap from a Bonaparte cousin who had to go into New Orleans for a while—" She broke off and looked up at Lord Robert. "I believe you are laughing at me, sir!"

"Not at all at you, dear ma'am, but with you! Your predicament reminds me very much of my own first Grand Tour, when I was packed off with a tutor, a fencing-master, a valet, a groom and a tour guide, all of whom were determined that I should fall into no trouble!"

"Had they but known!" Lydia Wingate laughed. "Jonathan and I have only each other and our servants—a most respectable couple!—to keep us from total ruin. But since George and Hannah are even grander Quakers than Grandfather, and have known us since birth, you may depend upon it that they are even more afraid of Worldly Pleasures than Grandfather, besides mistrusting all foreigners in the worst possible manner!"

"My own valet is a Methodist," Lord Robert reported gloomily. "I believe Jenks stays with me only because he has known me since my birth and he hopes someday a miracle will occur and I will reform my rum and ramshackle ways!"

"Oh, dear me!" Miss Wingate said again.

With a flourish the waltz ceased and the dancers applauded. As if some spell had been broken, Lord Robert and Miss Wingate drew apart, their applause joining politely with the rest of the company's, their eyes unable to meet one another's, as if each had betrayed too much to the other, a perfect stranger.

Two

It was as Lydia had expected; having employed every degree of persuasion at her command to entice her brother to attend the contessa's *bal masque* against his arguments that his health would not stand the strain of such strenuous activity, that they would find none of their acquaintance among the company at Villa Orsini, that they had no costumes, and no means, in this rural district of Italy, of procuring any; through the arts born of long practice in nursing him through his long bout with the yellow fever she must now use this knowledge to convince him that it was past time to leave the gathering.

Still, they were among the last guests to find their craft at the foot of the broad marble stairs that swept down to the waterfront, and as their admittedly rickety craft was being piloted back across the waters in the moonlight which poured down from the mountains, Jonathan was still marveling that he had been singled out to dance with the future Queen of England.

"Although she isn't what you would expect, is she?" he asked his sister thoughtfully, watching with an expert eye as their pilot reefed the mainsail above their heads. "If we were home in New York, Lyddie, you might have thought her to be one of those women like Madame Jumal! Now, old girl, you will have something to write about!"

Miss Wingate absently agreed with her brother that, indeed, Her Highness had proved to be a very civil princess indeed, speaking English with a heavy German accent and standing upon as little ceremony as her rather amazing consumption of wine would permit, and that the lady was very much like the famous Madame Jumal.

That she had expected, and had not been overly surprised to find that in general, the contessa's ball was very much like those she had attended in New York. Under the watchful eyes of duennas and mamas, the young ladies present had behaved with the sort of decorum that would have passed muster on Madison Square. Beneath the watchful eyes of husbands and wives, such flirtations and intrigues as had occurred had been very discreet indeed, and upon the whole, everyone had acted in a most depressingly conventional manner. She had danced with her brother, with the elderly Conte d'Orsini and with one or two other gentlemen who had been presented to her, and twice with Lord Robert Marchman.

And it was not the Princess of Wales who had caught her imagination, although she was certainly worth a few pages of description, but Lord Robert Marchman.

Having never before had a chance to observe a despoiler of female virtue, she had found the experience intriguing, of course, and rather deliciously dangerous. In all of her thirty-one years, she had never found herself *flirting* before, and certainly not with a masked man who proclaimed himself a hardened libertine. She was more than a little vexed with herself for succumbing so easily to the charm of a man who must have cut his teeth upon such females as herself, and a little put out at her own spirited defense. Within the bosom of the Family, Lydia was frequently characterized as the eccentric for the frankness of her manners and her predilection for setting pen to paper, but not even the severest of her sisters could have ever castigated her for *flirting!*

She had matched sally for sally and felt that she had come off rather well, for from the very moment she had met Lord Robert, it had seemed to her as if she had known him forever, and that they must needs be comfortable together in the easiest manner, almost as if they were old friends....

But when the midnight hour had come, and they had all removed their masks, she was surprised, not only that her eyes had immediately sought out Lord Robert's across the crowded ballroom, but also that his had sought her own, and his face had betrayed the slightest smile, as if inquiring if she liked what she beheld of his countenance. That she had, very much, in no way comforted her. What might be permissible behind the security of costumes and masks and dominoes was suddenly rather too real when people were presented to one another in their true form, and she had suddenly understood how every sort of license was generally supposed to occur at costume parties.

She supposed that she had rather been expecting a gaunt-faced, saturnine man with all the marks of dissipation writ large upon once-handsome features, rather like her brother-in-law, Cyril, who was notorious for kissing the housemaids behind Sister Priscilla's back, and could be most tiresome at family gatherings. Instead, Lord Robert's countenance was almost boyish, despite a certain vague look of sadness in his deepest blue eyes, and showed the deeply tanned skin of one who is accustomed to spend much time out of doors. His hair was a shade between brown and gold, and curled around his head, except, she had noted, upon his forehead, where it was displacing a tendency toward recession in a manner that was by no means displeasing, but rather added to his attractions, for it gave him a look of maturity and intelligence. Beneath a rather pronounced nose, his lips, when he was not paying attention to his reputation as a rake, tended to lie in a rather gentle line, and when he smiled, it was as if he were illuminated; it was a great deal too bad that he did not smile often enough. But dark, threatening and Byronic he was not, and Miss Wingate was pleased to be relieved forever of that image.

But it was almost as if one must needs substitute a mask of papier-mâché and wax with one of attitude, for the second time they had danced together, although it had passed agreeably enough, had been by no means as lively in conversation as the first.

With a little sigh, Miss Wingate recalled the warm, tender feel of his hand placed against her waist as he guided her across the black and white marble floor to the strains of the orchestra's music, and gave her head a little shake. To think that she, a grown woman of thirty-one, well past the age of romantic daydreams, a woman with a reputation for poking irreverently with her pen at *everything*, should fall prey, even for a few moments, to the practiced charms of a man who made a career out of seducing women, roused her to her usual common sense.

"Dear me," she murmured aloud, turning her thoughts away from Lord Robert with a bit more effort than she might have expected. Perhaps, she thought a little sardonically, that is why he is so proficient at his chosen occupation! He makes you believe it is true! She ruffed out her simple gray merino skirts, as if shaking away an unpleasant thought. When one was disguised—and not a very good disguise at that!—as a simple Quaker miss, how easy it was—how incredibly easy!—to believe that one was being oneself. But now, with the cool breezes of Como against her face, and the moonlight pouring down from the mountains across the water, dancing upon the waves in a thousand diamonds, she knew herself to be Miss Lydia Wingate of New York City again, and however erratic her pen might be, Miss Wingate was never so! Or never had been so, until tonight.

She felt rather like Cinderella, however, coming home from the ball, without even the fortune to leave behind a glass slipper for the prince to trace her through. No, she would never see Lord Robert Marchman again, and that was just as well, for she would be embarrassed to encounter him as

31

herself—or the self she chose to present to the world.

That perhaps, in the course of a single waltz, she had allowed the real Miss Wingate to peek out from behind her excellent mask for a man she had never met before and would never meet again was a thought she did not permit herself to consider.

"Hey, Lyddie, I don't think you've heard a word I've been saying!" Mr. Jonathan Wingate rallied his sister.

Miss Wingate have a little start and turned toward her brother who was leaning back in the stern of the boat, his neck propped into his clasped hands, his legs thrust out before him. "I'm sorry, Jon—my mind must have been in the moonlight! Are you chilly? Do you wish me to wrap a blanket about your shoulders, my love?"

"Lyddie, pray don't wrap me in cotton wool!" Jonathan pleaded, although when it suited him, he could be very ill indeed, particularly if there was something he did not wish to do. "I'm perfectly fine, really! Well, perhaps just a little tonic before I turn in, but otherwise—Lyddie, I was just saying that if Grandfather knew we'd been having *fun* tonight, he would have sent us for packing home immediately!"

Miss Wingate stifled a giggle and leaned back against the cushions provided for her comfort. "That is no way to speak of Grandfather," she managed to say, however half-heartedly.

"Perhaps not," Mr. Wingate agreed carelessly. "Only, Lyddie, it seems as if all we have done since we came to Europe has been tramp from spa to spa, drinking the elixirs and bathing in dirty waters and seeing a pack of doctors I wouldn't send

32

my dog to! And the people we've met—I suppose ambassadors and shipbuilders and so forth are all very well in their own ways, but none of them were as exciting as the people at the contessa's tonight! Did you happen to meet M. Farouche? He was with Napoleon, and told the most amazing stories about being in Egypt. It is too bad that we missed Byron and Shelley, I suppose—but I do like it here."

"I am glad," Lydia said gratefully. "Because I do, too. And I think that these few weeks of sun and fresh air have done more for you than all of those doctors and waters! You are quite restored, my love!"

"Well, not quite," Jonathan said, shifting a little and looking at his elder sister. "I should hate to be well enough to have to go home, wouldn't you?"

Lydia smiled. "Jonathan, you were supposed to enter Princeton in September, you know," she reminded him gently.

"Yes, and dull I can imagine it to be! Lydia, should you like to go on to Greece when the weather turns chill?"

"We shall think upon it," Miss Wingate replied noncommittally.

Jonathan, who had never in his nineteen years been denied anything by his indulgent family, nodded and stretched again. "Perhaps the air would be good for my lungs," he murmured.

"Perhaps the young ladies would be good for your pride, you peacock!" Lydia responded with a laugh. "It was not M. Farouche in whom you were interested, but his very pretty daughter!"

"They think of removing to New Jersey to join

33

their relatives in Monmouth," Jonathan said lazily. "She is pretty, isn't she though?"

"And so was Frauline Heinrich in Baden-Baden, and so was that blonde lady in Zurich, and so was—"

"Oh, don't pour it out on my head, Lyddie!" Jonathan implored his sister. "That's why you are my favorite, you never preach or prose or ring the bells over me!"

"And that is why you are my favorite," Lydia replied. "I never *need* to! Unless you are languishing, of course," she added, but there was an undertone of seriousness in her voice, for having nursed Jonathan through the almost fatal bout of fever, she was never quite certain when he was pretending ill health and when his natural spirits were actually depressed.

"Listen, Lyddie," Jonathan said after a brief silence. "It ain't my place to comb your hair, either, sister, but I couldn't help but notice that you were dancing twice with Marchman! You couldn't be expected to know, of course, but Colonel Schulmann mentioned to me that the man was—well, a terror with women! I hope he didn't try anything rude with you, did he?"

Lydia stiffened for a second, but her voice was smooth. "Oh, of course not! If you had asked me about Signore Bergmani—I had to turn him about! But Lord Robert was all that was proper, I assure you."

"Well, Lyddie, you may think yourself an old maid, but Schulmann says you're exactly in his style, except you ain't married, and Lyddie, I don't know how to fight a duel—I am not Hamilton or Burr!"

"Oh, Jon! Don't talk such nonsense! As if you would have to fight a duel over me! Really, I am quite old enough to take care of myself! I was dancing with worse men than him long before you'd left nurse!"

"Well, you are my sister, Lyddie, and I certainly don't want any rakehell thinking he can take liberties with you! I might not be up to my full weight yet, but I can defend you!"

"If there is any need, brother dear, I will instantly inform you," Lydia replied seriously, seeing that Jonathan meant his words. But she could not resist adding, "Only I hope you will not take lessons from those silly Heidelburg boys—imagine thinking it the mark of a gentleman to have a dueling scar! I never heard of anything so ridiculous in all of my life, for besides making them look like someone you would see hanged on Cherry Street, it seems to me to be a great waste of time to go around picking out fights."

"You don't understand, Lyddie," Jonathan sighed in that voice which indicated he would provide her with far more enlightenment than she required. "It's a matter of honor!"

"Honor," Lydia repeated, trailing her hand through the water, which was far cooler than she might have expected from such a warm spell of weather.

"Actually, it's very much a matter of Schuyler's honor," Jonathan continued.

The thought of the stolid widower with whom Miss Wingate was supposed by her Family to have an Understanding had not intruded upon her thoughts in some days, and now, without much enthusiasm, she conjured up a vision of his ruddy,

35

somewhat disapproving countenance. "Charles does not enter into this," she said rather primly. She did not need to add that Mr. Schuyler was one of the reasons she had not protested too strenuously when it had been proposed that she accompany her youngest sibling upon his restorative tour of Europe. It was not that he was unpleasant, or that she minded becoming stepmother to the four lively offspring of his first, tragically ended marriage; it was rather that whenever Mr. Schuyler looked at her, she had the uneasy feeling that it was not Lydia Wingate whom he viewed, but the alliance between his family's fortune and her own. Thirty-one, Miss Wingate might protest herself to be, and well upon the shelf, but all of her sister's protestations that the status of a married lady was far superior to that of a single woman had not yet induced her to look as favorably upon Charles' suit as the Family might have wished.

But upon such a wonderful night, so full of moonlight and mountains and the fragrance of flowers borne upon the wind, Mr. Schuyler was easily dismissed back to his Hudson River mansion and his brood of children, far across the Atlantic. That Lord Robert's handsome face rose up to replace Mr. Schuyler's stolid countenance in her imagination was not, however, calculated to insure her peace of mind, nor her rapt contemplation of the scenery.

As if he had read her thoughts, Jonathan looked up at the sky. "It is a night, isn't it, Lyddie? Those old Romans might have been bores, going on forever in Latin about the dullest subjects, but they certainly had the right idea when they decided to build their summer places up here! Not to mention all those Renaissance people, of course. You know, when you think that you're used to thinking a building is old when it was built by the Dutch at home, and when you come to Europe, where things are thousands and thousands of years old, it really does make you think, doesn't it?"

"Indeed," Miss Wingate said comfortably, her smile hidden in the darkness.

"Well, at any rate, encountering that fella ought to give you something to write about besides ruins and cathedrals and the other tourists."

"Perhaps," Miss Wingate murmured.

"Although it does seem as if one meets the oddest set of characters everywhere—since they put Napoleon away, it seems that everyone is traveling. In England we met the French, in France we met the English, and the Germans were in Spain, and the Spanish are in Milan, and the Dutch are in Florence, and the Milanese are in the Netherlands—and, well, it just goes to show you, Lyddie, that we ain't the only tourists!"

"*Aren't* the only tourists," Miss Wingate said absently.

"And recall, sister, how on the voyage over, we were certain that we would be the only gawkers around, and how we would be discreet by not tramping through the museums and the palaces with our Becker's GUIDE, gawking at the frescoes."

"And what was the first thing we did, 'ere we landed in Portsmouth, but go out and *gawk*," Lydia laughed. "We must have looked like a pair of frontier settlers on our first trip downriver!"

"Of course, now we're above all of that, bein' seasoned travelers," Jonathan announced loftily.

37

"Why, I imagine you can complain about damp sheets and indifferent food in four languages now."

"Oh, we have grown quite sophisticated *for a pair of American rustics!*" Lydia responded airily. "I was certain that Lady Sidmouth thought we would eat with our fingers and drink from the handbowls when she had us to dinner that night in London. Such looks as she gave us all through the meal! I was very glad that you managed to tell her that New York has gas lighting upon all the principle streets and that Broadway is the longest paved thoroughfare in the world."

Jonathan Wingate shook his head. "But you have to admit that you do get annoyed, Lyddie, when people regard us as provincials simply because we are Americans."

"I am afraid that I allow myself to become slightly acerbic," Miss Wingate admitted. "One does not want to be patronized, after all."

"But you always stick your pen into them!" Jonathan added complacently. "And speakin' of stickin' your pen, Lyddie, when next you write to Grandfather, will you mention how salubrious the air of Greece is generally supposed to be?"

"I shall. Although, brother, it seems to me that you could at least contribute your mite to the correspondence."

"Oh, Lyddie, you *know* I don't feel well enough to write anything! It makes my brain hurt, tryin' to think of something to say, and I know they like your letters far more than mine." As if to emphasize his point, Jonathan coughed into his fists, and instantly, Lydia forgot everything else in her efforts to place a blanket about her brother's shoulders, and solicitously inquire after his lungs.

38

"Oh, Lyddie, pray don't wrap me in cotton!" Jonathan protested, but rather weakly, for he was by no means as robust as he had been before the yellow fever. So close had he come to death that occasional symptoms of illness still had the power to affright him, and being of a somewhat self-centered nature, he found it simple enough to accept his sister's dictums that his health was not quite restored.

Although his cough subsided as swiftly as it had arisen, Miss Wingate was still relieved to see the dim Renaissance shapes of Villa Solario hove into view above the cliffs, and the lanterns at the foot of the steps illuminating their path upwards to the house. Gladder still was she to see the large, comfortable shape of Friend George Pennington looming above the craft, his lantern held aloft.

"Thee should know better, Friend Jonathan," he said in his rich West-Indian-tinged English, "than to be staying out until the morning hours! And thee, Friend Lydia, should not keep him so! Thy grandfather would hardly approve!"

"I am sorry," Lydia said humbly, for there could really be no other reply to give to a man who had boosted her upon her first pony and pulled her down out of her grandfather's cherry trees when she was still in short skirts. "Italians keep later hours, you see! Will you fix Friend Jonathan a toddy? He coughed on the way home!"

"I cleared my throat!" Mr. Wingate felt moved to protest, but he was very glad to have George bundle him up the steps toward his rooms and the comfort of his own bed. "And a real toddy thee shall have, Friend Jon, from American whiskey, and none of this heathen foreign swill!" George was saying firmly.

"Friend Lydia!" Hannah was bustling down the steps, her plain black dress rustling as she moved toward her charge. She was as large and powerful as her husband, but her skin was the color of coffee-and-cream, in contrast to his mahogany complexion, and her West Indian was softer. She inspected her charge critically and shook her head. "Jaunting about in the plain clothes, Friend Lydia, for a *costume*! Thee should be shamed! Come now, it's past three of the morning, and thee should be in thy bed, not strolling among these foreigners!"

"Indeed," Miss Wingate replied meekly, but Hannah was not taken in. A firm hand was placed beneath Lydia's elbow, and she was escorted to her own bedchamber beneath a severe stricture upon late hours and those that the Penningtons were pleased to castigate as heathen foreigners.

Once the door had closed upon that room, Hannah instantly began to undress her charge, despite Lydia's protests that she should really be in bed. Working her stays with expert hands, Hannah made a clucking sound with her tongue.

"Well, did thee have a good time? And there's no need to tell me thee didn't, for I haven't known thee for all these years without being able to tell when thee's pleased with thyself."

Lydia smiled as she stepped out of her pantalettes and dropped her nightdress over her head. "It was very interesting!" she admitted cautiously, seating herself at the vanity table and peering at her face in the gilt-framed mirror.

Friend Hannah Pennington picked up her hairbrush and began to remove the pins from Lydia's hair, allowing it to fall over her shoulders. In the mirror, dark brown eyes met gray-blue and two slow smiles were shared.

"Oh, Hannah!" Lydia sighed. "I have been very, very wicked! I have danced all night, and *flirted*! I felt as if I were eighteen again!"

Hannah shook her head and clucked her tongue again as the brush fell through her charge's hair, but there was the ghost of a smile in her eyes. "And high time it is, Friend Lydia, that thee enjoyed thyself! Was there a dancer you liked above the others?"

Lydia smiled. "A very wicked man, Hannah—a duke's son, I believe, who told me he was an abandoned rake! Lord Robert Marchman."

"English," Hannah said sourly, shaking her head.

"Yes, but an exile!"

"Oh, I know about him! Depraved these Italian servants may be, and not at all what I would want to keep under my household at home—but they do gossip, Friend Lyddie, and I've had to learn enough Italian to speak to them! A very dangerous man indeed, and thee should not have encouraged him! Why, that girl who makes up thy rooms told me that he is part of that English princess's party—and she is no better than she should be, for all of being a princess!" Hannah dropped her voice. "That duke's son is being where he ought not with the wife of that old German baron, the young baroness, thee and Friend Jonathan had met with that contessa Tuesday last?"

"Baroness Galtzalter," Lydia repeated, her brows rising slightly at the thought of that voluptuous

41

Frenchwoman with the dark eyes and the very amply exposed bosom.

"That's the one! Why that man is supposed to have—well, *thee* knows!—with half the married ladies in this heathen place! That, Friend Lydia, will not do!"

Lydia's face fell into its serious lines. "No," she said softly, "that will not do! But it would make such an interesting *sketch*, don't you think?"

"I think, Friend Lydia, that thee ought to go to thy bed and think no more upon duke's sons tonight! Thee knows the English are no better than they should be!"

"No," Lydia said meekly.

The former occupant of the Villa Solario had been created a prince by Napoleon. Before that interesting event, he had been a silk merchant, and being a good Frenchman, had decorated the chambers which now were occupied by Miss Wingate.

Alone in her vast, carved bed, she found that sleep quite eluded her, and that try as she might, her thoughts could not be removed from that night's events, or from one particular guest.

Again and again, she reminded herself that she was well past the age of romance. When she had been of an age to be courted and married, her parents had died and she had found herself to be cast into the role of caring for her several sisters; their claims to her attention seemed to have naturally superseded her own, and her grandfather, a widower, had naturally looked to his eldest granddaughter to replace her mother as his hostess, housekeeper and *chargé d'affaires* for the remainder of his grandchildren. A man who has taken a small boatyard and built it into a vast Yankee shipping empire, after all, must needs have a female who can preside upon his home board and insure his comfort. Her sisters needed to be chaperoned, to be guided away from fortune hunters and steered toward the proper sort of husbands, weddings, and subsequently, children and households. She had been an aunt many times over, and enjoyed a vast popularity among her nieces and nephews that quite puzzled her elders, for there you had it, Miss Wingate mentally addressed the moonlight. She had always been considered a bit, well, *pixilated* within the Family. She read as voraciously as her grandfather, and had found herself at the age of fourteen to be far better educated than the preceptress of the expensive and excellent Ladies Seminary through which the Wingate Ladies passed one after the other; she knew politics as well as any of her grandfather's friends and had never hesitated, when at the head of the board, to express her opinions to those very much her senior; she had not hesitated to refuse several very good alliances with other Families who sought to align their fortunes with those of the Wingates, saying with simple honesty that her heart and head must both be engaged at once before she could consider living with a man, and she had a deplorable tendency to contract friendships with persons of whom the Family could only disapprove, particularly those associated with the periodicals published in the City. The radical publisher William Legget and the writer Washington Irving had been the first to encourage her to set her wit to paper, and very soon, her anonymous squibs were appearing in the EVENING STAN-

DARD satirizing everything from the overopulence of Miss VanderGelt's debutante ball to the excitement caused by the new steamboats blowing their way up the Hudson in a cloud of smoke. Something inside of Miss Wingate, so long supressed or dismissed with the port and cigars upon the board, had emerged when she set pen to paper, and it had not been long before SKETCHES AND SCENES OF A LADY OF NEW YORK CITY was discussed everywhere. Some were outraged, others amused, but Miss Wingate was astonished to find that she was universally read, and that had more than made up for the two pennies a line Mr. Legget saw fit to pay her for her services.

It was unfortunate that in addition to those other vices associated with gentlemen of the press, Mr. Legget also like to drink; and when he drank, Mr. Legget liked to talk, and when he talked, Mr. Legget unfortunately liked to argue with his political opponents, and that upon one particular evening in Fraunces' Tavern, Mr. Legget's political opponent happened to be Miss Wingate's grandfather. Lydia could only imagine what sort of a scene had ensued upon Mr. Legget's informing Mr. Wingate that his granddaughter Lydia was the Lady of the Sketches, but in the ensuing domestic confrontation, she had been obliged to own to the truth of the matter.

"Why did thee not tell me?" Mr. Wingate had demanded of his errant granddaughter.

"Because you never asked," Miss Wingate had replied calmly, and the Family had immediately been called in.

All of the tears and remonstrances of her sisters had been to no avail; the threats and dire predictions of her many brothers-in-law had fallen upon deaf ears. Not even the sacred name of the Family could sway her from her decision to be an authoress, and the very next day, Miss Wingate had signed a contract with Scrope and Company, Book Publishers of 12 Light Street, to publish her Sketches together in one volume, with a promise of a second.

Being packed off to Europe as nurse to her youngest brother Jonathan had been the result; it was hoped that upon her return, the scandal would have dimmed, and Mr. Charles Schuyler, of a cadet branch of that illustrious family, would be in a more forgiving mood. The cementing of bonds between the Schuylers and the Wingates was something earnestly hoped for with the Family; Lydia's feelings in the matter were to be of little concern.

That Miss Wingate had continued, upon her travels, to employ her pen to no very good end for those who happened to be at its point, had probably delighted Mr. Legget and Mr. Irving and her many readers at home. Since the Family had never mentioned the affair, once it had passed over, she could only guess, with all too fair a degree of accuracy, at their several reactions.

Only consider then, she thought moodily, what their reaction would be if they had known that she was flirting with a notorious English libertine.

That she would probably never again encounter Lord Robert Marchman was cold comfort indeed.

Three

In the morning, beneath the wash of the yellow sunlight, with late summer flowers blooming everywhere along the terraces and the plazas, Miss Wingate was prepared to dismiss the previous night's revels as a sort of sweet and colorful dream, as illusory as one of Turner's paintings of the Venice canals.

Both Lydia and Jonathan had slept quite late into the morning, and when they first met upon the terrace for breakfast, the hour was closer to noon than morning.

Jonathan was stretched out upon a chaise, carelessly attired in his shirtsleeves and breeches, reading an English language newspaper and seemingly contented to stare up at the sun. He greeted his sister lazily, casually informing her that there was hot chocolate upon the table.

Miss Wingate, attired very simply in a round dress of thin jaconet muslin over a peach-colored sarsenet slip, trimmed with Frenchwork and cut low at the throat, a little cap placed over her hair, poured herself a cup of that now lukewarm liquid from a Limoge pot and strolled to the edge of the terrace, looking out across the lake toward the high shore where Villa d'Orsini's ornate spires gleamed in the sunlight. She sipped her chocolate and thought about peeling an orange, at which thought, her stomach revolted slightly, and she pressed a hand against her forehead.

"I shall never, ever drink champagne again," she declared firmly.

Behind her, Mr. Wingate chuckled. "You drank enough last night, sister! Lord, Lyddie, it was a fine thing to see you so!"

Miss Wingate shuddered delicately, and sat herself, with a great deal of decorum, upon a marble bench in the shape of a seashell facing her brother, whom she regarded with mock severity. "You were no better, if I recall!" she replied.

Mr. Wingate rubbed his hair and shrugged. "Probably not," he agreed happily. "But it was fun, was it not, Lyddie? Perhaps we should entertain, sometime."

"Heavens! Don't allow Hannah and George to hear you! If they knew that they were to supervise all of these poor heathens in putting together an entertainment, they would be on the first packet back to New York!"

"You'll take care of it, Lyddie," Jonathan replied with serene confidence. "Hullo, what's that sail?"

Lydia turned to follow her brother's gaze down toward the water, where a *bâteau* propelled by two boatmen was putting into their dock.

"It looks to me to be the contessa's gondola," she said. "I only hope that I may attain her age and entertain all night, only to pay morning calls the very next day!"

The contessa, protected from the injurious effects of the sunlight by a lace parasol and a very large leghorn hat trimmed with a great deal of silk ribbon and velvet flowers, waved quite gaily toward them, saying something in her native language which Lydia did not understand.

"I believe she's brought us some company," Jonathan murmured, and Lydia frowned against the sunlight to see a second person disengaging himself from the gondola. She blinked, unbelieving, and uncertain of her own feelings, somewhere between hope and annoyance, for was it—*yes!*—Lord Robert Marchman who gallantly assisted the contessa from the boat to the landing, turning for an instant to look up the steps toward the terrace, framed in the sun.

"*Buongiorno*, Lydia and Jonathan!" the contessa called as she swept majestically up the stairs to place a kiss on each of Lydia's cheeks, shaking Jonathan's hand in the American manner, twirling her parasol and acting, in every respect, as if she had pulled off an interesting *coup*. "You see, I have brought you a visitor who speaks English! Lord Robert, you will recall Miss Wingate and Mr. Wingate!"

Although Marchman raised his brows slightly as Lydia politely shook his hand, in no other way did he betray the least discomfort in his situation. But Miss Wingate was not entirely certain that she had missed the smile that lurked in his eyes, nor the way in which he held her hand for just a second longer than absolutely necessary. "Your servant, Miss Wingate!" he said very correctly, however, and turned to shake Jonathan's hand also.

"Lord Robert, is it, sir?" Mr. Wingate said stiffly.

"We welcome you to Villa Solario!" Lydia said quickly, plumping up a cushion on the long settle for the contessa. "Would you care for some chocolate? I could send for another pot—or perhaps something stronger! We had some ice brought from the mountains two days ago, so I may at least offer you something cool!"

"One of your mint juleps, with that extraordinary American whiskey! Have you tasted American whiskey, Signore Robert? It is amazing, I believe."

Lord Robert seated himself upon a marble bench, shaking his head. "I have not yet had that pleasure," he said gravely.

Scarcely aware of what she did, Lydia rang the bell. "It is rather strong," she said a little dubiously.

"Oh, let him have it!" Jonathan said a trifle petulantly, seating himself beside the *contessa* and looking at her beneath his lashes. "I shall have one also."

George, in his apron over livery, came into the doorway, frowning very darkly indeed at the contessa and Lord Robert. "Thee called, Friend Lydia?" he asked, wiping his hands on a rag.

"Yes, Friend George! Would you be good enough to make three of your mint juleps for our guests— and I shall have an orange ice!"

George shook his head and exited back into the villa again, muttering to himself.

Lydia fluttered into her seat and clasped her hands together in her lap. "I'm afraid Friend George does not approve of liquor," she said with a nervous little laugh. Really, Lydia Wingate, she thought, get a hold upon yourself! One would think that you were excited!

The contessa beamed upon the company. "Such a lovely day," she said. "I think to myself this morning, the conte has his doctor come in, he is occupied all morning with the medical baths and the leeches, what can I do? And then, Lord Robert comes walking over the cliffs—*walking*! And I say, well, I see that my young friends across the lake are awake, let us take the gondola and go to pay them a morning visit!"

"You had a truly fine ball last night, contessa!" Jonathan said with his engaging smile. "I actually got a dance with the Princess!"

One delicately green-tinted lid dropped over the contessa's large brown eye. She was as fond of good-looking young men as her friend Her Highness of Wales. "She is *stesso*—" the countess waved one mittened hand delicately in the air, allowing her sentence to dangle, "is she not? But so droll, and such a good friend to have! I am glad that you liked her, for you know that she was very taken with the Wingates! The charming Americans, she calls you!"

"The highest compliment," Lord Robert said drily, and Lydia wondered again if he was smiling at her. He flicked an invisible speck of lint from his nankeen jacket and crossed one elegantly shod leg across the other. Unlike so many men she had met in London whose lives rose and fell upon their shirt points, he was tastefully attired. She could

50

find no fault with the cut and color of his coat, a very fine shade of chocolate, nor were his biscuit-colored breeches cut so tight that she need fear for his comfort as he sat down. His neckcloth was arranged with neat propriety, and he need not fear to turn his head lest he wilt his shirt points. From his watch chain there depended only one fob, and his waistcoat was a plain affair of subdued green. Certainly not the powdered and perfumed fop she might have expected, enticing women into his toils with all manner of flashy sartorial splendor. In fact, she thought, a little critically, he looked just a slight bit *mussed*, as if his appearance were of no major concern to him.

While the contessa idly conversed with Jonathan over the state of his health (always an interesting subject to him), Miss Wingate sat demurely waiting for Lord Robert to open the conversation.

"Did you enjoy the ball last night, Miss Wingate?" he asked at last.

"Yes, very much. I thought it was very amusing. I have never before met a princess, you know."

"Ah, live long enough in Italy and you will meet enough princesses to fill a ballroom!" Lord Robert replied.

"Oh, I think that would be far too many, for then there would be no room to dance," Lydia replied quickly.

Marchman's eyes crinkled, and he nodded. "Perhaps they could make up their own orchestra; that would leave the floor free for you and me, Miss Wingate, and other lesser humans."

"Perhaps," Lydia agreed, laughing at the thought

51

of an orchestra of princesses. "I must write that down! Only think of the confusion it would cause!"

"Only think!" Marchman agreed soberly. "Princesses, their tiaras slipping as they grind away at violas and blow upon their French horns!"

"And of course, Princess Caroline must lead all of them!" Lydia flashed.

Marchman nodded, leaning back into his chair. "Of course! But, Miss Wingate can you imagine anything more dreadful than that black wig of hers falling askew as she waves her baton?"

"Indeed not! She would throw off the royal time most dreadfully! The confusion would increase!"

Lord Robert laughed. If anyone had told him that he would be sitting upon a terrace with an unremarkable-looking American female, conjuring up a vision of a dance orchestra of the crowned females of Europe, he would have pronounced such an activity a dead bore. But it was he who had requested that the contessa pay a morning call upon Villa Solario, and even though he was here, he was still not quite certain *why*. He only knew that he was enjoying himself very much, and that Miss Wingate, this odd American female, could do what no other female had ever been able to do for him before—she made him laugh. And that was unusual enough. Clearly, this stay in Como would prove to be more interesting than he had expected when he had accepted the Princess of Wales' Invitational Command, and not because of the Baroness Galtzalter, either, although he had originally accepted the invitation in order to remain close to that very dashing female.

George emerged from the house with four tall glasses. As he presented the tray to Lord Robert, he gave him a most peculiar look, and made a sound deep in his throat.

Lydia, accepting her glass, cast George Pennington a most frightful look, but he shook his head and marched back into the house again, muttering beneath his breath.

"You have most unusual servants, Miss Wingate," Lord Robert murmured as he lifted his glass to the ladies.

"They are a little bit more than just our servants, sir," Jonathan said stiffly. "Friend George and Friend Hannah have been with us forever—well, since Lydia was born!"

"And that might as well be forever," Miss Wingate sighed. "They were once slaves, you see, and George escaped and came North, then worked and bought Hannah's freedom. They are very devout Quakers, and Friend George does not approve at all of drinking spirits—unless one is ill, of course!"

"But he does mix a fine punch, for all of his abstentions," Lord Robert said. "Very smooth stuff, your American whiskey—and mint! Quite original!"

"And quite, what is the word, Lydia?—potent!" the contessa added, sipping her own beverage with a great deal of enthusiasm. "I believe it is distilled from corn?"

"Corn," Lydia nodded.

"A better drink than blue ruin," Marchman said, holding the frosted glass up to the sunlight.

"And every bit as deadly," Lydia added.

"But you do not drink, Miss Wingate?"

"Never in the morning—and never, ever after such a night! I consumed far too much champagne last night."

53

"Ah," Lord Robert said. "The best cure for the blue-devils, Miss Wingate, is more of the same!"

Lydia made a most unladylike grimace. "No, I thank you!" she protested. "Enough is enough!"

"But this talk of blue devils and *mal da capo* is all very dull! Me, when I was your age, Lydia, I danced all night and rose in the morning to take the air in my carriage! And," she added with a wink, "perhaps met a young officer in the time before luncheon, like so!" She shook her head. "*Giovinezza*! It is a great deal too bad!"

"It comes, contessa, of being raised in colder climates," Lord Robert said easily. "We are cold-blooded creatures, Miss Wingate and I."

The contessa looked as if she did not agree, but she nodded and patted Jonathan's hand. "This one, is not to say coldblooded! He has the *passione* of Byron."

"Heaven forefend," Lord Robert murmured.

"Do you know Lord Byron, sir?" Lydia asked. "He is one of my favourite poets!"

"And I assure you, ma'am, had you his acquaintance, he would be among your least favored friends," Marchman said. "Brilliant perhaps, but difficult—very difficult."

"Lord Robert is too modest. He has lately visited with the romantic Lord Byron—such a beautiful man!" the contessa sighed. "Such eyes!"

"Such manners," Marchman said. "No, ma'am, I do not mean to disillusion you over Byron—my fellow exile; suffice to say that he and I parted company under a severe strain upon our friendship!"

Jonathan looked interested, but Lydia swiftly interposed. "I am certain that it is all very inter-

esting, and we must hear more about Byron someday, but perhaps you have not seen our borrowed
villa, sir? I am told that it is all in the first style
of Empire elegance, and that the Renaissance architecture is most interesting."

"Indeed," Lord Robert said, raising one eyebrow
slightly.

"Oh, *show off*, Lyddie," Jonathan said lazily.
"It's a great pretentious nouveau riche pile, and
as good as the circus!"

"Then indeed, I must see it, if Miss Wingate will
be good enough to be my guide," Lord Robert said,
rising politely from his chair.

"Go," the contessa said. "I have seen it already,
and I will not exert myself again. Rather I shall
sit and talk with Jonathan, if he is agreeable."

"Perfectly so, ma'am," Mr. Wingate said, giving
his sister a mischievous look.

Lydia bit her lower lip and looked at Lord Robert. "If you would wish to follow me, sir...." she
suggested.

Inside the halls, it was several degrees cooler,
and she felt the flush draining from her cheeks as
he followed her down the corridor.

"Forgive me! I did not think that Lord Byron's
situation was—suitable for discussion!" Lydia said
in a low voice.

Lord Robert's lips curled slightly. "Perhaps not,
but it would seem to me that everyone is at least
aware of it! *Lady* Byron made certain of that! Bella
Millbanke always was a prosy little tale-bearer!
Of course, my situation is only a little better than
Byron's," he added thoughtfully.

"This," Miss Wingate said, opening a set of
French doors which led into a vast room, "is the

Salle de Napoléon, which you might be able to tell by the number of times the letter *N* is worked into every object in the chamber! You will also note the bee motif, and the amazing amount of gilt alligator's feet—"

"Crocodile's feet."

"What? Oh, yes! Quite! Crocodile-footed furniture! It quite gives me the chills, if you must know, and I never come into this room unless we are obliged to entertain someone we *do not* like, which of course means almost *everyone*—and then we bring them in here, hoping they will become so depressed by all this faded splendor that they will leave!"

"Particularly if they are Bonapartists!"

"Exactly so! You see, however, that there is a David portrait of the Emperor over there—"

"He looks dyspeptic, I fear; not one of the master's best."

Lydia stifled a giggle. "M. Gombard assured us that this villa was *impregnated* with history, sir!"

"That serious, then?"

"Oh yes—well, at least it was to poor M. Gombard, who seemed to feel the climate of New Orleans was better suited to his health than Italy. Shall I show you the Empress' suite? Josephine was to have stayed here, I believe, but something—perhaps a very refined sense of taste—restrained her."

"It is a bit, well, modern," Lord Robert admitted, shying away from the enormous gilt Pharaoh's head that seemed to have placed itself in his exit.

"All very modern—except the plumbing! You can have no idea how inconvenient it is to have only one pump for all of this house—"

"But I am certain that your American servants remind you daily."

"Oh, yes! At home you know, we have an excellent system—everything is of the very latest—and an enclosed stove, also, which I fear Villa Solario is sadly lacking. I fear that M. Gombard's taste for redecorating did not extend into such imperatives as his kitchens and his closets. Very primitive."

Lord Robert, who had never considered looking into his own kitchens, stole a look at Miss Wingate's face. "And of course, here we have a Vigée-Lebrun of Mme. Gombard. She seems to have been rather formidable! Or Mme. Vigée-Lebrun took a dislike to her, I know not which!"

"Looks bracket-faced to me," Lord Robert said humbly. "Of course, I have no right to talk. M'father's house has a great many unflattering portraits of my ancestors. Of course, they were all rather rum, so I suppose it don't signify."

"Grandfather sat for Mr. West, and we have Copleys of my parents, and each of my sisters had her miniature taken on her come-out, but I fear Wingate House lacks an ancestral gallery—so far," Miss Wingate said. "Of course, if my nephews and nieces continue to arrive, I am sure we shall have something in no time at all."

"Do you have your likeness, Miss Wingate?"

"Oh, yes! Both Jonathan and I had to sit for Mr. Lawrence when we were in London, but the paintings were to be shipped home. Grandfather particularly wanted Jonathan's likeness taken, you see, he is the *heir*, and Grandfather's particular favorite...and here we have the dining room—and a very nice Angelica Kauffman over the man-

57

telpiece. I am only thankful that Napoleon does not stare down at one while one is dining—that would be most uncomfortable, I think!"

"Then Lawrence is still all the rage in London?" Lord Robert asked.

Miss Wingate nodded thoughtfully. "He is—what do they say—hideously tonnish! One must make arrangements to sit for him quite months in advance, and we were given to understand that we were quite fortunate that he was condescending enough to squeeze us in between Princess Lieven and an East India Nabob! I think that Grandfather's money had a great deal to do with it, however," she added a bit naively.

"Doubtless," Lord Robert murmured. "Does Lawrence still court Mrs. Siddons's daughters in tandem?"

"I believe so! Was there anything ever so much out of a comedy? They say his heart goes first to one, and then the other, and he is quite unable to make a choice. I think that his heart really belongs to Mrs. Siddons herself, although she must be twenty years his senior....I pity the lady, however, to make shift to support such a family as she has!"

"It is amazing how one yearns for news of home," Lord Robert murmured, then shook his head. "Ah, this room is—er—remarkable!"

"Ah, but then you have yet to see the rooms of some of our newly made people in New York! Not that Grandfather's house is meager," she added thoughtfully, scanning a dining suite that seated forty with ease, and a silver epergne the size of a shoe-bath centered upon the board. "But like many Quakers, Grandfather prefers that everything be of the quietest style, though the best quality."

"I must admit my own preferences are for something less grand," Marchman admitted, clearly a little awed by the amount of rosewood inlay and gilt sphinx heads ornamenting the furnishings. "But you have not seen the Villa d'Este!"

"I am assured that the Princess lives in the very best style, however," Miss Wingate twinkled a bit. "I am certain that we must look quite shabby in contrast."

"I should not have said so," Lord Robert admitted with a grin at his guide. "But doubtless you shall discover for yourself, in time. The princess was quite taken with your brother—and yourself, of course!"

"Oh, dear," Lydia said, pausing in the act of throwing open yet another set of enormous French doors. "There is something about an invalid boy that always attracts older women! I know not what it might be, but there you have it. The contessa dotes upon him!"

At this description of Jonathan as *invalid*, Marchman raised his brows slightly, but said nothing, only remarking that Jonathan appeared in tolerably good health to his view.

Miss Wingate shook her head. "He must appear so, for I am convinced that the salubrious climate of Italy has done very well for him, I think—but he coughed last night, and that was enough to throw us all into the greatest anxiety! We came so near to losing him, you see...."

"Of course," Lord Robert said quietly, and changed the subject. "How long do you mean to linger on in Como?"

"And this is the withdrawing-room—please note the lamé work in the curtains and the carpets—the effect by candle light is considered to be *blinding*, I assure you! Only Carlton House rivals the splendor of such elegance!" she added, tongue firmly in cheek, turning to face her guest. "To answer your question, sir, I think that when it becomes cold, we shall move on to Greece—Jonathan feels the climate must be good for his health. Although I worry somewhat about the political situation—it cannot be salubrious for mere travelers."

"No, I think not, from what reports I have received. I might suggest Rome, of course—it is a place that I have always enjoyed—there is much to recommend it."

Miss Wingate's lips drew upward quizzically, but she merely nodded, keeping her thoughts very much to herself, for she could imagine what sort of pleasures Lord Robert Marchman must find in Rome, that ancient and very sinful city.

"I understand the Two Sicilies are to much be admired," she said a little breathlessly, rustling on before him.

"Much scarred by war," Lord Robert replied. "But an amazing court. Perfectly amazing."

Miss Wingate allowed that remark to slide past her without comment.

For Miss Wingate knew exactly what sort of a court was maintained by Ferdinand and Maria Carolina.

"Here," she announced, throwing open yet another set of doors. "We have the music room. Note, if you will, the harp and the pianoforte, both made to specification by Russo. M. Gombard desired particularly that his daughter be musical. The youngest, I fear, became a little *too* musical, for M. Gombard allowed it to drop that after Waterloo, she eloped to Switzerland with the dancing master!"

Lord Robert shook his head. "M. Gombard's troubles seem to have overflowed his cup."

"Oh, I would imagine the youngest Mlle. Gombard to be very happy. The music she left behind her is all of the finest—and the most difficult, so I think perhaps that she was very much musically inclined. At least, I would like to believe that she is happy, now...." As she spoke, Lydia ran her fingers across the erstwhile Mlle. Gombard's harp; its clear, pure tones filled the still air.

"Do you play, Miss Wingate?"

"Me? Oh, no! You have but to see my sister Prudence in an attitude before *her* harp to know that I do not! I have no drama, you see, and must needs limit myself to the pianoforte."

"We have an excellent instrument here—may I?" Lord Robert asked, seating himself at the stool before the instrument, his fingers producing the first few bars of a sonata.

"But you play!" Lydia exclaimed, surprised.

Marchman shrugged. "Only a little—and only before those I may feel comfortable among. When I was younger, I thought perhaps to compose—but nothing came of it."

"There is a Haydn duet, somewhere in here," Lydia said, rifling through the music scores in the standbox, "Jonathan is not at all musical, and I have been dying for someone to play it with me—here!"

She produced the score and sat down at the instrument next to Lord Robert, studying the music.

"Do you think you can feel it out? I have been trying for such a long time to *synch* out both parts—"

Marchman studied the piece. "I think perhaps, but I must take it slowly at first—" He pounded out the lower bass octaves, and Miss Wingate joined in upon the upper octaves.

"I think we are getting it now," he laughed, and together, they launched into the piece *con brio*, making many mistakes, but laughing so over their lack of aptitude that they barely noted the erratic sounds issuing from the instrument, hardly what the great composer had intended.

"We are both much in need of practice!" Lydia finally exclaimed, striking the keys with a great many fingers.

"Indeed!" Lord Robert agreed laughing. "Two musicians such as we belong in the Princess Orchestra!"

Lydia shook her head, seeming to recollect herself and her company. "But I fear that we are ignoring—or *inflicting*—the worst sort of caterwauling upon Jonathan and the contessa! We really should join them you know—I think you have seen all of Peale's Museum that there is to see, sir!"

Lord Robert bowed his head in assent. "As you wish, Miss Wingate."

For the remainder of their visit, Lord Robert did all that was proper, but over her conversation with the contessa, Lydia noted that Lord Robert exerted himself a great deal to please her brother, involving himself in a long discussion of the various merits of sailing craft, particularly those smaller vessels used in racing, a particular enthusiasm of Jonathan's. Miss Wingate could not help but be impressed with the style and spectrum of Lord Robert's knowledge of sailing and ships, or with the way in which he drew Jonathan out, soliciting the younger man's opinions and listening to them with a great deal of respect.

When at last the contessa rose to go, Lydia was secretly pleased to see Jonathan shake the other man's hand warmly and invite him to Villa Solario soon.

"He's not such a ramshackle character after all," Jonathan said complacently as they watched the boat sailing away across the lake. "As a matter of fact, I quite like him!"

Four

Miss Wingate was suffering from a condition not unknown to all writers who desire to control their thoughts when their minds have perversely strayed elsewhere. Seated upon the shell chaise on the terrace, a magnificent view of the blue lake and the mountains beyond, a cup of lukewarm chocolate on the table beside her, a light summery morning dress of sprigged muslin gathered genteelly about her ankles and a white straw hat shading her fair complexion from the injurious rays of the sun, she had, since morning, been endeavoring without much success to make an account of the contessa's mask. Tapping her pencil against her cheek, Lydia reread for the third time the manuscript she had begun to draft, with many crossings and deletions and additions. It was a sad scratch indeed.

Present at this fantastic fête were several persons of whom the Europeans are pleased

64

to call Rank, and verily, our heads were spinning to keep track of the number of barons, Lords, contessas and suchlike folk as we were introduced to meet. Because of the recent upheavals after Waterloo, one was sore pressed to determine who was not upon terms with whomever else, and this, combined with the international rivalries, intrigues and stores set upon precedence, caused great confusion among the Company, for being disguised as Gryfins and Pierrots, who was to know who was to be snubbed and who to be toadied to in the most obsequious fashion? We were much amused by this international confusion, but no more so than our hostess, a delightful contessa whose main amusement in the summer months is to create just such an international gathering of ill-assorted persons. If Contessa d'O—i were an American, she would be considered a premiere hostess in one of our major metropolises. Perhaps the most astounding guest at this ball, however was *a lady* whose age must have been closer to *fifty* than *forty*, whose figure was certainly matronly and appearance most startling, for her face, already ruddy was covered with such a quantity of rouge as to make one believe she had purchased out the warehouse, and whose dress and style were of a young girl who has just done up her hair and let down her skirts. Perhaps this lady had borrowed her white silk gown from just such a young chit, for it was barely adequate to cover both her amazingly full *legs* and her very ample *bosom*. Upon her head this lady wore a black wig, so full of curls, rats and fringes that one might have thought she had snatched up her lap-dog instead of her hat, had it not been for the astounding number of plumes to which she had appended a number of pink silk garlands. This striking ensemble was accented by a great number of diamonds which would have done better for a good *cleaning*. It is to be hoped that the Reader will understand the surprise felt by the Authoress when informed this creature was the unfortunate *Princess of Wales*. An English lady, much embarrassed by the odd appearance of Her Highness, ventured to remark, *sub rosa*, that such eccentricity was no doubt the result of marriage to such a notable Original as the Regent. The Author understands that a certain *poet*, exiled to this shore, refers to the Royal Couple as the Prince and Princess of *Whales*. It is not to be wondered at, for, if the Reader will recall previous Sketches from London a meeting with His Highness was rendered interesting by the audible creaking of that gentleman's stays...."

Miss Wingate bit her lip, crossed out some words, replaced others, and nodded. "That should keep Legget happy," she murmured to herself. If there was one thing Americans, so insecure in the newness of their country, liked more than having their own public figures held up to ridicule, it was an opportunity to reassure themselves that the Old World was a place of decadence and profligate activity. A demon of genius crossed Lydia's path and she scribbled a few more Legget-happy lines.

In all fairness, however, one must admit that both the Royals are charming persons, very gracious and standing upon as little ceremony as our own Presidents. But the Author, now having made the required curtsy to both of this Royal Darby and Joan pair, cannot help but feel grateful that her own country is separated from the government of such as these.

That was a line certain to make the banty-rooster in Mr. Legget's press-personality happy. Patriotism is never out of place, especially in foreign climes, Lydia judged wisely. She looked back through the pages of her notebook, reading over the comments on the post-Napoleonic government of the Italian provinces as she had observed it, and was about to apply herself to some description of the antiquity and beauty of the northern provinces, when she found her mind had wandered away from her again.

Quite unaccountably, her mind strayed toward Lord Robert Marchman. Since the morning he had appeared with the contessa, the Wingates had heard nothing from him, and Lydia, with time upon her hands to reflect, had decided that the contessa, in that remarkable spirit of mischief that Miss Wingate found at once so charming and exasperating, had merely dragged the English gentleman along, doubtless under strong protest, to visit the so-much *originales américannes*.

Sternly, she reminded herself that the English-

67

man had made his career from seducing and pursuing women (and *what* had been the scandal that drove him from England, she wondered?) that Lord Robert was a self-confessed rake whose profligate habits were the natural consequence of a system of inherited wealth and rank that could only lead to the idle pursuit of the most depraved pleasures; in a system where a gentleman, instead of being put to some suitable occupation or profession where he might advance himself, his family and the commerce of his nation, must needs spend his days upon the selection of a neckcloth, the wagering of fabulous sums upon the most ridiculous circumstances, the idle leisure of far too many balls and parties, and far too many women of dubious virtue—in a system where men who made their fortunes through trade and commerce and their own hard labor and brains were looked down upon and called Cits and Mushrooms, instead of being properly lauded for their endeavors and successes—well! To the strict, American mind of Miss Wingate, it made very little sense indeed to bring up generation upon generation of persons in the best circumstances and education, with the finest opportunities to advance themselves, only to withhold that privilege and challenge by custom. Had she been brought up in the South of America, amidst landed gentry, her attitude might have been different; but Miss Wingate was the daughter of a long line of industrious folk who prided themselves as much upon their enterprise as their morals, and from the custom of having long been the mistress of a large household of her own management and occupation, found it very easy indeed to deplore the scenes of gaiety that she had witnessed in London. If she ever stopped to consider that the management of vast landholdings upon which these fashionable fortunes were based, or that many gentlemen of that class were respectably occupied in such ways as even she must find industrious and unexceptionable, she did not allow those sentiments to enter into her reflections. Her chief though unconscious aim at that point was to stave off the first serious attachment she had ever formed within her very secret heart, and her chief weapon was a formidable intellect based upon democratic and very Quaker principles. For all of her wit, and for all of her yearning toward Worldly Pleasure, Miss Wingate had far too long been in the habit to view herself as Above It All to allow herself to slide into a romantic decline over a libertine's practiced arts. Indeed, she was just considering some sort of squib upon her meeting with the notorious (at least in Como) Ld. R—t M—n and nibbling the end of her pencil when her attention was distracted by her brother.

Jonathan's cough, as she had dreaded, had developed into a slight inflammation of the chest, and although the contessa's excellent Italian physician had pronounced three leeches and rest as the cure, Mr. Wingate had rebelled after only a few days of this treatment, and was now stomping about the house in that sullen, martyred manner that his sister and the Penningtons had come to dread. It was never that he was rude, or precisely out-of-sorts, of course; he simply seemed to withdraw into himself, moving restlessly from room to room, staring longingly out across the blue waters and angelically refusing a plaster upon his chest or just a hot posset such as Friend Hannah had nursed him with in the days of his yellow fever. An outburst, however, was never far from the surface at times of confinement, and the whole household had been treading eggshells for several days, for such a tantrum as Jonathan was capable of, when his short temper was strained to the breaking point, was liable to result in the tedious business of having to hire several new servants.

That Lydia was also beginning to feel that the peace they had originally resorted to Como to attain was becoming downright dull tended to make her own nerves a little sharper, and communication between brother and sister had been, of late, almost elaborately polite and restrained. Cosset her brother Lydia might do, but in her role of surrogate mother to her many sisters and brother, she could also be strict, and from force of habit, Jonathan generally ended either bending to her will or behaving in such an invalidish manner that she was forced to give in to his own, this latter a new trick he had learned in his convalescence.

Hearing Jonathan's footsteps on the terrace behind her, Miss Wingate deliberately pretended a great occupation with her Sketches, until she could determine his mood and act accordingly.

But fortunately, something else had seized upon Mr. Wingate's attention, for as he drew nigh his sister's couch, he waved the telescope in his hand. "Lyddie, have a look at that ketch! Have you ever seen such a *yar* craft on these waters? None of your hogged *puntas* there, but a real boat!"

Miss Wingate obediently took the glass and put it to her eye, picking out the fine lines of a small, well-made sailing vessel under mainsail and bright orange jib, cutting easily through the lapis lazuli waters of the lake. She was enough her grandfather's child to appreciate the size and style of the vessel, so very different from the usual rather awkward, jury-rigged craft that passed for transport upon these waters, and said so in admiring terms.

"By Jove, Lyddie, wouldn't it be just the thing to have such a fine boat as that to sail here? Much better than that piddling gondola that comes with this house!"

"Indeed!" Miss Wingate agreed warmly. "I wonder to whom it belongs—I have not seen it before."

"Either the English or the French, I would say, to judge by the rigging and the bowsprit," Mr. Wingate ventured with some expertise. He continued on, enumerating the finer points of the vessel for several moments in a manner that was much above Miss Wingate's comprehensions of such matters, but she thoughtfully tapped her pencil against her cheek, only half-listening, for she was certain that the yar vessel was making its way into their port.

For a moment, she frowned in puzzlement, for none of their friends were possessed of any craft half so fine, relying, as they did, upon the pokey native craft for transport, but having surrendered the glass to her brother again, she could only hold up a hand against the glare of the lush Italian sunlight and attempt to pick out the sailor of such a craft. All that she perceived, from that distance, was a vague, masculine shape but as the jib was reefed into a billow of orange across the bow, and the boat expertly glided into the mooring at the foot of their steps, she drew in her breath a little, unbelieving that the sailor who so nimbly dropped the mainsail and threw the lines to their boatman could possibly be...Lord Robert Marchman.

But Jonathan confirmed her suspicions with a boyish exclamation of joy. "Famous! It's Marchman! He *is* a complete hand, Lyddie, to sail that boat by himself in such a way!"

"Oh, dear," Miss Wingate said, uncertain whether to make immediately for her bedchamber with a sick headache, or to rise in greeting. Marchman, turning to wave as he gave his instructions to their boatman, seemed oblivious to any sort of discomfort his appearance might be arousing in Miss Wingate's breast. He was stripped to the waist against the heat, like any common sailor, only a spotted tie knotted carelessly about his throat. She was, even from that distance, able to observe that his suntan extended further than his face, and that his tailor had no need to pad his jackets with buckram, nor his shirt shoulders with muslin wadding. As he spoke in rapid Italian to the boatman, he hastily pulled on his shirt, slinging his jacket over his shoulder as he took the steps two by two, approaching them with the sort of smile Lydia had frequently observed upon her young nephews' faces when they had acquired some fine new toy.

"Hallo! Forgive me for just dropping in, as if I were illbred enough to run tame, Miss Wingate, Wingate," he said a trifle breathlessly, shaking their hands and tucking in his shirt tails all at once. "But the contessa told me that you'd been down, Wingate, old man, and I thought, knowing how much you like to sail, that a turn about the

72

lake, down to Como and back, might be just the ticket!"

"She's—well, she's truly *yar*," Jonathan said admiringly. "Marchman, you are a prince of good fellows to think of me, for there is nothing I'd like more. Do you think we could get up a good breeze? She must cut all of ten knots under full sail—"

Marchman shook his head. "We'll soon see, old boy! Thought of you immediately as she came into my possession—daresay there's not another true sailor to be found on this curst pond!"

"And how did you manage to come across such a yar vessel, Lord Robert?" Miss Wingate asked, just a little drily, aware that her hair must look quite disordered in the breeze, and her sprig muslin, although good enough for a morning's sunning on the terrace, was hardly elegant enough to receive company in. Especially if that company doubtless preferred his women in jewels and silks and grosgrains, cut low across the bosom and high about the hem.

But the look Marchman gave her seemed to convey that she was looking splendidly. A roguish grin crossed his face. "Well, ma'am," he said in an amazingly good imitation of her own American accents, "it happened that Billy Austin and myself became involved in a friendly wager last night, and Dame Fortune chose to smile upon me!" He looked, Lydia thought almost sheepish, as if he were not used to the smiles of that one elusive lady, but she refused to be charmed. She could imagine what sort of a wager had passed between the Princess's young, spoiled ward (and there were those who said that Austin was more than her ward) and Lord Robert Marchman, across the waters last night at Villa d'Este.

"Well, then Dame Fortune did right by you, Marchman! M'sister and I have little enough reason to like Mr. Austin," Jonathan said, unable to remove his eyes from the magnificent craft bobbing at mooring.

Lydia flushed slightly at Marchman's inquiring glance. "We chanced to encounter Mr. Austin one afternoon at the contessa's—he made his opinions of Americans unpleasantly clear to all of us," she explained quietly.

"Then you must consider yourself avenged, ma'am," Marchman said, "for it cost him a small fortune to have that boat brought first from England to Milan, then overland to Como. Or rather, I should say, it cost Her Highness a fortune, perhaps."

"A fool, Lord Robert," Miss Wingate said primly, "and his money are soon parted." But still and all she could not help but feel a certain sense of triumph for herself and her brother and had she not been a practical woman, she would have regarded Marchman as a sort of Avenging Knight. Austin's remarks had not only been cruel, they had also been vulgar—and they had hurt. The suspicion that he might have gleaned some knowledge of this unfortunate experience before the Wingates had confided it in him seized her at that moment, particularly when he was grinning at her in such a manner, and the thought that he might attempt to pursue his flirtations with such a gesture made her compress her expression into severe lines.

"I really do not know if *il dottore* Sprangia would

approve of Jonathan's actions in taking such strenuous exercise—" she began, but catching sight of her brother's stormy expression, caught her own tongue. Fresh air and sunshine and, yes, the company of men was exactly what he needed right now. She knew he had spent far too much time being cosseted by females and confined to exactly the sort of inactivity that was liable to lead him into mischief. "But *I* do!" she managed to finish just in time.

"Capital!" Jonathan said. "As if I need you to tell me how to go on, Lyddie—after all, I'm not in cotton wool anymore!" he added, in a show of independence before this older man.

Marchman grinned and clapped him on the shoulder. "Go and fetch your sailing gear, then, Wingate! And we'll be off to Como. I was going in to fetch up my letters, so perhaps there are some errands you might wish me to perform also, Miss Wingate?"

Lydia thought of her Sketches, but they must yet be copied over in her best copperplate before they could be presented to Mr. Legget's editorial scrutiny. "Lord Robert, it is excessively kind of you to offer to take Jonathan sailing with you— there is nothing more that he loves, you know, being brought up almost upon deck, but I am sure that looking after a sickly boy cannot help but be a great bore to you—"

"You mean to such a dissipated rakehell as myself, I trust?" Marchman asked her quizzically, his grin quite taking the sarcasm from his words. "To tell truth, Miss Wingate—and I hope that you and I shall always stand upon truth with one another, I like your brother very much! He reminds me of my own younger brother—and there was a time I was sent down from Winchester with the influenza and forced to spend my days much as he has doubtless been forced to spend his own. Leeches and laudanum and magnesia are no great restoratives for a young man of his age, if you will forgive me from saying so. I speak, you see, from my own experience. Perhaps you might like to accompany us, Miss Wingate, then you could be assured that I would neither lead Jonathan into my more wretched excesses, nor cast his health to the peril of the elements."

Lydia looked at her notebooks. "I really should be writing, you know. The muses, sir, are capricious and—"

"Sitting about all day in this great rambling pile is certainly not what you came to Europe for, Miss Wingate. It seems to me that you cheat yourself as well as Wingate of a great deal of the pleasure of this place."

Lydia's expression was shaded by her large straw hat, but she scraped a sandaled foot along the marble terrace, torn between an urge to deliver Marchman a strong setdown and an acknowledgment of the truth of his remark. She looked down at the lovely little craft, bobbing in the water, and thought of the wind in her face and the swift, light speed of sailing again, so close to what it must be like to fly, and she thought of being in the company of Marchman.

Lydia straightened her shoulders and lifted her chin, the Authoress quite prepared to defend her heart from idle flirtation. As if he had read her thoughts, Marchman pursued. "A writer, if I understand these things correctly, Miss Wingate, is expected to have Experiences from which to draw her material. Only look at Mrs. Shelley!"

"Oh dear!" Lydia said, not quite able to hide the laugh which sprung to her lips. "I suppose, for Jonathan's sake, I ought to come, but I am certain that he will think that I am trying to protect him—"

"Nonsense; I shall tell him, man to man, of course, that you are in as much need of recreation as himself, and that he must come along to protect you from my reputation!"

"Lord Robert!" Miss Wingate exclaimed, but the look that passed between them was of such amusement at the rest of the follies of the world that she meekly said that she would only fetch her reticule and shawl.

Aboard boats, Miss Wingate had frequently had a chance to observe, even the mildest of men became variable buccaneers, Nelsons of the sea, and underwent such transformations of character as to be quite different persons entirely, having little time for females and less for any talk that did not concern the most esoteric of masculine concerns. Jonathan and Lord Robert were no exception to this rule, and Marchman, having placed cushions in the stern seating and assured himself that Miss Wingate had her parasol, her shawl and her comfort assured, immediately turned his attentions to Jonathan, the two of them reefing and luffing and talking of such oracular things as battens, sheers, chimes, oakum, sheets and blocks as they performed various activities designed to set the little ketch under weigh at a very good rate of speed. Lydia, settling back to enjoy alternately the lush scenery and the sweating efforts of someone other than herself, only occasionally asked to take the tiller or grasp a sheet about a winch, was able to watch with amusement as Marchman ordered Jonathan about in a way he would never have accepted from his sister, his man or any of his tutors. Quite forgetting her presence, they talked of such things as cockfighting and boxing and horses, and if Miss Wingate found herself to be adrift in a sea of cant, she was certainly not bored by this most interesting glimpse into what men *really* talked of when there were no ladies present. It had been a long time since she had seen Jonathan so alive and so happily occupied, hopping nimbly across the deck at this task or that, going shirtless and barefooted in the same manner as Lord Robert. She was interested in the discovery that Marchman had sailed the Atlantic waters about his homeland extensively, and that his father's estates marched with the Irish Sea; that he had sailed the Caribbean after selling out of the army and found it was a capital place, and that he had always thought such sailing as Jonathan had done, from Halifax to Spanish Florida, must be interesting. They agreed that the Pacific must be a place to go, and both expressed interest in exploring the Orient, although Marchman protested that Hellespont was not all that Byron had made it out to be, although the Aegean was good enough in its own way. The infamous Barbary pirates, as well as the unfortunate Mr. Lafitte, came under scrutiny and it was discovered that both gentlemen had been fed upon tales of pirates as boys and had often dreamed of unearthing a sea chest full of Spanish treasure.

But it was not long before her thoughts drifted

away again, and she watched the lake shores passing them in all of their beauty. The farther south they sailed, the less mountainous became the region, and the more that lush and beautiful foliage, so brightly flowered, so exotically entangled began to claim the shores, dotted here and there with the villas and houses that must have stood, some of them for two thousand years and might stand for two thousand more. Everywhere there was color—the kaleidoscopic infinity of color was almost breathtaking, and everywhere one looked, there seemed to be as Becker's GUIDE had promised, "one view yet more beautiful than the last, until it must seem as if the very senses would reel from so much visual pleasure as is to be found in this charming region in the warm months of the year." For once, Becker had underestimated, Lydia thought. It was almost *too* beautiful, too lush and fertile, warm and bathed in sunlight—it was almost, she thought with a little blush, *erotic*. This was a countryside made for lovers, a place that must have been created for people to fall in love, to seek one another out like the old Roman Gods were said to have done. From beneath the brim of her hat, she stole a glance at Lord Robert, shirtless, shoeless, his pantaloons rolled to his knees, that spotted kerchief tied about his brown throat, standing on the bow, staring out across the channels. Again, as if he had read her thoughts, he suddenly turned and looked at her. Their eyes met for one second, and then he smiled his boyish smile.

"It is beautiful, is it not, ma'am?" he asked simply, sweeping one arm to indicate the mountains and the water and the terraces of flowers.

Lydia could only nod and pretend a great absorption in the carved ivory handle of her parasol.

Their approach to the city of Como was sighted long before they actually made port. In the distance, the ancient city seemed to rise out of its verdant surrounding vineyards and chestnut trees like an enchanted kingdom. The dome of the marble cathedral, the broken stretches on its ancient walls, the first glimpses of its pale ocher buildings and narrow, transepted arches almost luminous in the sunlight, was splendid to the New World eyes of the Wingates, and even Jonathan was pleased to remark that it was much different in the daylight than upon their first arrival, late at night, after a long and tiring journey by coach through the Swiss border.

Fortunately, there were many foreigners sojourning there in that year after the Great Peace, and the presence of three Anglos attracted little attention as they allowed Lord Robert to guide them from the harbor through the narrow, cobbled streets of the town, peering with unabashed curiosity into the gates which closed the courtyarded houses away from the bustle of the street.

"It is rather like New Orleans," Lydia remarked, particularly attracted by an establishment erected in the best tradition of the High Renaissance, peering unashamedly through the wrought iron gates at the landscaped courtyard where several fountains played merrily among the marble nymphs and fauns.

"I regret to say that I never had the pleasure of actually visiting that city, although I was very near," Lord Robert said.

"Perhaps now you might, that circumstances

are different," Jonathan said good-naturedly, his attention distracted by a public square watering trough where a stream poured from the open mouth of a bearded man carved in marble. "Looks like Blake's idea of God," he remarked, pushing his hands into his pockets. "That is to say—well, one wishes that one could sketch or draw these things, everything is so beautiful."

"Oh, yes!" Lydia breathed, quite taken with the color and variety of marble to be found everywhere in the quiet streets through which they passed.

"I am stunned, Miss Wingate! Surely a lady of your accomplishments must be well armed with watercolors and portfolios!" Marchman said, taking her elbow to move her out of the way of an approaching carriage.

Lydia shook her head. "I cannot even endeavor a straight line, I fear. And we will not talk of my stitchery, if you please. Jonathan is the artist in the family."

Mr. Wingate shrugged. "I can draft a bit—plans and such-like, like any boatbuilder, but looking at this—this beauty, I'm wishing that I had a sketchbook—"

"That can be easily arranged," Lord Robert said comfortably. "I happen to have been given a commission by Lady Anne Hamilton to procure her some papers at a particular stationer. They also sell English periodicals there. But first I thought we might have a luncheon—there is a very good hotel not too far from here, and then we shall do our errands and see the cathedral. I believe their St. Sebastian is considered to be excellent. Quite unexceptionable—I believe the gentleman is wearing a loincloth, Miss Wingate."

Lydia gave him a droll look, but said nothing, for everywhere she looked, there was something else to attract her attentions.

"When one is accustomed to a city where three hundred years are considered ancient, one is quite moved by a city that was flourishing at a time of the Caesars!" she said involuntarily.

"Pity poor Como, once a republic, and now a fiefdom of Milan," Marchman remarked. "Although if you look about you, from time to time you will see the wriggling viper that was the emblem of the Visconti when they ruled the roost."

"Rum sort of fellows, those old Italian princes." Jonathan remarked cheerfully, "Always going to war with each other, or carrying on a *vendetta*, or poisoning each other off in the oddest ways. I wonder if they enjoyed it?"

"Most probably they did. Some people find power a most enjoyable thing," Marchman said thoughtfully. "The Coldstones—that's my tribe, you see, were used to be quite ruthless, I understand. Border feuds and all of that. Probably little better than bandits, most of them, but they had the good sense to choose the right side at Culloden, so there must be something to be said for the prosperity of the wicked. Of course now, they're all quite respectable—excepting yours truly, of course."

It was upon the tip of Miss Wingate's tongue to ask Marchman what he had done that he must be exiled from his cold Northern home, but she thought better of it.

With only a few stops in shops purporting to sell classical antiques and some rather unsanitary-looking relics of long dead saints to the credulous, Miss Wingate insisted that some little souvenirs must be purchased for each of her many sisters, brothers-in-law, and nieces and nephews, and with the aid of Lord Robert's fluent Italian in bargaining for such interesting items as a small head of Diana that would certainly look very lovely in Prudence's drawing room, and a topaz and silver brooch that would certainly please Charity, and a book of scenic etchings that must edify the schoolroom of Verity's large brood, the party at last made their way to a very modern-looking and pleasant hotel whose antecedents were betrayed by the interesting name of Murat.

The French maitre d' who greeted Lord Robert at the doorway with every degree of respectful familiarity immediately made it clear to the Wingates that their host was by no means a stranger to this city or this establishment. Despite what Lydia felt must make a less than fashionable appearance by a sailing party, they were treated with such a degree of civility as the little man led them through the cool marble archways and into the lush beauty of a courtyard spread round with tables covered by striped awning, each discreetly made private from the others by hedges and shrubbery and the omnipresent flowering trees and bushes circling around a large and graceful fountain set in the center of the yard, she thought that she might have died and passed into heaven, as Hannah would have said.

They were not the only diners present, she noted as a chair was placed beneath her by a wigged footman. Indeed, this seemed to be a very popular spot, for an international babel of language played a contrapuntal harmony to the music of the bubbling fountains.

"I hope you do not object to dining *alfresco*," Lord Robert said, and Lydia wondered at the manner in which he had transformed a sadly wrinkled shirt and a spotted kerchief, with only the aid of a well-tailored coat of blue superfine, into the very model of what a gentleman should wear to a luncheon in Como.

"Not at all! Lyddie, this is famous! If only we had known about this place when we came into Como, we should not have had to put up at that miserable inn!"

"It is all that is lovely," Miss Wingate said sincerely. "We are very much in your debt, Lord Robert, for being so kind as to become our *cicerone*."

"The pleasure is mine," Marchman said in a very gentlemanly fashion. "Should you care for seafood? I can recommend the cuisine here—French, but the chef was one in the service of the Empress Josephine."

Lord Robert ordered a bottle of light German hock and procured lemonade for Miss Wingate with a twinkle in his eye.

After due consultation with the maitre d', a menu consisting of a watercress soup, *trifle aspérge*, *mussels Napoléon* and some dish with what appeared to be shell-shaped pasta, a light cream sauce and tiny bits of delicately spiced fish whose name Miss Wingate was never quite certain of were elaborately presented.

To her surprise, she found that she was very hungry, and was even more gratified to see that Jonathan was making a good work of his own meal also.

Throughout the meal, Lord Robert managed to entertain both of his guests with an amusing flow of small talk about the history of the various ruling families of the Italian city-states, and Miss Wingate, who had suspected that her friend was a trifle more bookish than he liked to allow others to believe, watched him with considerable amusement, intensified, perhaps, by the amount of hock she was consuming with her *cavatelle*. In fact, she was so occupied with the conversation, in which she was taking a very lively part, that she did not notice a voluptuous female in ruby red and a large, fashionably plumed hat of *gros de Naples* seating herself directly in their line of vision across the courtyard, in the company of a much decorated and gilt-braided military gentleman, until Jonathan gave Lord Robert's sleeve a tug.

"Marchman, old man, do believe I see Baron and Baroness Galtzalter over there, waving at us."

Marchman's smile stiffened slightly. "Yes, I do see them. You will excuse me? I will go and make myself civil to them."

"Of course," Lydia said a trifle stiffly, sipping her wine.

Jonathan watched as Marchman crossed the courtyard, bowing to the old Baron, and kissing the Baroness' hand. "That's supposed to be his flirt, you know! Must say she's a very dashing piece!"

"Yes, I suppose so, in that rather overblown way of some Frenchwomen," Lydia replied cautiously, trying not to stare at the dark, lush beauty. We must be much of an age, she thought, and yet she seems so much—more sophisticated. More in his style, you mean, what she was pleased to term her Authoress voice whispered inside, very tartly.

The Baroness was laughing at something Lord

Robert had said, twisting a long strand of pearls about her low-cut neckline as if to call attention to the charms reposing there. Whatever Marchman had said, it evidently passed over the old Baron's head, for he merely shook his mustaches, looked over at the Wingates and rose, doing what Lydia did not doubt that he felt to be the courtesy of exchanging a few words with the Americans.

It was indeed so, and though his English was almost as bad as their German, he managed to spill out some anecdote about his experiences with the Hessian Army in the Revolutionary War, evidently under the assumption that the Wingates were Tories. Since it was as dull as it was incomprehensible, Lydia was able to allow her eye to wander toward the other table, where Lord Robert was plucking a flower from a shrub behind him, and pressing it, in the most flirtatious manner, into the Baroness's hands.

If she had believed for a moment that her sense of pique stemmed not from the impropriety of such an incident, but from a strong wish that Lord Robert would press a flower into her own hands, perhaps she would not have allowed her glass to be refilled once again.

She almost choked over her wine, however, when the Baroness looked over and smiled upon her in the most condescending way possible, one long slender hand twining itself insidiously into Lord Robert's for just a second. Since Marchman's back was turned away from her, Lydia could not see *his* expression, but her imagination allowed her to *guess* exactly what sort of an exchange was being made between that couple.

It was fortunate that Jonathan, who had always

been taught to be polite to his elders, was giving over his attention to the elderly Hessian Baron's military memories, and had managed, without causing the old officer any grave discomfort over the true status of the Wingate Family in the American Revolution, to bring his memory toward the more fortunate events in which he had played his role at Waterloo under Blücher. Since Jonathan's German was tolerably better than Lydia's, the Prussian officer's mustaches were directed mostly in Mr. Wingate's direction, and he called for another bottle of the *liebfräumilch* hock before transforming the cutlery into Napoleon's troops and the bread baskets into those of Wellington and Blücher.

With rather more interest than she wished she was displaying, Miss Wingate continued her observation of Marchman and the lovely Baroness over her wine glass, wondering rather wistfully why nature had seen to make her a rather washed-out blonde of spare figure instead of a raven-tressed, black-eyed beauty with all the beauty's arts of flirtation at easy hand. At that moment, Miss Wingate might have seriously considered trading all of her Intelligence and Wit for just one iota of the Baroness' obvious physical charms. So long had Miss Wingate stood aside for her younger and prettier sisters, she had never really had the time or the inclination to consider herself much above the ordinary. A chatelaine, a surrogate mother, a hostess and an Authoress, yes, but never a Beauty. Years of putting her sisters before herself on the dance floor and in the drawing room might have made her an excellent educationist in those arts which must please men, but faced, for the first time in thirty-one years of composed living, with the ugly specter of jealousy—and over *such* a man and *such* a woman at that—all of her Quaker training rose up to confront her with guilt at such an unbecoming emotion, only to find itself doing battle with all of her natural instincts as a warm and needful woman. The end result was that, as always, her commonsense and her humor restored her (but not without cost to her Wretched Pride) and she bestowed a rather bleary smile upon the Baroness.

Whatever passed between Marchman and the Baroness after that, Lydia was not quite certain. Politeness dictated that she turn her attentions to the Baron's very dull and almost totally incomprehensible story, and since Lydia had had a great deal of practice with her grandfather's friends in listening to very dull and nearly incomprehensible stories, she managed to give the appearance of being interested in the defeat of Bonaparte based solely upon the fact that the Emperor was suffering from disordered bowels upon the fateful day of Waterloo. It was not what she wished to hear, even as an Authoress, but the Baron was so stricken in years of military training as well as wine that he seemed not to care for the delicacy of ladies, and Jonathan was too sure of his sister to attempt to turn the conversation in another direction, merely grinning at her in just such a devilish way.

It was therefore almost a relief for her when Marchman and the Baroness suddenly appeared at the table, declaring that the two parties should combine for cappucino and pastries and perhaps just a bit more wine. If Marchman looked a little tense about the eyes and mouth as he seated the Baroness, her flower now tucked in her cleavage, between her husband and Miss Wingate, Lydia chose to put it down to the fact that he had not wished his *tête à tête* with the lady interrupted. For her part, Baroness Galtzalter was all amiability and smiles, complimenting Lydia upon her sprig muslin dress and cottage bonnet, and nearly rendering Jonathan speechless with a dazzling smile and a droll French compliment upon the handsome masculinity of *l' homme américain*, as well as with the heavy muskiness of her scent, thicker than the perfume of the flowers all around them.

The conversation, conducted in three languages, did not truly lend itself to anything deeper than the beauty of the area and the charm of the company to be found upon the lake that summer, subjects upon which all could agree. In company, the Baroness' manners were not so ramshackle as to allow her the slightest degree of over-familiarity with Marchman, Lydia noted, but she did once or twice catch the woman looking at her brother as if he were a succulent piece of beef and she a starving lioness.

Clearly, the Baroness was in complete control of the situation, for she rather sweetly quizzed Miss Wingate, was it true then, as Lord Robert said, that she was an Authoress? A fact to which Miss Wingate was forced to agree with a little more emphasis that she might have wished. The Baroness declared that she herself had never been able to put pen to paper for much more than a gaming vow, but had known Madame de Staël when she had been at the Imperial Court, a most interesting woman, did not Miss Wingate agree? Miss Wingate, who thought Madame de Staël a little too indiscreet in her enthusiasms, politely agreed that she was an interesting female and an agreeable conversationalist. But, added the Baroness, fingering the flower in her bosom, a sadly homely woman.

Miss Wingate could not bear to look at Lord Robert, but a slight flush rose to her cheeks, as if by calling Madame de Staël homely, the Baroness had implied that all females who wrote must needs compensate for a lack of beauty. Slowly, she placed her wine glass upon the table and took the side of her fork, cutting delicately into the pastry before her, leveling her gaze at the Baroness. "Queen Elizabeth of England you know, was no beauty, but she once declared, Baroness, that such was her cunning, that if she were turned out of her Kingdom in her petticoat, she would prosper anywhere in Christendom," Lydia said quietly.

For a single fraction of a second, the Baroness' lovely face allowed a shadow of sadness to pass over its features, and she glanced at her elderly husband, his mind clearly somewhere many years ago, many miles away. As swiftly as it had come, the look was gone again, and the hard brittleness had settled upon her dark features again, but Lydia knew that her own barb had gone home, and she felt an unexpected pity for this woman, married for money and position to a man as old and older than Grandfather Wingate whose loneliness and boredom must be the force which drove her into intrigues with men like Lord Robert, into flirtations with boys like Jonathan. She had understood, and when her beauty faded, she would be as vain and empty as poor Princess Caroline.

But Lydia did not want to feel sorry for this woman who so clearly beheld Miss Wingate to be an Anecdote; after all, *she* had Lord Robert, and Lydia Wingate had...her writing.

The remainder of the party passed off without too much incident, and if it was a little noisier, because of the forced gaiety of both ladies, than it really needed to be, not even Lydia could have said that it surpassed the bounds of propriety. The bad moment had passed, and as if to compensate for it, everyone, even the Baron, became more jocular, and Lord Robert did his best to keep the trilingual conversation light and amusing for all of them, often deliberately mistranslating a phrase or two for everyone's amusement.

If as they rose from the table upon the end of the repast, neither lady quite wished to fall into the other's arms, they had achieved a tacit respect for one another that Lydia, at least, hoped would last, so that they might at least treat one another with civility, if not great friendship. But she had a strong intuition that the Baroness was not fond of other females at all. Besides, she told herself firmly, it was none of her concern whom Lord Robert chose to make the object of his *affaires*.

They were just passing from the courtyard back into the hotel again when Miss Wingate heard her name being called in the accents of her native land, and she did not need Jonathan's muttered "Oh, Lord!" to tell her to whom that familiar voice belonged.

"Why fancy that, Isaac! Did you ever expect to see Jon and Lydia Wingate in Como, of all places?"

A rather stout dowager in a dove-gray turban and a severe traveling dress of purple merino was making her majestic way across the marble tiles toward them, followed by her equally rotund spouse.

"Why, it is Mr. and Mrs. Schuyler, Jonathan," Lydia exclaimed in rather too hearty accents, her heart sinking at the sight of Mr. Charles Schuyler's brother and sister-in-law, whose very sight was sufficient to recall to her memory the unprepossessing countenance and style of the almost forgotten suitor left behind in New York. "How do you do, ma'am, sir? We certainly did not expect to see you abroad! That is—we have had no word that you had planned a journey!"

Mrs. Schuyler looked down her Roman nose at Miss Wingate, taking in every detail of her sadly crumpled muslin, her hat set at a rather rakish angle, and her suspiciously foreign looking company. If Lydia had not been precisely drunk, she now felt herself, beneath that disapproving dowager's stare, to be so.

"And Mr. Wingate also! How very pleasant a surprise to see you looking so well, Mr. Wingate. From the last report we had, you were still feeling quite peaked," Mrs. Schuyler said in her funereal tones, matching the Baroness's amused stare with one of her famously frigid glares. "Well, I must say, we were wondering who was making up such a merry party on the courtyard—we could quite hear it within the dining room. We do not believe in eating outdoors. Mr. Schuyler feels that it is quite injurious to the health and digestion. Well, we shall certainly have something to write home to New York about, meeting you in such a fashion, Miss Wingate!"

"Now we *are* in the soup," Jonathan murmured dismally.

Five

There was nothing for Lydia to do except make all of the ill-assorted gathering known to one another. If anything, she reflected unhappily, Charles' brother and his wife (née Cornelia VanWyck) were even more disapproving of her SKETCHES and the subsequent scandal than Grandfather had been. And she knew for a fact that Mrs. Biddle Schuyler was the grandest purveyor of gossip in New York City.

The sight of a Jonathan looking healthier than any time since his yellow fever, albeit a bit disheveled, Miss Wingate a little sunburned, slightly tacky in dress and in company with persons whose rank and wealth did not deter them from having the unfortunate status of *foreigners*—indeed, in the Schuyler mind titles and rank could only increase the likelihood of something not quite *correct* upon them—would certainly be duly reported home. A VanWyck of Van Wyck married to Biddle

Schuyler was after all, not expected in the least to be impressed with a sunburned duke's son and a rather senile Prussian Baron, while the Baroness, seen through their eyes, Lydia thought unhappily, could only be castigated as an Adventuress.

What the Duke's son, and the Baron and Baroness must make of such a pair as the Biddle Schuylers was far more than Lydia even wished to contemplate. She cast an appealing look at Jonathan, but he seemed to find a marble cupid upon the frescoes of far more interest than the company.

After acknowledging the introductions with a sniff, Mrs. Biddle Schuyler seemed perfectly ready to consign them all to some place outside of her knowledge.

"Pray, ma'am, tell me how you left my grandfather and the Family?" Lydia immediately demanded. "I worry that he will not go on very well without me to hold house for him you know, and Verity's youngest had the mumps when last we heard."

Mrs. Schuyler inclined her head slightly. "Mr. Wingate is a very remarkable gentleman for a septuagenarian, and holds house tolerably well. His health is, as always, brisk," she continued with faint disapproval for the liveliness of a man of seventy-one summers. "And his mind as clear as water, of course. I understand that one after the other of your sisters has attempted to lure him to her household, but he refuses to leave Wingate Place, and has hired and fired a series of housekeepers." She made a tsking sound. "I must say," she added grudgingly, "that no one holds Wingate House as well as you have done, Lydia."

"He made a pile on that Erie Transport System," Mr. Schuyler put in with a slight shake of his head. "Saw him at the Fifth Avenue Hotel and told him he was senile to sink his dollars into that bubble, but he bid anyway, and made thrice his investment within a week." There was a slight trace of resentment in his voice, and Lydia guessed, correctly, that her prospective brother-in-law had been one of those who had not seen the glorious future in steam engine boats.

"Grandfather has never lacked for shrewdness," she said a little stiffly. "And I should never call him senile."

"Grand's sharp as a tack," Jonathan told the marble cupid. "Not like some I could mention."

"Undoubtedly. But you just wait until one of those bellowing boats explodes on the Hudson, then you'll see! If God had wanted men to travel about in steamboats, He would have given them engines," he finished somewhat pompously, hooking his thumbs into his waistcoat.

Jonathan had that look in his eye, and Lydia swiftly turned the direction of the conversation. "But I have been so anxious to know of the Family that I have not even inquired as to what brings you to Como."

"The silk trade, Lydia, the silk trade. Why these Eyetalians just about have it wrapped up. Makin' a deal to import fifty thousand bolts a year, and if they don't rob your eyes, they'll steal you blind. But I said—" Here Mr. Biddle Schuyler, who was by way of being one of the premiere importers of New York City, launched into what appeared to Lydia to be the beginning of a long and totally incomprehensible description of his business that

96

threatened to be even more dull than the Baron's reenactment of Waterloo.

"Well, that is all very interesting!" she managed to interject when he had paused for breath, "and indeed you must tell us more about it at some other time! Perhaps you'd come to dinner some evening, if you plan to make a stay here?"

"Lyddie," Jonathan murmured beneath his breath, but Miss Wingate nobly ignored the fact that she shared his sentiments exactly.

"Perhaps we shall," Mrs. Schuyler said with a great deal of condescension. "The Hotel Murat is of course in the first style of luxury—for these parts, at any rate, although I am certain that the chambermaids steal and one could certainly wish that foreigners would make more use of soap and water....

"*Papists*," she added in a slightly lower tone, as if that explained it all. "You have to watch all of these people, all the time or they will try to cheat you. Well!" She drew herself up to her full height and smiled a wintry smile. "I took care of that soon enough! I do not think we will make out a long stay, but of course we do wish to see the antiquities while we are here—only a short visit, but one must remember that one represents America abroad and maintain the strictest propriety. We shall call upon you. I believe we have your direction." With another nod, she sniffed again at the rest of the company and proceeded up the staircase, loudly complaining to Biddle that she was certain the beds had not been aired properly and that it was not at all what one was used to.

Lydia sighed with relief. She was a little surprised to find herself more in charity with Marchman and the Galtzalters than the Schuylers. At home, they had always seemed so proper; encountering them abroad, she was slightly embarrassed by their provincial bigotry.

"Reminds me exactly of my Aunt Penistone," Marchman said, a slight twinkle in his eye, as if, again, he had guessed at Lydia's thoughts. "She's certain that no place outside of Bath is entirely safe."

"That's Mrs. Schuyler exactly," Jonathan exclaimed. "Lord, Lyddie, wouldn't you put them off somehow, tell 'em we were going to Greece tomorrow or something?"

"You know very well Jonathan that I would not," Miss Wingate said severely. "That would never do! They are friends of the Family!"

"Well, I wish they were not! You wait and see what she goes home and tells Grandfather—"

"We'll discuss it later, Jonathan," Lydia said severely, rustling out the wrinkles in her skirt. "We need only have them to dinner, and then you may be ill, if you wish!"

"I don't believe I'll have to pretend," Jonathan muttered. As they had spoken, the party had been moving in the direction of the doorway toward the street.

As they stood politely telling the Baron how much they had enjoyed his company, Lydia was certain that she overheard Marchman and the Baroness murmuring about meeting at a certain time and day. So, she thought, this is where they have their assignations. She wished that her Authoress voice would allow her to accept it just a *little* less jealously. After all, what the Baroness and Marchman did, if discreetly conducted, was none of *her* business. She had been abroad long enough to understand that infidelity, especially in European marriages of arrangement, was the accepted norm, and that all over Como, other couples were stealing just such moments together. Everyone knew and no one discussed it, but it was certainly not like New York, where there were women who were *not* ladies; or at least she naively believed that to be the case.

She was able to shake the Baroness's hand with a cool civility as they parted with insincere murmurs that they really must call upon one another, their villas so close, but she rather thought that lady took Jonathan's hand just a shade too long, and gazed into his eyes with far too fetching a look. And suddenly a new cloud appeared upon Miss Wingate's horizon. Jonathan was her younger brother by ten years; although she was wise enough to know that he was a healthy enough young man to take a decided interest in the opposite sex, his affections had always been for young ladies of his own age, as naive and inexperienced as himself. But standing there in the hot Italian sun she saw her brother, truly *saw* him for the first time in many years. He was no longer a schoolboy but a young man. The traces of his illness had left him with a slightly more mature look than most men of his youth, but he was not, she decided, unattractive, and certainly there was something of his mother's beauty about him that must make him attractive to women. The idea that she might be called upon to protect him from the advances of an Older Woman had never occurred to her before, but suddenly confronted with the problem, she knew instinctively that it was a situation Grandfather, and not she, should have handled long ago, for Jonathan was not about to listen to an older sister upon such a delicate subject. It fluttered across her mind that Marchman was exactly the person who would be able to handle that role, and at that point, the irony of the situation struck her so forcibly that she had to suppress a laugh.

Marchman, offering her his arm as she opened her parasol, gave her a quizzical look, but fortunately did not ask her what had caused her suppressed mirth. Perhaps he guessed correctly, perhaps not; Lydia was never certain about such things with Marchman, but his uncanny knack of seeming to read her mind at times discomfited her for a little space of time.

However, nothing could have been more exceptionally civil than the way in which he patiently adopted the role of *cicerone* in showing the Wingates about the beautiful and very ancient city of Como. Several times, viewing an historic building or strolling through one of the exceptionally lovely Cathedrals, she was certain that he must be bored almost to tears and deeply regretting his offer to show them the city, but if such were the case, he was far too well-bred to betray the slightest impatience or restiveness as the Wingates viewed everything that was there to view, from altar pieces to architecture, both Italian Gothic and Renaissance, and was certainly more interesting than any guidebook, for in spite of himself, he betrayed a great deal of knowledge about the history of Italy both ancient and modern. Such a fund of expansive information could have only been derived from serious study, and again, Miss Wingate was forced to alter her opinion that Marchman led a life of idle pleasure.

For her part, she was also much too well-bred to make any sort of comment upon this unexpected and very pleasant facet of her guide, but within the cool confines of the Broletto, when he briefly and in a most interesting manner, informed them of Como's origins as a sovereign republic, before it had been seized by the Visconti, she must have cast him a look, for he broke off and shook his head slightly.

"I am afraid I bore you both. My tutor was an excellent man—he had to have been such to have filled me with an interest in history! You have no idea how many long and tedious journeys I have whiled away, lost in a book."

Jonathan protested that Marchman was not at all boring, and though he himself was not bookish in the least, he imagined it might not be such a bad thing if it allowed one to understand so much about one's surroundings.

Miss Wingate again suppressed a smile, and quietly expressed admiration of the variety and color of the marbles which had been employed in the construction of this thirteenth-century edifice.

The rest of their tour proceeded in the same spirit, and after a small repast of Italian ices, the frozen base of this delicate treat being brought down from the high mountains, in a very charming little cafe with pots of bright geraniums, striped awnings and a large and very contented tabby cat who seemed to take a liking to them, they returned to the boat.

The sun was slowly setting over the mountains,

spreading a brilliant orange and pink fire across both the sky and the lake.

Again, Miss Wingate was settled in the stern with her cushions, and her purchases stowed neatly away beneath her seat. This time, she was glad enough to allow Jonathan and Marchman to sail the boat and talk of masculine pursuits, for it had been a long time since she had spent such an active day, and the wine, which had been playing in her head all afternoon, gave her a sleepy sense of perfect contentment. Not even the unhappy thought of dining with the Schuylers at some nebulous and hopefully very distant date could quite depress her spirits. Indeed, it had been a long time since she had been in such a glorious sunset, in scenes of such beauty, and, Lydia admitted to herself, stealing a look beneath her lashes up at Marchman's profile as he took the helm, in such good company.

As if he had felt her look, Lord Robert glanced around at her for a second, and smiled. "This is the time of day that I like the best, wherever I am—sunsets are always somehow more beautiful to me than sunrises." There was a faint trace of yearning in his voice, as if he spoke more to himself than to her, and he looked out across the bow again, setting his jaw. "The sunsets in Italy are beautiful, but not as beautiful as the sunsets at home, over the hills—nothing but hard, barren crags and cairns perhaps, but home..."

Miss Wingate preserved her silence, unwilling to intrude into her companion's thoughts. Somehow she sensed that any attempt to draw him out upon his homeland would meet with a civil but firm rebuff. Whatever the scandal had been that had driven him from England, it must have been very serious, she thought, for never before had she heard a sailor speak with such longing of a distant home. Sailors, she knew from her own experience, always spoke of other ports, exotic places, future sojourns; rarely of the places from which they had sailed away to escape…and she wondered, but kept her silence, only watching his rather surprisingly gentle profile, relaxed and freed of the tight and cynical lines he usually adopted in company—like a mask…so very much like a mask, she thought, and turned away from him, as if she had been given an unexpected and intrusive glimpse into the very secret soul of another, unsuspecting human being. There was enough of the cynic in Miss Wingate's character to make her recognize the hidden undercurrents in another's outward appearances.

Slowly, the dusk stretched between the strip of mountain that separated sky and water, deepening from the fires of orange and rose to long purple fingers and azure casts. Along the hillsides, the docks of the villas and houses which dotted the shore of the lake were beginning to light up from within, rather, Miss Wingate allowed herself poetically, like the jack o'lanterns she and her sisters had carved at Harvest Home when they were children. The yellow and green lamps at the foot of each villa awaited arrivals, signaled departures. This was a place where life did not begin until late afternoon, after the worst heat of the day had passed; now the fashionable internationals of Como would just be beginning their days, really, with a dinner that should have been luncheon and a supper that should have been dinner, served nearly at midnight. All morning they would dance or play cards or perhaps merely sit in company with one another, and when the dawn was breaking over the eastern mountains, they would sleepily sail their way home again, to sleep then rise again at noon or later to begin the rounds again.

As they passed the imposing structure of the Villa d'Este, quite the largest and most ornate mansion on the lake, the red lights of the punts and gondolas, just setting out, began to glow in the heavily gathering dusk, almost a full darkness now that summer was growing old.

A strong and steady breeze blew down from the mountains, and Lydia wrapped her thin cashmere shawl a little tighter about her shoulders, feeling the chill of the wind through her thin muslin gown.

Jonathan, who had been setting the jib, clambered down the deck, and Marchman relinquished his place at the helm. "Bring her in, Wingate!" He called cheerfully, and Jonathan, barely concealing his pleasure in the older man's confidence in his ability, nodded and grasped the wheel.

With a little sigh, Marchman flung himself down beside Lydia on the stern seat, curled a sheet neatly into a coil, tightened it at the winch, and began, with some difficulty, to attempt to strike a spark from his tinderwheel in order to illuminate his stern running light, a brass-bound kerosene lantern, held between his knees as he attempted to strike the spark from the flint against the wind.

"Oh, dear," Miss Wingate said, and moving closer, wrapped her shawl about both of them to provide a shield against the breeze that continually extinguished the flame.

Marchman leaned against her, turning his own body so as to provide a further screening, fumbling with both wick and flintwheel.

In such a close proximity of contact, Miss Wingate was not only aware of the smooth hardness of muscle beneath Marchman's coat, but also of the faint and not unpleasant—not unpleasant at all—scent of the man himself, of sunburned skin, good leather, and that peculiarly attractive smell of clean, ironed linen from his shirt. Indeed, she was conscious of a sudden and quite improper impulse to want to bury her face into the clean front of his chest, where just a bit of golden hair was visible above his opened Byronic collar.

"Oh, dear," she repeated, trying to force herself to deal with the task at hand, that of lighting the stern running light, holding her shawl open about them both like a set of wings, leaning against the wind, watching the lines and planes of his face glimmering in the dull flicker of the recalcitrant firewheel, his expression one of complete concentration upon the task at hand.

Miss Wingate was not naive in the formalities of romance; having assisted at the birth of most of her numerous nephews and nieces, having patiently listened to the most intimate marital problems of her sisters and having had to explain these facts of life to them one after the other through most of her own growing years, she was aware of the deeper passions between men and women, but her own experience in these deeper passions was sadly limited. When she had first let down her skirts and done up her hair, she had, of course, been kissed, and like most young people of that age of first emerging into the adult world had even experimented a little further. But only *so far*, of course, and always in the greatest haste and stealth, in some dark corner at a party, or a stolen moment alone in the park or the parlor. But she was intelligent enough to comprehend that what she was feeling at that very moment for March-man was far from the way she felt when Mr. Charles Schuyler would have been substituted in his place, and not only was that feeling quite *novel* to her experience, it was also most unusually pleasurable. Had Lord Robert been less conver-sational, less *simpatico* with her as a person, she knew that she would not be experiencing these very unmaidenly feelings, and wishing that that *damned* spark would never strike! Well, at least not the one in the lantern...

But, perversely, the wick chose just that mo-ment to catch fire, and in the flare of the light, as her eyes met his, Miss Wingate was forced to look away instantly, less he see her feelings reflected therein.

Without looking at him, however, she had the oddest feeling that he was studying her for just one second before she again wrapped her shawl about herself and he leaned away, clipping the lantern to its slide.

She found the moon, just beginning its waning, to be of the utmost interest, and looked upwards at that silver-gold globe, hanging just above the mountains, all the while aware that though he had moved to the opposite end of the seat, he was still regarding her. At that moment, she would have traded back the very best and wittiest of her

SKETCHES to see the expression on his face, and to know what his thoughts might be, but even had she been immodest enough to steal a glance in his direction, and she would not, could not do so, for it went against every carefully ingrained instinct of her rigid upbringing to be so bold, she knew perfectly and commonsensically well that his features were obscured by darkness.

The Baroness, Lydia thought rather resentfully, now the Baroness would lean back against the cushions and turn herself just so, displaying all of her charms to the fullest, and without so much as a word, only that lazy, dark-eyed smile, deliver her message with perfect clarity. For a flickering moment, Miss Wingate wished she were the Baroness. But as soon as the idea struck her mind, it also struck her humor, for the picture of Miss Lydia Hope Jane Elizabeth Wingate of Wingate House, Cherry Street, New York City, positively *lolling* against some cushions, with her hair a fright and a sober sprig muslin morning gown, with a seductive smile upon her rather serious face was truly ridiculous. And not at all in her style, her Authoress voice added mentally, Lydia Wingate, you've had too much sun and too much hock! Remember who you are! Jamie Legget does not publish sketches from women like the Baroness Galtzalter.

But still....

"You must be cold," Marchman's voice, rather gruff, cut across her thoughts as he stripped off his coat and placed it impersonally as a footman, across her shoulders, standing up and moving forward to perform some mysterious and, he knew, totally unnecessary function with the mainsail.

Miss Wingate touched the bath superfine with the tips of her fingers, and unconsciously perhaps, wrapped the overlarge garment a little closer about herself. It smelled of those same exotic masculine scents of clean shirts and leather as its owner, who now stood in the bow, looking out across the waters into the darkness, where there was nothing that the eye could truly see, the wind ruffing through his shirt and his hair. He lifted his face toward the sky for a moment, one hand clutching a shroud, as if he were greeting the moon, then shook his head and quickly began to reef the mainsail.

It was only then that Lydia noticed that they were approaching the docking steps of Villa Solario, and with a slight letdown, she instinctively knew that Friend Hannah and Friend George would have been watching for them from the terrace, certain that they had either been drowned or waylaid by *bandetti* in Como, and would even now be making ready to come down and bring herself and Jonathan in to their dinner as if they were two children who had played too long outside. And with that thought, all the other realities came crashing back upon her again; there was a stack of mail beneath the seat that she had picked up at the receiving office, most of it directed in the various hands of the Family. Without even as much as breaking a seal, Lydia was fairly certain that she could guess the contents and style of each one of those dutiful epistles, but somehow news of her Grandfather's latest business triumph and the various plagues and joys of her sisters, their husbands and their numerous offspring did not quite make itself as attractive or as strongly redolent of certain homesickness and pages of re-turn-posted sisterly advice as it once had done, not so very long ago. Perhaps as much to her own surprise as to theirs, her various Family was discovering that it was quite possible to manage a way out of their tangles and tribulations without her guiding hand. For the first time since her parents' death, Lydia Wingate had almost been freed from the responsibilities that had played so large a part in creating her secondary role as an authoress and her primary role as a professional aunt. Now that Jonathan was so much stronger and no longer in need of nursing, she had also been freed of that burden; and quite suddenly, freed of the somewhat restricted (and yes, rather provincial) society of New York, set adrift in the Old World, so wise in so many ways beyond her years and so naive in others that fell easily to youth, Lydia was beginning to feel as if she was in the process of becoming a stranger to all that was old and familiar and respectable about herself.

Only a month ago, she would have greeted even so stuffy a couple as the Schuylers with welcome relief to see a familiar American face.

But now, as Marchman and Jonathan were mooring the boat, she sat as if in a daze in the stern, suddenly confronted with the novel thought that she cared not a whit if her little teapot tempest over the SKETCHES had died down or not, nor that she should be grateful that Charles Schuyler was willing to overlook the fact that she had been eccentric enough to publish, nor that Wingate House was being sadly mismanaged in her absence, or that Prudence could not possibly travel to Charleston with her Harvey unless Lydia would come and supervise her nursery in her absence.

Hearing Friend George's voice at the top of the stairs, slightly reproachful, overanxious, slightly resentful of this beautiful and exotic place and its influence over his charges, Miss Wingate suddenly wanted to cry, to shout, to scream and to forever protest the role that her life had confined upon her.

She knew what she did *not* want in an illumination as sudden and clear as the flare of the wick of the running light.

Even as she gathered up her purchases and parcels, and made ready to hand them over to Jonathan on the dock, she heard Friend Hannah not far behind, carrying her pelisse, already worrying that the temperamental Italian cook had ruined the dinner with too much spice and sauce, and she heard herself, as if she were someone else, moving through long habit, of the motions of soothing, comforting, setting to rights, smoothing out her hair and her skirts as if she could smooth away this sudden and unexpected emergence of open rebellion against everything she had been reared to believe in.

A month ago she would have preferred to eat dinner with the Schuylers, properly under a roof, rather than with an elderly Prussian Baron, his rather risqué Baroness and a self-acknowledged rakehell in the bright sunlight of a courtyard.

What had happened to bring her up so short, she wondered, suddenly conscious of the fact that she did not want to eat a plain American dinner, that she did not want to have to read all of those letters and compose suitable replies, that she did not want to pass the remainder of the evening playing the pianoforte while Jonathan gazed moodily out of the window, that she did not want to be put to bed with the motherly admonitions of Friend Hannah, clucking over her sunburn and her tangled hair.

"Miss Wingate?"

Lydia snapped out of her brown study and looked up at the dock where Lord Robert, faintly outlined in the dim glow of the lantern, stood tall and waiting, his face hidden in shadow, his arms outstretched to lift her the short distance from gunwale to steps.

As he picked her up in his arms as if she were no heavier than an eiderdown quilt and gently set her upon her feet on land, Miss Wingate realized quite suddenly, not with very much astonishment, that she knew what she *did* want.

The unthinkable, the unattainable, the impossible. It did not even bear consideration that his arms lingered just a second too long about her waist, or that she felt a little breathless in the space of that second.

Very quickly, she removed his coat from about her shoulders, handing it back to him, forcing herself to smile. "Thank you so very much, Lord Robert—you have been so kind—"

"The pleasure, Miss Wingate, was mine, truly."

"Indeed, Marchman! Thank you so much! She is a yar boat and was such a yar day, and well, I don't know when I've had so much fun since I left school! Will you stay to dinner, sir?"

Miss Wingate held her breath, looking away, wishing that Friend Hannah would not choose that moment to insist that she take off that shawl and put on her pelisse, nice and warm.

Lord Robert shook his head. "No, I thank you. I have another engagement this evening."

Lydia thought that she knew with whom that engagement was, and where it would be. Breaking free of Hannah's ministrations, she suddenly picked up her skirts and ran up the steps, calling over her shoulder, "Excuse me! I seem to have developed the most dreadful headache—too much sun—thank you, Lord Robert, no Hannah, I do not need my pelisse!"

"Ah," said her Authoress voice inside her head, "but you do know what you do need, don't you, Lyddie! Foolish, foolish girl!"

Indeed, Miss Wingate told herself, running into the house. But she did not cry. Lydia Wingate had not cried in ten years. There had been no time for her own tears. And now, when it seemed that she had all the time in the world, tears were not enough.

She would write. That always helped before.

But somehow, Lydia knew she would not write a line that night.

Six

Grandfather was full of his latest triumph with the Erie Transport System; Mr. Fulton was a fine fellow, full of what it took; he had discharged his third housekeeper and rather querulously wanted to know where Lyddie had put his leather-bound copies of Virgil, and had so many anxious questions about the state of his heir's health and so much advice to render his eldest granddaughter upon this subject that she quickly turned to the letters from her sisters, reading them in descending order of age. Prudence, expecting her fifth little Clinton, had a houseful of guests and had been repulsed by the slavery system she had witnessed in South Carolina; Charity was still doctoring herself against all manner of imaginary complaints which she had forced Lydia to pay several lire to read about, and *her* husband, he of the philandering nature, was prospering in his land speculations in the Ohio Territory. Since Charity also added a line or two to the effect that Lydia's *transgression* was spoken less and less of these days since Miss Vandergelt had eloped with a penniless schoolmaster from Baltimore, Miss Wingate was able to toss Charity away with her grandfather and Prudence. Verity, only married to her William a year, blushingly confided that she had laid off nursing since she was expecting another Blessed Event and added rather wistfully, Lydia thought, since Verity was inclined to *embonpoint* that she had been most dreadfully craving Hannah's rum-and-raisin cakes. She was inclined to take Lydia's authorship as a vastly good joke, and added one or two little items of interest that she thought might *sharpen her sister's pen.* The last letter, in Mr. Charles Schuyler's precise fist, expressed his continuing forgiveness of Lydia's Little Mishap with that scoundrel Legget, and apparently operating under the assumption that her brief and dutiful letters, thinly spaced, arose from penitence and shame, hastened to assure her that she need not feel his wrath was upon her head, that even *he* had been known to make a mistake. In the most formal terms possible, he expressed his genteel and continuing affection for his *dear* Miss Wingate (and her Family's fortunes, Lydia thought tartly) and added that all five of his little Schuylers continually wanted to know when their New Mama would arrive in the Hudson Valley. Since he also appended a rather hideous description of a family visit paid to his late wife's final resting place in Sleepy Hollow before closing as her most affectionate and considerate Charles A. Schuyler, Esq., Lydia ended up laughing out loud as she tossed the letter on the pile. The news was all three or more months old, of course, but she had a very strong suspicion that nothing of great consequence had altered within that space of time in Old New York. That Mr. Schuyler had not even thought to warn her of the proximity of his brother and sister-in-law to Como was rather annoying, however, and so typical of Charles, as typical as the fact that not once, either in person or in letter had he ever mentioned the word love as an emotion existing between them.

However much she might try over the course of the next few days to ignore them, or to find some new and more devious method of forcing her brother to make suitable replies, finding his excuses as entertaining as they were also exasperating, she knew that the letters remained reproachfully piled upon her writing desk.

There had, however, been a slightly more recent communication, carried by packet delivery, from Mr. Legget, and Lydia was much heartened to discover that Scrope and Company had received the first EUROPEAN SKETCHES with a great deal of enthusiasm, and that Mr. Legget had been, as usual *in the soup* over one of his numerous editorial scandals. The affair had evidently started in Fraunces' Tavern and ended, quite predictably, with a double development in Weehawken Heights, and seemed to have been settled to the satisfaction of both parties in a rather roisterous manner set in a bordello on the Jersey Side, which, of course, Miss Wingate should have quite deplored, but so briskly cheerful and drily witty was Mr. Legget's description of the event that she had quite ended up in laughter instead, and determined that it was something to be shared with

Lord Robert, who would *certainly* find it as amusing as she had.

But this brought up the rather unfortunate and deeply suppressed thought that there had been no sign of that gentleman at the Villa Solario since their journey to Como; and once she had allowed herself to openly consider that day and that gentleman, she could not quite dismiss him from her mind, and once or twice even caught herself casting a rather yearning look across the lake, as if she were not old enough to know by now that wishing did not make it happen, as Friend Hannah had frequently said.

But Mr. Legget's letter had inspired her with the happy idea of burying herself in her writing, and when she was not copying out a fine hand, she and Jonathan found time to take long walks in the mountains, visit and be visited by the contessa, upon whose friendship they had come to depend, and even attend one or two small evenings and suppers in the villas of their neighbors. Though Lydia might enter the room looking in vain for Lord Robert among the company, by sheer force of will (and the visual reminder of those unanswered letters, representations of her *true*, her *real* world) she was able to suppress any overt displays of emotion or melancholy. She had been so long in the habit of placing her commonsense and intelligence above her heart and imagination that it was not a terrible task for her, but she alone was aware that it was requiring a great deal of effort and all of her strong will to prevent her from lapsing into either daydreams or any assertive plan of action by which she might accidentally place herself in his path.

But that spark, once ignited, refused to be extinguished, and almost as an act of rebellion, those letters remained day after day, unanswered, while she cut flowers in the garden or allowed the contessa to bring her to her dressmaker, or punt about the lake with Jonathan, or dance until quite scandalous hours of the morning with the series of German military men who seemed to find her vaguely attractive because they could not believe that she could find them so amusing for all of the wrong reasons, with their dueling scars and their stuffy, braid-and-brass uniforms, as precise and starched as their manners. Once or twice she encountered the Baroness, always in the company of a different and dashing escort not the Baron, but the difference between them was too vast for more than a few civil exchanges of compliments upon gowns and the state of the weather or the style of the music. And too, Lydia noticed that whenever the Baroness was present, Jonathan was one of her court. While she was far too wise a woman to speak to him about that lady, she did feel a certain need to be watchful whenever they were in company with her. But she could not wrap Jonathan, as he had said, in cotton wool, and being of a naturally gregarious and, when it suited him, energetic temperament, it was not long before he had found companions of his own age and interests among the other lake dwellers, and was frequently off on some lark of his own where the presence of an elder sister would have been a very sad detriment indeed to the merriment of a cockfight or a falcon hunt or a day-and-night sailing trip. Or whatever. And though Lydia had her suspicions about whatevers, she placed enough faith in Jonathan's concern for his state of health to hope that he would not land in some scrape too deep to extricate himself from without a great deal of trouble. And at any rate, she was certain that his escapades were no worse than any he might have encountered at Princeton, for the set into which he had fallen all seemed to be likable young men who were not likely to gamble too deeply or frequent the establishments of females likely to communicate anything more unpleasant to their clients than rather heavy toll charges.

And besides, she rather liked having the house full of lively young men from time to time, eating healthily and regarding her in much the same light as her own brother; it was a novel and different change from so many sisters all those years, after all; and equally pleasant to have entire days solely to herself, a luxury she had never before in her life enjoyed, and now found rather peaceful, even if sometimes it was *too* peaceful for her own state of mind, for it was then that the image of Marchman was most liable to steal, uninvited, into her thoughts, leaving her fingers suspended over the keys of the pianoforte, or her pen dripping ink across what had been a neat page of copy.

But Contessa d'Orsini was not only a good friend; she was a shrewd woman, and very fond of her young American friends, especially Lydia, whose air of grave reflection she found very droll. Even if Miss Wingate's written wit entirely escaped her, it was, after all, only to be regarded as a mild eccentricity, such as her other friend Princess Caroline's black wig and short skirts, or the Baroness' entourage of adoring (if unrequited) young men.

It was upon the pretext of her own dressmaker's coming from Rome that the contessa invited Lydia to come and spend the afternoon at Villa d'Orsini, sending her gondolier across the lake for just such a purpose as she knew would instantly repel the brother from accompanying his sister. And indeed, Grasini was a modiste of the very first order who did not undertake to travel with bolts of fabric and several members of her staff for just *anyone* at all, but the contessa suspected that the elder Mr. Wingate's pockets would no more be put to let by Grasini's outrageous prices than her own. And besides, the contessa, while having decided that Miss Wingate's simple and elegant style was all very well in its own way, also had made up her mind that her young American friend could definitely use a little *fòggia,* what the English called a new touch. It might be all very well for her to have a wardrobe of round gowns and carriage dresses such as were suitable for travel, but by the contessa's standards of opulence, *eposito*! the girl might as well be a Quaker for so many muslins and somber colors as Miss Wingate chose, just as if she were on the shelf and an ancient spinster, rather than a very attractive young woman just coming into mature bloom, a bloom that became her far more than her young budding must have ever been allowed. Americans! Really, sometimes they were past understanding, like their cousins the *Inglese*, but in her opinion, all Nordicos were slightly mad and overcautious, anyway. And since the contessa was the contessa, as majestically surmounting all obstacles in her path as a clipper ship cutting through the ocean, Miss Wingate found herself with no choice at all in the matter.

A new touch she would have. And Lydia was not bluestocking enough, nor without some dim flicker of unspoken hope, really to resist. It was true that her sturdy wardrobe, while all very well for travel, and of the best quality, lacked a certain *stile di moda*. Once the thought had been put into her head, she was not unfeminine enough to resist the temptation of new gowns, even her commonsense assuring her that her old ones had endured quite a bit from the strains of travel.

She was known simply and internationally as Grasini, and she was a small, spare woman, dark and more given to shrewd looks than smiles, but Maria Theresa Luisa Maggio Grasini was a woman possessed of a rare genius, and the contessa did not begrudge her expenses in bringing not only the Grasini but her own entourage of assistants and servants all the way from Rome any more than she resented the modiste's commandeering of the Blue Saloon as her field camp. Theirs had been a long and mutually agreeable relationship based upon a perfect understanding of the contessa's needs and Grasini's tastes; and once she had unpacked a carriage load of showroom dresses, shears, threads and needles; conferred swiftly with the contessa over the latest editions of LA BELLE ASSEMBLEE and A LA MODE, for Grasini would rather have been caught without her rosaries than the very latest Paris plates; set her seamstresses to work on five new gowns for Contessa d'Orsini; and sold her four of the ten hats she had brought from her own milliner in Rome; she turned her oblique dark eyes upon the person of Miss Wingate and tapped her measure thoughtfully against her wrist.

Lydia, quite unused to the temperamental ways of Roman *modellas* of *personas del bella moda*, shrank a little beneath that appraising stare, feeling that her ecru morning dress of light muslin trimmed modestly with bands of blue silk corsages that she had formerly thought quite stylish must certainly look very dowdy indeed. Her hair was done in simple bands, a braid wound around her head and concealed beneath a morning cap of Brussels lace; she was certain that her deplorable tendency to freckle in the sunshine must put her far beyond the pale; and she cowered a little on the white and blue striped couch, quite unable to face that stare, certain that Grasini would any second throw up her hands and pronounce that nothing could be done with such a one as the American Lady, that she was beyond hope.

But Grasini, who did not number too many *Nordicos* among her clientele, magnificently rose to the challenge of dressing a blonde with a positively martial gleam in her eye. Miss Wingate was stripped of her gown and made to turn this way and that as her measurements were taken and dutifully written down by the two assistants who were if anything even haughtier and more intimidating than their employer, while the Grasini, her eyes never leaving Lydia, strode this way and that, her hands clasped behind her back, her lower lip set, obviously *thinking*. Even the contessa, perpetually voluble, was usually silent before Grasini out of respect for true genius. The Grasini, the Great Grasini was designing.

Suddenly, she threw up her hands and looked heavenward, spilling out her words far too fast for poor Lydia to follow, although the assistants nodded knowingly and the contessa clapped her hands.

"What is she saying?" Lydia demanded anxiously as the three women withdrew to a trunk of silk, conferring in low tones and expansive gestures.

"Reste, reste," the contessa replied, handing Lydia LA BELLE ASSEMBLEE and admiring her own reflection in the mirror in a plumed traveling bonnet of madeira silk and silver-shot lozenges. "You will see soon enough."

A bolt of first one color then another were held up to Miss Wingate's complexion, and more conferences were conducted. Lydia was rather glad that she could not follow the dialogue, for she did not particularly think she would like what they were saying about her, as if she were a horse being decked out for a parade, but she dutifully studied the plates of the French fashion journal, and glumly noted that all the styles seemed to be set upon ladies who must be at least seven feet tall and as thin as pencils. Hems were deeper, sleeves were fuller, hats were larger, she noted, and the waist, which had reposed somewhere beneath the breasts for as long as she could recall, was slowly descending again to its natural position, right above the hips, while skirts were becoming fuller once again, and slippers, having passed from points to rounds were once again going to points. Jewels, she was assured by that magazine, were now worn even at country houses from dinner onward, and full dress was expected from the last meal of the day on through the night, even *en famille.* Since she generally sat down with her brother in exactly the gown she had been wearing since breakfast, Lydia felt a little intimidated by this information, but having no jewels to speak of beyond her mother's diamond-set and her own presentation pearls, she was not overly concerned with what was proper in the Bourbon Restoration Society, a circle within which she definitely did not move.

She had wandered, rather lazily, for she disliked reading in French and translating the image into English, into a long piece on the new fashions at the Bourbon Court, when Grasini gruffly presented her with a series of sketches.

With Lydia's indifferent Italian, the contessa's translations, and mutual French, as well as a great deal of nodding and sign language, Lydia beheld what had been mapped out for her new style.

Five gowns had Grasini created for Miss Wingate; the first, a morning dress was to be made up from jaconet muslin, featured a *pèlerine* and trimmings of just such a certain shade of rose silk ribbons drawn through sarcenet easings, the second a summer walking costume, featured a rather close body and a high collar, half sleeves and a deep hem trimmed in point lace; it was to be made from *zephyr* figured silk of a delicate and unusual shade between pink and lavender, and trimmed in deeper blue-lavender *gros de Naples* with lavender rosette closings down the front, the third gown was for evening, and featured a rather low *corsage*, certainly much more daring than anything Miss Wingate had ever worn before, with capped and trimmed sleeves and a full falling gored skirt that fell easily into deep lace-tiered flounces, caught up by silk bouquets of flowers and leaves, to be made from a deep sea-green tint of urling's net over a white satin slip, and white silk trim and lace, the fourth of Grasini's inspirations, a pelisse with a *pèlerine* that tapered from the set of the sleeve to the waist, where it met the closing of wadded silk, the half-caps of the oversleeves also wadded, and a simple band of wadding about the hem. This was to be made up in an azure *gros de Naples*, and the wadding, an ivory silk shot with traces of *lamé*, was counterpointed by a *lamé* series of knottings down the front closure. The fifth dress was obviously Grasini's final stroke of genius, for the woman seemed near to tears of triumph as she illustrated it to Miss Wingate. It was a ball gown, and Grasini conveyed to Lydia, of such style and color as only her American client could possibly do full justice. It was a low gown, with a square-cut *corsage* that almost seemed to slip away from the shoulders, decorated around the bust with a wreath of crepe leaves, and folds of lozenge-beads, cut rather lower at the waist, finished at the back in a heart shape caught by a crepe-lozenge bow. The skirt was cut rather short, and instead of the usual deep ruffs, was ornamented by three deep bands of the same fabric as the skirt, caught up in drape by little crepe-lozenge hearts. This gown, Grasini informed Miss Wingate, *must* be made from the bolt of orange-pink fabric known as *marguerite* crepe, shot through with a figure of spiderwebs in a deeper orange and pink variation contrast, made up over an orange satin slip, and trimmed with crepe in those two colors. No one but a corn-blonde such as Miss Wingate could carry it off, she declared passionately, and fell into such transports as made

124

it necessary for a glass of wine to be procured for her.

Miss Wingate had exclaimed in admiration over all of the previous four gowns, but such a daring dancing dress as this last masterpiece left her with a vestigial Quaker doubt; the neckline was too low, the skirt too short, it was far too fashionable and far too dashing for *her*, she said dubiously, with only the faintest hint of longing in her voice. Why, she would look a quiz, if she were to appear at a ball in New York in such a gown.

"You are not in New York, and you are no longer a schoolgirl to be wearing little pastels, and besides, when you do go back to New York, I assure you everyone will copy your style, Lydia," the contessa said, overriding all of her objections by sheer force of will. "Besides, if you do not accept it, Grasini will go into hysterics, and that I will not have! She is far too valuable to me, you know!"

No, Lydia thought, paging through the sketches and fingering the materials longingly, she was not in New York, and she was no longer a schoolroom miss, if indeed she ever had been. Neither was she a lady of fashion—but she did want, she understood suddenly, allowing a length of ribbon to slide through her fingers, to dress beautifully, to wear bright colors and walk about feeling herself very much *up to the knocker*, as Lord Robert would have said. And perhaps it was the thought of Lord Robert that decided her. Clothing was meant to be enjoyed, just as food and wine and dancing and —and other things—were meant to be enjoyed. Life was for the living of it, and she, Miss Lydia Wingate, had come very much to want to live it to the fullest.

She held up her head. "Please convey my deepest thanks to Grasini—please tell her how very— satisfied I am with her designs, and," Lydia added humbly, "how very grateful I am!"

These sentiments were duly conveyed, and Grasini nodded, accepting her due. It had been difficult but not impossible; when other pale *Nordicos* saw what she had wrought, from the sweat of genius upon Miss Wingate, it would certainly bring her more custom. Why these Americans, with their money, hardly knew how to dress, living as they did in a wilderness populated by ruffians and wild Indians, no wonder. But now, when they came to Italy, they would remember Grasini, and dollars would mix with lire, francs, and pounds in her accounts.

The thought of dollars in her account books edified Grasini enough to be able to rise to her feet and dismiss her patroness and her Galates imperiously. Summoning her assistants and her seamstresses, she announced majestically that there was work to do—cloaks and bonnets and shoes and stockings could all be discussed later; while the tide of her inspirations was at full flood, she would create without any assistance from outsiders, she loftily informed them, shooing them away.

Restored to her own ecru morning dress, Lydia felt a little like Cinderella after the ball. As the door of the Blue Saloon closed behind them on Grasini's curt orders to her underlings, Lydia heaved a sigh. "Lord, ma'am, I don't believe I have seen such a performance since we saw Mr. Kean in London," she whispered to the contessa.

That lady laughed indulgently and took Miss

Wingate's arm. "It is *trés drôle, non*? But genius is genius, and you will see that Grasini does not make mistakes! Now, my dear, if you will be so good as to come to my dressing room with me, I have a little surprise for you!"

Mme. Contessa's "little surprise" turned out to be her maid, already aproned, her cutting shears and curling irons laid out upon the cutting table, her underling standing by with a copper of hot water and several jars of mysterious looking creams and lotions.

Seeing this scene, Lydia tried to back out of the giltleaf doorway. "Oh, no, contessa—not my hair, if you please!" she exclaimed. "Not my hair—Grandfather would kill me if I cut my hair!" she cried, putting both hands over her cap.

"*Sciocchezza!*" the contessa said firmly. "*Fòggia* from head to toe, my dear! What a quiz you would look with those bands and braids and such lovely new dresses! Josefina, *per piacere! A ituo!*"

There was nothing for it, and besides, Miss Wingate did not protest too strenuously, only wondering aloud what Friend Hannah was going to say as the contessa's abigail placed her firmly in the chair, wrapping one of her mistress's own elegant dressing gowns about Lydia's shoulders and brandishing her brush in a most professional manner, pulling the pins from Lydia's tresses with swift fingers, clucking over the masses of corn-gold hair that fell over her shoulders, nearly to her waist.

Meekly, Miss Wingate sat still while maid and mistress argued amiably about what to do with her coiffure, twisting her hair and her head this way and that, until the first snip of the sharp shears; the feeling of lightness as a long strand fell away upon the floor was almost an anticlimax.

Josefina was not as histrionic as Grasini, but a half an hour later, when Lydia allowed herself to open her eyes and look in the mirror, her expression and the hand she raised to her new curls, as if to be sure this was really herself she saw and not some stranger, forced that stolid female to laugh.

"You see?" the contessa asked simply as she presented Lydia with a gold hand mirror, and indeed, turning this way and that, Miss Wingate *did* see. Her hair, so long used to the severe confinements of bands and braids now fell softly about her face in little ringlets, and was swept up in the back and held in place by a tortoise comb. "Josefina only needed to use the curling irons a little, and she says that you may arrange it yourself without a great deal of trouble, and she will be glad to show your woman how it is done."

"Grazie," Lydia said simply, but the gift of a gold coin pressed discreetly into Josefina's palm probably was the true cause of her deep curtsy and her smile.

"Now, we shall have lunch!" the contessa announced, sweeping Lydia down the stairs again to the little dining room. "I don't know how it should be, but clothes always make me want to eat, when one knows from that look on one's modiste's face that eating is exactly what one should not be doing!"

That any human being could not only set out but consume so many fruits, fishes, cheeses, pastas, breads, salads and pastries as the contessa and call it *a light repast* fascinated Miss Wingate;

Jonathan had declared himself frankly in a state of awe the first time they had been invited to luncheon at Villa d'Orsini. Since the contessa also liked to wash all of it down with several kinds of wine, finished off by cappucino and brandy, luncheon could not only be a long affair, *con brio mucho* (again, Mr. Wingate's opinion) but also by the time a final plate of sliced oranges and chocolate rusks arrived, a somewhat stunning experience.

By the time Miss Wingate was able to follow her hostess from the table, she was just a little unsteady upon her sturdy kid slippers and more than willing to join the contessa upon one of the several chaises ornamenting the solarium.

After politely refusing one of the many shawls offered to her as a wrap by her hostess, and reclining herself with a contented sigh upon an orange and green striped sofa with several cushions to keep her from any possible discomfort, she watched lazily as the contessa's two footmen arranged their mistress's couch of repose with an even greater number of cushions, pillows, shawls and drapes, a daily ritual which had at first fascinated Miss Wingate, but now that she had spent some time in her friend's company, seemed very sensible indeed.

"Contessa," Miss Wingate said after a brief and comfortable silence while luncheon was allowed to settle itself, "you shall positively turn me into a sybarite, if you are not careful! I shall go home dreadfully spoiled and quite useless, and very haughty and fashionable and spoiled beyond repair! Grandfather will turn me out of the house!"

"Signore Wingate sounds to me as if he needs

to come to Italy. Besides, if he does, you may come and live with me, and I shall do what he would have done and find you a good *sposo*, a handsome man with much money and the taste to adore you, like my poor Orsini," she sighed, dismissing both Mr. Wingate and her late husband with the same gesture. "By the time I was your age, Lydia, I had buried two husbands and was looking for a third!"

"Oh, Contessa!" Lydia protested lazily. "Grandfather has found me a *sposo*—a husband, that is to say."

"This Signore Charles Sky-leer? He sounds very *stuffy* to me, and you do not sound at all like a woman in love when you speak of him."

"Charles and I are not precisely—that is to say, we have an Understanding."

"Then you must marry so that you may have a lover," the contessa said matter-of-factly. "One should not reach thirty whatever years and not have an *amore* unless one is very holy like my sister Rosalba, who went into a convent and is now an abbess."

"Oh!" Lydia said, turning a little so that she could see the contessa's Roman profile. "In America we do not do such things! It is *most* improper!"

"If you marry this Sky-leer, you will need a lover. I will send you one of my footmen—Mario, perhaps. He is young and very handsome. And alas, very *stupido*, also, but one cannot have everything."

Lydia, thinking that a month ago she would have been quite shocked to hear this sort of talk, laughed at the thought of introducing the faunlike Mario into Mr. Schuyler's Hudson household as her "footman."

There followed a long and far more comfortable silence, during which Miss Wingate found herself in that pleasant state between wakefulness and dozing.

She was just drifting down a lovely stream in a skiff rowed by Lord Robert Marchman when the contessa suddenly sat bolt upright, spilling a great many shawls, pillows and cushions across the Persian carpet.

"Tarot!" she said enigmatically.

Miss Wingate started and her daydream popped like a soap bubble. "What? I beg your pardon, ma'am?" she asked, blinking in the shady darkness of the heavily curtained room.

"Tarot!" the contessa repeated. "Why did I not think of it before? Never mind that—the *écartes, d'accord!*" She rang the little bell upon the stand at her elbow and lay back down again, snuggling herself comfortably into her cushions and closing her eyes.

Now, Miss Wingate, thoroughly puzzled, sat up. "Contessa, you know that I do not play cards well enough to compete with you!"

Her hostess waved her down again with one lazy hand, not even bothering to open her eyes. "Not to play—to do the *divinazione* with!" She chuckled.

"Do you mean, to tell fortunes?" Miss Wingate demanded, utterly astounded.

"I mean to tell your fortune, Miss Lydia Wingate! I am *strega*, all of the D'Avrazzoes have always had the second sight, as you call it, in English. So, rest now, and let me have my little sleep, because I will not read them until they are brought to me, and that will take Josefina and Mario forever, because everyone is resting now, so we might as well compose ourselves for a little wait. But I am *strega*, and I will look into your future!"

"Dear me," Miss Wingate said.

Seven

This, Miss Wingate supposed, not without humor, was where it all ended, rather like that series of etchings Mr. Legget had tacked to the walls of his office on Light Street, THE RAKE'S PROGRESS. First it was foreign travel, then foreign friends, then masques, then flirtation, then strong drink and spicy foods, then vanity and fripperies, then witchcraft. Grandfather would have no doubt had an attack of the gout if he could have seen his eldest granddaughter's latest aberration—divination! Not, of course, that she believed for one moment in such things, she thought a little doubtfully as she watched the contessa's beringed fingers shuffling the pasteboards on the table between them. The cards were very old, and, she noted, not at all like the decks that were used for loo or whist, but full of strange pictures and strange symbols that somehow made her a little uneasy, as if there were actually some *power* in those old woodcuts.

"If Rosalba had not become a *mònaca,* our old *bambinaia* used to say, she would have been the best strega of all the sisters—there was talent! *Ecce!*" The contessa clipped the deck into three piles at her elbow. "Choose ten cards, anywhere at all, and hand them to me, face down, if you please. No peeking! *Si,* Rosalba could always *see,* but she was called by God, so I suppose that He needed her more than we, and of course, the Church does not like such things—unless it comes from our saints, hey? *Le vecche religione,* though, it still runs strong in Italy—the old gods, the old ways...." As Lydia chose her cards, the contessa's voice droned on, low and soothing in the darkened room, and the older woman leaned forward on her elbows, losing her scarves and shawls as she intently watched Lydia's face.

With a little sigh, Miss Wingate picked the tenth card and handed the pack to the contessa, who began to turn the cards over in a pattern, making little noises in the back of her throat as she studied the esoteric symbols on the pasteboards.

In spite of herself, Miss Wingate leaned forward also, rather anxiously wondering if the contessa really could see her future in hanged men and chariots, hermits and lovers. "What do you see?" she whispered into the silence.

The contessa laid down the last card and sat studying the spread, a small crease appearing between her brows. "Is not *clear,*" she murmured, "so much confusion inside, outside....I see many journeys...a long wandering, a long search for

134

something, something you do not know of here—"
she touched her head, "but here," she added,
touching her heart.

Lydia smiled. "Perhaps," she said.

The contessa studied the cards again. "I see
great changes, changes that you never
expected...they will challenge you—caught between the old and the new, you will be tried, Miss
Wingate, sorely tried...but there is no escape
from your destiny, remember, and what will be
will be."

"Dear me," Lydia murmured, a little frightened
suddenly.

"I see darkness and light...darkness and
light...how strange, usually the cards are more
specific...but they say the darkness comes before
the light, then the darkness comes again...."

"Oh," Miss Wingate said, pondering this mys-
tical pronouncement.

"I also see," the contessa continued on in a more
businesslike tone of voice, "much gaiety—I see a
party, many parties, but one grand ball, very elegant—dancing and music, and a dark man who
will come to your aid when you least expect it—
I also see unexpected visitors. They bring trouble,
they bring a long journey...but never must your
courage fail you. You have three chances to attain
the wish of your heart; you have already passed
one chance by without even noting it; two more
will come, and you must take courage, Lydia, and
follow, for once, not your head, but your heart."

She leaned back in her chair and sighed, pressing her fingers against her forehead.

Miss Wingate, who understood none of this at
all, and was trying to sort it all out, also leaned

back in her chair. It could mean everything—and nothing, she thought. That she so desperately wanted to know what would happen to her, however must indicate something was amiss in her well-ordered life.

"Darkness... in the darkness you will find your light. Things are not always what they seem, and all about you, there are—people who will attempt to bend you to their will, *tu comprends*?" The contessa sighed, and swept the cards back together into a meaningless pile. The spell was broken.

"You must have your party, Lydia...." she said, regarding her young friend from beneath her lashes. "You must have your ball... because there your heart will be revealed."

Lydia blinked. "My heart will be revealed," she repeated. "If only it were so!"

"There comes a messenger, bringing tidings... a messenger you have long awaited..." The contessa's voice was trailing away; she seemed to almost be asleep.

Suddenly, she gave a start, and smiled at Lydia, patting her hand. "The cards are usually much clearer when they speak to me, but the heart, while a very admirable thing, can frequently cloud the inside of the head, where the old knowledge lies... when we want to know something very much, it is precisely that information which is denied to us."

"I think I understand," Lydia replied thoughtfully. "Did you see anything about Jonathan's health, and my Family in there?"

The contessa shook her head. Always, Lydia thought of others before herself. *"Tout va bien,"* she said airily. "But I will help you to plan your party and everything will be of the first style of elegance. Why, I believe you might even have a request to extend an invitation to Her Highness!"

"Oh dear!" Lydia said, smiling again.

"But you will—wait I see, now that Her Highness will first extend an invitation to you and Jonathan to attend a ball at Villa d'Este! I see the messenger—he ascends the steps, he knocks for admittance, he is ushered in—"

At that moment, a familiar voice said, just outside the door, "Don't bother! I can show myself in, *grazia!*"

And Miss Wingate gave a start, looking at the contessa in such a way as to assure that other lady that there would be no need for a comfortable gossip; she had seen all that she needed to know in that single reaction to the sound of a certain voice.

Lord Robert Marchman rather carelessly allowed himself into the room, and made a bow. "Good afternoon, ladies! I trust I have not interrupted your slumbers? Forgive me, contessa, but Jonathan directed me to fetch home his sister to dinner—it would seem that we have a very fine couple of fish to set out for the good Friend Hannah's hand—I understand her baked fish is heaven!"

"We do not need you, Mario," the contessa said, extending a lazy hand for Lord Robert to kiss, "but as long as you are here, you may open the curtains."

"Ah, Miss Wingate! How do you—" At that moment, Mario drew back the heavy velvet drape and a shaft of late afternoon sunlight fell across Lydia's person. Lord Robert's expression altered only slightly, and he skipped but a beat, but Lydia noted that he was pleased by her new hairstyle, and put a hand to her head again, as if to assure herself that it was still there. "Do," he finished, shaking her hand and nodding. "Quite becoming, ma'am! Yes, quite becoming indeed! And I suppose we owe this to your good offices, ma'am?" he asked the contessa.

She nodded lazily, giving her half-smile, gesturing him to a chair.

"No, I cannot stay—Jonathan's below, hungry as a bear, which a day's fishing will always do to a young man! I am directed, Miss Wingate, to fetch you instantly home!"

"Oh dear," Lydia murmured, rising, "that sounds precisely like my brother—I have imposed upon you long enough today, ma'am—and I cannot thank you enough for all that you have done for me!" Impulsively, she threw her arms about her hostess's neck, and the contessa smiled and patted her back.

"If I had a daughter, I would have her be like you, my dear," she answered. "Now go and fetch your bonnet and shawl, and tell Mario that you are to have a bottle of that soave my late conte laid down to go with your fish tonight! Run along now—we do not keep the little prince waiting in the hot sun!"

When she had gone from the room, Lord Robert turned his stare away from her retreating back and looked down at the cards upon the table, flipping them idly over. "Fortunetelling again, contessa?" he asked idly.

Their eyes met. "It is necessary to see the future, as well you know, Robert. But the cards were most sullen today! Fortunately, Josefina was not! I think Miss Wingate shall do very well with her new *fòggia*, do you not?"

"She looks quite beautiful," he responded, still playing with the cards. "But *I* have always found her beautiful, even in bands and braids. The Wingates are a very charming pair, I think."

"Quite so," the contessa murmured, her lazy glance missing nothing, like a hawk in yarak. "But now, perhaps other men will also think her beautiful, my friend. *Pensez!*"

Lord Robert gave her a strange look, but said nothing, only shook his head slightly. "I am not a complete cad, not yet, by any rate, ma'am! I have never plucked a rose that was not in full bloom! Which reminds me," he added, reaching into his jacket pocket and producing a cream-colored card, "Her Highness has charged me to present this to you, and to demand that you see to it that the Wingates do not refuse to attend. Especially Mr. Wingate," he added a little sardonically.

The contessa accepted the card and laid it upon the table without glancing at it. "*Buono,* Robert, I think that they shall enjoy themselves immensely, but we shall watch them, no? Was it difficult to convince Caroline to invite them?"

"Not at all. For all of her faults, she is extremely good-natured, you know, and also quite fond of lively young people."

"Young men, you mean!" the contessa snorted, shrugging her shoulders. "Well, I have told Miss Wingate that she would be receiving her invitation to a grand ball at Villa d'Este, so please do not forget to give her her cards, or she will lose all faith in my abilities as a *divinata!*"

In spite of himself, Lord Robert laughed. "Ma'am,

you are *the* complete hand!" He kissed her fingers again, and shook his head as she continued to smile at him.

"Tell me, Lord Robert Marchman, do you ever think of putting an end to plucking other men's roses and planting a tree of your own?"

Almost imperceptibly, his face darkened, then lightened again. "I have thought upon it, ma'am, but I doubt that the plant would grow in the poor soil I have to offer it," he drawled cynically.

"Roses," the contessa said firmly, addressing some point above Lord Robert's head, "are amazing plants. I have seen them growing out of what would appear to be solid rock cliffs; only give them a little air and sunlight, and they take root instantly."

"But some roses, ma'am, are more delicate than others; one dare not touch their blossoms, let alone attempt to transplant them."

At that moment, Lydia returned to the room, and no more was said, but as they thanked her and left, chattering away amiably, the contessa leaned back into her chair and snapped open her fan.

It had been an exhausting day, for one who disliked bestirring herself as much as the Contessa d'Orsini, but it had been well worth it.

A small, satisfied smile crossed her face and she rang the bell for Mario, wondering what her chef had in mind for her dinner.

The fish, as Friend Hannah had promised, was a foreign fish, and not at all what she was used to, but when it arrived upon the dining room table, it was noted that she had worked her West Indian magic upon it, and the eating of it, Jonathan pronounced, was almost as good as the catching of it.

Since Lydia had heard little more than descriptions of the day's sport, and the details of each fresh catch, she smiled upon her brown brother, looking healthier than he had in nearly a year.

Over his wine glass, Jonathan frowned slightly, looking at his sister in a puzzled way. "Doing something new with your hair, Lyddie? Looks very becoming, I must tell you. The contessa's giving you some style, sister. But as I was saying, I thought that a Bachman's fly might work on such waters, and a light trolling, you know, and we had such a good *strike* right off the point at Bellagio—"

"That reminds me," Lord Robert put in, smiling in response to Miss Wingate's look, "I have been directed to present you with this—" From his inner pocket, he withdrew two more of the cream-colored cards bearing the Princess's crest, and handed them to the Wingates.

Lydia glanced down at hers and bit her lip, her eyes growing large. Jonathan laughed and pushed himself back from the table, tossing his napkin carelessly on the plate. "Her Highness The Princess of Wales *commands* your presence—" He began to read aloud, then laughed again. "If that doesn't beat all! The old girl's asked us to a ball, Lyddie! Now you will have something to write home upon!"

"Oh, dear," Miss Wingate said doubtfully. "Lord Robert, I hardly think that—"

"Then do not think, ma'am! You need only to go! Imagine how your grandchildren will berate you for missing such an opportunity to *go and see the lions!*"

"It's not my grandchildren, but Jamie Legget," Miss Wingate admitted ruefully. "He would have my liver and my lights, as he is fond of saying, if I were to miss a chance to squib Royalty. Oh! That is—"

"Quite all right. Her Highness may be Princess of Wales, but she is still a Character," Lord Robert said smoothly.

"I'll say!" Jonathan exclaimed. "But I suppose you will have to tell us how to go on, Marchman! Is it very different from the Prince?"

"Very different," Marchman assured him gravely. "Much less—er formal. But the contessa will lend you her countenance, and I shall be there, and many of your friends, I am sure, so you need not put yourself out unduly. Only come in knee breeches and enjoy yourself!"

Miss Wingate looked at Lord Robert gravely. "I fear, sir, that you must have extended your influence over the Princess on our behalf, and Jamie Legget's newspaper is hardly worth such a trial. We could not!"

"Ah," Marchman replied, his eyes dancing, "you have been commanded. You *must.* Besides, the Princess was presented by an admirer with a copy of SCENES AND SKETCHES, and now nothing will do but that she must also *come and see the lions!*"

"Dear me," Miss Wingate said. This put her in mind of their own proposed entertainment as she turned to Jonathan to discuss the plan, and inform him that the contessa had offered her support.

"Do what you like, Lyddie," he said carelessly,

spooning into the *mousse à l'orange* placed before him, "you always do these things so well, anyway. All you need do is apply it to our letter of credit on that bank in Milan, and I'll sign it."

Since it had not been Jonathan's idea, Lydia could reasonably have been expected to feel slightly put out at his lack of participation in the actual execution of the entertainment they planned, but she merely smiled and said that she would put her mind to it, and he only need make out a list of his particular friends.

Since they were dining informally, Lydia did not withdraw after the covers had been removed, and was pleased to note that Lord Robert easily balanced his conversation between helpful plans for Miss Wingate and the contessa and Jonathan's plan for another fishing expedition.

However, when the ormolu Napoleon clock on the mantel below the Angelica Kauffman struck nine, he rose very politely and declared that he must take his leave.

"Ah! Can't you stay a bit?" Jonathan demanded a trifle sulkily.

But Lord Robert shook his head and smiled. "I have another appointment this evening, I fear," he said smoothly, "and I fear it would not do to keep the party waiting overlong."

Miss Wingate would be perfectly able to imagine whom that party might be, but she rose to accept his gracious thanks and walked with Jonathan to see him to the top of the steps, without the least betrayal of the slight tinge of jealousy she felt in her breast.

But Marchman grasped her hand within his own for a second and smiled at her. "I particularly enjoyed the description of the Ohio family visiting the city for the first time," he murmured.

"You read it!" she exclaimed.

"Delightful! I only wait to see how you will cut me to your style, Miss Wingate! I quake in my boots!"

With those words he was gone before she would see the sadness in his expression, only leaving her to wonder what he had meant, if he thought of her when he saw the Baroness.

But it was to seem that he was not as afraid of her pen as he had indicated, for not above three days had passed before he called at Villa Solario again, and not two days after that. Each time there was some pretext for the call; some sheet music for the pianoforte that he thought she might enjoy, his own copies of the latest novel from Miss Austen which she had expressed a little impatience to read; as the escort of the contessa, or to propose a sailing for herself and Jonathan. In no way were his attentions toward her any more partial than those of a good friend, and he was always gone by nine o'clock, but Lydia was grateful for his company, and grateful that he genuinely seemed to enjoy Jonathan's company as well as her own.

He had even gone so far as to arrange an inland trip through the mountains by mule, the only animal capable of negotiating the steeps and valleys of the mountains, and if she had hoped that they might be set upon by bandetti, and he would be forced to nobly rescue her from a fate worse than death so that she might fall into his arms, she was forced instead to settle for a visit to an ancient monastery with a breathtaking view of the lake

far below and a luncheon at a very good little inn.
Try as she might, she could not fault his conduct,
for his behavior was everything that was proper,
and they were never alone, not even in the relative
privacy of Villa Solario.

Perhaps Miss Wingate, who had been used to
managing not only her own affairs but a large
household for years, who had never known anything but the freedom granted to American females rarely granted to their European sisters,
and who at the age of one-and-thirty would have
laughed at the idea that she needed to be chaperoned, would have been incredulous if she had
known how very scrupulously Lord Robert was
guarding her reputation in that small and gossipy
community. Certainly a Wingate did not give two
snaps of the fingers for such a thing as servant's
gossip, but Lord Robert Marchman, more up to
snuff in these matters than Miss Wingate, certainly did; and if anything he was more than doing
his best to prevent any of the less savory aspects
of his own repute from sullying her own.

But Miss Wingate, experiencing, for the first
time in her life, a set of emotions she had never
previously dreamed existed, and finding that it
would seem, quite reasonably, that these emotions
were not returned, was determined to maintain
her self-control, and to make the best of the situation in which she found herself. And that was
not at all unpleasant, for it had to be admitted
that the man was the easiest company in the
world, and the most companionable human being
she had ever spent time with before in her life.
Their senses of the absurd were similar, their
tastes in everything from literature to politics ran

in the same courses, they enjoyed the same occupations, and certainly found no loss of employment or conversation whenever they were together.

Miss Wingate, who would no more dream of revealing her own feeling than of flying to the moon, never allowed herself to even consider throwing herself upon Lord Robert in an excess of passion, though often she wished that she could do so. Outwardly, she maintained her calm, and no one need ever know what it cost her to do so.

It took a great deal of the contessa's persuasive powers to convince her that she must spare Grasini's ball gown for her own party and wear another to that to be held at the Villa d'Este. But Miss Wingate had a clever needlewoman in Friend Hannah, and when she and Jonathan joined the contessa and Lord Robert for dinner at Villa d'Orsini before proceeding onward to that very grand affair, the contessa was satisfied to see that her charge's white silk had undergone an interesting transformation from pink trim to embroidered tendrils of green ivy, and was cleverly concealed beneath a voile slip and three tiers of Russian lace at the hem, quite a different ball gown entirely, and very charming. Over her shoulders, Miss Wingate had draped a spangled shawl, and upon her wrist she carried an ivory carved fan ornamented with medallions. Her feet were encased in green and white striped slippers, and her pearl set, a very handsome affair of droplet earrings, a necklace and a double bracelet completed her outfit admirably. Indeed, it was not her clothes, but something else that seemed to create a new Miss Wingate, a Miss Wingate who could be the belle of the ball instead of the chaperone of three hopeful sisters and a lively brother.

The contessa was pleased to note that that certain aura of transformation had not escaped Lord Robert, either, although he was doing his level best, as he escorted Lydia into dinner, to conceal it beneath his customary drawling manner.

No fault could of course be found with her own ball gown, a stunning Grasini creation of deep mauve watered silk, elaborately trimmed in deep billows of rose satin and crepe. Her own diamonds were quite admirably set up by this toillette and she knew that she was looking her best, but nothing could quite detract from her pleasure in seeing Lydia in such high bloom, for once—not even her own considerable vanity.

Both of the gentlemen were looking quite handsome in evening dress of somber black and white, and she would have been hard pressed to choose which man was the more elegant, for when he was persuaded to dress, Jonathan turned himself out quite well. The Princess, she decided, would be very pleased.

Indeed, Her Highness, if anything, even more *outré* within the confines of her own magnificent palace, resplendent in pink and white satin stripes and a mass of towering white plumes above the royal wig, seemed very pleased indeed to receive the Wingates, graciously accepting Lydia's curtsy and Jonathan's bow by extending her hand and speaking to them in her guttural German-accented English about her longing to visit America, a country of which she had heard so much. If her eyes tended to stray toward Jonathan Wingate with a certain predatory glimmer, Lydia was able to breathe easily, for Jonathan, with an American's distrust of royalty, behaved just as he ought, with exactly the correct degree of respect for a woman elderly enough to be his mother.

Lord Robert, who knew his Princess well enough to understand that the idea of a voyage to America would have been the last thought to enter her head, merely smiled sardonically at the easy way in which she immediately found a way to put the Wingates at ease. There were those who would say that the woman was half-mad, and who would not think so if they had seen the menagerie of flotsam and jetsam that formed her entourage, but she was, for all of her faults, a Princess of Brunswick and, when she chose, as charming as her equally disreputable husband. That she had chosen, after her long and unhappy stay in England, to separate from Prinny and had found consolation with the heavily mustachioed, rather oily Bergmani who stood by her side tonight, rather too resplendent in his bottle-green satin coat with the Order of St. Caroline pinned to his breast, who was to fault her? In middle age, she had found some kind of happiness, after all, in her Italian exiles and her journeys to Jerusalem, and that, he thought, was a far happier fate than the one that awaited him. ...

As if to shake that thought out of his head, he turned to offer Miss Wingate the next dance, only to frown slightly as he noted that she had already been swept into a sea of international admirers, and was laughingly trying to arrange her dance card to suit them all. Since he had previously claimed a waltz, Lord Robert was at least assured that he would glimpse her once tonight before it came time to escort her home again. But a dry and rather sardonic smile played about his face as he watched her accepting the hand of a handsome Italian prince for the quadrille making up at that moment, and with only the slightest of shrugs, he turned away, pretending an indifference that he was far from feeling.

Jonathan had already claimed the hand of the contessa, and one would have thought that they made an odd couple, this woman of sixty and a youth not yet in his twentieth year, but there was some bond of affection between them that made the sight almost gentle—certainly a loving one. The contessa, he knew, did not often put herself out for others; she was far too spoiled and lazy for that, however good-natured she might be. That she had gone to so many pains to introduce the Wingates into what passed for Polite Society in Como, that she clucked over Jonathan like a mother hen and waved her fairy godmother's wand over Lydia—and O, God, how he wished she had not, now that he thought upon that; in her severe aspect, Miss Wingate had been charming enough, but transformed into Cinderella, she was almost unbearably beyond his reach. The unaccustomed emotion of jealousy rose up in his breast, and he shook his head, wondering why this particular woman, above all others, should have captured first his head and then his heart. The distance between them was as vast as the huge ballroom of the Villa d'Este, and as crowded with obstacles as this room was with people. Not for the first time, he cursed himself for the flippant manner in which he informed her of the evil reputation he enjoyed that first night they had met. Until this moment, he had regretted none of his many scandals, nor had he felt much pain about his exile from home and grace. What had he to offer her, he wondered bitterly, but a shared life of eternal wandering and the unhappy prospect of being forever cut off from the Family she held so dear? He almost laughed aloud, thinking of the reception he would have received if he had called in Wingate House on Cherry Street in New York City and asked an old Quaker shipbuilder, a selfmade man of those depressingly American moral standards, permission to pay his addresses to his eldest daughter. Doubtless the elder Mr. Wingate would order him thrown out of the house. Lord Robert Marchman, who since his majority had become suspicious of the motivations of the entire female sex, had suddenly and unexpectedly found love with the most unlikely member of that band. She had cast out no lures, she had employed no great charms, her fortune must certainly be more than his own, and her intellectual discipline was a great deal stronger than his own, and in every way she was totally opposite to the voluptuous, cynical females to whom he generally found himself attached. Would he have given her a second look in Edinburgh or London or Paris, he wondered a little savagely, and knew that the answer was *yes*, that he might have encountered her anywhere and suddenly and cruelly lost a heart that he had never known that he possessed....

"You do not dance, Robert?" A voice at his elbow cut across his thoughts, and he looked down at his shoulder to see the Baroness Galtzalter standing there, lushly fragrant, draped in emeralds, smiling up at him as she placed one gloved hand against his arm.

"I was only waiting for you," he replied, gallantly offering her his arm and hoping, like a sulky schoolboy, that Miss Wingate had noticed.

The music started, and the Princess, together with an archduke of Russia, opened the ball.

As the other couples joined the two highest-ranking members of the company on the dance floor beneath pink silk tents and garlands of roses, the Baroness smiled up at Lord Robert. "She is becoming very lovely, you know," she said softly, an amused smile playing across her face. "But the brother, Mr. Wingate, I think is also very lovely. *Un homme très beau.* I shall dance a waltz with him tonight, I think, and see what will come of it."

"What?" Lord Robert asked, directing his attention at his partner from a great distance away.

The Baroness pouted a little. "I was saying, Robert, that I think since you have been neglecting me so sadly of late, that I will flirt a little with Mr. Wingate."

His crackle of laughter was hardly gratifying. "Do as you wish, Yvonne. You could hardly say that you and I have any ties upon each other, could you?"

Her smile was a little hard, but she shrugged easily enough. "*Non*, between you and I there was but one thing, Robert. And you have begun to bore me, you know. It must be that bluestocking female you visit so often that has made you so dull."

"Perhaps. But then I do not visit the bluestocking lady for the same reasons that I visited with you, Yvonne. Do you wish to cast me off?"

"Ah! How charming you are—I know you, Robert—you seek to make me cast *you* off first, like a gentleman. But you are no gentleman!"

"Neither are you a lady, Yvonne, but let us not quibble! I am sure that you have other, more entertaining suitors than I."

She nodded. "Did I not tell you that I was to dance with young Mr. Wingate? Such a pretty young man, so fresh and full of life."

"I fear you will have to stand in line, Yvonne—the Princess has set her heart upon the young American," Lord Robert returned easily.

"We shall see," she murmured. "Mr. Wingate is not uninterested, you know."

Lord Robert shrugged. "As you wish. But I warn you, Yvonne, trifling with striplings is a dangerous business! They lack discretion as well as logic."

"Ah, but such *passion*!" she returned, licking her lips like a cat. "Such *jeunesse* should have its reward, do you think not?"

"Tread lightly, Yvonne, lest you trip over your own schemes!" Marchman retorted.

"Ah, but I might say the same to you, Robert. I never thought that a little American Nobody would ever capture *you*!"

His grip tightened on her hand and she winced. "Tread carefully, Yvonne—you know better by now than to cross swords with me!"

The Baroness winced slightly, but smiled. "Try me, Robert," she breathed as the figure broke apart and they were separated.

Lord Robert bowed.

It was midnight before Lord Robert was able to claim his waltz with Miss Wingate, and even then, it was necessary for him to politely but firmly disengage her from a gaggle of gentlemen clustered closely about her, all of them vying in a babel of languages to see who would have the honor to procure her a glass of champagne. The prince was just about to use his rank to influence the outcome of the contest when Lord Robert gently stepped between him and Miss Wingate, offering her his arm. "Our dance, I believe?" he asked with a slight bow at the prince, leading her away from them before she would reply.

He had never seen her so animated before; she was flushed and laughing, her eyes aglow with the excitement of a girl in her first season. As they took their places on the floor, she smiled up at him in a way that almost wrenched his heart for the life she must have led before. "I have not sat down once all evening! Is this not a wonderful ball! All the gowns and everyone here and Her Highness so civil—"

"Quite so," Marchman said, returning her smile with one of his own.

"That is why I am so glad that you rescued me! Now I may be comfortable and say exactly what is on my mind, and not have to translate into French, or German, or Italian and try not to be *too* witty!"

He relaxed slightly. "You could never be too witty for me! You are a sharp-tongued shrew, ma'am, and that is precisely what I like!"

It was on the tip of Miss Wingate's tongue to retort that she was nothing of the kind, but the remark had been made with such a quizzing smile that she instead retorted, "Oh, no! I have a very good idea of what sort of shrews you prefer—and their tongues are not the sharpest things about them!"

The minute she had uttered this remark, she regretted it, even though she had uttered in the same teasing tones as he had used upon her.

For his part, Lord Robert could have wished himself at purgatory for exposing his own jealousy in such a sullen manner, and with a little laugh, attempted to pass off the whole incident as an example of wit.

But both were uneasily aware of a sudden uneasiness rising up like a specter at the fête between them, and both knew that something must bend—or forever break.

Eight

Although relations remained civil between Miss
Wingate and Lord Robert, an interested spectator
might have noted that in the weeks which followed
the Princess's Ball and preceded the Wingates'
fête, there was a certain degree of reserve existing
between them.

Between Jonathan Wingate and Lord Robert,
however, everything remained cordial and aboveboard, and if that young man made excuses several times to absent himself from some proposed
expedition with a vague excuse, Lydia at least was
able to put this down to his occupations with
friends of his own age. That he had begun to absent
himself more and more frequently from Villa Solario upon some errand or another, and seemed
withdrawn and slightly restless she was able to
put down to the fact that he disliked having everything at sixes and sevens, and, having proposed
the idea of a ball, was more than willing to find

any excuse to avoid having to participate in the long and elaborate preparations that went into making up such an entertainment.

With the aid of the contessa, however, she managed very well, and kept herself occupied and safely away from any but the briefest moments of reflection upon Lord Robert Marchman.

Since one of her grandfather's favorite maxims had always been that idle hands were the devil's plaything, Miss Wingate threw her attentions into preparations for her own ball with an energy that made the more lethargic contessa slightly dizzy.

By the behavior, however, of both of her friends, the contessa shrewdly guessed without even having to fish about that matters had somehow come to a standstill. Of its style and nature she could guess, but knowing that any approach upon her part to either party would result in the unhappiest rebuff—pair of *touces* that they were, walking about smelling of April and May and thinking no one could guess how things stood!—Well, something would come of it, of that she was certain. But exactly how to bring it about, even the contessa did not know. Some things were out of even *her* hands. But she lit a candle to St. Theresa, just to be sure that the matter would be brought to the attention of those with even more determination and power than the Contessa d'Orsini, promising a new altarcloth to Rosalba's convent if the matter came to a conclusion that pleased her.

But *only* if it pleased her.

Whether or not St. Theresa heard the contessa's petition was still a matter of some doubt by the evening of the ball. Her Highness had very graciously agreed to attend, if of course, Signore Bergmani was also invited, and Lydia's mind had been set to rack by the totally novel experience of hostessing a Royal Personage.

But this was the least of problems for her ingenuity. At the close of a long season, there had been many balls and parties given, and how to distinguish her own as a memorable occasion for so many people that she would never see again after September but would always wish to remember fondly taxed her somewhat. In her experiences as a hostess, she had found that people were generally more than pleased with a party if one only provided an excellent table and a very good wine selection (and plenty of both) and allowed them to conduct themselves comfortably.

To this end, she ordered vast quantities of staples up from Como and put her head together with Friend Hannah's, deciding that a good American menu would be best for the dinner and doubtless a fine novelty for their forty guests at table. Unfortunately, it was not the season to provide such delicacies as oysters, and quail was unattainable in Europe, but George declared himself satisfied that several varieties of local turtle, fish, mussels and shellfish would do well enough to make up a fine seafood stew, while thirty chickens could be cut and fried in the Maryland style, would be a treat, and a solid venison roast could be procured if one knew where to look among these heathens. The baking of biscuits and cornbread deployed a full day in itself, while Friend Hannah found a squash that would pass admirably for pumpkin custard. Of these and many other things American did Miss Wingate plan her menu, pronouncing herself satisfied with seven courses and three removes, while refreshments at the ball would consist of such things as a tolerable imitation of a crab patty, thick slices of ham, several varieties of cakes and pastries and a compote of apples, oranges and pears soaked in rum and spiced well with clove and nutmeg.

On the wines, Miss Wingate did not hesitate; they must be French and there must be plenty of them, particularly champagne, and lemonade for those who did not care for spirits.

The decoration of the vast ballroom, so redolent still of the days of the Empire, must tactfully cover up all reminders of that period of recent history, and at the same time, not be another pink silk tent. After some thought, Miss Wingate directed that flowers and silk ribbons would do very well, and ordered both the vast chandeliers polished until they shone like diamonds. The ordering up of candles, linen, tallow wax and a hundred other details occupied her for two days, and since she had decided upon two hundred for the guest list, and expected only one hundred and fifty, she was a little surprised when the total number of acceptances finally tallied one hundred and seventy-seven persons.

It was decided that the contessa's favorite orchestra would be imported from Milan for the evening, and her red carpet generously loaned to grace the ancient stairs where the guests would arrive to the light of twenty stone lanterns, to be greeted at the top of the stairs by their host and hostess.

Each of the Wingate sisters had in turn been presented to New York City with a ball, Lydia reflected as she looked over her lists, but truly this would be the finest she had ever planned, for freed of the necessity of squeezing four hundred into a ballroom designed to accommodate two hundred, and freed of the rather dreary conventions of New York society, she was able to give herself free rein and, for the first time in her life, do exactly as she pleased.

Here there were none of the rather Puritanical constraints of entertaining in a city as small as New York, where one must never invite certain people to sit at the same table or dance at the same ball, where one must always recall who was related to whom by ties of blood or marriage, and *must* be issued a card of invitation. In Como, everyone was more or less known to everyone else, but it was as if the outside world did not exist, that they were all stranded together upon some distant and paradisiacal planet, far from the realities of their day-to-day considerations. Barriers were down, and all sorts of people mixed freely— ah, it would be quite a party!

For a fortnight before the event, she was able to fall into her bed, exhausted, immediately drifting off into a deep sleep, and if it was not quite a dreamless sleep, it was at least a slumber so intense as to preclude the more disturbing of the dreams which had plagued her previously.

The night before the ball had been a particularly full one, coming as it had at the end of a day filled with a thousand last-minute details that must be dealt with one by one. With the final assurance that between the three of them, Friend Hannah, the contessa and herself had managed to tie up almost every conceivable detail, Lydia retired to bed a little after ten.

That Jonathan had been absent since that afternoon and had not yet returned bothered her not; she had barely had time to give him overmuch consideration in the past fortnight, and was able to put his absence down to his preference for friends of his own age and sex to the company of a household of women bent upon planning an entertainment.

She had read for a while in Miss Austen's latest novel then dropped off to sleep, the candle on her nightstand still flickering, the book opened against the silk coverlet. The household, as exhausted as its mistress, was not long in following her example, and a funereal silence had settled over Villa Solario long before the midnight hour had arrived.

She was never precisely certain what had awakened her; at first she had thought it was the sound of matins or lauds bells from the monastery, echoing across the mountains and the lake, except that she was dreaming of bells pealing out beneath the water, a sonorous, muffled chiming. Whatever it was, it brought her full awake, and she lay in bed for a second, holding her breath and listening.

The candle guttered in its socket, throwing the shades of the first empire across the room, the memories of another, happier day for Villa Solario. She shuddered slightly, thinking for a blurred second of *fantasmas* of the unhappy Empress Josephine that one of the scullery maids had claimed to see, before her sturdy commonsense reasserted itself.

Someone was coming up the stairs, dragging a heavy burden—it was exactly that sort of sound, she told herself, accompanied by the muffled sound of voices; human, living voices.

Housebreakers and servant's assignations, however awful they might be, were at least real, and better than ghosts. Seizing up the candlestick beside the bed for as much a weapon as a source of illumination, Miss Wingate slid silently from her bed and padded on bare feet across the floor, pressing herself against the doorway. With trembling fingers, her hand sought the ornate crystal knob, and she turned it slowly, cupping the candle flame against her shadow.

"Oh! Good God, Marchman—"

"Steady, m'boy—only a few more steps—"

With an angry exclamation, she threw open the door, and the dim light flickered across the two shapes in the hallway. At first she thought they were both more than a trifle foxed; Marchman's cravat was gone and his shirt was opened to the waist, his fair hair plastered to his head with sweat, as he supported Jonathan's limp body across the carpet. Her brother was a total loss, absolutely castway, glaring at her from black pinpoints of eyes in a pale face, his hair disheveled, his coat stained with wine—

No, blood.

"Good God," Miss Wingate said simply, fighting down the panic that rose up in her throat, her iron will asserting itself from a lifetime of dealing with scrapes and bruises, falls from horses, carriage accidents, boating mishaps, all demanding to be patched and cared for, fussed over and calmed and soothed by a clear head. Her eyes met Marchman's as she supported her brother's other shoulder, helping him down the hallway, oblivious to the spreading red stains on her white nightdress.

Her brother winced, but did not cry out, and even in the faint light, she could see that he was deathly pale beneath his tan.

She bit her lip, however, and kicked open the door to his bedchamber, half-leading, half-dragging him to the bed, where he collapsed with a groan.

"I'll need scissors and rags and a bowl of water— do you have any sulphur powder in the house?" Marchman said abruptly, pulling Jonathan's coat gently away from his shoulders. Against the white shirt, the stains seemed enormous and flowing, but Lydia merely nodded, flying down the hall to her own room where she rifled her sewing box and without hesitation, dragged one of her petticoats from the press, only pausing to sweep up her writing-lamp before she returned to her brother's room.

Marchman nodded. Jonathan, his head propped up against the pillows, tried to give his sister a smile, but it turned into a grimace of pain as Marchman began the unpleasant task of cutting his shirt away from the wound.

Lydia was automatically ripping the petticoat into long strips, fetching the washbowl from the stand, holding it while she dipped the long shreds into the water and handed them to Lord Robert.

"Lyddie—" Jonathan gasped.

"Don't talk!" Marchman said curtly, sponging at the blood. "The light, Miss Wingate!"

Lydia's hand was amazingly steady as he lit the wick and brought the oil lamp to the bed. There seemed to be so much blood—

And yet, beneath Lord Robert's fingers, sponging and wiping about the wound, she was able to see that it was not quite so bad, and had not touched a vital organ. Unconsciously, she sank against the edge of the bed, giving a small sigh of relief. Marchman looked sharply up at her, and evidently, having assured himself that she was not about to faint, asked her for sulphur powders, which he sprinkled generously over the gash, closing it with his hands, with fingers that were quick and sure, before laying a piece of her ruined petticoat over the wound.

Jonathan moaned aloud this time and grit his teeth, but Lord Robert merely shook his head. "Be thankful I don't have to dig a bullet out of you, my lad! Then you would have cause for complaint! Miss Wingate, bring me a needle and some clean thread—take it from the inside of the spool, if you please—and leave that damned lamp here—I need the light."

Without thinking, Lydia did as she was told, and brought also a bottle of eau-de-cologne and her laudanum drops. She handed the threaded needle to Marchman, who tied off the ends and, with a deep breath, laid three long basting stitches into the wound, closing its red lips.

Lydia watched Jonathan's face, bathing his temples with the cologne, forcing him to drink back water mixed with the opiate. He seemed to relax, once the stitches had been set, but Lord Robert took the cologne and poured it liberally over the wound, making the boy hiss with pain. "Damn, Marchman!"

"Better than an infestation. If you could have seen the wounds we sustained in New Orleans—"

He broke off and with expert fingers began to bandage up the shoulder. "You just rest easy now, old man. You'll feel more the thing in the morning."

He looked sharply up at Lydia's face, a mask of rigid self-control. "Brandy—or whiskey, Miss Wingate—and three glasses!" he commanded.

Jonathan's hand grasped toward his sister's and she took it in her own, feeling the coolness of it, and the fragility of his bones. His pained, drugged eyes sought out hers. "Sorry Lyddie—didn't mean—thought we could bring it all off without bothering you...."

"Don't talk. You may give your sister a very contrite apology tomorrow, when you are more the thing, Wingate!" Marchman said. "Right now, I am going to undress you and get you into bed—and pray that no one hears of this night's work!"

Lydia fled for the brandy, stumbling down the dark stairs, moving in stealth across the vast, empty floors. If Friend George or Friend Hannah caught as much as a sleepy glimmer of this scene, she reflected, there would be hell to pay, and such nursing and disapproval and questions and—Grandfather. With that uneasy thought, she grasped up bottles and glasses in the darkness, cradling them against her bloodstained nightdress.

When she returned to Jonathan's bedroom, she saw that Marchman had undressed him, somehow put him into a nightshirt, and was covering him with the sheets.

"Is he—" Lydia asked, approaching the bed fearfully.

Marchman shook his head. "You saw it—it is not too deep, and it will pain him for a few weeks, but it's no more than he deserves, foolish pup. God! Even in my wildest times I never fell into such a scrape!" He shook his head and smiled grimly.

Lydia looked down at her brother. He was falling into a restless slumber, the dreams of opium taking him out of his pain, but there was not, as she feared and knew too well, the look of death about him.

She barely felt Lord Robert's hands removing the bottles and glasses from her own lifeless fingers, nor his sure but gentle pressure as he seated her in a chair, drawing another quietly across the floor. "Drink this," he said, "it will make you feel better."

Lydia accepted the glass, unable to take her eyes from Jonathan, absently pouring the white-hot liquor down her throat. It burned, but she did not choke, and she was barely conscious of the hot tears spilling down her cheeks, only shaking her head from side to side, as if she would deny what she had just witnessed.

Marchman tossed off his whiskey, eyeing her with an unfathomable expression on his face. He wanted very much to put his arms about her and have that dear fair head resting upon his chest, but instead, he withdrew his own pocket handkerchief and handed it to her.

"T-thank you," Miss Wingate said, drying her eyes and blowing her nose. "Thank you very much, Lord Robert," she added, composing herself with effort and meeting his gaze.

He shrugged. "It was nothing. If you could have but seen the wounds we sustained in New Orleans—this was nothing. He'll awaken tomorrow with a terrible case of the blue-devils and repentance in his soul, but beyond that, I think he's all right, Miss Wingate." A slight, sardonic smile twisted his lips. "It would be better however, if we arranged some story to explain it all away—"

"Exactly what happened?" Lydia demanded. "How did he come by such a wound?"

Lord Robert leaned back in his chair and poured himself another drink, noting with distaste that there was dried blood beneath his fingernails. Absently, he rubbed his hand on his coat.

"Lord Robert, I am no child, so if you please, you will tell me what has passed." Lydia's voice was firm, but he knew her well enough to detect the angst below the surface, and again, suppressed the urge to comfort her in his arms, to give her that comfort she so desperately needed.

He stroked the beard stubble on his chin, and stretched one long leg out across the other, turning his glass in his hands. "Apparently Jonathan and Mr. Billy Austin got into a duel over the affections of a lady."

"B-Billy Austin," Lydia repeated, recalling that unpleasant, long ago afternoon at Villa d'Orsini when the Princess's ward had rudely made his opinion of Americans known. She had not seen much of him since then, and did not care to, but now, reflecting upon it, she understood that being of much the same age, Mr. Austin and Mr. Wingate must have more than once rubbed together in company, and doubtless rubbed together very badly. Mr. Austin was as spoiled by the Princess as Jonathan was by the Family.

"D-dueling?" She asked next, twisting his handkerchief in her lap, her eyes very wide, but her voice clear and unemotional.

166

"Dueling. Personally, I don't think either of them really wanted it to come to that, but those Prussian lads are so hot on the trigger—to them a duel is nothing—a game. They do not see it as we see it—it would have been simple enough to pressure both of them into it—you know what boys are like when they are all thrown together...."

Lydia grasped the arms of her chair. "And what is Mr. Austin's condition?" she asked.

"Only a little worse than Jonathan's, I think," Marchman said drily. "It apparently started as a duel with rapiers—"

"Jonathan is no swordsman! He is terrible!" Lydia started, and Marchman gestured for her to keep her voice low. "That is, he has been taught, but I should have chosen pistols for him! At least he has a good eye—he can hit the side of a barn door—"

"Ah, well, Mr. Austin is no better a duelist than Wingate," Lord Robert said slowly, a faint, ironic grin lighting up his deep-set eyes. "From what I can gather, the affair soon degenerated into fisticuffs. By the time I got there and was able to break it apart, it was a rare mill! Your brother has a great deal of science, Miss Wingate, and he's handy with his fives! I'd like to be able to take him to Jackson in London and allow him to really have a go at some training—"

"Boxing?" Miss Wingate repeated. "Fighting?"

"Like the pair of spoiled schoolboys that they both are," Lord Robert assured her gravely. "And the claret was flowing. They'd both managed to stick one another, but I think that their tempers were more suited to having it out in a mill—and that opened their wounds, you see. Merely scratches, but the bloodshed could put you off, I suppose."

"Jonathan, brawling?" Lydia repeated. "With Austin—Good God, the Princess—"

"Is dealing, I have no doubt, very severely with her ward at this very moment. Unofficially, since of course, we must all agree that none of this happened, she sends her most abject apologies, and hopes that you will forgive her for exercising so little discipline over her household. She was actually quite distraught—Her Highness is quite fond of Wingate."

"Yes, I know," Lydia said. She did not object when Lord Robert refilled her glass. Indeed, now she was shaking almost uncontrollably, whether from fear, anxiety or laughter, she was not quite certain, for she had a lively imagination and now that she was assured that there was no danger, had a very clear picture of the night's scenes. "I am sure, Lord Robert, that you must know exactly what sort of a response I am to make to Her Highness, and you'll convey the proper sentiments for me. Dear me, we owe you so much, so very much—"

"Easy, my de—my friend," Marchman said. "No need for you to get wiped up over this. Wingate will be right as a trivet, and none the worse for his scrape...and that was all it was, a schoolboy scrape, you mustn't ring too hard a peal over his head, if you please! I think both of them have had a very good scare and the incident won't repeat itself."

Lydia cast a look over at her brother, snoring slightly in his sleep. "Lord Robert, I don't know how to thank you—there are so many questions

I have to ask you—things I imagine I am better off not knowing—but I do thank you, sir! You have been much more than a friend to both of us—and how I shall ever repay you for this night's work, I do not know!"

"If you really wish to repay me, Miss Wingate—" Lord Robert said softly, and she looked up at him, meeting his eyes for the first time that evening. He saw fatigue and shock and concern in them, and mistook their sources. "You will endeavor, if you can, to keep the boy from being wrapped so much in cotton wool!" he finished, much more brusquely. "I know that he came as close to sticking his spoon in the wall as makes no difference, but he's been recovered for a long, good time yet, and well, frankly, Miss Wingate, and I think we need right now to speak directly, I think I know Wingate—and his circumstances—well enough to know that he's been pretty well kept in leading strings all of his life. I am a younger son m'self, you know... but that don't signify; I didn't come at the tail end of a pack of sisters with an anxious grandfather hovering over me from the moment of my birth, either, keeping me from every rig and row in town. You've got to cut slack, Miss Wingate—and make your grandfather cut slack with him also! He's a high-spirited boy, and he ought to be given some direction for all of that energy—I think the lad might like the Navy over a term at Princeton College, you know. He's not bookish, Miss Wingate, but he's not evil, either." He stopped, and his head sunk to his chest. For the first time, she saw how exhausted he himself was. "Forgive me! I didn't mean to ring a *peal* over you, either—God knows, you don't deserve it,

Miss Wingate—you've done the best you can, and better with the boy—more than anyone should have expected out of you—that is—" He flung up his hands and threw back his head, closing his eyes so that the light caught only the outlines of his profile. "What I am, Miss Wingate, I lay to an upbringing like Wingate's...as a child, I incurred an illness at Winchester, and I was sent home, cosseted and nursed and terribly spoiled by my family and my servants...long past the time I was recovered. I rebelled, Miss Wingate—I rebelled in every way I could think of, and in the end, I created such a tangle of my life that it was better to leave England than leave others to face the consequences of my actions...and for the first time in thirty-five years, Miss Wingate, I have finally faced the consequences of my own follies— I punished no one but myself, and never have I seen it more clearly than in this night's work! The rake's progress...." He laughed bitterly, and shaded his eyes. "God! I would rather have drowned the lad than see him facing such a life as I've led...."

"If you were one half as black as you like to paint yourself, Lord Robert," Miss Wingate said gently, "you would be a very Gothic villain, indeed. But for all of your warnings and your posturings, sir, you have dealt no one any harm—and indeed, a great deal of assistance! Tell me now that you have a heart of stone, and I shall be forced to laugh in your face, sir. But I understand that analogy you draw between yourself and my brother and I thank you for it! I only wish that he may turn out to be the man you are!"

"Precisely what your grandfather would wish, I am certain," Marchman retorted drily.

"I think perhaps, that I have some influence with him. And—Good God, if I ever talked to Jonathan as if he were more than a child, perhaps he would have confided these things in me!"

"Miss Wingate, believe me, you have done everything and more for the lad that you can do! He needs a man—if his father had lived, perhaps—"

Lydia nodded, thinking of her relationship with the contessa, of Jonathan's relationship with Lord Robert. "I see," she said quietly. "Dear me. I have tried—I have tried so very hard—so very very hard, and all I have been is selfish, thinking only of new gowns and balls and—and my own pleasure, of Worldly Sins. And now I have been punished!" The tears, so long pent up, could no longer be dammed, and Miss Wingate suddenly found herself sobbing as if her heart would break.

It was more than Lord Robert could stand. In an instant, he was kneeling beside her chair, his arms about her, his fingers stroking her hair, holding her and rocking her in his embrace as if she were a child, murmuring soothing words into her ear, tender words he thought he had forgotten forever. Crying females, he had discovered from long experience, were not among his favorites, but never before had he confronted a woman who cried not for herself, for some lost vanity or lover, but who cried for others, out of a deep and abiding love.

It had been a long time since anyone had simply *held* Lydia, an age since anyone had offered her comfort, lifted her burdens from her shoulders. To be upon the receiving of comfort was a novel experience for her, and she sobbed herself out, her own arms stealing about his shoulders, her head resting against his chest as if it were the natural thing in the world for him to offer her comfort, for her to accept it. Long after her crying had subsided, and she was struggling to catch her breath, he still held her closely, rocking her as if she were a child, his cheek against her hair, his eyes closed.

"I am so sorry...." Lydia murmured when she trusted herself to speak. "You really do not need my vapors...."

She lifted her head and looked at him, and he at her.

"Robert...."

"Lydia...."

She swallowed, meeting his eyes, wrapped in his embrace.

"Robert, I want—*I want*—" The very sound of the words filled her with wonder. *Lydia wants...Robert.*

"No," he whispered. "Don't even say it, Lydia. Not tonight. Not now. You're tired, you've had a shock...you must think upon it...think carefully...I won't offer you a *carte blanche*, Lydia...I'd offer you my life...it cannot be any other way between us, all or nothing...." Gently, he lifted her fingers to his lips and pressed a kiss against them, disentangling her reluctant arms from his shoulders, rising, bringing her up with him.

"Robert—I would take anything—*anything* you offered me," Lydia heard herself saying, clinging to his fingers, his hands turning about her wrists, keeping her from embracing him again.

"You hardly know what you're saying, Lydia,"

he replied. "Don't—sleep upon it all, think upon it all—but let me go before I—I do not want for anything in the world to harm you, do you understand, my love? My boat stands at your dock— I must go—though God knows it's the last thing I want to do—"

"Stay." Lydia was almost pleading, turning her hands in his grasp. "Oh, Robert, stay—"

"No. You must understand how much I love you, Lydia—enough to let you go—for tonight, at least. If your feelings are the same tomorrow, then I shall sail to New York and call upon your grandfather instantly. It must all be proper and aboveboard! My reputation must *not* sully yours, do you understand? I want to protect you—you're a lady, Lydia, and I would not have it any other way!"

"I'm not a lady!" she almost cried. "I'm not! I'm not! And I want you, Robert, now and forever, if only you'll have me."

He smiled, and seemed to waver before he gently disengaged her. "Understand, Lydia, that I want you now and forever, too. More than you could possibly understand right now—but for you, I want everything to be proper—to be right. Now let me go, my love—until tomorrow night. Then you may give me your answer—and I pray to all of the contessa's saints that it will still be *yes*."

Lightly, he brushed her forehead with his lips and was gone.

173

Nine

It was much as Lord Robert had predicted; Jonathan awoke quite late, and with a very sad case of the blue-devils indeed, and complained, somewhat sheepishly, that his shoulder ached something fierce. But Lydia had too many other things upon her mind to ring a peal over him, and beyond changing his dressings and telling him that she had no wish to know the intimate details of the event, since she could not approve of dueling, and would have far enough trouble on her hands explaining it all away to Grandfather as it was, barely listened to his recounting of the night's events, except to agree that Marchman was an exceptional fellow indeed before she bustled off, still wrapped in her own daydreams, to attend to the last-minute details of the ball.

Miss Wingate had herself risen quite late in the morning, somewhat refreshed by a night's slumber, but by no means changed in her feelings of the previous night. Not even Jonathan could quite distract her from her happiness, and once she had ascertained that he would be fit enough to attend the ball and even dance, despite his wound, she was content to drift automatically through the day's chores, serenely directing the decoration of the ballroom, overseeing the preparation of the dinner, the arrival and setting up of the musicians, and all of the other last-minute details with the ease of long practice. No one could possibly have detected, by her calm demeanor, that inside, she was bubbling over with joy, but there was no way that she could ease the glow of happiness from her face, or prevent herself from moving with a light, airy step through the house.

But the contessa was not just anyone, and when she arrived, a little early, bringing Josefina along with her to do Miss Wingate's hair, she knew in her heart that something had been resolved. Miss Wingate, in general so reserved in her behavior, instantly requested that the contessa be sent to her. She had just emerged from her bath, and, wrapped in her dressing gown, instantly dragged that lady into her inner chamber for a short, but quite intimate conference.

The contessa clasped Miss Wingate against her bosom, regardless of her magnificent and very ancient emerald-set, and some tears were shed upon both sides, but today they were tears of joy. The contessa, noting that Miss Wingate had slept with Lord Robert's handkerchief upon her pillow, was inclined when she looked in upon Mr. Wingate to tell him he was a very naughty boy, but that Mr. Austin had long been deserving of something more than a genteel set-down, and wished, in fact that she had witnessed it all. Mr. Wingate, allowing her to assist him to shrug his shoulder into his corbeau evening-coat and do up his cravat in a *trône d'amour* in a way that he would have forbidden to his sister, much less his valet, was inclined to take her teasing in good part, and felt secretly relieved that Como seemed to be passing the whole affair off as a very good jest.

Although the contessa was discreet, and did not as much as breathe a hint of Miss Wingate's confidences to her brother, Jonathan had a vague sense of the direction from which the wind was blowing, but, being Jonathan, was far too occupied with the interesting figure he planned to cut with the lady who had been the source of the duel than with Lyddie's romances. He expressed a fervent hope that Mr. Austin had *the guts to show up, and with both eyes black at that,* but otherwise seemed to express no more ill will toward his contemporary; in his mind, and presumably Mr. Austin's, the matter had been settled with satisfaction given to both parties and Anglo-American relationships at Como, if not treatied, at least somewhat patched. Billy wasn't all that bad a fellow, he was inclined to say generously, being nautically inclined and damned good with his fists, for a foppish Brit, with more style than sense.

· The arrival of a messenger from Villa d'Este with an enormous bouquet of flowers and a very kind note in the Princess's own hand directed to both the Wingates was a matter to be gratified about, Lydia decided, since she had no more desire to be involved in some dreadful tangle of an international incident than her brother. Only think of what the Family would say about that! It did not bear thinking about, however, Lydia decided, because a second, and, to her mind, a far more important package had arrived from Villa d'Este, and although it was only a corsage of white roses and a brief cryptic note in Lord Robert's fist, she cherished it far and above the more opulent gift from Royalty.

Of course, she was not so far gone as not to note that several other nosegays had also been delivered for her, but it was all that the contessa would be able to do to dissuade her from immediately crushing the roses against her bosom and staining them with her tears.

Dusk was just gathering as Lydia and the contessa descended the stair to wait the arrival of the first guests. With a certain maternal pride, the contessa noted that Miss Wingate was tonight a true beauty. The glow came not from Josefina's arts, but from within. Nonetheless, the elder woman shrewdly decided, it did not hurt that her young friend was attired in Grasini's inspiration of a ball gown which set off her face and figure to perfection in such subtle tones of valencia and rose, nor that she had clasped her mother's diamonds about her throat and ears, and their sparkle was only dimmed by that in Lydia's eyes. She wore white satin slippers upon her feet and long kid gloves to her elbows, and upon her head Josefina had dressed her curls very high, so that they spilled over her ears and her temples, softening her somewhat angular face. Upon her very low corsage, she had pinned Lord Robert's roses, and carried an orange fan of painted chickenskin over one elbow, depending from her wrist on its silk cord.

The contessa, who considered herself very well turned out in English Green watered silk and a great deal of blond lace with *gros de Naples* trim and several towering plumes in her hair, knew that Miss Wingate would never be the beauty she had once been, but shining, as she had never seen her shine before, with first love, she was as lovely as a Botticelli painting, and far more animated than any of those passive Renaissance damsels had ever been.

The contessa was satisfied. Rosalba would not only get her cloth, but it would be the best that could be found, with gold thread and the *Ave* worked in silk bargello, from the best religious embroiderer in Roma.

Standing at the top of the stairs to greet her guests, Miss Wingate was almost alight; before her there passed a parade of faces that she had seen all summer, and yet tonight, she knew that as the season was closing and they would all soon go their separate ways, that she might never see many of them again, that they had become her friends—and what an assortment of friends they were, she thought, shaking hands, bowing, dipping a curtsy here and there to an older lady; everyone from a Royal Princess of England to a down-at-the-heels Bonapartist with barely a sou (but so much charm!) to his name. And yet she had become fond of each of them for their own virtues and fallacies, and now bathed in the light of love, they became almost luminously precious to her, as if somehow she could make them each a present of some of her own happiness, as joy were a contagion that could be spread like a rumor.

The Princess arrived, with all of her entourage, but even as Lydia was making her bow and shaking that strange woman's hand, listening to her robust pleasantries in her guttural English-German accent, her eyes were seeking out Lord Robert's.

She had never seen him take so much care in dressing as he did tonight; from his burnished locks to the high gloss of his dancing-pumps he was all that was perfection in a man to her eyes, his corbeau evening coat a masterpiece of Weston's art, his cravat for once not twisted away from his neck as if he could not bear the confinement of so much linen about his neck, but neatly and elegantly arranged in the style known as the *coeur-perdu*, lost heart, his knee breeches correctly buckled in silver.

A little behind the Princess and Signore Bergmani, he lifted up his quizzing glass and stared at the white roses she wore against her breast, and his face was illuminated in a way that she had never before witnessed, as if the sun had suddenly burst out from behind a cloud, and at that moment, Lydia loved him so dearly that only her discipline allowed her to continue her conversation with Her Highness without the smallest catch of attention, graciously bowing Her Highness on to what that lady must certainly believe to be the more pleasant task of conversing with Jonathan, whom she playfully slapped on the arm with her fan and called a *very naughty boy*.

Lydia bowed to Lady Anne Hamilton and Lady Mary Lambert, the Princess's two ladies-in-waiting, accepting their compliments upon her gown and freely crediting it all to the contessa and Grasini, and then as Lord Robert took her hand in his own and raised it to his lips, their eyes met in perfect understanding.

"I would like to sweep you away this instant," he murmured.

"And I would like you to sweep me away this instant," Lydia returned, touching his fingers with her own for a brief moment.

"Later, when we are supposed to waltz, ma'am..." he murmured, allowing the next guests to claim their hostess's attention.

It seemed to Lydia as if that waltz would never come, at that moment, but she only gave him one backward glance before she smiled and welcomed M. Bertan and his daughters to her house.

Although it might generally be held that the Wingates' manners were somewhat odd and old-fashioned in some ways and very forthcoming in others that puzzled their Old World neighbors, they were generally well liked, and with the contessa to lend them her countenance, they had somehow, without quite knowing it, come into fashion over the summer, and there were no lack of guests to fill up that vast dining table.

Quite correctly, Lydia had placed Her Highness at the head of the table and herself at the foot, hoping that no one would notice that she had placed her brother to the Princess's right and Signore Bergmani to her left, or would at least put it down to *odd American manners*. In this way, she was certain that her Royal guest would be quite comfortable, and in setting the tone for the rest of the table, make others comfortable also. She held her breath as the first course *à l'américain* was served, wondering up to the last moment if she had committed a serious error in placing such simple fare before such sophisticated company, but from the moment the Princess tasted her soup and nodded agreeably toward her hostess, she knew that she had a Success upon her hands, and relaxed to give her attention over to the Prussian officer she had seated to one side and the Italian prince upon the other, very correctly alternating her conversations with the courses. She was pleased to note that more than once, the footmen were forced to circle the table with second helpings, and that the conversation seemed to glitter in a babel of languages. The contessa, seated next to Lord Robert and that rather down-at-the-heels Bonapartist with so much charm, caught her eye and nodded slightly, indicating to her that her cuisine had been, after all, well chosen.

Once or twice she allowed herself to look up and find Lord Robert catching her eye, but beyond bestowing a radiant smile upon her beloved, Miss Wingate did nothing so hoydenish as attempt to converse with him across several other persons. She was content that he was there, where she could look up and merely feast her eyes upon his presence, exchanging those small secret smiles over their wineglasses.

Later, spun about the ballroom in the arms of a Hessian colonel, Lydia caught a glimpse now and then of Lord Robert, leaning against the wall, watching her with a faint, amused smile on his face. It was so clear to her that he was proud of her, that he loved her... *he loves me and I love him*... Lydia's mind whirled as much as the dance; her cup of happiness was full to overflowing.

In spite of his shoulder, Jonathan was bearing

up well, she thought; perhaps the admiration of his friends for being brave enough to engage in a duel and the tender ministrations of so many young ladies went a farther distance than all the opiates in the world to ease his pain; certainly he was being very gallant and brave, an amusing change for a young man who, until a few weeks ago, had seized every opportunity to take on the character of an invalid complaining of every ache and pain.

Once or twice, she thought she saw him dancing with the Baroness Galtzalter, her ivory skin set off to advantage by a deep gown of teal blue, sapphires glittering in her dark hair, and she heaved a sigh that they would soon move in to Greece, safely away from that woman, whom she could not, would not trust with either her brother or her *beau*.

But even as she moved among her guests, greeting someone here, stopping for a chat there, a snatch of conversation, did someone wish for more champagne or perhaps a crab patty? Lydia was certain that Robert's eyes followed her about the room, that whatever he might be doing, he would always know exactly where she was, as she knew exactly where he was, without even having to look.

But at the first strains of the waltz, she was still surprised when he appeared like a specter at her shoulder, gently but firmly placing her hand in the crook of his elbow and disengaging her from the knot of people with whom she was conversing.

"My dance, I believe," he said and delivered her of a small bow, leading her into the tangle of dancers on the floor.

"We shall sit this one out, Miss Wingate! I shall, I hope have the rest of my life to dance with you and right now there are other reasons for seeking out the company of the most beautiful and intelligent female in the room," he told her as they discreetly slipped out the door into the blue-silver moonlight on the terrace.

Lydia allowed him to guide her away from her guests and seat her upon the shell-shaped bench. She watched as he made a turn about the terrace before returning to her, seating himself beside her and taking her hand between his own, smiling down at her. "Miss Wingate, I believe that you and I have spent a great deal of time together, enough to make our feelings toward one another conformable. While I have not yet made a formal offer to your father to pay my addresses to you with the intention of marriage firmly upon my heart, I would wish to do so now."

"Silly," Miss Wingate giggled at the high-blown formality of his language.

Robert laughed also, looking into her eyes. "How," he asked severely, "do you expect me to properly court you, within the bounds of propriety, if you keep collapsing into levity?"

"Because it is so funny, Robert!" With a little sigh, Miss Wingate rested her head against her beloved's shoulder. "Don't you know that I'd have you under any conditions at all? I am a blue-stocking, sir. Don't you know that I am, therefore, a believer in free love, that a woman must love where and how she chooses, and still maintain her own independence?"

"Miss Wingate, I must severely chastise you for such improper thoughts! Here I am, becoming

183

quite respectable, a rake reformed by love of a good woman, and you are speaking of free love?" He shook his head, and took her chin with his thumb and forefinger, so that she looked up into his eyes.

"But my dear Robert, I am sacrificing all my high-held principles by marrying you! Dear me, Robert, do, please allow me to shift my views, reformed by love!"

"That is my role, Lydia!" he said tenderly.

"Then I suppose we must compromise, Robert. I shall become a little less—so very respectable and dull and you shall become a little more so!"

"Agreed, although it is clear to me that I shall forever live beneath the cat's paw, and find all of my sins punished in matrimony with an abandoned hoyden whose every lark will etch futher lines into my highly moral brow!"

"Dear me," said Lydia, her eyes dancing. "And doubtless, you will lock me into a deserted tower to repent heartily of my escapades—Robert, you would not make me forsake my writing, would you?"

Lightly, he brushed his lips across her own. "Don't be a goose, my love! You shall continue— shall I have all the wrath of the muses upon my head for preventing your genius its natural flow?"

Miss Wingate sighed with relief. "I was perhaps afraid that you might have become so respectable that you would instantly suppress my deplorable tendencies the moment the ring was upon my finger."

"My darling foolish female! I would wish to give you every opportunity to create! Perhaps I shall take up something creative myself—embroidery or bargello, I wonder? Lydia, should you like to go to Greece for our honeymoon? The islands are so beautiful—last night I tossed and turned in my bed, thinking of you and me in Greece together, wondering how I could have ever enjoyed that country without you—how I could bear to endure my life without you, now that I've met you. Do you understand Lydia, how hopeless I believed my suit to be? What would a female like you possibly find to love in a man like me? And what evil spirit possessed Fate that we should have to wait so long to find each other?"

Miss Wingate sighed, pressing both of her hands into Marchman's, snuggling happily into his shoulder. "So many times, I dared not believe or think that you might see me as anything more than a friend! What could a man like you see in a poor old spinster like me?"

"Lydia, if you do not immediately desist referring to yourself in those terms, Miss Wingate, we shall have our first falling-out! You are the dearest and most wonderful creature nature has ever created, and surely I am blessed to be loved by you!"

"Not half as blessed as I feel to be loved by you," Lydia sighed. "Shall we come to blows over the superiority of one another's style and character, my love?"

"Undoubtedly we shall render our honeymoon hideous with our rows!" he promised lightly, stroking her cheek, his face turning suddenly grave. "Lydia, listen to me—I am struck by moon madness, but I am not so blind as to not consider what our situation must be. I have severed all ties from my home, my family—I am an exile, Lydia, an outcast. That is the life I am asking you to share with me, a life of wandering in foreign countries, among strangers—for you know, Lydia, you know that your Family will certainly consider you as one dead if you should marry a luckless wretch like me."

"I know," Lydia said clearly. She smiled and shook her head. "Robert, they don't need me any more—not as much as I need you, as you must need me. This summer has been as if I were released from a cage, released into a world I never dreamed existed—anywhere, Robert, would be paradise, if you were there with me."

He searched her face. "I only want your happiness, Lydia. I only want you to understand fully and completely what our life together would mean—"

"It would mean my greatest happiness," Lydia said softly. "Pray do not tease me, Robert! Don't make me think about the past—only our future, together."

"Lydia, I love you—I love you far more than I ever dreamed it possible to love, I love you on every level of my being—I love you enough, Lydia, to allow you to go—to go back to what is real and safe and known to you—"

"I love you, Robert—oh, will you just *kiss* me?"

Lord Robert was more than willing to comply with his beloved's request, bringing his lips to hers, searching her out hungrily, finding in her response the mirror of his own desire. Miss Wingate's arms were about his shoulders, her gown sadly forgotten in the crushing embrace they wrapped about one another, all forgotten in the final consummation of their love.

"Lydia Wingate! Have you become so depraved by this lascivious, abandoned scene of every ancient vice as to forget that you are a Wingate of Wingate House?"

The flat, American drawl that sliced across Lydia's bliss like a guillotine blade was all too familiar. It harkened every iota of her ingrained training and instinct back to her with the unpleasant and horrifying force of a beautiful dream suddenly turning into a nightmare, and she broke away from Robert, full of blushes and stammers, automatically preening at her hair, smoothing the curls into the neat bands that no longer existed. Not even love could perform a miraculous transformation of a lifetime of discipline and habit at that moment, and as Lydia turned to see the large and forbidding shape of Cornelia Schuyler looming like an avenging fury of Virtue's Protection above her, awful in a puce gown and a purple turban, she shuddered. Mrs. Biddle Schuyler never raised her voice—possibly had never raised her voice in her entire lifetime, and yet she had no need to. Her tones of iron harkened back some dreadful semblance of sanity to Lydia's mind, as if a trumpet had reawakened the spellbound and slumbering forces of generations of staid New York Quaker blood in her veins.

For a single, terrible second, Mrs. Schuyler seemed to loom above her as the embodiment of all of her former training, her rigid upbringing, then the woman took a step, and Lydia sighed, rallying a little.

"Really, Cornelia—" she begun.

"Really, my foot, Lydia! A fine—might I add a very fine piece of work you have created this season! When Mr. Schuyler and I returned to Como, it seemed as if the whole city was buzzing with talk of the Wingates! A Wingate, being spoken of in these heathen parts! I should have known what would have happened, I should have done my Duty before, but I believed that your aberrations were of a temporary nature—how could I possibly have believed, even within my heart of hearts, that a Wingate would give herself over to such scenes of sybaritic depravity as I have witnessed, now, with my own eyes! And I am not a moment too late, praise the Lord, to rescue you from—from this hardened rakehell, this libertine—this seducer of poor, innocent women! You sir, shall remove your person from touching a Wingate! I shall have you know that this lady is betrothed to my brother-in-law!"

"How do you do, Mrs. Schuyler?" Lord Robert asked drily, his grip tightening as Lydia automatically sought to pull away beneath this tirade.

Mrs. Cornelia Schuyler gave one of her famous damning sniffs; it might have been enough to depress the pretenses of some poor individual in New York, but Lord Robert merely leaned back, regarding her with amused eyes, unaware of the reaction she was producing in his beloved's breast.

"Really, Lydia! It is disgraceful—disgraceful! Biddle and I return from Milan with the wonderful news that your Grandfather and Charles are even now awaiting our arrival in London—Charles' regard for you was such that he did not wish to wait until you had returned to America to join with you in matrimony!"

"Grandfather—and Charles—in London?" Lydia demanded, rising from the bench, pressing a hand to her heart, oblivious now to Robert's hand, reaching out for her own.

Mrs. Schuyler gave a small sour smile and nodded, full of satisfaction. "I believed it to be my Duty to inform your Grandfather of the sort of company I had encountered you among in Como—certainly not the sort of persons We are used to! The result was fortunate and immediate—he and Charles sailed at once from New York! And not a moment too soon! What did I come here for, but to give you the happy news that Charles had decided, despite your Disgrace, to offer you his hand—most generous of a Schuyler of Schuyler, a patroon of Ancient Standing, you will agree, Miss Wingate—and what do I find? Persons of what I may only believe to be a very depressingly decadent style—The Princess of Wales, and no better than she should be!—dancing the waltz—the waltz!—in a Wingate House! And Jonathan creating an international incident—dueling with some young British fop over a female who is but no better than she should be either, this Baroness—this dear friend of yours, Lord Robert—with whom I have seen with my own eyes—I have seen you conducting a flagrant intrigue with that female in the Hotel Murat—"

"The Baroness?" Lydia spun around and looked at Lord Robert, open-mouthed. "Jon and Mr. Austin dueled over the Baroness? Oh, dear!"

"Exactly so, and well might you say 'oh, dear,' Lydia Wingate, allowing someone of Jonathan's delicate sensibilities, his uncertain health—to engage in a duel and be wounded, and almost creating an international incident, of course I felt it to be my Duty to report the affair to the United States Consul in Milan—"

"You go too far, ma'am, in your Duty!" Lord Robert cut in sharply, rising to his feet. "Do you realize that if this trivial matter was put into diplomatic hands, it could indeed create a great deal of unpleasantness between our two countries? And that unpleasantness, coming so recently upon the last war, is hardly what is needed at this point? Have you no consideration, no thought for the position you may have placed not only the Wingates, but Her Highness into? Your Duty, Mrs. Schuyler, has led you to meddle in affairs not of your concern!"

Mrs. Schuyler trembled with indignation. "Don't you dare address me, you—you profligate scoundrel! If it had not been for you—*seducing*—and don't believe for a moment that I didn't see what was going on out here in the moonlight, because I did—every disgusting bit of it!—an innocent American woman betrothed to another—but also seducing a young man into taking up every vice in which you so flagrantly indulge, including your cast-off mistress?"

"Charles and I were never really engaged—we only had an Understanding," Lydia murmured. "Only an Understanding...."

"And you are most fortunate for that! Do you wish to put your grandfather in the grave with your scandalous behavior? To disgrace all of your sisters, your sister's husbands, your nieces and nephews with your dreadful folly? Really, Lydia, if you were not a Wingate, one would not know what to think! It can only be madness—a temporary madness brought on by innocently mingling among such decadent company that would lead you into this—this scene of Sodom and Gomorrah!" With one hand, she indicated the sedate scene in the ballroom behind her, as if she turned her back upon Roman orgies.

"I–It is not madness!" Lydia cried, but there was an edge of uncertainty in her voice, as she struggled valiantly to maintain that which she had won against all odds. "I—Lord Robert and I are to be married!"

"Married?" Mrs. Schuyler demanded shrilly. "You actually entertained the idea of marrying this—this wastrel when a Schuyler has offered for your hand? Do you wish to kill your grandfather, Lydia? Do you wish to put him into the grave? This is his wish—that you should return at once to London, under the escort of myself and Mr. Biddle Schuyler and be properly married to a man of a family and fortune to equal your own, not—not some depraved, decadent nobleman's son, lost over to every vice!"

"Lydia!" Robert cried in a low voice, but she could not turn toward him, she was rooted to the spot, unable to tear her eyes away from Cornelia Schuyler's frosty disapproval.

"I cannot believe that a Wingate of Wingate would refuse not only the requests of her Grandfather, a man who has given her *everything* but the hand of a man like Charles Schuyler, so respectable, so upright in every American virtue—to—to toss herself away upon an uncertain life with a hardened libertine! And what, Miss, will you do when he casts you off, after his empty promises, upon some foreign city, to pursue another female? For your Grandfather will do his Duty, I assure you—and cut you off utterly without a cent! Without your own dear sisters, your brother—all of New York—A very pretty mess, indeed! Why, the alliance of a Schuyler and a Wingate will cement two of the greatest Families in New York— two of the greatest fortunes? And what, I wonder does he have to offer you in the way of a fortune? You, you cad, must have known from the start that Miss Wingate is a considerable heiress—"

"My fortune is doubtless not the equal of her own, but I believe in a quiet way that it is adequate to support us both," Lord Robert said. "Lydia— please, look at me—"

Gently he turned her about, and felt as if he looked into the face of death. All animation had fled from her countenance, leaving her expression that of stricken angst, guilt, confusion. "R–Robert—" she pleaded.

"Lydia, do you hear what this woman says? If you marry me, you become as I have become—an exile, a wanderer, I cannot assure your future with me, I can only tell you that I love you, Lydia, and that shall never change. That is all I offer you against everything you have been brought up to believe in, every precept in which you have been reared. All I can offer you is the promise that I shall always love you, always cherish you. Is that enough? Lydia, I love you enough to try to allow you to make a choice, do you understand that?"

She nodded, numbly staring into his eyes.

"Very pretty speeches, my lord! And with your reputation, vastly amusing!" Mrs. Biddle Schuyler retorted. "Lydia, you have been promised to my brother-in-law—you have given your word. Think of the Disgrace you have already brought upon your Family—of what further disgrace you shall heap upon their innocent heads if you elope with this—this *vastly unsuitable man!* Not only shall you put your grandfather in his grave, but you shall violate every Principle upon which Persons of New York must pride themselves! If you accept this madness, you shall forever regret it, I promise you. And only consider what your grandfather's reaction will be when I inform him of your brother's goings-on!"

"You wouldn't dare!" Lydia retorted.

"Wouldn't I? It would be my Duty! But if you return to London, I am sure that you would lay your version of these events before Mr. Wingate and Charles far better than I."

"Blackmail, ma'am, think on!" Lord Robert said softly.

Mrs. Schuyler drew herself up to her full height. "*I* need not respond to that, from you, sir! God only knows what wiles you have used to seduce this woman away from her family and friends—I am sure that blackmail is the least of your black arts!" She added, "Well, Lydia?"

Miss Wingate looked at Lord Robert. He shook his head. "You must come to me of your own heart, Lydia," he said softly. "Knowing all of my sins, all of the consequences. The only thing I could possibly find to agree with Mrs. Schuyler about is that it must be your own decision."

Lydia turned to Mrs. Schuyler. "Lydia, come to your senses! Can't you see what injury you will do to the Family if you go with this man, what great benefits they shall all reap if you return, like the very commonsensical girl I know you to be to New

York as Mrs. Charles Schuyler? The *Family*, Lydia!"

Slowly, she turned back to Robert, who regarded her steadily, but made no move.

It was as if someone had wiped away all of her will; the past was too strong, too great an instinct to be so easily overcome.

"I—I am sorry, Robert—I c-could never m-make you happy!" she whispered, and without a word, brushed past Mrs. Schuyler, who nodded triumphantly at Lord Robert.

"This is a great day for the Wingates!" she almost crowed. "To marry a Schuyler is a very great honor indeed."

Marchman inclined his head. "I am certain," he said drily, "that is as near to apotheosis as a mortal may achieve in this world. And ma'am, I hope you may sleep well at nights, thinking upon how you have destroyed the happiness of two people upon the altar of money and pride! I bid you good night, madam!" Without as much as a bow, he turned upon his heel and strode down the stairs.

Blindly walking through the ballroom, Lydia only saw the figure of the Baroness through a mist. She withdrew as the woman sought to put a hand upon her arm. "Miss Wingate! I am truly sorry," the Baroness gasped. "Truly, I had not meant that it should have gone as far as it had between your brother and Mr. Austin—I only wanted to make Marchman a little jealous, to hurt him as he hurt me—you must—"

Lydia drew herself up; a cold, ironic smile flickered across her pale face, and she regarded the other woman not with hatred, but from a vast pity. "It is of no consequence, I assure you! Your schemes were all in vain! Doubtless as soon as the good Baron sticks his spoon in the wall, you and Lord Robert will be able to make a very fine match of it! Now, if you will excuse me—"

She rushed blindly away, unable to hide her tears any longer, leaving the Baroness staring after her with a haunted look in her dark, beautiful eyes.

The contessa—witnessing this exchange and the triumphant return from the terrace, not of Marchman, but of that dreadful American woman, a self-righteous smile upon her wattled face—darkly withdrew her promise. Rosalba would not have her altarcloth after all.

Unless. Setting her face in the most charming of smiles, the contessa approached Mrs. Schuyler and her husband. If either of them knew how much this regal and elegant lady wished them both in *Purgatorio*, they might have felt very differently indeed.

Ten

London was gray, foggy and damp; a high contrast indeed to those last sunny glimpses of Italian shores that the Wingates had been afforded, rather like Lot's Wife, over their shoulders as they were ruthlessly borne away by the Biddle Schuylers, back to London. It was a journey rendered hideous for Lydia, not only by Jonathan's sullen resentment of the Schuylers' overbearing ways, but by Cornelia Schuyler's voluble complaints upon every subject from the cabins assigned them by the packet-company to the rough weather they endured upon their northern voyage. If Mrs. Schuyler had decided to Say No More upon Lydia's transgressions, it was a very eloquent silence indeed, and it said a great deal for Miss Wingate's self-control that she sustained her temper as well as she did, her nerves already sadly frayed by events at Villa Solario.

But if Miss Wingate shed tears, she shed them

in private, exhibiting to the outside world only her calm demeanor and a certain thoughtful silence, only allowing some indication of her inner turmoil to surface in the long chess games she wiled away the endless seabound days with Jonathan by allowing him to beat her soundly several times, if only to keep the peace.

While neither Lydia nor Jonathan spoke of their feelings about having their independence thus rudely snatched away from them, for both of them were very fond of their grandfather and understood the filial duty they owed this gentleman, there was an unspoken tension, a cloud of gloom that surrounded both of them. Not even to Jonathan did Lydia confide her true feelings about events at Lake Como that summer, but if by the time that the packet boat put into Plymouth she had indeed come to regard her season abroad as a temporary madness in an otherwise well-ordered life, the last fling of a lonely bored spinster whose head had been turned by the sophistication of European ways, it would not have been surprising, for Mrs. Biddle Schuyler, with one purpose in mind, had been steadily hammering away at Lydia for well onto a fortnight by that time.

The only indication she gave of her true feelings was a smile when Jonathan muttered rebelliously of *being brought to Rome in chains*.

It was perhaps fortunate that they reached Grillion's Hotel in London at an hour well past midnight for Lydia could not have sustained either an interview with her grandfather or Mr. Schuyler after a day spent in the closed confines of a post chaise with Cornelia Schuyler and her vacant echoing husband, a Jonathan growing more sullen and raw-tempered by the moment, and the grim stoicism of the Penningtons, suspicious as always of foreign travel.

It would not perhaps have been expected that such an august and elegant establishment as Grillion's Hotel would have removed every obstacle to the pleasant and comfortable stay of such a plainly dressed and plainly spoken American gentleman as Mr. Perryman Wingate of New York City, but that gentleman was an old and valued patron of that fine place, and his dollars spoke far louder than his words. While his tastes may have been simple, his ideas of comfort were not, and the suites of rooms that he had engaged for his expected party occupied almost an entire floor. Miss Wingate was immediately escorted to her own chambers, and left with the message that at eight-thirty, she would be expected to breakfast in her grandfather's suite, a few doors down the corridor from her own. It at least gave Miss Wingate a night, Mrs. Schuyler said, to meditate upon her sins, and that lady would have been afforded very little satisfaction if she had known that Lydia's head touched the pillow and Miss Wingate was asleep.

She had never been anything in her life but a dutiful and loving granddaughter, and that next morning she was not to deviate from her patterns of a lifetime, her Italian fineries packed in the bottom of her trunks, her hair knotted simply at the crown of her head. Attired in a simple round dress of dove-colored cambric ornamented with knots of white silk, she knocked firmly upon her progenitor's door, to all outward appearances perfectly composed in her first interview in six months with the elder Mr. Wingate.

A little to her surprise, it was Perryman Wingate himself who threw back the door and opened his arms in welcome to his eldest. "Lyddie!" he said simply, and Miss Wingate embraced him with a vast feeling of relief, and all the affection she felt for a progenitor who had served as both parents to her for many, many years.

As they drew back to regard what six months' separation had done to change one another, it could have been seen by an interested spectator (and the waiter laying out the lavish breakfast was an interested spectator in all aspects of the American Nabob) that there was a close Family Resemblance between grandfather and granddaughter. The elder Mr. Wingate, with seventy-odd years upon his dish, stood as straight and tall as any man half his age. Time had set a firming sculptor's hand upon his angular features, and had turned his leonine mane from corn-gold to snow-white, but there was a distinct warmth in his blue eyes, normally described by his business associates as being as cold as the North Atlantic waters his ships plied, and a certain unexpected softness in the generally thin and tight line of his lips. Despite the severity of his dark and somber attire, no fault could have been found by the most censorious critic with his style, or the quality of the materials upon which his tailors had built his wardrobe. His religious beliefs may have demanded that everything be of the plainest, but his own beliefs insisted upon quality in all things. "Lydia! Thee looks quite well, Granddaughter— thee has done thy hair in a different way, I see!

For a second, when I beheld thee, I thought that I beheld thy mother—but, come, our breakfast awaits us, and I imagine thee is hungry! How is Jonathan? Did thee take good care of thy brother? I thought it best to allow him to sleep in this morning."

"Jonathan is quite well, Grand, and so are you! I have never seen you look handsomer!" Lydia affectionately linked her arm into his as they approached a table set with a vast English breakfast for two.

Mr. Wingate tried to frown, but the effort was quite lost upon any of his grandchildren. "Thee speaks of a man well past his prime, Lyddie! But I go on well enough and better than that poor scoundrel Burr, whom I could give fifteen years or more! He was here last night and begging money, Lyddie, 'twas a sad thing to see any man fallen so low, after rising so high...."

Miss Wingate, who knew better than most how hard a shell held so soft a heart, imagined that Perryman Wingate had been generous with his old enemy, but wisely did not press this side of the issue, merely allowing him to seat her before himself and helping them both to vast amounts of grilled kidney and eggs and cold muffins.

"Thy chef has made a mistake, my man! We want coffee, not tea, if you please!" he said to the waiter, who bowed low and offered many apologies as he jumped to rectify this mistake.

When they were alone, Wingate shook his head and regarded Lydia, a faint crease appearing between his magnificently sweeping brows. "Now, no roundaboutation, if you please, Lyddie! Thee knows that I have no more use for Cornelia Schuyler than for a red silk petticoat to call my own, but it would appear that thee has fallen into a scrape?"

Lydia carefully buttered her toast, and took a bite, chewing thoughtfully, before she spoke, as her grandfather did, without roundaboutation. "I think, Grand, that she exaggerates the case. It would have passed off without incident if it had not been for her meddling. As it was, it took a very stern note from the Princess of Wales to put a period to the matter." Very carefully, she described the incidents leading up to the duel with Mr. Austin and Mr. Wingate, only infrequently, and as a last resort mentioning Lord Robert Marchman's part in smoothing out potential difficulties. But the old man regarded her shrewdly, seeing the light blush rise and fall in her cheek, and, having a much better idea of which way the wind was blowing than his granddaughter would ever have dreamed an elderly Quaker gentleman capable of, only nodded.

"So you see, Grand," Lydia finished calmly as the waiter returned with a silver pot of coffee, removing the offending tea service, "it was only a schoolboy's prank—the sort of thing Jonathan should just have worked out of his system long ago, if he had not fallen ill and been so cosseted. I think perhaps you ought to give consideration to Marchman's suggestion that he be allowed to join the Navy—but you should speak to *him* about that score."

Mr. Wingate waited until the waiter had bowed himself out of the room before he poured them each a cup of steaming brown liquid, stirring sugar thoughtfully into his cup. "And who, I may ask of thee, is this Lord Robert Marchman who bobs in and out of this story like a *deus ex machina* in a play?" he asked casually.

Miss Wingate bit her lower lip and cast down her eyes, a gesture her grandfather had not seen her make since her schoolgirl days, and only then after she had committed some grievous outrage. But her voice was equally casual as she made her careful reply. "Oh, he was a friend of ours, much like the Contessa d'Orsini—he ciceroned us about, here and there, you know."

"Cornelia seemed to think there was a great deal more to it than that, Lyddie. Lord Robert Marchman apparently does not enjoy the love of all of his fellow men in his own country. Some scandal or another is attached to his name."

Lydia threw her grandfather a very sharp glance. "Dear me," she said simply, and the old man suppressed a smile.

"Lyddie, thee and I have never minced words with one another. It might surprise thee to know that I was once a young man, and sent to Oxford to continue my studies. There I happened to meet a young miss, the sister of a friend of mine—no, they were *not* Quakers, in fact they were minor aristocracy, as full of worldly pleasures as could hold. I was a young man, and I fancy, a bit of a blood, in my own way," He smiled at this memory and Lydia, somewhat shocked at the idea of her grandfather ever being a *bit of a blood*, stared at him. "But, it was calf-love, only, and she far better off married to an earl's son than to me, and I of course married thy grandmother, may she repose in peace, who was of my circle and who understood all of my needs as easily as I myself." He leveled a glance beneath his brows at Lydia. "It was a bit of calf-love only—she was a great beauty, and a lively miss, but sadly devoted to worldly pleasures. Our worlds were very different, Lydia, very different indeed. Oh, at the time, I thought my heart was broken and I should never recover from the wound, but I was halfway home to America when I knew that my place was New York, just as hers was London." He sipped his coffee. "Does thee understand what I am trying to tell thee? Thee will be a great heiress, Lyddie—I like to think that all of my grandchildren will be left warm and snug when I finally stick my spoon in the wall, but I have kept thee, selfishly, perhaps—"

"No, Grand! Never!" Lydia protested. "What would we have all done if you had not taken us in?"

"There was no other question, child, where else would thee all have gone if not to thy grandfather? But my point, Lydia, is that thee has been kept back from such experiences by the circles in which thee moves in New York, else thee would have been more aware of the motives of others...."

Lydia hung her head, feeling quite wretched. "I am such a Disappointment to you, Grand," she said miserably, and quite without her usual tartness.

He patted her hand. "Nay, thee has never disappointed me, Lyddie, as it is with Jonathan, so with thee; I have kept thee wrapped in cotton wool far too long. It should have been my duty to warn thee of the snares and traps of the old world—thee should have had a mother for such a role. Thee has done thy best, always, and thee knows that thy Grand wants only the best for thee. Always, Lyddie, I have tried to be impartial, to be equal among all of my offspring, but thee—thee, Lyddie has always held a special place in my heart." He leaned back in his chair and hooked his thumbs into the sleeves of his waistcoat, a faint smile breaking the severity of his expression. "I am not so old as not to feel the Spirit moving me in the error of my ways, child. While I was in meeting, right after thee and thy brother had departed for Europe, I meditated profoundly upon thy career as an Authoress, and asked the Spirit for guidance. I was moved to speak, and I said, 'I have committed a worldly sin out of my own vanity, for I have cast off my beloved granddaughter for expressing the movement of the Spirit inside herself, all because I dared to disagree with the way in which the Spirit chose to move another.'"

It took Lydia a moment to work out the logic of this in her head, and when she had, she rose and knelt beside her grandfather's chair, taking both of his hands in her own, burying her head in his lap as he stroked her curls. "Truly, child, it is thee for whom I must ask my forgiveness. The Spirit has also revealed to me that there is much truth and not a little humor in what thee writes, once I was guided to sit down and read thy works."

"Oh, Grand!" Miss Wingate sighed. "I have been such a dreadful trial to you—"

"Eat thy breakfast, Lydia, I would not have thee starving for my vanity and pride. I shall read thee no sermons this morning, upon thy life at Como, for I hold myself to blame for all of that far more than either of thee. It was my duty to speak to thee both, and I was so caught up in worldly affairs that I failed beside my own hearth. Thy own discomfort is far more than enough punishment, I suspect. But it shall be a warning to thee in future to avoid persons given over to a life of pleasure, those who reap nor sow not, toil nor spin not, and who are members of the aristocracy. It is a very bad thing, this system of titles and rank, and against all that thee has been brought up to believe."

Lydia nodded listlessly, but could not help but add, "Lord Robert Marchman was a most estimable man, Grand! No matter what his repute might have been, nothing could have been more considerate than the manner in which he treated Jonathan—and me."

"Perhaps so, but thee recalls that thee must never overturn a stone without expecting to find the worms beneath. Tell me, child, could thee see thyself living in New York with this man? Could thee truly picture a Wingate of Wingate House married to such a person as this Lord Robert appears to be? Or 'twas it just the spell of the time and the place?"

Miss Wingate looked thoughtful. Whatever opinion her grandfather might cherish of Cornelia Schuyler, that woman had done her work well. And with ample time in which to exert her influence and her will upon Miss Wingate's training, it had almost taken. For just a second, the rebellion flickering up from within Miss Wingate's bosom seemed about to flare out, but recalling that it would never do to contradict her beloved Grandfather's opinion, for his thoughts in general always had a depressing way of turning out to be correct over the long run, she settled down again, dropping her eyes meekly. "I suppose it was the time and place, Grand," she said. "But I would not have traded it for all of the world. Just once, Grand to be loved—really and truly loved, not for being a Wingate of Wingate House, not for being a great beauty, which I am not, and never will be—but for being simply Lydia—"

"Ease off, child! Never did I think to see thee having the vapors like Verity!" Mr. Wingate said soothingly. "'Tis but a flame that rises and dies, this love thee speak of. I know, believe me Lyddie, that of which I speak. Thy grandmother and I never felt the deep passions, but we have had something far more comfortable between us, and that grew over the years. Does thee understand?"

Lydia nodded. The sparkle had died from her eyes.

"Now, thee is one-and-thirty, Lyddie, and far past the age of missishness. But I will not force thee to marry where thee has no inclination. Whatever thy state, spinster, widow, or married, thee will be well provided for in thy own right. But Charles Schuyler, while not precisely the man I should have chosen for thee, loves thee in his own way, and his ways are our ways, his people our people, his manners our own. He will provide thee with a life thee knows thyself to be secure in, among thy own people. He feels such for thee that he has come to London to secure thy hand, Lyddie, and before this event, thee was not unpartial to his suit. But I will not force thee to marry where thee does not wish to do so."

"Charles," Miss Wingate said, rather dully, "is a most estimable man!"

"Exactly so! And his fortune will more than match thy own! I do not marry off my granddaughters to suit my convenience, but I do not toss them lightly away upon useless wastrels, either." Lydia, trying to picture any of her sisters meeting anyone in the circles within which the Wingates moved who could be classified as a *useless wastrel*, only nodded.

Mr. Wingate evidently took this as an assent to his opinion. "So, then! In time thee will see that thy decision was wise, Lyddie. Thy head has been turned a little by worldly manners, but at heart, thee must know that thy true directions lie in the well-rutted paths."

Miss Wingate bit back a bitter smile at this thought and her grandfather's innocent pun, particularly in relation to the widowed Mr. Schuyler and his pack of offspring.

Unfortunately, Perryman Wingate mistook this smile for one of sunny agreement, and more than relieved that the unpleasant task of setting his eldest granddaughter back upon the straight and narrow path had been accomplished, merely abjured her to finish her breakfast and grant her anxious fiancé an interview, as he was expecting the Minister of Trade to call upon him at ten. From that point on, the conversation was turned to more general topics, and there was so much news for Mr. Wingate and his daughter to share that he did not notice Lydia's undercurrent of rebellion.

Mr. Charles Schuyler was not, unfortunately, an imposing figure. Like his brother, Biddle, he was inclined to be red-faced and more than a little stout, with an underslung jaw and a pair of slightly protuberant eyes. All morning, he was nervously awaiting the close of Lydia's interview with her grandfather, and while it may have said a great deal for his sense of propriety that he did not seek an interview with her himself until she was sent to his sitting rooms, it also said very little for his sense of the romantic.

He had been nervously pacing the room, in conversation with his brother and sister-in-law when Lydia made her entrance. With a rare degree of license, however, Cornelia soon allowed the lovers to be private, masterfully shepherding Biddle out the door before her and smiling upon them both in a rather self-satisfied manner.

She need not, however, have entertained a great deal of fear that Lydia's virtue was in jeopardy from a closeted *tête-à-tête* with Charles. With the greatest possible propriety, he strode ceremoniously across the room and took one of Miss Wingate's hands within his own, bowing so slowly over it that she heard the audible creak of his stays. "Dear, dear Miss Wingate!" he wheezed, a little out of breath from tight lacing. "I can only say that it is a deep, deep pleasure to see you again, looking so well."

"Hullo, Charles," Lydia replied listlessly. "How very nice to see you again."

Since this was precisely Mr. Schuyler's idea of correct conduct in courting, he permitted himself a smile and the pleasure of pressing Miss Wingate's hand to his lips.

"My poor, poor Lydia! Cornelia has been telling me that you have been much racketed about by some goings-on of your brother's at Lake Como. Not at all what one would wish for, oh, no! Most improper, most improper indeed, to send you junketing about when a tutor would have done as well for the boy! You must be quite fagged to death! I find foreign travel so exhausting! I have not had a wink of sleep upon my bed since I left the Hudson!"

"I'm sure," Miss Wingate allowed, letting him lead her to a sofa. After she had seated herself, he seated himself at a proper distance from her, only showing his deep ardor by again clasping one of her hands within his own. Lydia supposed it was not his fault that his palms sweated so, or that he had not changed for the better in six months' time, but indeed, seemed to have resorted to the dye-bottle to stain his graying locks a jet black, one curl plastered against his forehead.

He gazed upon her for several seconds, then attempted a silly sally of what passed for humor. "I understand you have been a naughty little puss, and you've been writing again! That will never do, never do at all! Why, women should never have learned to read and write! It can only detract from their feminine and helpless charms in the eyes of any truly chivalrous male. My poor Lydia, what horrors you must have been subjected to, without me to protect you from this hot-bed of foreigners."

Since Miss Wingate had the choice of acerbically pointing out they were foreigners here or holding her tongue, she wisely chose silence.

Mr. Schuyler, perhaps worried about allowing such a desirable quarry to slip away again, taking with it its fortune and Family Connections, did not allow the inclement silence to last above a minute. "But we shall have time and more to discuss all of that later! I am prepared to forgive you, Lydia, after all, you cannot have been expected to know what was proper and what was not—you have never enjoyed the benefits of such an excellent mother as I have had, and certain excuses must be made for that fact."

Since Mr. Schuyler's late mother was, to the best of Lydia's recollection, far worse a dragon than her daughter-in-law, this might have been expected to elicit some remark from her, but she merely stared out the window at the dripping autumn rain.

"Lydia, there is no need to discuss the advantages of our alliance—of our fortunes and our families! Most excellent! Most excellent indeed! It only remains to make this alliance a reality! Tell me, will you consent to marry me now? Truly, I cannot wait any longer! My children need a mother, my house needs a hostess, my business needs—needs you to stand behind me! The American ambassador had made all the arrangements for us to be married this very afternoon—we may return to New York as man and wife! Could anything be better than a long sea voyage, you and I and all of our families together in great and happy intimacy?"

Miss Wingate could imagine few fates worse than further confinement in enclosed spaces with Cornelia Schuyler, but she put it down to her recent disappointments, and forced herself to smile. What did it matter what she did now, she wondered? Her life was over, just as it was about to begin; it had lived and died as swiftly as fireworks.

"Whatever you like, Charles," she replied tonelessly.

Her reward was to have her hand covered with moist kisses. "Dear Lydia, you have made me the wealthiest—that is to say in happiness! Yes, the wealthiest man in happiness in New York! Only allow me to tell Biddle and Cornelia and your Grandfather!"

She barely felt the transfer of his moist lips from her hand to her cheek. "Dearest Lydia!" he crooned.

Dearest dollars and cents, she thought, and a single tear trickled down her cheek.

"This should be the happiest day of thy life!" Friend Hannah clucked as she wound Lydia's hair out of the curl-papers. "And thee looks as if thee is going to a funeral!"

Lydia looked at her reflection in the mirror. Above the happy flair of Grasini's gown, her face looked strained and corpselike. Like a condemned prisoner, she stole a glance at the clock. Three-thirty. At four, they would all depart in the chaise waiting below for the American Embassy—and her wedding.

"It may as well be a funeral," Lydia sighed, watching without any great enthusiasm as Hannah dressed her hair high upon her head and fastened her pearl-set about her ears and throat.

Friend Hannah made a little sound in the back of her throat as a gentle knock fell against the door. "What I say, Friend Lydia, is that you've been sold down the river! Girl, you haven't had time to catch your breath!" Still fussing, she walked to the door, opened it and exchanged a few words with the person who stood outside. Lydia, totally uninterested, propped her chin in her hand and continued to stare sightlessly in the mirror, hearing the ghost of a waltz long played out.

"Lyddie! Hssst!"

She gave a little start and turned about to see her brother, dressed in his wedding finest, tiptoeing across the floor. Their eyes met in the mirror and Lydia picked up her silver brush.

"Really, Jon," she said a little snappishly. "Everyone is waiting downstairs. Can't *you* respect my desire for a little privacy, at least?"

Jon ran a hand through his hair and smiled. "I've got a surprise for you," he said in that tone he had used to use to present her with a garter snake or a dead cat in a velvet box.

Lydia frowned. "Well, I'm sure I don't want it! Now, Jonathan, please!

"Jonathan!" Lydia then shrieked, automatically folding her arms protectively over her head.

When she had waited several seconds and nothing had been poured upon her or was slithering down her back or had leapt out at her from one of his pockets, Miss Wingate peeked out from the crook of her elbow.

In the mirror, her eyes met those of Contessa d'Orsini, and with a cry, she whirled about to embrace her old friend.

"Oh, dear!" Lydia almost wailed, enfolded comfortingly in that embrace of musk and mantua. It was several seconds before she noted that the room contained a second unexpected guest, and slowly, she broke away from the contessa and held out her arms, openly and simply.

The contessa watched this with a little interest for a few seconds before giving Jonathan and Friend Hannah a businesslike nod.

"Tout va bien!" she announced to her companions making a satisfied rubbing gesture with her finely gloved hands...her vast hat's enormous plumes trembling with self-satisfaction. "Now, Friend Hannah, you will please to pack Miss Ly-

dia's things and your own! Jonathan, *vite*! you will go downstairs and how d'you say in American—stall them off at the pass! Keep them in the parlor and well away from the door for fifteen minutes. No less, no longer! We do not want them to have a look at the staircase! And then, when I descend, Jonathan, you will please allow me the pleasure of announcing that there was a slight alteration in the wedding plans of Miss Wingate! For I have promised St. Theresa that Rosalba shall have not only a new altarcloth but a whole silver communion set for her convent if I may but see the face of this grandfather—not to mention this La Scee–ler woman!—when I break them this news! *Vite, Vite!* And you two, *mes caritoes*, must save your reunion for another time! Right now there is not a second to lose."

"You loved me enough to come to England, after me!" Miss Wingate said in a smothered voice.

"Lydia, I loved you enough to venture into hell unarmed, if only for this moment," Lord Robert Marchman told his beloved fondly. "But the contessa is right! We must hurry if we're to make a start for Scotland, my darling bluestocking!"

Epilogue

A chill north wind had been blowing all day, but with the coming of nightfall, it had increased its autumnal force, rattling the study windows in their casements and sending billows of smoke down the ancient chimney, giving the dimly lit study a foggy ambiance that was really, Lydia thought, quite Gothic.

With the small writing table drawn up before the fire, a shawl wrapped closely about her shoulders and several pieces of paper spread out on the blotter before her, she was not giving too much thought to what she was supposed to be writing. Rather she was chewing the nib of her pen and watching Lord Robert Marchman, lounging in his chair, his feet propped up on a footstool, reading the OBSERVER. Her expression was quite tender.

Sensing that he was being watched, Lord Robert dropped his paper and peered at her over the headline. "Do you regret your decision, now that you have seen Iverston, my love?" he asked fondly.

Lydia shook her head. "No! Although I was just sitting here thinking that I ought to write a series of positively Gothic novels with this pile as my inspiration. Your housekeeper's tour included the fact that there is not a sheet in the house that has not been darned, and that the kitchen stove belches smoke worse than all of the chimneys. And your plumbing, Robert, leaves much to be desired. All in all, a perfect setting for Scenes of Horror."

"More likely scenes of Domestic Discomfort. I have carried you off to a moldering house where everything is under dust and holland covers."

"Hardly romantic, my love. I am sadly abused and will immediately apply for redress as the very picture of Outraged Innocence, coming into a house unoccupied for five years and finding a nest of squirrels in the bedroom eves."

"My darling Lydia. Should you prefer to go back to Italy?" he asked with some concern.

She shook her head. "Not when there is so much that needs to be done here. And you do love this house, do you not?"

"It's been in my family for three hundred years. It was passed on to me from my Aunt Serena, who kept a hundred cats and talked to the shades of her dead lovers. I was terrified of her as a small boy, my brother and I were certain she was a witch. If you listen carefully, you can probably hear her ghost wandering through the gallery."

"Looking for her cats, no doubt! What a banbury tale! Mrs. Marty told me that your Aunt Serena was a very clean little old maiden lady who would

215

have a spin in her grave if she'd seen the way in which you have allowed your house—her house!—to fall into ruin," Lydia said with a severity that did not quite reach her voice.

"Humbug! I should have taken you to one of the hotels instead of bringing you here. The place is a ruin!"

"But, Robert, my love, it is your home and say what you will, I know very well how much you love this house and how glad you are to be back here."

Robert looked at her, and slowly smiled. "I never could bamboozle *you*, Lydia, could I? Doubtless you think it's a queer old place, and damp and musty, but yes, I do love it. And I love being home—if you're here!"

"Dear Robert, wherever you are, there I shall be, until you are quite tired of seeing me! No, I love it very much, and I think that it only needs to be lived in and well, *improved* a little—" She paused to watch as another puff of smoke spit down the chimney.

"A little!" Robert laughed, tossing aside his paper. "Come here, you mistress of understatement. I shall keep you warm!"

Lydia abandoned her writing table to perch indecorously upon Robert's lap with a happy little sigh. He stroked her hair and gazed thoughtfully into the fire. "I only want you to be happy."

"Then you will oblige me by buying me new sheets and an enclosed stove for the kitchen, my dear, for I mean to become a chatelaine and rattle my keys in a perpetual bustle of domesticity." Miss Wingate sighed. "I shall always be underfoot, and shall quite ruin you with plans for redecoration and modernization."

"What? And all the guidebooks describe Iverston as *a charmingly ancient house*! Will you have me throw up a Nash facade and erect a Gothic ruin in the Park? No, we already have a Gothic ruin, did I show it to you? It was the old castle that once stood here when my ancestors were border lords."

"Yes, and the Park that Queen Elizabeth stripped of deer on her visit here, also," Lydia said when she was not being kissed. "Your American lady, Robert, will make heads shake and tongues click with her modern ideas."

"I am no stranger to talk. But my lady, like Caesar's wife, will be above reproach. Within a fortnight, you will have had cards left by everyone of consequence in the neighborhood."

"Ah! Then I shall further drive you into ruin by insisting that you purchase me a very grand carriage in which to return all of these calls. And a phaeton, also, with a matched pair of grays, I think, so that I may cut a dash and run races with Letty Lade! I intend to be a Sporting Peeress, I assure you!"

"Then I shall have to be kinder to Lord West, who is the Master of Hounds, for you will need to become a member of the Quaghorn Hunt!"

"Dear me!" Lydia said, and was kissed again.

When she had emerged from his embrace, she held her head up. "Robert, I thought I heard a carriage on the drive."

She was kissed yet another time. "Only the ghost of Aunt Serena's lover, who is said to arrive

217

headless, together with his headless pair on such nights as this!" he assured her.

"Thee will not need to announce me, I say! I have come after my granddaughter and thee will stand aside!" a familiar voice said.

Lydia slid from Robert's lap. "Oh, *dear!* It is Grandfather at last!" she exclaimed.

"Come to beard the lion in his den, no doubt. Well, Lydia, I suppose that we ought to send down for some sort of dinner for him! I imagine in addition to being very out of sorts, that he is cold and tired and hungry and much in need of a toddy!"

"Exactly so," Lydia murmured, pulling the bell.

At that moment, the study door burst open and Mr. Perryman Wingate, in a full drab coat, strode into the room, his brow thunderous, his lips pressed together in a tight line. "At last I have found thee, thou despoiler of females! I may have seventy years, but I'm still a match for thee, sir! My principles forbid me to call thee out, but— but?" Mr. Wingate in the act of shaking his fist at Lord Robert, in a dressing gown and carpet slippers, a newspaper across his chest, faltered a little. His fantasies of scenes of depraved decadence, nurtured over the two-day gambit of his runaway granddaughter and her lover, had not included such a placidly domestic scene as was now presented to his eyes.

"Touché!" said the contessa, very fine and none the worse for wear in a velvet traveling pelisse and a very large hat with several purple plumes, coming in behind him. "If you please, Meester Wingate, I have endured quite enough of your tantrums upon this journey and now I would like some

218

hot arrack punch and a very good dinner and Josefina will warm my bed for me! Good evening, Robert and Lydia!"

"T-tantrums?" Mr. Wingate faltered, looking at the contessa in a very strange way. "Thee says that I am throwing tantrums! Thee, madam, will stay out of a matter that is none of thy concern!"

"Pish!" the contessa replied, stripping off her gloves and looking about the room. "For two days, I have listened to you, Meester Wingate, and I am bored with your anger! You will allow me to make you known to Lord Robert Marchman, and you will be a gentleman!"

Much to Lydia's surprise, her grandfather did calm down, if only a little, shaking Lord Robert's hand.

"How do you do, sir? Contessa, this is an unexpected pleasure! We had only ordered one extra bedchamber made up, you know, in anticipation of your visiting us, Mr. Wingate," Lord Robert said equably.

Mr. Wingate stared at him, growing very red in the face. "Thee is a despoiler of innocent females, and I will not stay in thy house! Lydia, thee will make thyself ready to return to London instantly!"

"Hullo, Grand," Lydia said, keeping a discreet space with her progenitor, but allowing the contessa to embrace her. "I think you would be much happier if you would pull your chair up to the fire and warm yourself! The northern journey is not a comfortable one and I know that you must be very tired! Contessa, do you desire me to show you to your bedchamber?"

"Oh, no! This I do not miss for the world!"

"Thee!" Mr. Wingate said, turning on the contessa. "If it had not for thee, none of this would have come about! Thee!"

"Do not fatigue me, Meester Wingate! All the way into this bleakness of the Nordico I have come with you, and you have been like the wasp trapped in the jar, buzzing to sting something! Now you will not sting anyone, I think, but you will be much happier if you have a good dinner and a bottle of wine and a warm bed."

"I agree with the contessa, sir!" Lord Robert said, assisting his guest to remove his greatcoat and leading him to a seat before the fire while Lydia gave the orders for a meal to be brought up instantly for their arrivals.

"To top it all off, that butler of thine should get the sack, behaving as if he were a Royal Duke!" Mr. Wingate growled, but warmed his hands nonetheless.

Lydia, assisting the contessa to remove her bonnet and pelisse, turned and smiled. "Oh, no! Marty is not a Royal Duke! The Prince himself has less formal manners!"

"Thee, miss, will hold thy tongue!" her grandfather roared. "Thee has caused me a great deal of trouble, forced me to travel for two days in the company of this—this woman!"

"Lydia, the scene at the Hotel was so lovely!" the contessa crowed. "I shall send Rosalba not only her altarcloth and a communion set, but also an altarpiece! If only you had seen the looks upon their faces when I informed them that you had changed your mind! That pig-woman fainted dead away, and your Charles made *such* sounds in the back of his throat! And your very naughty brother laughed in such a way!"

"I may imagine!" Lydia retorted drily, suppressing a chuckle.

Mr. Wingate was thus able to vent a considerable amount of his spleen in describing his journey. It would have appeared the contessa, upon making her pronouncement to the company that there would be no wedding, had immediately insisted upon accompanying the outraged father on the northern pursuit, which was not at all to Mr. Wingate's liking. Since the contessa had done her level best to give Lord Robert as long a head start as possible, it was some hours before the fuming shipbuilder was able to start out from London on the Great North Road.

It seemed at each posting house, they had just missed his errant granddaughter and her lover by a few hours, and since the journey into Northumberland took two full days, even with the fastest horses and the most frequent changes, Mr. Wingate's forced confinement with a lady in every way his opposite had not improved his temper at all. "Although I will admit that Friend Olympia knows how to make you comfortable on a journey!" he admitted grudgingly. "Heated bricks and hot wine!"

The contessa bowed with dignity toward her companion. "Meester Wingate knows how to travel in the first style of comfort, also!" she added, nodding brightly.

"F—Friend Olympia?" Lydia asked, suppressing a laugh.

Her grandfather's brows drew together. "Aye,

Friend Olympia! Would thee have me address her as contessa, and I a Quaker?"

"No sir, indeed not!" Lord Robert said swiftly. "It is just that my wife and I never knew that the contessa's Christian name was Olympia!"

"It is," Mr. Wingate said, bristling. "And what's more, I find it a very attractive name, Olympia!" Suddenly, he frowned and made as if to draw himself out of the chair. "Thy *wife*?" he demanded in awful tones, looking from Robert to Lydia.

Marchman nodded. "My wife, sir, Lady Robert Marchman. We were married over the border this morning."

"Good Lord," Mr. Wingate said, digesting this information. "I will not have it! None of my granddaughters will marry an English aristocrat!"

"But it's done, Grand," Lydia said quietly.

"I was hoping that you would not hold my title against me," Lord Robert said. "In all other respects, sir, I hope to make your granddaughter a very happy woman. Before—circumstances er, intervened, it was my full intention to sail to New York and make a formal application for your permission to court my wife. At that time, I would have laid out my circumstances fully to you, and I will be glad to do so now if you wish. My income, sir, is not inadequate to support your granddaughter in the style to which you have accustomed her, and I believe, is quite sufficient to provide for her, should anything ever happen to me, in that same style. We have not yet worked out the settlement lines, but if you would wish to speak to my brother, the Duke of Coldstone, he will assure you that all is as I have said. He witnessed the marriage lines for us."

"And he was as disapproving as you, Grand, that his brother should be marrying an American."

This remark wrought a wonder upon Mr. Wingate. "What? What? Some nobby British duke thinks that a Wingate isn't good enough? Why, Lydia may look where she pleases for a marriage, for there's good blood on both sides of her family and so I shall tell this Duke!" He looked about the room. Fortunately, the gloom also concealed the shabbiness of long inhabitation. "This house is yours?"

"Yes sir. I have the freehold. It is out of the lines of entail."

"You could fit Wingate Mansion and the summer house into this old pile," Mr. Wingate said musingly, and Lord Robert knew that he had his grandfather-in-law; the rest would only be a matter of winning the old man over.

At that moment, Marty chose to enter the room and inform the company that dinner would be served for four in fifteen minutes' time.

Since he had the forethought to bring up a very good bottle of Madeira from his lordship's cellars, Mr. Wingate's choler began to subside somewhat and his granddaughter was summarily dismissed to see to Friend Olympia's needs, as there was business to be discussed that did not concern her.

As Lydia escorted the contessa to her bedchamber, the older lady sighed. "Really, Lydia, you are a great deal of trouble, the pair of you, smelling of April and May! Making me come all the way to England with Lord Robert in tow—that is very bad of St. Theresa, when she must know that I do not like cold climates! But, however, I was not prepared to like your grandfather—and I was so surprised to find Friend Perryman such an excellent gentleman! And so handsome, also! I have never had an American husband before....I wonder...."

Before Lady Robert had time to recover from the shock of this oracular pronouncement, she overheard the gentlemen's voices floating up from the study.

"Well, Friend Robert," Mr. Wingate was saying, "if she wants thee, that must be good enough for me! Truth be told, I never did much care for that Schuyler sprig for her! But—yes, thank thee, I will take a little more of the Madeira—thee must tell me, what was the scandal that thee left English soil?"

What Lord Robert replied, Lydia could not catch, strain as she might to hear.

But Mr. Perryman Wingate had, and he gave a great burst of laughter. "That is very good! Very good indeed, sir! Thee is to be toasted! To my grandson-in-law, the reformed rakehell!"